AMELIA PEABODY'S EGYPT

AMELIA PEABODY'S EGYPT

A COMPENDIUM

Preface
by
ELIZABETH PETERS

Edited
by
ELIZABETH PETERS
& KRISTEN WHITBREAD

Designed
by
DENNIS FORBES

Contributions by Numerous Authors

WILLIAM MORROW
An Imprint of HarperCollinsPublishers

HarperCollins books may be purchased for educational, business, or sales promotional use. For information please write: Special Markets Department, HarperCollins Publishers Inc., 10 East 53rd Street, New York, NY 10022.

FIRST EDITION

Designed by Dennis Forbes

Printed on acid-free paper

Library of Congress
Cataloging-in-Publication Data

Amelia Peabody's Egypt / preface by Elizabeth Peters; edited by Elizabeth Peters & Kristen Whitbread; designed by Dennis Forbes; contributions by numerous authors.
1st ed.
        p. cm.
ISBN 0-06-053811-2 (acid-free paper)
        1. Peabody, Amelia (Fictitious character). 2. Detective and mystery stories, American—History and criticism. 2. Historical fiction, American—History and criticism. 4. Excavations (Archaeology)—Egypt. 5. Women detectives in literature. 6. Antiquities in literature. 7. Archaeology in literature. 8. Egypt—In literature. 1. Peters, Elizabeth II. Whitbread, Kristen.

PS3563.E747Z56 2003
813.45—dc21

                                                                2002192182

03 04 05 06 07 RRD 10 9 8 7 6 5 4 3 2 1

Front jacket image: "Iconoclasts." *The Graphic*, July 1890.

Preceding the title page: General view of Cairo with the Great Pyramids in the distance. Engraving, Georg Ebers, *Egypt:*

Descriptive, Historical, and Picturesque (London, Paris, New York, 1878).

Mummy cases on display in the Opet Temple at Karnak. Engraving, Ebers, *Egypt.*

FOR THE DEAR READERS OF:

Crocodile on the Sandbank (1884-85 Season, published in 1975)

The Curse of the Pharaohs (1892 93 Season, published in 1981)

The Mummy Case (1894-95 Season, published in 1985)

Lion in the Valley (1895-96 Season, published in 1986)

The Deeds of the Disturber (Summer 1896, published in 1988)

The Last Camel Died at Noon (1897-98 Season, published in 1991)

The Snake, the Crocodile & the Dog (1898-99 Season, published in 1992)

The Hippopotamus Pool (1899-1900 Season, published in 1996)

Seeing a Large Cat (1903-04 Season, published in 1997)

The Ape Who Guards the Balance (1906-07 Season, published in 1998)

The Falcon at the Portal (1911-12 Season, published in 1999)

He Shall Thunder in the Sky (1914-15 Season, published in 2000)

Lord of the Silent (1915-16 Season, published in 2001)

The Golden One (1916-17 Season, published in 2002)

CONTENTS

*A street scene in
Cairo, ca. 1905.*

People, Places & Things
A Handy Reference to the Journals

Feluccas on the Nile.

PREFACE

The story of how I was first offered the opportunity to edit Mrs. Emerson's journals is too long and unbelievable to relate here. When I began, I had no idea the labor would extend over so many years. The original source material consisted of only eight volumes, but they required careful editing, since the handwritten text was in some cases blurred by the ravages of time. Mrs. Emerson's sporadic emendations and interpolations presented additional problems.

I was working on the last of these volumes when a wholly unexpected and equally unbelievable chain of circumstances brought into my hands another collection of Emerson papers — not only additional journals but a motley lot of miscellaneous material. It was immediately evident that even more arduous study and analysis would be necessary if these documents were to be put in proper order. I felt obliged to take this task upon myself. Thus began the addition of Manuscript H and other documents to the basic text of the journals.

But, one may ask: what does all this have to do with the Compendium? The answer should be obvious. The wealth of the material inspired many Readers to request elucidation, amplification and explanation of innumerable petty details. This proved that the Readers of the journals were persons of remarkable intellectual ability; it also provoked the Editor into periodic states of intellectual confusion. She determined, therefore, to provide a reference book that would satisfy the most assiduous questioner and, so to speak, "get her off the hook."

She deems herself fortunate indeed to have found so many talented contributors. Kristen Whitbread has nobly taken it upon herself (following a number of forceful hints) to edit this collection. A decade (which may have seemed longer) of experience has made her thoroughly conversant with the material and the vagaries of the Editor. Dennis Forbes, the distinguished editor of *KMT, a Modern Journal of Ancient Egypt*, brings to this collection not only his talents as artist and designer, but his vast knowledge of Egyptology. The authors of the articles are experts in their own fields, as their brief biographical notices will make evident.

It only remains to repeat my thanks to the contributors and express my hope that this modest volume may prove of interest to Mrs. Emerson's many admirers.

Elizabeth Peters

Opposite, late-19th Century engraving of tourists being assisted by locals during their ascent of the Great Pyramid at Giza.

LOVE AMONG THE RUINS

Excerpt from the Unpublished Journal of Professor Radcliffe Emerson January-February 1885

10 Jan. 1885

Boulaq Museum with Walter. Place is a damned disaster. M. is an ass. Found a confounded woman trying to dust the pots!!! Could strangle T. Cook for starting his tours. Egypt overrun with babbling idiot tourists. Women are the worst. Why the devil don't they stay home? This one had the audacity to shout at me after I stopped her handling the artifacts. Walter made me come away.

S. after dinner. Bloody place. Walter made me go. Said I owed the lady an apology. Nonsense. She started it. Suspect W. is soft on the girl — Miss Peabody's companion. Pretty little thing in that washed out English style. Nothing washed out about Miss P. She is as swarthy as a gypsy and as opinionated as a man, black hair, eyes like daggers. Admirable figure, though.

I cannot imagine why I am wasting paper and ink on the woman. Tomorrow we leave for Amarna. I'll never set eyes on her again.

3 Feb. 1885

That damned woman is here. THAT woman. What have I done to deserve this? I had been a trifle under the weather for a few days when they turned up — don't tell ME that was a coincidence! Now she's moved in, bag and baggage, and there's no getting rid of her, or the companion. Walter spends half his time mooning over the girl and the other half jumping to obey Miss P's orders. She and W. will have it that her nursing brought me back from the brink of death. Bloody nonsense. Must get on my feet before she takes over the expedition. She's gone dashing off to inspect my pavement. My pavement!

6 Feb.

I expected Miss P. would be trouble, but this goes beyond normal bounds even for women. It must be her fault. Never encountered a situation like this one. I may have been a trifle unjust when I accused her of stealing the mummy Walter found; hard to picture even the indomitable Miss Peabody creeping out of camp in the middle of the night with the mummy tucked under her arm. Nor do I suppose she invented that wild tale of seeing the cursed thing strolling around. She is too hard-headed to believe in such nonsense, or to expect anyone else to believe it. Furthermore, the villagers claim to have seen it too. When they failed to report for work I went to the village to talk some sense into them. The old mayor and the rest of the villagers seem to be intimated by his son, who had the effrontery to inform me we must leave the site because it is accursed. He then made an abominable remark about leaving the women. Walter dragged me off him. Absurd to lose one's temper over something so trivial — but how did such a crawling, spineless creature gain courage enough to challenge me? Can it be he who is trotting about disguised as the missing mummy? Someone must be, but I would not have credited Mohammed with sufficient imagination.

7 Feb.

Have to give Miss P. credit for nerve if not sweetness of temper. Made a practical suggestion — the same scheme I would have proposed, except that I had intended to get her and Miss Evelyn away before we set an ambush for the "mummy." Might have known she'd not agree to that. She is set on taking part. Thinks she can do anything. I was strongly tempted to take hold of her and carry her off to her dahabeeyah. But I have never laid violent hands on a woman, and this one wouldn't go without a struggle.

Later. The ambush was a failure. We did not catch the thing. Must confess the costume makes an impression, especially in the pale moonlight. We did learn one useful fact: Mohammed was snug in his bed while the mummy was rambling about. I never believed he was the one.

So who is it?

8 Feb.

I had just become resigned to having the place overrun with women when another cursed busybody turned up — a friend of theirs, naturally. Supercilious ass of an aristocrat. There's something odd about the fellow. He's after Miss Evelyn, who is related to him in some fashion. That explains his coming here, I suppose, when one takes into consideration the corrosive effect of sexual attraction on the brain, and Lord Chalfont's brain isn't much to begin with. He smirks and smiles when I address him obsequiously as "my lord" and "your lordship." Sarcasm goes right over his swollen head. But he knew about the royal tomb. How? The locals have known its location for years, and so have I, but I've made damned good and sure not to pass the information on to any of my colleagues. Chalfont's not the sort who hobnobs with "natives," nor, if I am any judge, is he interested in Egyptology. An interesting little puzzle.

Two days later.

Justice compels me to admit that I cannot entirely blame Miss P. for a sudden increase in the severity and frequency of our misadventures. The destruction of my painted pavement could have been an act of malice on the part of Mohammed or another of the villagers, and a minor avalanche at the Royal Tomb while she and I were within could have been an accident. Neither of these incidents caused actual harm. However, the reappearance of the mummy night before last led to an injury to Walter that might have been even more serious than it was. Chalfont claimed he was firing at the mummy and that Walter, moved to rashness by danger to the girl, ran into the line of fire. In fact, I do not believe Chalfont meant to kill him. No one would make a fuss if he had "accidentally" murdered one of these poor Egyptians, but shooting a fellow Englishman would result in an inquiry — and I think he has learned to know me well enough to realize that the matter would most probably never get to court. It was an accident. Another accident. To make matters worse, we have lost one of our most loyal servants — Amelia's dragoman, Michael. Chalfont claims he has fled. Bah. Must talk with Reis Hassan. We will visit the dahabeeyah tomorrow.

Next night.

Bad to worse. I persuaded Amelia to keep Miss Evelyn on board the dahabeeyah overnight, to see if "the mummy" would follow her there. It did, and Chalfont put on a performance that seems to have convinced our superstitious crewmen that the mummy is invulnerable to bullets and capable of hurling curses. Confound it, the bastard must be involved somehow, though it is obviously not he who has played the part of the mummy. His motive eludes me, but he has almost convinced Evelyn that she is some sort of jonah, who has brought us all into danger. Greatly as I dislike interfering in such matters, I believe it will be necessary for me to force my ineffectual brother into a declaration. I've never seen him in such a state. There can be no objection to the match; they are both young and poor and utterly besotted with one another. Yes, why not? She may be fool enough to give in to Chalfont, and I am convinced the man is a villain, even if I cannot prove it. And she has the makings of a competent artist.

Later.

Hell and damnation! I'm in love with the woman! I never supposed such a thing could happen to me, but it is the only possible explanation for my present state of confusion. So addled is my brain that I could almost believe it was Fate rather than coincidence that brought me to her room in time to kill the cobra that lay coiled at the foot of her bed. I am not ashamed to admit I felt weak kneed and tremulous afterward. Anyone might feel so. It was such a near thing! But only a man who loved her would have taken advantage of her obliging and uncharacteristic swoon to snatch her up and hold her close and shower clumsy kisses on her face. Madness!

The advent of the others brought me to my senses before she returned to hers. I am glad of that. She is a wealthy woman and I have nothing — but I have too much pride to risk a blistering rejec-

tion. She's got a tongue that could raise welts on a man's soul, does my darling Amelia — and intelligence and fortitude and courage and loyalty — and she makes me laugh. I cannot resist stirring her up. She has no idea how enchanting she is when she faces me down and snaps back at me, as if she were seven feet tall instead of barely five.

I want her, and I cannot have her, but perhaps I can get her out of this business alive. Matters are coming to a head. Throwing Evelyn into Walter's arms settled that matter, but it didn't have the effect I had expected on Chalfont. What the devil is driving the man? He will act tonight, I think. I must tear these pages from my diary and conceal them before I go out to face him. I do not know what the night may bring, and if any of the others survive me, they must not read these maudlin sentiments.

(*Apparently Professor Emerson carried out his intention and then forgot to retrieve the pages, which is not surprising, considering the ensuing events, described in the first volume of Mrs. Emerson's published memoirs. The crumpled manuscript was found in a crevice in one of the northern tombs at Amarna in 1997 by a member of the Egypt Exploration Society's expedition. Since they were of no interest to that organization, they were eventually handed over to the present editor.*)

Page 14 & left, watercolor copies of painted-plaster decoration found at El Amarna.

Opposite, 1896 tourist photograph of the excavation of the First Courtyard of the Luxor Temple, a colossal statue of Rameses II partially revealed.

THE EMERSON ERA: I
The Historical Background to the Journals

A SPLENDID OVERVIEW OF EGYPTOLOGY

Napoleon to World War I

When English brothers Radcliffe and Walter Emerson arrived in Egypt in 1884, for their first full season of excavation, the relatively young discipline of archaeology had been practiced there only since the early years of the 1850s, and during that time had been limited pretty much to the wide-ranging activities of a single individual. This was a Frenchman named Auguste Mariette, founder of the Egyptian Antiquities Service (or Service des Antiquités d'Égypte, more correctly).

From the time of Napoleon's ill-fated Egyptian Expedition (1798-1801) until Mariette's arrival in Egypt in 1850, "archaeology" along the Nile had been by-and-large the domain of treasure-hunting agents of European museums, foreign epigraphic missions, local tomb robbers, and souvenir-collecting travelers. The scholars and artists who accompanied the Napoleonic forces had inevitably acquired portable antiquities, though these ultimately were surrendered as war booty to the victorious British and are today housed in the British Museum (the most notable of which is the famous Rosetta Stone, key to the decipherment of Egyptian hieroglyphic writing).

Although a military failure, Napoleon's Egyptian Expedition and the subsequent publication, *Description de l'Égypte,* resulted in widespread European interest in the long-ignored ancient pharaonic monuments, most particularly those objects and architectural elements which could be transported back to the Continent to grace the galleries and vitrines of the great museums there. This was facilitated in Egypt by its Macedonian governor-general, Mohammed Ali Pasha, who was eager to modernize his adopted country and therefore welcomed European visitors interested in acquiring, for a price, the plentiful artifacts of its ancient past. In the rush to assemble Egyptian collections, the British Museum and the Musée du Louvre engaged the services of on-the-scene antiquities agents. Chief among these were the British consul-general in Cairo, Henry Salt, French consul-general Bernardino Drovetti, and, most significantly, an Italian-born adventurer named Giovanni Battista Belzoni.

While Salt and Drovetti were chiefly bureaucratic middlemen interested in assembling (*carte blanche*) large collections of significant Egyptian antiquities for sale to their overseas museum clients — acquiring these from lesser agents and locals — subcontractor Belzoni was of a different stripe. Today the adventurer might be regarded as a

The Rosetta Stone — found by the soldiers of Napoleon Bonaparte (inset) in 1799, during the French occupation of Egypt, & confiscated by the British who defeated the Napoleonic forces in 1801 — proved to be the key to the decipherment of the ancient Egyptian hieroglyphic script. It is today in the collection of the British Museum in London.

proto-archaeologist, although his somewhat primitive excavation techniques left much to be desired, and publication of his finds was limited to his memoirs — and far from scientific. While acting as an in-the-field employee of Salt, the Italian strongman (he had once been a circus performer) actually dug in the Valley of the Kings (1817), discovering eight tombs, most importantly that of the 19th Dynasty king Seti I. His explorations ranging the entire length of Egypt and into Nubia, Belzoni also eventually excavated on the Giza Plateau (1818) and succeeded in entering the Pyramid of Khafre, penetrating to the burial chamber and leaving his name emblazoned on its ceiling.

European interest in the antiquities of Egypt shifted from wholesale collecting to scientific recording, with the arrival in Luxor in 1821 of the Englishman John Gardner Wilkinson, who — along with his fellow countrymen James Burton and Robert Hay — spent the mid-1820s through the mid-'30s observing local customs and documenting the *in situ* monuments of the ancient capital, (which is not to say that these English savants necessarily refrained altogether from personally collecting smaller objects offered to them by enterprising *fellahin*). It was Wilkinson who began the numbering of the tombs in the Valley of the Kings, a sequence which was continued as later tombs were discovered. It is still being followed today.

Antiquities collecting was likewise engaged in by two 19th Century scientific missions to Egypt, the Franco-Tuscan Expedition of 1828-29 and the Prussian Expedition of 1842-45. The former was the joint venture of the Frenchman Jean-François Champollion (principal decoder of Egyptian hieroglyphs) and Tuscan scholar Ippolito Rosellini, who with a team of a dozen architects and draughtsmen explored the length of the Nile into Nubia. Excavation was not the objective of the Expedition, but rather the recording and collecting of that which was already exposed. Regrettably, this included the removal — for transport to France and Italy — of two wall reliefs from the Belzoni-discovered Tomb of Seti I.

The Prussian Expedition to Egypt, 13 years after the departure of Champollion and Rosellini, was led by the pioneering German Egyptologist Karl Richard Lepsius. It was more extensive than the earlier Franco-Tuscan effort, and Lepsius's subsequent gargantuan publication of the Expedition's documentation, *Denkmäler aus Aegypten und Aethiopien*, still remains a valuable resource today. The Prussians did not only record what they saw: when they returned home they took with them thousands of artifacts (and casts of less-portable objects), some of them actually gifts from Egyptian Governor-General Mohammed Ali Pasha to the Expedition's sponsor, the king of Prussia, Friederich Wilhelm IV.

By the middle of the 19th Century, a staggering quantity of artifacts, statuary, wall reliefs and paintings, and architectural fragments had left Egypt to grace the great museum collections of Europe, in what might be described as officially sanctioned looting of that country's ancient legacy. But clearly, Egyptian portable antiquities were ultimately exhaustible, and as early as 1835 Champollion (who had removed the Seti I reliefs, as he claimed defensively, in order to preserve them) called for the establishment of a French-directed Egyptian commission to conserve the pharaonic monuments. It was not until 15 years later that this began to be a reality.

The aforementioned Auguste Mariette, a junior curator at the Louvre, arrived in Egypt in 1850, as an agent of the French Bibliothèque Nationale, with a six-month mission to acquire antique Coptic manuscripts for the institution's collection. However, he encountered

Two scientific expeditions to record Egypt's ancient monuments were led by Frenchman Jean François Champollion (above) in 1828-29 & Prussian Karl Richard Lepsius (below) in 1842-45.

Enterprising fellahin turned to wholesale antiquities looting, in order to supply the ever-increasing demands of 19th Century European collectors, both institutions & private travelers seeking "souvenirs" of their sojourn along the Nile.

Opposite, A fellah & mummies, which, ground up, were in great demand during the 19th Century for their perceived medical properties.

the unwillingness of the modern Church's higher clergy to part with further texts (a great quantity had left Egypt in the 1830s), and so the 29-year-old Mariette turned his full attention to acquiring pharaonic antiquities for his principal employer back in Paris, the Louvre. It was not long before he discovered the Serapeum (catacomb burials of the sacred Apis Bulls) at Sakkara, thereby launching his new career as the first true Egyptological archaeologist.

For 30 years until his death at the age of 60 in 1881, Mariette traversed Egypt, from Giza to Elephantine, employing hundreds of local workers and formally overseeing excavations at up to 35 sites simultaneously. Since he obviously could not be at more than one dig at a time, much of the actual supervision was left to his various foremen (*reises*). Mariette thereby took credit for discovering a staggering number of previously unknown ancient monuments, including some of the most important Egyptian sculpture and jewelry ever to come to light. Among these finds were the burial of King Kamose at Dra Abu el Naga (Luxor); the collective burial of the priests of Montu at Deir el Bahari (Luxor); the coffins and jewelry of Queen Ahhotep (Luxor); the so-called Hyksos statues later reassigned to Amenemhat III of the 12th Dynasty (Tanis); statues of King Khafre in his valley temple (Giza); the 3rd Dynasty Tomb of Hesyre (Sakkara); and the 5th Dynasty Tomb of Ti (Sakkara), to name but a few of the better known.

In 1858 Egypt's Ottoman ruler, the Khedive Said, officially

The Boulaq Museum, Cairo

As director of the new Antiquities Service, Auguste Mariette began to assemble an Egyptian national collection of antiquities. In 1863 the buildings of a former Nileside railway station in the Boulaq warehouse district of Cairo were converted into a museum to house & display this collection. Mariette considered the site as only a temporary facility, however, and when in 1878 a high Nile flooded the premises, it was clear that a new location was needed. It was not until 1889 that the collection was moved to another temporary site in a former palace of the khedive in Giza, the grounds of which today are the location of the Cairo Zoo.

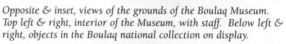

Opposite & inset, views of the grounds of the Boulaq Museum. Top left & right, interior of the Museum, with staff. Below left & right, objects in the Boulaq national collection on display.

EGYPTIAN MUSEUM, CAIRO

In 1897 construction began on a new national museum of antiquities designed by French architect Marcel Dourgnon in the neoclassical style popular at the time. Work on the immense structure — the first anywhere to be built specifically as a museum — was completed in 1902, and in July of that year the recovered relics of Egypt's ancient past were transferred from the khedive's former palace in Giza to their new home on El Tahrir Square. On November 15, 1902, the Cairo Egyptian Museum of Antiquities officially opened under the direction of Gaston Maspero, who was head of the Antiquities Service once again.

Above, facade of the Cairo Museum &, right, one of its galleries.

Following his death in 1880, Mariette was entombed on the grounds of the Egyptian Museum in Cairo, with his bronze portrait-statue atop the tomb.

Frenchman Gaston Maspero, above, a student of Auguste Mariette's, was selected to succeed to the directorship of the Antiquities Service & the Boulaq Museum upon the death of Mariette in 1880. Soon thereafter, in the summer of 1881, the existence of a cache of royal mummies near Deir el Bahari was revealed by a family of Luxor modern-day tomb robbers, initiating what has been called the "golden age" of Egyptian archaeology under Maspero & his successors. Location of the cache, known as DB320, is shown in the engraving above right; the entrance shaft is the darkened area just left of center in the scene.

appointed the Frenchman director of the newly established Antiquities Works, the immediate predecessor of the Antiquities Service. By late 1863 Mariette had opened the country's first antiquities museum, a converted railway station in Cairo's river-port district, Boulaq. Therein Mariette assembled the hundreds of ancient objects he had already found (and eventually those he discovered during future excavations), thus forming the basis for a national antiquities collection. The Boulaq Museum was flooded by a high Nile in 1878; and, while most of the artifacts were rescued, all of Mariette's excavation records were regrettably lost.

Mariette died in 1881, to be succeeded in the directorship of the Antiquities Service (and, subsequently, of the museum) by his assistant and chosen successor, another Frenchman, Gaston Maspero, a serious but charming Egyptological scholar, who also possessed considerable administrative and diplomatic skills. Whereas Mariette had personally monopolized archaeological activity in Egypt during his three decades of extensive digging, his successor — although also interested in hands-on searching for new monuments and artifacts — expanded archaeological exploration from the Delta to the First Cataract by encouraging foreign excavators to come and work in Egypt, thereby initiating a "golden age" of Egyptology and antiquities discovery. This was done through the system of the *firman* — an exclusive contract with the Antiquities Service to excavate a specific site, with a subsequent division of any objects found between the Service and the excavator.

This "golden age" may be said to have begun at the very outset of Maspero's watch, with the discovery (revelation, more accurately) in mid-1881 of the Royal Mummies Cache in the cliffs near Deir el Bahari at Luxor (DB320). This ancient group-burial of 40 mummies — royal, non-royal, and anonymous — actually had been located accidentally some 10 years earlier by a Qurna Village family of professional tomb robbers, the three brothers Abd er Rassul: Ahmed, Hussein, and Mohammed. When the suspected existence of the royal cache was finally acknowledged by the eldest sibling, Mohammed, Maspero was vacationing in France; and possession and clearance of the precarious cliff tomb fell to his German assistant at the Boulaq Museum, Émile Brugsch. Removal of the many mummies and their coffins and additional grave goods for transfer to Cairo was effected in a matter of only six days, or 48 hours of actual labor. (Brugsch feared that the local villagers, believing the tomb contents to be their personal property, would attempt to retake the prize.) Thus, documentation of the find and subsequent clearance was non-existent or, at best, dependent on Brugsch's recollections well after the fact.

Record keeping would prove to be the obsession of a new figure on the archaeological scene in Egypt, one of the first Europeans to take advantage of Gaston Maspero's foreigner-friendly policy of controlled excavation, an Englishman named W.M. Flinders Petrie. The young man made his initial visit to Egypt in 1880, as a disciple of the early "pyramidologist" Charles Piazzi Smyth. Petrie's accurate measurements disproved the latter's belief that the Great Pyramid was a "prophecy in stone," and he turned from the metaphysical to the archaeological. By 1883 he was in possession of a *firman* to excavate at El Nebira in the Delta, site of the ancient Greek trading center of Naukratis. There the Englishman was able to put into practice his penchant for focusing on the lesser finds of excavation — the potsherds, beads, amulets, corroded coins, and other fragments of everyday life — meticulously recording all those scraps of evidence which other diggers of the day passed over or tossed aside without interest. They moved massive amounts of earth to expose buried monuments and statues; Petrie sifted for minutiae.

In 1884 Petrie was exploring in the Delta when two of his countrymen and contemporaries, brothers Radcliffe and Walter Emerson, arrived in Cairo late that fall and headed directly up the Nile to an archaeologically virgin locale in Middle Egypt that would later come to be famed as El Amarna. While the epigraphically inclined

Key players in the Royal Mummies Cache revelation were Ahmed Abd er Rassul (l., in his old age) & Maspero's assistant at the Boulaq Museum, German-born Émile Brugsch (r.). Ahmed & his brothers discovered the group reburial in 1872 (or perhaps even earlier); &, when its existence finally was made known, Brugsch took on the task of emptying the tomb of its 40 occupants.

Englishman William Matthew Flinders Petrie (seen above in his later years) is regarded as the father of Egyptian archaeology, because of his long field career & numerous excavations, & because of his work techniques & meticulous attention to detail in recording his finds. He also devised a dating system based on pottery types.

The Royal Mummies Cache

Gaston Maspero (reclining at right above) visiting the Royal Mummies Cache with Émile Brugsch (center) in January 1882.

Gaston Maspero was vacationing in France in July of 1881 when word reached Cairo that suspected tomb robber Mohammed Abd er Rassul had revealed the existence of a cache of royal mummies near Deir el Bahari at Luxor. Maspero's assistant at the Boulaq Museum, Émile Brugsch, rushed south to take charge of the clearance of the cliff-tomb of its 40 occupants (not all of them royal, it turned out), their coffins, and grave goods. This was quickly accomplished and the congregation of mummies was taken by steamer to Cairo & deposited in the Museum. Maspero visited the site of the discovery in January of 1882, accompanied by Brugsch and Mohammed Abd er Rassul (above). Over the next few years, until Maspero's retirement from the Antiquities Service in 1886, the royal-cache mummies were unwrapped individually (often as special events for visiting dignitaries, as opposite), examined, and photographed. A second cache of mummified royalty was discovered in 1898.

Above, the royal mummies displayed in their coffins after arrival at the Boulaq Museum. Above right, museum assistant Ahmed Kamal & huge outer coffin of Queen Ahmes-Nefertari. Below, Maspero & Brugsch officially unwrap a royal mummy for British observers.

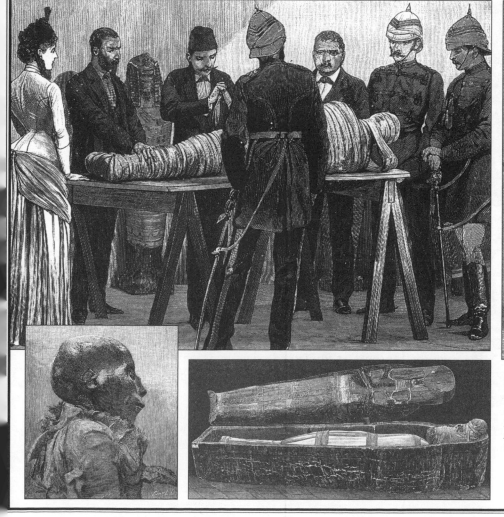

Bottom far left, DB320 mummy originally identified as "Pinentem II," now thought to be anonymous. Left, coffin with wrapped mummies of Princess/ Priestess Maatkare & a pet baboon. Above, the unwrapped mummies of father & son, kings Seti I (l.) & Ramses II.

E.A. Wallis Budge.

Walter recorded inscriptions in the nobles' tombs in the eastern cliffs, archaeologist Radcliffe (who preferred to be called by his family name of Emerson) focused his attention on digging at the largely disappeared town-site in the immense half-moon bay between the river and the encircling range of low mountains. It was there that the elder Emerson found a marvelously painted-plaster pavement in what had once been a dwelling of royal dimensions. Not until seven years later, in 1891, did Flinders Petrie, working the El Amarna concession, locate the same pavement. Emerson had uncovered and then reburied his find in 1885 (the actual first floor-painting which he and English tourist Amelia Peabody — his self-appointed assistant at the time — had cleared having been destroyed by vandals). The intentional destruction of this exquisite pavement (as subsequently described by Peabody [later Mrs. Emerson] in her first Egyptian journal) clearly led the great archaeologist to an epiphany, for he would follow this practice of discovery and concealment throughout his career.

It was in 1886 that Antiquities Director Maspero took charge of the clearance of the amazingly intact 19th Dynasty Tomb of Sennudjem in the necropolis of the royal tomb-builders' village at Deir el Medina (west bank, Luxor, where the Emersons and American amateur archaeologist Cyrus Vandergelt were to dig 20 years later), the actual discovery having been made by a bedouin, Salam Abu Duhi, digging with a government license. It was not long after this marvelously painted sepulcher was emptied of its several occupants and their burial goods (which were added to the national antiquities collection in Cairo) that Maspero fell ill, resigned his position with the Service, and returned to France to recuperate. He had wanted his successor as director to be the Swiss archaeologist Édouard Naville; but politics ruled the day, and another Frenchman, Eugène Grébaut, a former student of Maspero's, was named to the post.

Emerson was not the only Egyptologist to regard this appointment as a mistake. Grébaut lacked Maspero's personal charm, possessed no diplomatic skills, and, unlike his predecessor, was a stickler for following the Service rules to the letter. Thus, he was viewed as anti-foreign and in particular anti-English, having repeated run-ins with Petrie, and with the recently appointed keeper of Egyptian antiquities at the British Museum, E.A. Wallis Budge. Budge was frequently in Egypt at this time, acquiring non-excavated objects (sometimes under highly questionable circumstances) for his institution's collection back in London. Other than clearing the massive group-burial of some 153 priests of Amen of the 21st Dynasty found at Deir el Bahari in 1891, Grébaut's principal accomplishment during his six-year tenure was moving the antiquities assembled by Mariette and Maspero from the museum at Boulaq to a new national museum in a former palace at Giza — although apparently some things went "missing" in the transfer process. The Frenchman retired as director of the Antiquities Service in 1892, but not before he discreetly managed to avoid locking horns with Radcliffe Emerson and his wife of five years, Amelia (Peabody), who were in Egypt that same year to investigate

mysterious goings-on regarding the Baskerville tomb in the Valley of the Kings.

Grébaut would be replaced as Antiquities Service director by yet another Frenchman, Jacques de Morgan, an engineer and geologist destined to become a great archaeologist, as well — the latter not without a little help from Walter "Ramses" Emerson. Although an unknown quantity, de Morgan was generally welcomed as Grébaut's successor. Perhaps due to his methodical scientific training, he was exceptionally organized and practical, not to mention highly energized. During his less than half-dozen years as Service chief (1892-1897), de Morgan made several significant discoveries: first, in mid-1893, at Sakkara, the exquisitely decorated adjoining mastaba tombs of Kagemni and Mereruka; followed, in three seasons at Dahshur (1894-95), by the spectacular jewelry finds of the princesses in the 12th Dynasty pyramid complexes, including the disturbed burial of a previously unknown king, Hor, and the undisturbed-but-decayed interment of another princess, Nubheteptikhered. The Emersons had requested the Dahshur concession, but de Morgan kept it for himself, sending them to work their 1894-95 season instead at the unpromising site of Mazghuna. Had it not been for the Emersons' inquisitive son, Ramses, a boy destined to be a great archaeologist/epigrapher in his own time, it is doubtful whether de Morgan would have discovered the jewelry caches of the 12th Dynasty princesses.

Antiquities Service director Jacques de Morgan & his men are depicted above as they discover the jewelry of a princess in one of the 12th Dynasty pyramids at Dahshur. De Morgan & a lady companion are shown in another fanciful newspaper illustration, below, visiting the site of the archaeologist's Dahshur excavations.

Having exhausted — so he hoped — the secrets of the Dahshur (or Dahshoor, as was the usual spelling in those days) pyramids, de Morgan relinquished the site to the Emersons in 1895 and moved on to work at predynastic Nagada in Upper Egypt. Later that same year, he resigned his post with the Antiquities Service and shifted his excavation venue to Susa in Persia, where he would subsequently make additional spectacular discoveries.

It should come as no surprise that his replacement as Service director was yet another Frenchman, unfortunately one more in the mold of Grébaut than of de Morgan. Victor Loret was a scholar and protegé of Gaston Maspero, but he was hardly a bureaucrat and decidedly no diplomat. His brief three years in charge of all things archaeological in Egypt were a trying time for everyone concerned. Fortunately for the Emersons, during the season of 1897-98 they managed to avoid complications with Loret by taking themselves off to the western deserts of Nubia to discover, as it happened, a lost oasis and a forgotten civilization, and there to acquire a young ward, Nefret Forth.

Although he had previously been but a *littérateur*, an "armchair" archaeologist, Loret could now satisfy the urge to become a real hands-on digger. He had done some epigraphic work in the Valley of the Kings at Luxor in the 1880s and decided that it might be a rewarding site to investigate systematically. How right he was: in just two winter seasons, using a method of hit-and-miss hole digging (*sondages*, in French), his workers (Loret himself was often elsewhere on

Two additional newspaper romantic depictions of Jacques de Morgan's activities at Dahshur: Opposite, the archaeologist lifts the crown of Queen Khnemit from her burial; &, above, the procession of the Dahshur treasures being carried to the Nile for transport to Cairo, with de Morgan & companion accompanying on horseback.

Successful archaeologist but failed administrator Victor Loret as he appeared in his later years as an academic in France.

33

Engraving of three anonymous unwrapped mummies, two women & a boy, found by Victor Loret in a side room of the Tomb of Amenhotep II (KV35), the 2nd cache of royal mummies. The possible identity of these individuals is still debated today.

Service business) found or refound an amazing 17 tombs, including those of three kings: Thutmose I (KV38), Thutmose III (KV34), and Amenhotep II (KV35), the last also proving to be the Second Royal Mummies Cache (which Emerson would claim that he had actually located years earlier, but left unrevealed). Among the 14 private or anonymous tombs to Loret's credit was the first minimally disturbed burial discovered in the Valley (in 1899), that of a noble mid-18th Dynasty half-Nubian fanbearer, Maiherpri (KV36). However, despite his indisputable archaeological successes — and his initiating of the important *Annales du Service* report-series — Loret was judged a failure as a bureaucrat; and that same year he was dismissed as director of the Antiquities Service by the British consul-general of Egypt, Lord Cromer. He subsequently returned home to France and a long career there as an academic, with an Egyptological institute being named for him in Lyon.

It was during Loret's watch that a young Englishman befriended by the Emersons, Howard Carter, made his first significant discovery while working for the Egypt Exploration Fund at Deir el Bahari in late 1898. Riding his horse one evening in the area in front of the ruins of the 11th Dynasty temple of Montuhotep II, the mount broke through the rain-softened ground crust, revealing evidence of a subterranean passageway. The site would not be excavated until over a year later (January 1900), after Carter had been appointed the antiquities inspector for Upper Egypt. Disappointingly, it would prove to be a cenotaph (or symbolic) tomb of the same Montuhotep II. It was known subsequently as Bab el Hosan ("Tomb of the Horse").

Because no other Frenchman was available or suitable for the Service directorship, Lord Cromer now offered the position to former Antiquities chief Gaston Maspero, who accepted, being once more in good health. His return to Egypt and his old post was generally well

A youthful Howard Carter, about the time he was befriended by the Emersons.

regarded, especially in light of the negative experience with at least two of his successors/predecessors. During his second term (which would last for 15 years until his retirement, again due to ill health, in 1914), Maspero enjoyed even greater influence than during his initial appointment. With him again at the helm, the climate changed and foreign archaeologists were once more welcomed, even encouraged, to work in Egypt. Service rules were relaxed and the Frenchman was generous (sometimes to a fault) in his division of finds made by European and American expeditions.

Maspero's welcome extended to the Emersons, of course (although he and Radcliffe had been on only civil terms back in the '80s). When they arrived (along with son Ramses, ward Nefret, and brother and sister-in-law Walter and Evelyn) for a winter 1899-1900 season, they were awarded the concession at Dra Abu el Naga (or Drah Abu'l Naga, as Amelia would write it), the 17th Dynasty necropolis on the west bank at Luxor, where they would successfully locate the previously unknown Tomb of Queen Tetisheri, grand matriarch of the very early 18th Dynasty — which finally proved, however, to be devoid of its intended occupant. The Emersons spent the next three seasons (1900-01, 1901-02, 1902-03) carefully emptying this tomb of its otherwise extraordinary contents. Emerson, in accordance with his principles, declined Maspero's offer of a division of the latter, prefer-

Dra Abu el Naga, with the peak El Qurn ("The Horn") in the background. This is actually the flood-plain level of the site with some exposed 17th Dynasty tomb entrances visible; the Emersons made their discovery of the Tomb of Tetisheri high in the cliffs out of view to the right.

THE VALLEY OF THE KINGS

With many of its monuments standing invitingly open, the Valley of the Kings at ancient Thebes attracted tourists even in the Roman period. Archaeological activity may be said to have begun with the explorations there in 1818 of Giovanni Belzoni, resulting in the discovery of previously unknown tombs, including that of Seti I. Formal excavations in the Valley were initiated by Victor Loret when he became director of the Antiquities Service in 1898; he managed to locate and clear several important sites, including the Tomb of Amenhotep II, the 2nd cache of royal mummies. Between 1903 and 1915 the *firman* to the Valley was held by American Theodore Davis, under whose auspices a number of major tombs were uncovered and cleared, among them the nearly intact joint-sepulcher of royal in-laws Yuya and Thuyu.

Two 19th Century views of the Wadi Bibân el Molûk, the Valley of the Kings.

Clockwise from top left: The Valley of the Kings in the 1870s; Valley guard & tomb entrance; Fellahin & tourists in the Valley in the 1880s; Workers carrying finds from the newly discovered Tomb of Thutmose IV, 1904; Theodore Davis excavations, 1909-10; 19th Dynasty royal tomb entrance; In situ sarcophagus of Ramses VI.

ring that all of the Tetisheri objects remain in Egypt. Overseeing the Emersons' clearance those seasons was their friend, Howard Carter, who was now chief inspector of the Antiquities Service for Upper Egypt, though not for much longer.

One of those foreigners whom Maspero encouraged to dig in Egypt was a retired American businessman (reportedly a millionaire) by the name of Theodore M. Davis, who became persuaded that sponsoring and overseeing an archaeological excavation — in which "treasure" was the ultimate reward — was a gentlemanly sort of amusement for his sunset years. The generous Frenchman granted him Loret's previously fruitful concession, the Valley of the Kings, and assigned to the crotchety Davis as his archaeologist the Service's youthful local chief inspector, Carter — who had wanted systematically to explore the royal necropolis for some time, but had lacked the funding to do so.

In his first season (1901-02) of working the Valley for Davis, Carter made the unusual discovery of a small, yellow-painted wooden box that was part of the aforementioned fanbearer Maiherpri's grave goods. It contained two gazelle-leather loincloths — not exactly "treasure" up to Davis's expectations.

But in the following 1902-03 season, Carter lucked out and found the previously unknown Tomb of Thutmose IV (KV43), which, while robbed anciently, still contained a quantity of fragmentary funerary furnishings, including the king's handsome intact stone sarcophagus and the second chariot body ever discovered in Egypt (the one found by the Emersons in the Tomb of Queen Tetisheri being the first). The mummy of Thutmose IV was lacking, of course, having been among those cached royals revealed by Loret in KV35 four years earlier. Davis was suitably encouraged to continue with this new hobby, archaeology.

Although the elderly American technically had the Service's exclusive *firman* to explore the Kings' Valley, in the 1903-04 season Maspero made a small exception to his rules and granted the Emersons permission to work there as well, though he limited them to investigating already known tombs. Davis was not much around that winter, in any case, as his archaeologist, Carter, was busy with the unglamorous task of clearing the flood-debris-filled, incredibly long corridor of KV20, the kingly sepulcher of Hatshepsut. Carter was engaged in this difficult work until March of 1904, his reward being the female pharaoh's quartzite sarcophagus and canopic-chest set, and the quartzite sarcophagus of her father, Thutmose I (who anciently had been reinterred in the same tomb). Maspero presented Davis with the latter object, which the dilettante digger subsequently gave to the Museum of Fine Arts, Boston.

Excavating in the Valley of the Kings for Theodore Davis, Howard Carter found the Tomb of Thutmose IV (view of the burial chamber above) during the 1902-03 season & he cleared the Tomb of Hatshepsut of flood debris the following 1903-04 season. The view of the burial chamber of the latter (below), with sarcophagus in place, is a watercolor by Carter, who had first gone to Egypt as an expedition artist.

When Davis arrived at Luxor for his 1904-05 season in the Valley of the Kings, he was confronted with a change of situation. First, those Brits, the Emersons, were apparently staying in England for the winter, so he would have the Valley to himself. Second, Howard Carter was no longer to be his official digger, having been

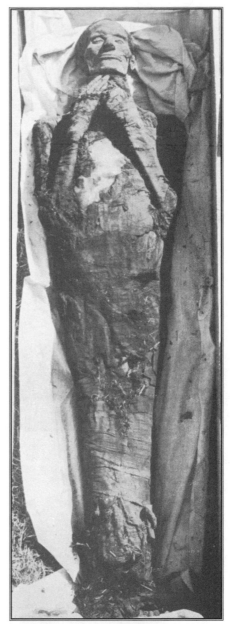

The Tomb of Yuya & Thuyu, found in the Royal Valley in 1905, was nearly intact, filled with grave goods (a chest & chair seen at left, awaiting crating), & still containing the well-preserved mummies of the tomb owners (that of Yuya seen at right, following its removal from the tomb).

transferred by Maspero to the Antiquities inspectorate in Lower Egypt, headquartered at Sakkara. Carter's replacement as chief Antiquities inspector for Upper Egypt was another young Englishman, James E. Quibell, who would take over where his fellow countryman had left off in the Valley. But as Quibell dug without the success of any finds that winter, he became convinced that his employer, Davis, was ultimately more interested in uncovering treasure than in purely esoteric excavation, and the young Englishman's patience with the impatient old American wore thin.

Finally, as the season was drawing to a close, Quibell requested a change of assignment from Maspero, which was promptly granted. Another young Englishman, a Flinders Petrie student named Arthur Weigall, was appointed to head the Upper Egypt inspectorate, and thus to serve as Davis's archaeologist in the Valley. While waiting for these new assignments to be confirmed in Cairo, Quibell's workmen made what would be Davis's greatest discovery in the royal necropolis, a violated but essentially intact nobles' burial place, the Tomb of Yuya and Thuyu (KV46), parents of Queen Tiye, chief spouse of the great 18th Dynasty pharaoh Amenhotep III and mother of the Heretic, Akhenaton. Quibell stayed on, Weigall looking over his shoulder, to supervise the clearance of this most spectacular — and treasure-rich — discovery to date in the Kings' Valley. Needless to say, the archaeology hobbyist was delighted!

The Theban royal necropolis was not the only scene of excavation activity and attendant successes in Egypt between 1902 and 1905. From the 1902-03 through the 1903-04 seasons, Scottish archaeologist John Garstang excavated a Middle Kingdom cemetery at Beni Hassan in Middle Egypt, finding numerous rock-cut tombs and their intact burials, the contents including everyday objects and large numbers of painted-wood tomb models. At Karnak in 1903, the French architect doing reconstruction work in the great Amen-Re temple, Georges Legrain, uncovered an amazing cache of some 17,000 statues, statue fragments, and statuettes from nearly all periods of pharaonic history, buried in the courtyard between the main temple and its 7th Pylon. From 1903 to 1905, an Italian team of excavators

John Garstang.

Egyptian workers under the direction of Georges Legrain (in fez at center) search in the water-table mud for ancient statuary discovered buried in a courtyard at Karnak Temple in 1903. Ultimately some 17,000 figures in stone & bronze were removed, ranging in size from truly monumental to just a few inches high.

Georges Legrain.

led by Ernesto Schiaparelli, working in the Valley of the Queens on the west bank at Luxor, found numerous previously unknown tombs of New Kingdom royal women and princes, most particularly — in 1904 — the tomb of Queen Nefertari (QV66), arguably the most beautifully decorated sepulcher ever created in ancient Egypt. All had been thoroughly robbed in antiquity.

In 1906 Ernesto Schiaparelli (above) found in the workmen's necropolis at Deir el Medina the totally intact tomb (burial chamber at left) of an 18th Dynasty architect, Kha, & his wife, Merit.

In early 1906 the Italians shifted their concession from the Queens' Valley to Deir el Medina, the nearby site of the village of the workmen who hewed and decorated the rock-cut royal tombs of the New Kingdom. Almost immediately, Schiaparelli and his colleagues located the Tomb of Kha and Merit (TT8), a mid-18th Dynasty architect and his wife. Although modest in scale and lacking decoration, this monument in the workmen's necropolis was in every other way unique, in that it had never been robbed and so was totally intact when entered by Schiaparelli and Antiquities Inspector Weigall, the first to cross the burial-chamber threshold since its wooden door had been closed and sealed some 3,400 years earlier. For reasons of his own, Gaston Maspero awarded almost all of the contents of this tomb to Schiaparelli and his Museo Egizio in Turin, keeping only a single piece — a floor lamp, one of a unique pair —for the Egyptian Museum in Cairo. This new building had been finished in 1903 and the national collection transferred from its temporary quarters at Giza.

Schiaparelli's workers carrying the contents of TT8.

When the American Davis sailed into Luxor on his *dahabiya,* the *Bedouin,* for the 1905-06 excavation season, in high anticipation of yet more treasures to be yielded by the Royal Valley, he found one thing the same from the previous year, and another quite changed. First, those Emersons would not be poking around "his" Valley; more significantly, he had a new archaeologist on his hands. Perhaps warned off by Quibell's bad experience the previous year, Weigall had persuaded Maspero to require that Davis employ his own archaeologist rather than use Weigall himself or another Antiquities staffer to direct the dilettante's digging. The man chosen for the assignment was a hapless, 24-year-old Englishman, Edward Ayrton, who — still somewhat archaeologically green under the collar — had been working with other British excavators at nearby Deir el Bahari. Davis could have been Ayrton's grandfather, and took every advantage of the youth's understandable deference.

While that first season with Ayrton in charge of the excavations failed to produce another "Iouiyu and Touiyou" (as the royal in-laws were identified in those days), the flood-debris-choked, apparently large Tomb of Siptah (a short-reigned boy-king of the late 19th Dynasty) was found. Davis decided to forego clearing it, on the assumption that the considerable effort and expense would be without suitable rewards; after all, what did he need with another huge, empty, stone sarcophagus? So Ayrton shifted his diggers to a different part of the Valley, with some resulting small successes: a series of pit-tombs (KVs 50-52) housing animal mummies, and also a faience cup hidden "under a rock," inscribed with the throne name of Tutankhamen, the first evidence of that then-little-known New Kingdom ruler in the Valley. The 1905-06 season ended in late February, Ayrton exhausted and Davis likely again having second thoughts about the point of his new hobby — dog and baboon mummies notwithstanding!

But return to the Kings' Valley Davis did, for yet a sixth winter season, 1906-07, discovering upon his arrival at Luxor aboard the *Bedouin* — to his chagrin, no doubt — that the Emerson lot were

Arthur Weigall.

Above, American dilettante digger Theodore Davis (foreground) & his youthful English archaeologist, Edward Ayrton, at the entrance to their 1907 controversial discovery, Kings' Valley Tomb 55, the so-called Amarna Cache; the rock-debris-cluttered entrance to the single chamber is seen below.

indeed back, and up to their old business of sticking a collective nose into the Valley's empty tombs and the American's business. Davis had learned in Cairo that Mrs. Emerson and her ward had tried to charm M. Maspero into taking his concession away from him, so as to hand it over to their own blustering "Father of Curses." But *baksheesh* always checkmates feminine wiles, which proved true in this instance, of course: Maspero had been good to his earlier word, and Davis was still in charge of new excavations in the Valley.

As luck would have it, Ayrton made his employer very happy that early January. Another royal tomb was found. In fact, the American was convinced — and so would publish — that it was the "Tomb of Queen Tîyi" herself. She, it will be remembered, was the daughter of Davis's "Iouiyu and Touiyou" (Yuya and Thuyu) and mother of the Heretic. Unlike the ransacked but relatively intact tomb of the royal in-laws, however, this space was a disaster zone. A cache of an odd lot of funerary furnishings and a nameless mummy rather than a true tomb, not only had it been entered and partially dismantled in antiquity, but it had been repeatedly invaded by water over the millennia and was in a sorry state of collapse and decay.

Notwithstanding the difficulties, Davis wanted KV55 (as it was numbered in the Valley tomb-sequence) cleared by the time his winter 1907 season came to an end, and this was accomplished, more or less, in a matter of just a few weeks — with consequences which would plague Egyptological scholars to the present day. Young Ayrton, as a result, would suffer an undeserved reputation as a slip-shod archaeologist. Emerson, a frustrated observer of the rushed and careless work, correctly attributed the disaster of KV55 to the failure of Inspector Weigall and his superior, Maspero, to exert their rightful authority over Davis.

Ayrton would labor for the American dilettante the next winter season, 1907-08, making several more significant discoveries, including, most importantly, KV57 — the magnificent royal tomb of Horemheb, which proved to have been thoroughly robbed in antiquity — and KV56. The latter was a simple single-chambered pit-tomb which contained, buried in the mud of ancient floodings, a considerable amount of jewelry datable to the late-19th Dynasty ruler Seti II and his queen (and subsequent female pharaoh), Tausret. Consequently, KV56 came to be known as the "Gold Tomb." By the end of this rather fruitful season, even the ever-patient Ayrton finally had had his fill of

The single chamber of Tomb 55 (above & left) was an archaeological disaster zone, due to an effort in antiquity to dismantle the funerary shrine which had been erected to shelter the tomb's occupant — one of the Amarna kings — & also because the space had been repeatedly invaded by water over the millennia, causing most of the wood of the grave furnishings & coffin to rot. This elaborately inlaid coffin (below) had fallen to the floor when the bier on which it rested collapsed, exposing the loosely shrouded body it contained. These photographs were taken by one R. Paul, part of only seven published in Davis's report on the discovery, which the American stubbornly — & mistakenly — believed to be the tomb of Queen Tiye, mother of the heretic Akhenaton.

E. Harold Jones.

George A. Reisner.

Davis and declined further employment as the American's archaeologist, moving on to dig at Abydos and El Mahasna, before quitting Egypt altogether in 1911.

Davis's new digger for the 1908-09 season was a young Welshman, E. Harold Jones, who previously had worked as the American's artist during the rushed clearance of KV55. Jones found another mud-filled pit-tomb, KV58, which contained a few scraps of gold foil identifiable to Tutankhamen. Davis wrongly concluded — as it would turn out — that this, along with the faience cup and a cache of embalming materials and funerary-banquet refuse discovered earlier (KV54), constituted all that was to be found of the burial of that shadowy king.

Jones continued to supervise Davis's excavations in the royal valley through the 1910-11 season. In 1912, his health on the decline, the elderly Theodore M. Davis relinquished his concession of the Valley of the Kings, believing that the site was now "exhausted."

There were other excavators in Egypt besides Davis and his diggers during the second half of the century's first decade. Another American, who was to become one of the finest archaeologists of his time, was busy on the Giza Plateau from 1908 through 1910. This was George A. Reisner, who had acquired plenty of excavation experience as field director of the Hearst/University of California Egyptian Expedition. In 1905 he had become a professor of Egyptology at Harvard University and headed up a joint Harvard/Museum of Fine Arts, Boston, mission to Giza. During his years digging in the pyramid and valley temples of the 4th Dynasty ruler Menkaure, Reisner located numerous sculptures of that king, many of which today grace the collection of the Boston museum. Reisner had received his Giza concession (which included part of the Western Cemetery) through a 1902 draw of lots between himself, the Italians, and the Germans. In 1905, the same year that his funding from Hearst/University of California ended, the Italians withdrew from Giza and Reisner was awarded their portion as well. Mrs. Emerson's comment that the Americans *"had got the lion's share"* of Giza was literally true, if prompted by envy. It was not until after the beginning of the Great War, when German expeditions withdrew from British-occupied Egypt, that Peabody got her chance to excavate near her beloved Giza pyramids.

Another excavator working at Luxor from 1907 through 1911 was, like Davis, an amateur who would depend on the expertise of a skilled archaeologist. George Herbert — the fifth Earl of Carnarvon, a wealthy Englishman — also had been encouraged by Maspero to take up excavation as a gentlemanly hobby. Initially, Lord Carnarvon dug on his own at Dra Abu el Naga, making a couple of small but important discoveries. But in 1908 he engaged the professional services of one Howard Carter, who happened to be at loose ends in Luxor, having quit the Antiquities Service a couple of years earlier, under the cloud of a minor scandal. Working together in the Theban necropolis over the next three seasons, they found several intact burials and, thanks to Maspero's generosity, accumulated numerous fine objects for the Earl's growing antiquities collection, housed at his family manor, Highclere Castle in England. When Theodore Davis gave up his concession to the "exhausted" Valley of the Kings in 1912, Carter persuaded Carnarvon to apply for that venue, believing that at least one more royal tomb remained to be found there — that of Tutankhamen, no less.

When the Emersons arrived in Egypt in December of 1911 to begin work at the pyramid site of Zawaiet el Aryan near Cairo, a German team under the direction of Ludwig Borchardt was engaged in a fifth season of excavation at El Amarna. The following December, 1912, the Germans found an amazing cache of artist-studies and unfinished sculptures in the ruins of the workshop of a sculptor named Thutmose. Maspero was otherwise engaged, so he sent a junior assistant to El Amarna to examine the season's finds and select the pieces to be retained for the national collection. Whether the assistant was, in fact, shown the most incredible of these sculptures, a painted limestone bust of Queen Nefertiti, and relinquished it to Borchardt can probably never be known for certain; in any case, when it was finally put on display in Berlin, in the 1920s, the Egyptian government protested that the bust had left the country fraudulently. By that time Maspero was long dead, so there was no one to dispute Borchardt's claim that the Egyptian Museum underling had passed on such a masterpiece, one of today's icons of antiquity. The Germans continued to work at El Amarna until the outbreak of the Great War in 1914.

Americans came somewhat late to the archaeology table in Egypt, but they were soon to take a prominent role, not only in excavation but in epigraphy and philological studies. To the name of Reisner must be added that of James Henry Breasted, who studied the language in Germany and collaborated on the definitive *Berlin Dictionary of Hieroglyphic Egyptian*, commonly known as the *Wörterbuch*. Breasted's survey of Egypt and the Sudan produced five volumes of translations of Egyptian texts, and he held the first chair of Egyptology in the U.S. at the University of Chicago, where he was later to found the Oriental Institute. It was not until the 1911-12 season that the Metropolitan Museum of Art Egyptian Expedition arrived, to begin excavating simultaneously in the royal cemeteries of the 12th Dynasty at El Lisht, at the Temple of Amen in Kharga Oasis and in Luxor at the palace-site of Amenhotep III known as Malkata. The latter dig was under the direction of 27-year-old Herbert E. Winlock. The next year, 1912-1913, found him moving dirt in an area known as the Asasif, near where Lord Carnarvon and Howard Carter were also digging. There the American found the causeway leading to the Temple of Montuhotep II at Deir el Bahari, and the foundations of a jointly shared mortuary temple of Ramses V and VI. The Metropolitan's final season before the outbreak of war, 1913-1914, was taken up with clearing the Monastery of Epiphanius, an early-Coptic site. The Museum's teams would not resume their Egyptian excavations until 1919.

What of Flinders Petrie in these years? In the winter of 1907-08 he was digging at Mit Rahina (Memphis), where he found, among other things, the great 18th Dynasty calcite sphinx. The next year he

George Herbert, Earl of Carnarvon.

Ludwig Borchardt.

James H. Breasted.

Herbert E. Winlock.

Pierre Lacau.

Opposite, entrance to the Tomb of Seti I in the Valley of the Kings. The world's attention would focus on archaeological activity in the Valley for much of the 1920s.

was first at Luxor, then returned to Memphis. The first half of the 1910-11 winter season found him at Meidum, dismantling — at Maspero's request — three 3rd Dynasty mastabas, for the purpose of removing their unique inlaid-relief decoration for safekeeping. He then relocated to Bedrashen in the Delta, to begin excavating the Palace of Apries. It was at this time that Maspero granted Petrie a truly huge concession: he could work any and all sites on both sides of the Nile from Dahshur to Ahnas, except for the pyramid fields of El Lisht, which were by then the exclusive venue of the Metropolitan Museum's Egyptian Expedition.

That next winter, 1911-12, Petrie was back at Hawara, where he found 70 painted-panel portraits in the Roman tombs there. He also further excavated in the so-called "Labyrinth," ruins of the Middle Kingdom pyramid-temple complex of Amenemhat III. Even though the Emersons had already been there years before, he next examined the "pyramids" of Mazghuna, confirming Emerson's late-12th Dynasty dating. Petrie also excavated Old Kingdom tombs near Kafr Ammar and in the Archaic cemetery at Tarkhan, then moved on to Matariya (site of ancient Iunu/Heliopolis), concluding his 1911-12 season there. In the 1912-13 season, he returned to Tarkhan, for further digging in the Archaic tombs. He had excavated at the 12th Dynasty pyramid-site of El Lahun in 1889-90, but decided to return there at the beginning of his 1913-14 season. A wise move, it turned out, as Petrie discovered the hidden treasure of Princess Sithathoriunet, a jewelry hoard to rival anything found at Dahshur by de Morgan (or rather, Ramses Emerson). It was to be the Englishman's last find before the war sidelined him at home for the next five years.

While excavation in Egypt did not stop entirely during the Great War, it slowed considerably; some of those archaeologists active in the field had gone to dig elsewhere, or else were involved in the war effort itself. George Reisner shifted his excavation activities to the Sudan, where he would work from 1916-20. The intrepid Emersons continued "going out" to Egypt each new winter season, braving the now dangerous trip there and back in order to excavate some of the private mastabas at Giza at the request of their old friend, the German archaeologist Herman Junker, whose group still held the concession. In July 1914, a month before hostilities began, an era in Egyptian archaeology came to an end when Gaston Maspero, 68 and in failing health, resigned the directorship of the Antiquities Service for a second time, returning home to France, there to die in 1916. His replacement, Pierre Lacau — yes, another Frenchman — was no Maspero, but rather a bureaucratic autocrat cut from the same bolt of cloth as Grébaut and Loret. The concession and division rules changed once again, as Lord Carnarvon and Howard Carter would soon discover when they returned following the Armistice to resume their Valley of the Kings search for the Tomb of Tutankhamen.

Dennis Forbes

A COMMANDING
PERSPECTIVE
The British in Egypt
1884-1917

The Peabody-Emerson Trust, recently formed by the heirs of the distinguished Victorian Egyptologists, Amelia Peabody-Emerson and her husband Prof. Radcliffe Emerson, have agreed to open Amarna House, the Emersons' residence in Kent, to the public. The fine Queen Anne house, which still retains many of its original furnishings, will not only display items connected with Prof. and Mrs. Emerson, and their discoveries and adventures in Egypt, but will also reflect Victorian and Edwardian social and political history.

While compiling an itemized inventory of the contents of Amarna House and its excellent library, a number of items of memorabilia have come to light which were evidently kept by Amelia Peabody Emerson as *aides mémoire* when writing her journals, or as keepsakes of important events, some of which originally may have belonged to the Emerson's equally famous son, the Egyptologist and expert on Middle Eastern affairs, Walter "Ramses" Emerson.

Some of the most interesting items include:
1. Medal commemorating Napoleon's conquest of Egypt
2. General Gordon's Khartoum Star
3. Medal commemorating the death of General Gordon
4. Newspaper cuttings from the *Morning Post*, 1897-98
5. Invitation to dinner at the British Agency, March 1895
6. Invitation to a ball at the British Agency, December 1913
7. Ashtray from Shepheard's Hotel
8. Advertisement for Cook's Tours of Egypt

By the time Amelia Peabody arrived in Egypt during her extended tour of the glories of the past in the fall of 1884, the country had already been under European influence for almost a century. In the previous two years Britain had gained the upper hand over her traditional rival, France, and a commission had been formed by both countries to investigate Egypt's disastrous financial situation.

(1) Medal commemorating Napoleon's conquest of Egypt in 1798.
Bronze, 1 inch (4 cm.) in diameter.
Obverse: Head of Napoleon surmounted by chaplet of lotus flowers.

Ignoring the solicitations of local beverage sellers, two British tourists enjoy a picnic repast prepared by their hotel, the Abbat, identified on the basket. Presumably they hoisted the Union Jack on a flag pole already in place there.

**Reverse: Napoleon as Roman general in chariot drawn by 2 camels.
Winged Victory above extending crown towards him.
Designed by J. Jouannin and L. Brenet.**
A card enclosed with the medal reads: "To commemorate your own 'conquest of Egypt' , R. E., 1st wedding anniversary, 3 March, 1886."

Since 1517 Egypt had been a province of the Ottoman Empire. Europe's involvement began in July 1798 with the invasion led by Napoleon Bonaparte (then only 28 years old), who had persuaded the revolutionary directors to back his campaign to take Egypt for France, and so deprive Britain of the possibility of opening up a land route to her newly acquired colony, India. Napoleon's ambitious plan was seriously compromised a month later, when almost the entire French fleet was destroyed by a British naval force under the command of Admiral Nelson in the Battle of Aboukir Bay. Nelson was knighted, with the title Lord Nelson of the Nile, while Napoleon, his 30,000 troops and 167 savants were cut off in Egypt.

After defeating a large force of Mameluke horsemen at the Battle of the Pyramids, where Napoleon encouraged his troops with the words, *"Soldiers, from the top of these pyramids, forty centuries look down upon you,"* (although the famous Pyramids of Giza to which he referred were actually about 10 miles away), the French entered Cairo. Expecting a romantic city of wonder and delight from "The Thousand and One Nights," they were bitterly disappointed. It was like stepping

Bonaparte as tourist, being shown a mummy in the vicinity of the Giza Plateau. He is accompanied by the "savants" of his scientific mission.

back into the Middle Ages, with all the accompanying squalor and discomfort.

Claiming to have freed Egypt from Mameluke misrule, Napoleon made every attempt to conciliate the Egyptians, but the Cairenes were not convinced and continued to be suspicious of the French and their strange ways. The clash of cultures was no doubt exacerbated by the behavior of the camp followers who had accompanied the French army, and shocked the Egyptians by their uninhibited conduct, going about the city unveiled and displaying a freedom totally unknown to Egyptian women.

In August 1799, Napoleon secretly left Egypt to pursue his political ambitions in France. Two years later his abandoned army, demoralized and reduced to half its strength by the plague, surrendered to the British after a joint British-Ottoman invasion; it was allowed to return to France with full honors. Although the military aspect of the French invasion of Egypt had turned into a complete fiasco, the most enduring legacy of the expedition was the study of all aspects of Egyptian culture, history, geography, flora, and fauna, by the scholars, scientists, and technicians of the Commission on the Sciences and Arts. When the army surrendered, the scholars were allowed to keep their notes, but had to hand over all the antiquities they had collected, including the famous Rosetta Stone, the key to deciphering the ancient hieroglyphs. Their researches were eventually published between 1809 and 1822 in the monumental 24-volume *Description de l'Égypte*.

Even after the French left, their influence continued for many years, especially in banking and law. Although Napoleon's plan for a canal through the Isthmus of Suez did not come about during his occupation of the country, it was eventually executed by a Frenchman. It was the French scholar Jean-François Champollion who initiated Egyptology with his studies of the ancient monuments and his decipherment of the hieroglyphic script. Another Frenchman, Auguste Mariette, set up the Boulaq Museum, which was the first national museum in the Middle East, and founded the original Antiquities Service, which had a French director into the 20th Century.

With the departure of the French, the British wished simply to restore Egypt to her Ottoman overlord, and had no intention of occupying the country, although they were also determined to prevent France from regaining a stronghold. In 1801 the British diplomat Sir William Sidney Smith commented, *"The great national objective is attained if we get the French army out of the country, even if they take the pyramids with them."* This policy was reflected in the actions of these two European powers for most of the 19th Century.

In 1805 the prominent citizens of Cairo, tired of the anarchy caused by the rival Ottoman and Mameluke factions and led by their religious leaders, the sheikhs, chose as governor (*pasha*) the commander of the Albanian mercenaries, Mohammed Ali. Later described

Frontispiece to Description de l'Égypte, *the 24-volume heavily illustrated scientific study of Egypt compiled by the Commission on the Sciences & Arts which accompanied Napoleon on his conquest of the Land of the Nile.*

Mohammed Ali, the "Father of Modern Egypt."

as the "Father of Modern Egypt," Mohammed Ali was Turko-Kurdish by birth, illiterate, but with qualities of genius and farsightedness.

By 1811 Mohammed Ali had completely suppressed his main opposition, the Mamelukes, and, recognizing the necessity for a strong military force, he modernized the army, assisted by French veterans of the Napoleonic Wars and Turko-Circassian officers. Native Egyptian peasants, the *fellahin*, were conscripted and ruthlessly whipped into shape as a powerful army of almost 250,000 men. Factories for textiles for uniforms, weapons, and other military supplies were established to make the new Egyptian army as self-sufficient as possible.

Conscripted *fellahin* also carried out Mohammed Ali's vast agricultural program, whereby 1,000,000 acres of new land were brought under cultivation, and the irrigation system all over the country was extended and improved. The administration was reorganized, and schools of engineering, military tactics, medicine, and languages were founded to create a new class of administrative and military officials. European experts were employed in various capacities, while entrepreneurs and professional people of every kind were encouraged to initiate projects or start up businesses as part of Mohammed Ali's grand scheme of modernization. Greeks, Italians, and Maltese, as well as British and French, came to make their fortunes in Egypt. Their numbers increased considerably throughout the 19th Century, but their presence eventually became a mixed blessing. The Capitulations, a long-established Ottoman system of concessions whereby foreign nationals were exempt from Egyptian taxes and justice, were initially designed to attract foreign merchants. However, as time went on, these privileges were abused by the foreign community, and caused resentment among Egyptians, who saw them acting outside the law of the land. It is only fair to say that this was also a constant source of irritation to the British police force in Cairo, who were unable to crack down on any of the crimes perpetrated by non-Egyptians.

Although many more Egyptians began to occupy government posts under Mohammed Ali, the most important positions in both the administrative and military spheres were held by Turks, a situation which was to prevail until the Egyptian Revolution in 1952. As for the rulers themselves, Mohammed Ali and his descendants who succeeded him as viceroy were essentially Turks living in a foreign country, who married Circassian women and spoke Turkish and French but not the Arabic language of their subjects.

Mohammed Ali's primary motivation was personal ambition, and his reforms were only achieved by ruthlessly exploiting the Egyptians, especially the *fellahin*. High taxes and government monopolies maintained the impoverished condition of many of the native Egyptians, and more than a third of the labor force was employed, chiefly by coercion, on public works or in the army.

The new Egyptian army came close to overthrowing the Ottoman sultan himself. Under the command of Ibrahim Pasha, Mohammed Ali's son, the army conquered Syria after the sultan refused Mohammed Ali's request for the governorship of that country in reward for his military successes on the sultan's behalf in Arabia and

"Recruitment" of the fellahin *under Mohammed Ali, as soldiers for the Egyptian army & forced labor for his many public works projects designed to modernize Egypt.*

Greece. Ibrahim then invaded Anatolia and marched on Istanbul, only halting on the orders of his father, who feared European intervention on the side of the Ottoman sultan. The defenseless sultan granted Mohammed Ali's request, and the Egyptian army withdrew.

Egypt's military achievements and expansion of control into Syria and Arabia alarmed the British, whose prime minister, Lord Palmerston, was anxious that Ottoman Turkey should continue as a barrier to Russian expansion into the Levant. In 1839 the British fleet attacked Ibrahim's position in Syria and blockaded the Egyptian navy in Alexandria. In 1840 Mohammed Ali was forced to sign the Treaty of London, under which Syria and Crete were returned to the sultan, the army was limited to 18,000 men, and the state-owned monopolies were converted into special trade concessions for the European powers. However, French intervention obtained for Mohammed Ali the hereditary right to rule as viceroy of Egypt, though still under the Ottoman sultan.

For the British this outcome was satisfactory, as long as French involvement in Egypt went no further. The French plan for the Suez Canal, which resurfaced in 1854, was vehemently opposed by Prime Minister Palmerston and his foreign secretary, Disraeli, although it was supported by an increasing number in Britain, including the Liberal leader, Gladstone. However, British investors refused to contribute to the canal, considering the scheme too expensive and well nigh impossible. Against all the odds, financial and labor problems, Ferdinand de Lesseps completed the canal in 1869, thus halving the journey from Western Europe to India and the Far East, which benefited Britain both militarily and commercially. However, the French-financed and -engineered canal also gave France a political foothold

French engineer Ferdinand de Lesseps (above) was commissioned in 1854 by the viceroy of Egypt, Said Pasha, to dig the Suez Canal (right), which was completed in 1869.

in Egypt, by which it could continue to oppose British influence in East Africa and the Middle East.

The agreement for the building and operation of the Suez Canal had been signed in November 1854 by de Lesseps and the then viceroy, Said Pasha, the third son of Mohammed Ali, who had been a boyhood friend of the Frenchman. On Said's death in 1863, the next viceroy was his nephew, Ismail, whose courage, charm, and intelligence compensated for his unattractive physical appearance.

Before he became viceroy, Ismail had the reputation of being a capable and successful manager of his private estates, but once he held the reins of power his ambition outstripped his managerial skills, and he was too proud to ask for advice. Early in his reign he was obliged to borrow money to pay off debts incurred by the Suez Canal. Then he borrowed more to finance his lavish celebrations to mark the opening of the Canal in 1869, which was attended by a number of European royalty, headed by Empress Eugénie, wife of Napoleon III of France. His grandiose projects for Egypt in irrigation and agriculture, harbor and shipping facilities, roads, bridges and railways, and schools (including the first for girls), as well as his creation of a new capital to the west of the old city in European style ("Paris by the Nile") all forced him to borrow more from European banks. By 1875 Ismail was no longer able to pay even the interest on his debts; and, in an attempt to raise money, he put his 44% share in the Suez Canal on the market. This was purchased for Britain for 4,000,000 pounds sterling by the prime minister, Disraeli, who was anxious to prevent such a large share going to a rival power. Several members of parliament were opposed to the purchase, including Gladstone, who foresaw serious implications of involvement in Egypt's internal affairs.

After a series of committees and investigations by various European powers, as Britain and France were the principal creditors, financial control eventually passed to them in what was known as the Dual Control. The British Commissioner was Captain Evelyn Baring, a member of the banking family, and former secretary of the viceroy of India, who was later to become the British consul general in Egypt. Severe measures were imposed on Egypt, but pay for government employees and troops lapsed many months in arrears, and the main burden of debt repayment fell as always on the long-suffering *fellahin*. Meanwhile the Turko-Circassian elite remained largely unaffected, and increasing numbers of Europeans were appointed to posts in the Egyptian civil service, on salaries which were extremely generous when compared with the meager payment accorded the Egyptians.

Unfortunately the judgment of history has linked Ismail inexorably with the loss of Egypt's independence, which he had so earnestly tried to win. The bankrupting of his country, caused by his grand schemes and insurmountable debts, has eclipsed his other notable achievements. In January 1876 the Alexandrian correspondent of *The Times* was moved to write, "*Egypt is a marvellous instance*

Khedive Ismail Pasha, whose lavish spending to celebrate the opening of the Suez Canal, as well as to improve & modernize Egypt, resulted in the country's bankruptcy & subsequent loss of independence to its European creditors.

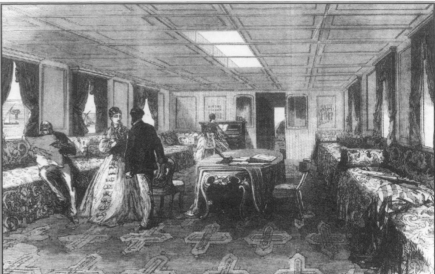

The preferred means of travel in Egypt by European tourists from early in the 19th Century on was by sail-powered river vessels called dahabiyas, *which could be modest in size, as above, or else quite grand, with a spacious salon for relaxing & entertaining, such as that seen above right.*

Above, crew of a dahabiya *relaxing on board. Below, sailors towing their vessel from the Nile bank.*

of progress. She has advanced as much in 70 years as many other countries have done in 500."

From the beginning of the 19th Century onwards, Egypt had become a favorite destination for the more intrepid traveler, as well as artists and antiquaries. The usual mode of transport was the *dahabiya* (a sail-powered riverboat), which was hired in Cairo, and sailed up the Nile at a leisurely pace to Aswan, or beyond into Nubia as far as the border with Sudan at Wadi Halfa. The artists David Roberts and Edward Lear and the historians Edward Lane and John Gardner Wilkinson, as well as Florence Nightingale and Amelia Edwards, all saw Egypt this way. This was also the mode of travel chosen by Amelia Peabody on her first visit to Egypt in 1884, when she hired a *dahabiya,* the *Philae,* to take her and Evelyn Barton Forbes to Upper Egypt. Thereafter she always considered sailing the best way to see Egypt, an opinion undoubtedly augmented by its romantic associations. Realizing and appreciating her fondness for the *dahabiya,* Emerson later purchased the *Philae* for her, renaming her the *Amelia Peabody Emerson.*

In 1830 an overland route through Egypt was opened up for passage to India, as an alternative to the long sea voyage round the Cape of Good Hope. Travelers would arrive by ship at Alexandria, then spend a few days (or sometimes weeks) in Cairo waiting for word that the ongoing steamer for India was approaching Suez, when they would then make a somewhat hazardous journey by wagon, horse, or camel across the desert to the small Red Sea port.

(2) Ashtray from Shepheard's Hotel

Porcelain ashtray, 5 in. square, decorated with red and green silhouette design of pyramid and sphinx, and inscribed "Shepheard's Hotel, Cairo."
Bought at Shepheard's in 1939.
Amelia Peabody Emerson was 87 years of age by then, but was still going

strong and continuing to spend part of each winter in Egypt. She pur-
chased the ashtray because of the outbreak of World War II in September
1939 and the uncertainty of when she might return to Egypt.

Hotels were opened in Suez and Cairo for the transit passengers, one
of which, the British Hotel founded in Cairo in 1841, was renamed
Shepheard's Hotel after its manager, and became a famous British
institution in the city. In 1849 the hotel moved to a larger building
around the corner on the site of an old Mameluke palace, which
Napoleon had used as his headquarters in 1798. This was Amelia's
favorite hotel in Cairo, where she and Emerson usually occupied a
room overlooking the Ezbekieh Gardens. Sadly, on January 26th,
1952, "Black Saturday," Shepheard's was burned down during anti-
British riots, which also destroyed the nearby Turf Club, another bas-
tion of British society in the city. Only a few minutes' walk from
Shepheard's Hotel was the infamous Red Blind district, Wagh el Birka
(where Nefret established her first clinic for distressed women in
1911-12). During the First World War, Sir Thomas Russell, the assistant police commandant for whom Ramses worked undercover, attempted to clean up the area but had only limited success.

*A paddle steamer of the type used
by Thomas Cook for his popular
river tours of Egypt.*

(3) Advertisement for Cook's Tours of Egypt

**Founded in the 1840s, the travel company of Thomas Cook first
began operating in Europe, and started running Nile cruises in
Egypt from 1869 onwards. "Cook's Programme," which was published annually, gave full information on itineraries, accommodations, prices, etc. As well as the popular paddle steamers, Cook's
also had luxury-class *dahabiyas* available for charter by those who
had the time and the money to make a prolonged tour.**

*Miss Gertrude Marmaduke, who was engaged in Cairo for the 1899-1900
season to tutor Ramses and Nefret, "had come out on a Cook's Tour and
fallen in love with Egypt."*

In 1869, an enterprising Englishman named Thomas Cook, who had
already operated tours to France, Switzerland, and Italy, at prices
affordable to the more modest income of the up-and-coming middle
class, conducted his first tour to Egypt. Using steamboats, which were
more reliable than the sail-powered *dahabiya*s, and charging an all-
inclusive price, with guaranteed comfort, Cook's first tour was a great
success. The following year his son, John, opened an office on the
grounds of Shepheard's Hotel, and business expanded rapidly. Some
independent travelers regarded Cook's success with horror, considering Cook's tourists to be "common."

In 1879 Ismail made a vain attempt to dismiss his European
ministers and establish control, but under pressure from Britain and
France, the Ottoman sultan deposed Ismail in favor of his eldest son,
Tewfik. The new viceroy was a weak ruler, who tried to cooperate with

Khedive Tewfik Pasha.

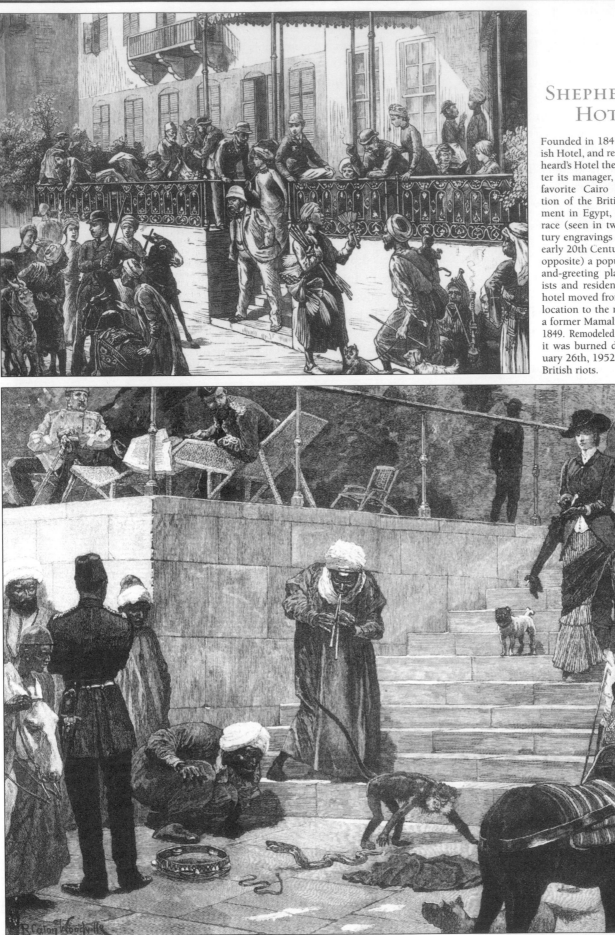

SHEPHEARD'S HOTEL

Founded in 1841 as the British Hotel, and renamed Shepheard's Hotel the next year after its manager, this was the favorite Cairo accommodation of the British establishment in Egypt, its front terrace (seen in two 19th Century engravings at left and in early 20th Century snapshots opposite) a popular meeting-and-greeting place for tourists and residents alike. The hotel moved from its original location to the nearby site of a former Mamaluke palace in 1849. Remodeled several times, it was burned down on January 26th, 1952, during anti-British riots.

As Readers of Mrs. Emerson's journals know, Shepheard's was the favorite hotel of the Emerson family when they arrived in Cairo for their nearly annual winter season of excavation. They always took rooms overlooking the Ezbekieh Gardens (above).

Nationalist leader, Colonel Ahmad Orabi, who in 1881-82 led an unsuccessful revolt to oust Khedive Tewfik & his European supporters, the British & French.

both the European powers and the Ottoman government, and was completely dominated by the European consuls, much to the dismay of a number of rich landowners, who had hoped to bring about a constitutional form of government. However, Tewfik had autocratic leanings, and when he dismissed his recently appointed prime minister, who had drawn up a constitution, opposition movements against the khedive and his European supporters began to ferment, with the aim of achieving "Egypt for the Egyptians." The leader of the movement was a native Egyptian colonel, Ahmad Orabi.

Although the Dual Control was gradually bringing about improvements in the *fellahin* situation, there was still discontent in the army. In February 1881 Orabi led a revolt against the privileged status of the Turko-Circassian element. Army officers were Turks or Circassians, while the bulk of the soldiers were from the peasant class. Orabi himself was of *fellahin* stock, and had obtained the rank of lieutenant-colonel under Said Pasha, who favored the *fellahin*; but under his successor, Ismail, who held such native officers in contempt, he had not risen in rank. He was finally promoted to colonel under Tewfik.

In September 1881 Orabi and his supporters marched to Abdin Palace and demanded action from the khedive to appoint a national parliament and increase the size of the army. These demands were backed by force, which meant that the khedive was humiliated by the army, and his authority was weakened still further. Orabi was appointed as minister of war. In January 1882 a Joint Note was issued by Britain and France assuring the khedive of their support, which was taken by the Egyptians to indicate further interference in Egyptian affairs, and military intervention. The two European powers regarded Orabi as a dangerous element and potential military dictator, who would not honor the country's debt. To the Egyptian people, however, he was a national hero, who would rescue them from foreign tyranny.

Nationalist demands continued, and in the summer of 1882

Riots & looting in Alexandria in the early summer of 1882 (above) led to a mass evacuation of the city by its European population (above left) &, at the request of the Khedive Tewfik, the bombardment of Alexandria by the British navy (left). Subsequently, British forces were dispatched to Egypt (below) to put down the rebellion led by Orabi.

Tewfik asked for military assistance, and a joint British and French fleet was sent to Alexandria. Tension in the city was high, foreign residents fearing they would be massacred by the native population. Riots broke out and were quelled by Orabi, but several people, Egyptians and foreigners, had been killed and parts of the city looted and set on fire. Tewfik suggested that the allied ships should bombard the city. The French refused and withdrew, but the British bombarded Alexandria on the pretext that Orabi was building up fortifications against the British fleet, although evidence suggests that these were

Overleaf, the Battle of Tell el Kebir, September 13, 1882, lasted just 35 minutes.

actually repairs being carried out on existing fortifications, which posed no threat to the British ships. (Observing the bombardment from the deck of the admiral's flagship was a young subaltern of the Royal Engineers, Horatio Herbert Kitchener, whose future career would be linked with Egypt.) The bombardment lasted for over 10 hours, until most of the forts were destroyed or seriously damaged, and parts of the city demolished. The Egyptian army left Alexandria in flames, and large areas were destroyed, as much by looters and native elements as by the bombardment. Order was restored three days later by a force of British marines, who took over the ruined city.

Orabi now declared that the Egyptians and the British were at war, and the country rallied to his support. The khedive proclaimed Orabi a rebel, while Orabi in his turn denounced Tewfik as a traitor. The British government under Gladstone voted to send an expeditionary force, not only to protect the Suez Canal, but more particularly to restore peace and order to Egypt as a whole. Twenty thousand British troops were landed in the Canal Zone, and in the Battle of Tell el Kebir the Egyptian army was defeated in just 35 minutes. The Nationalists surrendered Cairo, Orabi was exiled to Ceylon, and the "temporary" British occupation of Egypt began. It was to continue until 1954.

The other European powers, France, Russia, Germany, and Turkey, were furious at Britain's intervention and demanded to know its intentions. The British said they would leave as soon as the authority of the khedive and financial stability were restored. However, there always seemed to be good reasons for staying. The two primary aims took longer to achieve; the Egyptians needed to be shown how to govern themselves, and there was the continuing importance of the security of the Suez Canal. There was also the question of Sudan.

In September 1883 Sir Evelyn Baring (later Lord Cromer) arrived in Cairo as the new British agent and consul-general. Forty-three years old, he had already served twice in Egypt, first as the British Commissioner of Debt in 1877-79, and then briefly as finance controller. He had just completed three years as financial member of Council for India, for which he had been knighted. While in India he had earned himself the nicknames of "Vice-Viceroy" and "Over-Baring" for his somewhat imperious manner. The impressions of his personality which these names implied were no less evident when he returned to Egypt as consul general, and he actually earned a third nickname as *El Lurd*, "The Lord."

In his 25 years as consul general, Baring steered Egypt through various financial and political hazards, and was a legend in his own time. He was an extremely able administrator and financier, a disciplined man with an appetite for hard work, whose seriousness could be unnerving, but nonetheless one who inspired devotion as well as respect in many of his colleagues. (When Amelia said his complacency reminded her of her brothers, she was no doubt referring to his air

Sir Evelyn Baring, later Lord Cromer, served as British consul general of Egypt for 25 years, beginning in 1883.

of "solid British respectability.")

Baring agreed with Prime Minister Gladstone that a lengthy occupation of Egypt by Britain was not wanted, and he believed at first that Britain could leave as soon as the finances were set in order and the authority of the khedive restored. He changed his mind within a year, having come to the conclusion that it would take a very long time, possibly centuries, before the principles of European civilization could be instilled into the native Egyptians, thus making them capable of ruling themselves. In his opinion, the only element of the population with any governing ability was the Turko-Circassian minority. He made no attempt to understand the Egyptian mentality or cultural traditions, and, although he spoke fluent French and some Turkish (the languages of the ruling class in Egypt), he did not try to learn Arabic, the language of the Egyptian people.

Baring's "eyes and ears" was Harry Boyle, an expert linguist, who joined the consular service in Cairo in 1885 at the age of 22. Given six weeks to bring his Arabic up to scratch, Boyle disappeared into the popular areas of the city disguised as a Turk, and reported back after just five weeks with an astounding grasp of the language. In spite of his eccentric ways and consistently untidy appearance, Boyle soon became Baring's confidante (the special title of Oriental Secretary was created for him in 1888). The two would meet almost every day and discuss matters while walking beside the Nile. This was jokingly referred to as *"Enoch walking with the Lord."*

The number of Britons and other Europeans taking up positions in Egyptian government offices steadily increased, and Baring was quite literally the power behind the khedival throne. Egyptian officials occupied the highest positions in the government, but there was always a British adviser or civil servant directing their actions and decisions. The phrase "Veiled Protectorate" was coined to describe this state of affairs, and this was essentially the way Egypt was run under Baring. In spite of the fact that Egypt never became a colony of the British Empire, Baring as consul general had more influence over government policy and running the country than the viceroy in India.

(4) Invitation to dinner at the British Agency, March 1895.
The new British Agency was constructed while Lord Cromer was consul-general, in the newly developed area of Garden City. The building was in colonial style, with a large garden leading down to the Nile at the rear. The English oak tree planted in the front garden by the second Lady Cromer is still there over a century later.
A note on the back of the invitation in Amelia's handwriting states: "The prawn curry lived up to expectation!" During Cromer's time as consul-general, the food at the Agency was legendary, and the prawn curry was especially famous. Prince George, one of Queen Victoria's sons, asked for it immediately on landing at Suez.

After the defeat of Orabi and his forces in the Battle of Tell el

Kebir in 1882, Khedive Tewfik had dismissed the army, and in 1883 the task of forming a new Egyptian army was entrusted to Major-General Sir Evelyn Wood, who was appointed its first *sirdar* (commander-in-chief). Among the other British officers was Kitchener, who himself became *sirdar* in 1892. The regular soldiers were mostly Egyptians and Sudanese, and although the number of both Egyptian and Sudanese officers gradually increased, the senior posts were held by British officers. Like the civil service, the Egyptian army came to be regarded as one of the best opportunities for advancement. It was this opportunity which attracted Amelia's obnoxious nephew, Percy Peabody, who joined the Egyptian army in 1911, though his "advancement" was short-lived.

THE SUDAN

In 1819 Mohammed Ali had sent a military force up the Nile to conquer Sudan, which thereafter had been governed by Egypt as a part of the Ottoman Empire. In the decades that followed, the Egyptian administration at Khartoum became increasingly oppressive and corrupt. A blind eye was also being turned to the activities of the Arab slave traders, although slavery had officially been abolished in Egypt itself. Southern Sudan was annexed for Egypt in 1870-73 by the British explorer, Sir Samuel Baker, under appointment from Ismail Pasha. His mission was to annex the Upper Nile to Egypt and abolish the slave trade there. This was a ploy on the part of Ismail, who wished to maintain the support of the powers in Europe, where the abolition of the slave trade had strong political backing.

In 1874 Khedive Ismail appointed Colonel Charles George Gordon as governor of Equatoria, the southern province of Sudan, again largely to allay foreign suspicion of Egypt's attitude to the slave trade. Already famous for his military exploits in the Crimean War and China, Gordon was a mystical and mysterious enigma, regarded by some as a maverick, a deeply religious man, whose courage, leadership, and selfless concern for all humanity inspired unshakable devotion in those who served him. He was a true hero of the age.

Ismail and Gordon planned to push Egyptian control southward to annex the Nile as far as its source in Lake Victoria. Gordon did not completely achieve this, but he did at least bring relative security to Equatoria, drove out the slavers, and converted the hostility of local tribes into friendship, all in only two and a half years. He resigned in 1876, perhaps partly because he was disillusioned that in spite of his own great success, he could see the enormity of the Sudan problem.

In January 1877 Ismail persuaded Gordon to return to the Sudan, and at Gordon's request appointed him governor-general of all Sudan, giving him *carte blanche* with arms and men. Gordon was unbribeable, energetic, and disciplined, frequently riding to trouble spots on a fast camel. The provinces of Bahr el Ghazal and Darfur were

General Charles George Gordon, governor-general of the Sudan.

taken by military force from the Arab chief, Zobeir. The governor-generalship of Bahr el Ghazal was given to the Italian Romolo Gessi, a long-standing member of Gordon's staff, while that of Darfur went to a young Austrian named Rudolf Carl von Slatin. After five years Gordon's drive and commitment to the Sudan and its problems was beginning to wane; much had been achieved, but much still remained unchanged.

In March 1878 Ismail had summoned Gordon to Cairo to preside over the board of inquiry into his financial affairs. The European creditors refused to forego the interest for a limited period. Gordon and Baring met for the first time, an uneasy encounter, as Baring represented the establishment and Gordon did not. Gordon returned to Khartoum but was increasingly nervous, lonely, and exhausted. The deposing of Ismail in June 1879 was the last straw for Gordon, and he resigned a month later.

As soon as the firm hand at the helm had gone, the government authority collapsed, and the country was ripe for revolt. Slatin was still governor in Darfur, the German Emin in Equatoria, and the Englishman, Frank Lupton, had replaced Gessi in Bahr el Ghazal; but the Europeans were powerless with the Egyptian governor-general, Raouf Pasha, who had previously been dismissed by Gordon for his maltreatment of Africans. Raouf Pasha was replaced in 1882 by Abdel Kader, who was a better man, but it was too late.

Mohammed Ahmed, El Mahdi, "Rightly Guided" leader of the revolt against Egyptian control of the Sudan.

Hatred of Egyptians was the primary cause of rebellion in the Sudan. There were about 28,000 of them in the country, and their attitude towards the Sudanese was very oppressive, harsh, and corrupt. Early in 1881 the stirrings of unrest had found a native leader in Mohammed Ahmed, who called himself the Mahdi, an Arabic word meaning "Rightly Guided" and referring to an Islamic deliverer. Mohammed Ahmed had great charisma and was a persuasive orator. He was worshipped as semi-divine by his followers (whom he called "Dervishes," meaning literally "poor men"), and people flocked to his banner in huge numbers. At first his army was equipped only with spears and sticks, but after laying siege to the large town of El Obeid, which had an Egyptian garrison, and finally taking it in January 1883, a store of weapons and a large sum of money was captured. The Mahdi then established his headquarters in Government House at El Obeid.

Egypt was slow to react to the growing Mahdi movement, but the fall of Kordofan, the richest province in Sudan, made the situation urgent. Britain wanted no part in it, so in the summer of 1883 the Egyptian government got together its own military force of approximately 6,000 men, under the command of an ex-Indian army officer, Colonel William Hicks. The force traveled up the Nile to about 100 miles south of Khartoum, and then headed west towards El Obeid.

Summer was the worst time of year for such a campaign, and mismanagement of the expedition produced constant problems. There was a lack of water, men and camels were dying, the lines of

Colonel William Hicks.

Khartoum.

supply were cut off by the Mahdi's men, and the troops got lost in the desert, possibly being deliberately led astray by their guides. The exact details of the battle which took place are unknown, as there were very few survivors, and all the senior officers, including Hicks, were killed. It was two weeks before the tragic news reached the outside world.

The Mahdi was now on the crest of a wave, with his popularity and support swelling by the day. Panic was rife in Khartoum, and many rich families fled to Egypt. Slatin was cut off in Darfur; and, after converting to Islam to keep the support of his troops, he eventually surrendered, as did Lupton in Bahr el Ghazal. Emin in Equatoria retreated further up the Nile.

Gladstone declared at the end of 1883 that Khartoum must look out for itself, and likewise the Egyptians in Sudanese garrisons must fend for themselves. But there were others in Britain who felt that action should be taken, and they were looking for a man to champion their cause. After leaving Sudan, Gordon had occupied several posts, but only for a short duration in each case, and his thoughts were constantly on Sudan. Members of parliament, journalists, and the public wanted action after the massacre of Hicks and his troops. It was suggested that Gordon should lead an expeditionary force.

Gladstone was over a barrel; in Cairo neither Baring nor Tewfik wanted Gordon, but the British government and Gordon did not realize the danger or seriousness of the Mahdi uprising. The Mahdi and his followers were not like earlier lawless tribesmen, but were at the head of a national religious movement. In order to find a compromise in the face of opposition from Gladstone and Baring, the foreign secretary, Granville, stated that Gordon would go to Sudan simply to report on the situation, would take his orders from Baring, and was only to report and evacuate the garrisons and civilians if possible. He was to play no military or political role. However, when Gordon was summoned to meet Baring during his brief stay in Cairo, he was reappointed governor-general of the Sudan.

Gordon made great use of the telegraph to report back to

Rudolph Carl von Slatin.

Baring, sometimes sending as many as 20-30 messages a day. Berber was still holding out against the Mahdi. Gordon was welcomed enthusiastically when he arrived in Khartoum on February 18th, 1884. He made concessions to keep the support and loyalty of the local people and all seemed well at first. Then Gordon began gradually to worry about abandoning the people to anarchy and the Mahdi, also arguing that, once he was in Khartoum, the Mahdi would be a threat to Egypt. Gordon pointed out that if a military force was sent to crush the Mahdi now, it would be much easier than if he were in Khartoum. On March 13th the tribes north of Khartoum went over to the Mahdi and Khartoum was cut off.

For the next 10 months, until January 1885, there was little news out from Gordon except by native runners, and then only scraps of information. Slatin, Lupton, and some other Europeans were prisoners of the Mahdi. In May Berber fell. For a time Gordon was not too badly off in Khartoum; there were 34,000 inhabitants, of whom about 8,000 were soldiers, and the town was not too difficult to defend. There was the Blue Nile to the north, the White Nile to the west, and, on the west bank, a strong Egyptian garrison was posted in Omdurman Fort. The siege of the town began, especially from the southern side facing the desert, but this was not a serious threat throughout the summer, and Gordon's confidence was an inspiration to all. As a way of keeping up the spirits of the soldiers and inhabitants of Khartoum, Gordon designed and issued a decoration for gallantry he called the "Khartoum Star."

(5) General Gordon's Khartoum Star
Decoration designed by General Gordon during siege of Khartoum 1884. Manufactured in Khartoum by local goldsmith Bishara Abdel Molak.
Obverse: Seven-pointed star with crescent and star in each angle. Grenade in center encircled by Turkish inscription, "The Siege of Khartoum, 1301 Hejira" (Islamic date equivalent to AD 1884).
Reverse: plain
Pewter, 2 inches (6 cm.) wide
Suspended by loop with crescent and star
Pewter version issued to all NCOs and men, female servants of troops, and school students. (Silver version issued to senior officers, notables, merchants, and civilian employees; silver-gilt version to junior officers.)
According to a note in the box containing the Star, it was given to Ramses by Amelia on his 11th birthday, partly because she was an admirer of Gordon, and also as a reward for Ramses' bravery and ingenuity during the Emersons' hazardous expedition to Sudan in 1897.

In Britain the feeling that Gordon should be rescued was gaining more

Fanatical charge of the Mahdists against Her Majesty's forces at Al Tab in February 1884. The primitively armed rebels were defeated.

and more support. Even Queen Victoria remarked so to Lord Hartington, the minister for war. Gladstone and Glanville were still procrastinating, and it is true that, up until September, Gordon could have escaped; but he was totally against leaving his soldiers behind. Baring also suggested a military expedition, but Gladstone was adamantly opposed to it. By July public opinion was too strong, and when Lord Hartington threatened to resign, Gladstone at last agreed. The relief expedition set out in September, under the command of Lord Wolseley, victor of the Battle of Tell el Kebir. (Serving as an intelligence officer with the expedition was Major Herbert Kitchener.)

The dramatic events of the next six months have all the elements of a Victorian melodrama: Gordon waiting on the palace roof in Khartoum, surrounded by the forces of the Mahdi camped in the desert; Wolseley heading up the Nile to the rescue; all three caught in the hand of fate; and over everything an air of impending doom.

In early September Gordon decided to send Colonel Stewart, his second-in-command, down river with messages to the advance column of the expedition in Dongola. The steamers departed on September 8th, leaving Gordon completely alone, although he almost seems to have wanted it that way. He spent hours on the palace roof with his telescope looking northward for any signs of rescue. By the last week in September there was definite news that the expedition was on its way, and celebrations were held in Khartoum. However, as the siege went on into October, misgivings increased, and there were

The British expedition sent to rescue Gordon at Khartoum is seen hauling a boat past the 2nd Cataract.

shortages of food. Gordon received two letters from Slatin, which angered him, (he felt Slatin had betrayed his religion to save his skin), but the second letter had the news that the boats with Stewart had not got through, and he and most of the other Europeans had been killed. A letter also came from the Mahdi himself offering Gordon surrender. As one would expect, however, Gordon sent a contemptuous reply, and the Mahdi moved up to Khartoum with his main force, encouraged by information on conditions in Khartoum described in the papers that had been captured with Stewart. He camped with his army near Omdurman, and on November 12th began shelling Khartoum. Omdurman Fort was cut off, so Gordon sent the remaining boats north to Metemma, the last on December 15th with his journal and papers.

Conditions in Khartoum were becoming more and more desperate: the water level of the Nile was falling, the enemy was getting closer, food supplies were running out, and the dead were lying in the streets. On January 5, 1885, Omdurman Fort surrendered. The Arabs were closing in, but Gordon still rallied his men under the constant bombardment. Egyptian and Sudanese soldiers and civilians were deserting to the Mahdi; still Gordon continued to give the impression of being fearless.

The rescue force was making its final push upriver to Khartoum, but encounters with the Arabs on the way, and the difficulties caused by the low water level at that time of year, made progress difficult. On January 17th in the Battle of Abu Klea, about 80 miles away from Khartoum, the Mahdists were defeated, unknown to Gordon. On January 24th a flotilla of two steamers with just over 200 men carried on upriver, but in Khartoum all hope of relief had been abandoned. At 3:00 a.m. on January 26th, the Arabs launched their attack on the town at the south side, where a ditch had filled with dried mud as the river level dropped. Little resistance was offered, and there was brutal slaughter of all encountered as the Mahdists forced their way into the town. Gordon was killed on the steps of the palace just before dawn, and his head was taken to the Mahdi at Omdurman, where it was shown to Slatin. In the two days of looting and slaughter which followed, about 4,000 inhabitants of Khartoum were killed.

Two days later, on the afternoon of January 28th — poignantly, Gordon's 52nd birthday — the British expedition at last appeared within sight of the town. When the boats were fired on, and no Egyptian flag was seen flying on Government House, it became clear that Khartoum had fallen, and the steamers retreated from the disaster under heavy fire. They then had a harrowing journey back to Metemma. Wolseley wanted to advance on Berber and prepare for a counter-attack later in the year, but London ordered him to return, so the expedition retreated ignominiously to Egypt.

(6) Medal commemorating the death of General Gordon.
Bronze, 2 inches (5 cm.) in diameter
Obverse: Bust of General Gordon wearing tarboosh, facing left
Inscription: GENERAL (left) GORDON (right)
Reverse: Wreath and sword above inscription: IN MEMORY OF
    "CHINESE" GORDON, BORN JANY 23 (sic), 1833,
    DIED AT KHARTOUM, JANY 26, 1885.

Gordon had been a household name in Britain since the siege of Khartoum began, and there was much public anger and distress at his

When Khartoum fell to the Mahdists on January 26, 1885, General Gordon was slain on the steps of the governor's palace & decapitated. His head was sent to El Mahdi, then displayed on a pike in the victors' camp (below).

tragic end. Gladstone was held much to blame for being slow to act. Queen Victoria wrote personally to Gordon's sister, speaking of *"the stain left upon England, for your dear Brother's cruel, though heroic fate."* He was even commemorated in a music hall song:

Too late, too late to save him,
In vain, in vain they tried.
His life was England's glory,
His death was England's pride.

While Amelia was too occupied with Emerson, Evelyn, and Amarna, from October 1884 to January 1885, to record the details of Gordon's fall at the time, no doubt she had the news on her return to Cairo. Before the end of 1885, Gordon's journals were published in two bestselling volumes, copies of which can be found in the Peabody-Emerson Library at Amarna House.

After taking Khartoum, the Mahdi began to live an idyllic life in his harem. Tribesmen were still flocking to Khartoum, where some order had been restored, but life was miserable for the inhabitants. On June 22nd, 1885, the Mahdi died, the exact cause of his death at the age of only 43 unknown. One of his lieutenants, the Khalifa Abdullah, was chosen as his successor. Cruel, but also energetic and shrewd, the Khalifa encouraged the veneration of the Mahdi, and pilgrims began to visit his fine, domed tomb. Slavery was revived as a major industry.

Slatin was employed by the Khalifa as an interpreter, sometimes being treated as a confidant, at others imprisoned and in chains. Omdurman was expanded into a city, while most of Khartoum was destroyed. The Khalifa became very powerful, adhering to strict religious practice, which helped to make the Arabs feel that they were invincible with divine help. Little news filtered through to Egypt and the outside world.

There was a feeling in Europe that Christianity was being defiled by Muslim fanatics, and the Anti-Slavery Society in Britain also painted a grim picture. However, the Khalifa's rule was accepted in Sudan, there was a coherent state, with no refugees, and the Khalifa actually controlled more territory than the Mahdi had. He wrote in turn to Queen Victoria, the Ottoman sultan, and the Egyptian khedive, asking for their submission. Britain, Turkey, and Egypt had no desire to invade Sudan again, although there was fear in Egypt that the Mahdists might make a move on Egypt, which was affirmed in summer 1888 when Emir Negumi with about 10,000 men advanced 60 miles into Egypt north of Wadi Halfa. However, a year later in August 1889, Negumi was defeated at the Battle of Toshka, which was a great victory for the Egyptians, as most of the soldiers were Egyptian. Thus the Mahdist threat to Egypt was ended.

By now Sudan was ravaged by continual war, the slave trade, smallpox and other diseases, famine, and a plague of locusts. From 1889 onwards the Khalifa's control was in decline, and first-hand reports on his weakened state began to surface. In 1891 the Austrian

Above, the tomb built for El Mahdi at Khartoum following his death in 1885. Below, ruins of the tomb after shelling of Khartoum by the British in 1898.

British calvary patrol skirmishes
with Mahdist warriors during
the reconquest of the Sudan in
1896.

priest Father Ohrwalder and two nuns escaped, and in 1895 Slatin also escaped. In 1897, just two years following his escape, Amelia, Emerson, and Ramses met him during their Sudan expedition. (A signed copy of his account of his life in Sudan, imprisonment, and escape is also to be found in the Peabody-Emerson Library. It has obviously been read several times, and, from pencil notes in the margin, the memoir was a favorite of Ramses Emerson.)

Britain was also beginning to press for another campaign in Sudan, on account of international politics as usual, and the age-old policy of keeping France out of Sudan. At last, in 1896, Cook's pleasure steamers were requisitioned to transport about 10,000 Egyptian soldiers and British officers upriver to the border at Wadi Halfa. In command of the expedition was General Kitchener, who had been appointed *sirdar* of the Egyptian army in 1892. Slatin was also on the staff, along with Wingate, the intelligence officer.

The journey took two years and was very carefully planned. In March 1896 the defeat of the Italians by Abyssinians at Adowa, in a failed attempt to expand Italy's Eritrean colony, raised the specter of the Khalifa attacking other Egyptian- and European-held posts in East Africa. Cromer was ordered to send Kitchener and the Egyptian army up the Nile to recapture the province of Dongola which was taken on September 23rd. Kitchener pressed for the Sudan Railway to be extended to Abu Hamed, a distance of 225 miles southward. The work began on January 1st, 1897, and by July 23rd 103 miles had been completed. An advance force took Abu Hamed on August 7th. Only a few Dervishes escaped, and Berber was abandoned to the invaders. It was this encouraging news that inspired Emerson to propose an expedition to Gebel Barkal in the fall of that same year in order to excavate the pyramids of Nuri.

Cromer and British Prime Minister Salisbury would not agree to Kitchener continuing the advance. On December 18th Wingate of the Intelligence Service warned Kitchener that the Khalifa was about to attack Berber with his entire army. Lord Salisbury authorized Cromer and Kitchener to take whatever British troops were needed. On January 4th, 1898, Kitchener was appointed supreme commander of all British and Egyptian troops south of Aswan. On April 8th, at the Battle of Nakheila, Emir Mahmud and a large force were defeated. The Egyptian army then moved into summer quarters around Berber.

(7) Sundry newspaper cuttings from the *Morning Post*, 1898.
Reports by W. S. Churchill on the campaign for the reconquest of Sudan.
Having promised Lord Kitchener that he would not send reports to a newspaper, he got round this by sending long, detailed letters to his mother, Lady Randolph Churchill, who then passed them on to the *Morning Post*.

More troops continued to arrive, including the 21st Lancers, to which young Winston Churchill had been attached as a junior officer. There was a certain amount of resentment towards him because of his critical remarks about the North-West Frontier campaign in India, and the fact that he had only got to Egypt through the influence of his charming mother. By mid-August the whole expeditionary force had assembled at Wadi Hamed, only 58 miles from Omdurman, and on August 24th the advance began. On September 1st Omdurman was bombarded from gunboats on the river and artillery on the east bank. The Mahdi's tomb was severely damaged. Dervish troops about 50,000 strong assembled on the plain, and just after dawn the following day the Battle of Omdurman commenced. Although outnumbered by over two to one, the superior training and more up-to-date artillery of the Anglo-Egyptian army wreaked great slaughter among the Dervishes. Gunboats firing on them from the Nile were also very effective, and by 11:30 a.m. it was just about over. Anglo-Egyptian casualties were surprisingly low, but about 10,000 Dervishes were slain and several thousands wounded.

Many of Kitchener's army felt great respect for the courage and tenacity of the Dervishes. Winston Churchill was among a group of officers who inspected the battlefield three days later and was moved to write, *"But there was nothing dulce et decorum about the Dervish dead; nothing of the dignity of unconquerable manhood; all was filthy corrup-*

General Herbert Kitchener.

tion. Yet these were as brave men as ever walked the earth. The conviction was borne in on me that their claim beyond the grave in respect of a valiant death was not less good than that which any of our countrymen could make." (*The River War*, London, 1899)

In the evening after the battle, when Kitchener entered Omdurman there was very little resistance, but terrible scenes greeted the soldiers, and the Khalifa had escaped. A small cavalry troop was sent in pursuit, but did not find him. He fled to Kordofan, where he continued to plan his return. (Eventually he was tracked down and killed, in November 1899, by a force under Wingate.) At last there was the feeling that Gordon had been avenged. A memorial ceremony was held on September 4th in front of the ruined palace in Khartoum, and the British and Egyptian flags were raised side by side on the roof.

(Slatin was rewarded with a knighthood after Omdurman, and became inspector-general of Sudan. Later he became head of the Red Cross in his native Austria and was much respected for his humane treatment of Allied prisoners in World War I.)

Kitchener received a hero's welcome back in Britain, which was somewhat soured by press accusations of desecration of the Mahdi's tomb and brutality to Dervishes. A compromise devised by Cromer was finally reached over Sudan. In January 1899 the Condominium was ratified, whereby sovereignty was shared between Britain and Egypt. Military and civil command was in the hands of a governor-general appointed by the khedive on British recommendation. Kitchener was appointed as governor-general, as had been suggested by Gordon years before, and established a civil service which gained a reputation for its justice, efficient administration, and concern for people's welfare. Khartoum was rebuilt. Kitchener's methods may have been rather peremptory, but they were effective.

Sudan prospered, but Egyptian relations with Britain worsened because of the khedive's anti-British sentiments, and the growing Nationalist Movement, which resented the British presence in Sudan. Britain, on the other hand, regarded the situation as proof of the imperial mission to spread civilization: peace had been restored to the lands of the Nile, France had been thwarted, and the security of the Suez Canal was assured.

Khedive Tewfik had died in 1892 and was succeeded by his 18-year-old son, Abbas Hilmy, who had been educated in Vienna and felt he did not need a British mentor. To add insult to injury, Cromer treated him as a master would a schoolboy. (Baring was now Lord Cromer, having been made a peer in 1892.) Abbas supported the new Nationalist Movement led by a young lawyer named Mustafa Kamil, a movement supported by professionals such as David Todros. Cromer considered the Movement unimportant, but strikes and demonstrations became a common feature.

By 1900 Cromer had succeeded in sorting out Egypt's finances and reducing the burdensome taxes of the *fellahin*. Cotton growing

Khedive Abbas Hilmy.

was strongly supported, as it was a profitable commercial crop, but the consul-general was criticized for doing more to benefit the Lancashire cotton industry than the Egyptian economy. Local industries were discouraged, as it was felt that these would result in a disastrous neglect of agriculture, but near the end of his term, Cromer realized that this policy would have to change because of population increase, which caused the need for alternative employment and created a demand for skilled labor.

Education also received little attention, partly because Cromer wished to economize, but also because he held to the Victorian liberal view that it was not the duty of the state to provide education, thereby reversing the policy of Mohammed Ali and Ismail. He was also anxious not to create a class of discontented Egyptian intellectuals with rebellious intent, and opposed the founding of a university for the same reason. (A university was eventually established in Cairo in 1908 under Sir Eldon Gorst, Cromer's successor as consul general.) However, he did not interfere with the religious schools attached to mosques, or the Islamic university of El Azhar.

One of the biggest and most lasting contributions to the welfare of Egypt during the British occupation was the work of the irrigation engineers, which was also much appreciated by the Egyptian farmers. Men such as Sir Colin Scott-Moncrieff and Sir William Willcocks supervised the repair of barrages (small dams) in the Delta, the digging and repairing of canals, and the building of two new barrages at Zifta in the Delta and Assiut in Upper Egypt. The crowning achievement was the building of the Aswan Dam, which was designed by Willcocks, and constructed between 1898 and 1902, to control the annual inundation of the Nile and increase crop yields.

In its mission to improve the lot of the underprivileged, the British Agency under Cromer did its utmost to abolish slavery, and what Cromer referred to as "the three Cs," *corvée* (the ancient system of forced labor, especially for clearing and maintaining irrigation canals), the *courbash,* or whip, and corruption. By the 1890s the slave trade in Egypt had been almost completely eradicated, *corvée* had been abolished, corruption reduced, and the use of the whip was prohibited but had not completely disappeared. The increase in crime, particularly in rural areas, during the British occupation was very disheartening. The whip had been a traditional part of the justice system in Egypt, as a way of extorting evidence or a confession. Cromer later concluded that its prohibition, along with reforms in the judicial system and the laws of evidence, meant that people went in less fear of the law, so controlling crime became more difficult.

British engineer Sir William Willcocks & the Aswan Dam (below) which he designed.

During the summer of 1906, an incident occurred in the Delta which became a turning point in the British occupation. Denshawai was a small village near Tanta in the central Nile Delta. Like many villages, it had large mud-brick pigeon towers where the villagers bred pigeons for food. In 1905 some British officers had gone pigeon shooting there for sport. The villagers protested, but the only agreement made was that no one could shoot pigeons in the village without the permission of the *omda* (village headman).

A year later, on June 13th, 1906, a group of five British officers were again at the village at the invitation of a local landowner. In the absence of the *omda*, his deputy agreed that they could shoot pigeons, but well away from the village. The villagers again protested the threat to their livelihood and tried to beat off the officers with their wooden staffs. In the scuffle a gun went off and three men and a woman were wounded. The villagers then stepped up their attack with stones. One officer went off to a nearby camp for help, but died of concussion and sunstroke on the way. A party of soldiers coming to help beat to death a *fellah* who was trying to assist him. The other officers all escaped.

Fifty-two villagers were arrested and tried before a special court two weeks later. The judges were three British officers (none of whom could speak much, if any, Arabic), and two Egyptians, one of whom, as president of the court, was the minister of justice, Boutros Ghali, a Christian. Very severe sentences were passed on the accused: four were sentenced to death, two to penal servitude for life, six to seven years in prison, and the remaining to 40 to 50 lashes. The hanging and flogging were carried out the next day, and the villagers were forced to watch.

The incident had spiraled out of control because of the insensitivity and high-handed attitude of the British officers involved in the first instance, and it was compounded by the misinterpretation of the situation. There had actually been no real threat of a general uprising, and the trouble had been spontaneous. However, Cromer and the majority of the Europeans took it as an example of Nationalist xenophobia and saw the punishments as a warning to the Egyptians against planning any similar attacks. Cromer was about to go on his summer leave when the incident occurred, so he was not in Egypt during the trial. He and several members of the British parliament, including the foreign secretary, Lord Grey, were shocked by the harshness of the sentences, but it was considered unwise to override the tribunal. From then on national sentiment against the British became much more widespread, even among Egyptians who had previously supported the occupation.

When a Liberal government came to power in England in 1907, Cromer realized that his authority in Egypt would be more limited; as his health was also failing, he decided to resign. In 1909 he published his memoirs of his period in Egypt in the two volumes, *Modern Egypt*, in which he expressed his views, and reasons to justify his policies and actions during his 25 years as consul-general. The five chapters on the "Dwellers in Egypt," with their condescending tone and the implication that the Egyptians would never be capable of ruling themselves by British standards, hardened the resolve of many educated Egyptians to end the British occupation. (The copy of this work in the Peabody-Emerson Library is liberally marked in Prof. Emerson's hand, with asterisks, exclamation marks, heavy underlining, and comments such as *"What rot! Codswallop! Absurd!"* etc.)

Cromer was succeeded by Sir Eldon Gorst, an experienced Anglo-Egyptian civil servant, who had served under Cromer, eventually becoming financial adviser. However, he was a very different man from Cromer, both physically and mentally. Of medium height and slight build, he suffered from a lack of self-confidence and feelings of self-doubt. Nonetheless, he was probably more in touch with Egyptian sentiments, helped by the fact that he spoke fluent Arabic. He inherited a difficult situation, because British prestige was much decreased after Denshawai, and nationalism was on the rise.

Gorst replaced senior British officials with Egyptians, and also attempted a reconciliation with the khedive, which worked at first to Britain's advantage, as it lessened the khedive's support of the Nationalist Movement. In February 1908 Mustafa Kamil died, aged only 34, so the movement lost some of its impetus. The prime minister, Mustafa Fahmy, resigned after 13 years in office, and the new prime minister was the Copt, Boutros Ghali, who had presided at the Denshawai trial. However, in general the new government was popular, the more so when the Denshawai prisoners were released in December.

In 1908, after 13 years in office, Prime Minister Mustafa Fahmy (above) resigned, to be replaced in that post by Boutros Ghali (below), who would be assassinated two years later.

Gorst's initial successes with khedival relations and slowing nationalism were countered by the uncooperative attitude of many Anglo-Egyptian officials, who resented the threat to their livelihoods which his reforms would impose. They saw his proposals as a reversal of Cromer's policy of establishing a British civil service in Egypt. There was a new crime wave in the countryside and Nationalist press attacks on ministers (an indirect way of criticizing the khedive). Gorst re-established the press law of 1881, which gave the government the power to suspend newspapers. Cromer had never agreed to this, because he thought it was better to allow the Egyptians to let off steam in the native press, and also because a free press was a symbol of British liberalism.

In 1909 Gorst had the Relegation Law passed, whereby troublesome elements could be deported to penal colonies in Kharga Oasis without trial. However, this law was used by village officials to settle old scores in personal vendettas. Then, in 1910, the Suez Canal Company proposed the extension of its concession (originally to end in 1968) for another 40 years (until 2008), offering a down payment of 4,000,000 pounds sterling to the Egyptian government, and an annual share of the profits. Gorst and the financial adviser (Lord Edward Cecil) supported the idea, but it was rejected by the general assembly, which called again for an end to British occupation.

Two days later, on February 10th, 1910, the prime minister, Boutros Ghali, was assassinated in the street outside his office by a young Egyptian Muslim, Ibrahim el Wardani. He declared that he had killed Ghali not only because he supported the Suez Canal Company's

Sir Eldon Gorst.

Built under Lord Cromer, the British Agency in Cairo was the nerve center of the occupation. Today it serves as the British Embassy.

proposal, but also because as minister of foreign affairs he had signed away Egypt's rights over Sudan in the Condominium Agreement in 1899, and as minister of justice he presided over the Denshawai trial in 1906. Wardani was regarded as a national hero, but he was sentenced to death and executed. Kamil el Wardani, the leader of the Nationalist group with which Ramses Emerson and David Todros became involved, adopted the name of Wardani as a gesture of respect to the cause and in defiance of the British authority.

Gorst's policies were criticized in the British parliament, and slackness and lack of enthusiasm developed among Anglo-Egyptian officials. Gorst himself was in ill health. In April 1911 he went to England on leave, and died there in July of cancer of the spine. The khedive actually went over from Paris to visit him on his deathbed.

Cromer expressed a generally held opinion that the failure of Gorst's attempts at administrative reform had proved that the Egyptians were still incapable of ruling themselves. It was now clear that a firm hand was needed, and Kitchener was appointed consul-general. He was instructed by Prime Minister Grey *"to keep Egypt quiet,"* but not to reverse Gorst's reforms. When Kitchener arrived in Cairo on September 10th, 1911, he was greeted enthusiastically. Tall, with a magnificent mustache, he had an aura of prestige, glamor, and style. He was courteous and friendly to Egyptians, but it was always clear who made the important decisions, and he rarely considered any other points of view. He did, however, inspire loyal service from many subordinates.

Kitchener was a sensitive man who hid this side of his nature behind an aloof, awe-inspiring manner. He was a keen collector of antiques and fine art, and, unlike Cromer, very interested in Egyptian antiquities. He had a taste for grandeur, building the huge new ballroom at the Agency and changing the servants' liveries to scarlet and gold. The marble lions beside the front steps of the Agency (now the British Embassy) were originally at the Gezira Palace (site of the present-day Marriott Hotel) and were somewhat highhandedly appropriated by Kitchener.

(8) Invitation to a ball at the British Agency, December 1913.
By the time Lord Kitchener became consul-general, the main building of the Agency was so crowded with administrative offices that its ballroom had to be used as a waiting room, so a new ballroom was built in the northern section of the front garden. Lord Kitchener enjoyed entertaining in the grand manner, which is reflected in the classical style of the ballroom, with its musicians' gallery and large crystal chandeliers.
Amelia had always enjoyed dancing, and once Emerson had mastered the waltz under the tuition of Ramses and Nefret, he also found such evenings more entertaining. No doubt he and Amelia would have appreciated the wooden dance floor in the new ballroom, which was the first sprung floor in Africa.

Kitchener's first priority was to restore order, so he struck at the power of the Nationalists, whose leaders were imprisoned or sent into exile. He felt only contempt for the khedive, so he found ways to curtail his power, such as removing the right to preside at cabinet meetings, which made the khedive virtually a constitutional ruler. The number of British officials in high positions increased, but Kitchener deplored British social exclusivity, and like Gorst, continued to invite many Egyptians to the Agency. He delayed bringing in further liberal political reforms, adopting a policy of "wait and see." Harvey was replaced as financial adviser by Lord Edward Cecil, who was not a skilled financier but could be relied upon to follow Kitchener's instructions.

Like Cromer, Kitchener was keen on practical reforms, mostly concerned with the conditions of the *fellahin*, and he toured the country accepting petitions and hearing grievances. His two main agricultural aims were to reduce *fellahin's* debts and to solve the drainage problem, one of the principal tasks of the Ministry of Agriculture, which was founded in 1913. His solution to the debt problem was the Five Feddan Law, which made it impossible to take a *fellah* to court for debt if he owned less than five *feddans* (a *feddan* is a little less than an acre). The law had limited success, but did boost *fellahin* morale, so that they felt the government was on their side. However, Kitchener was unconcerned with education, and did nothing to improve the police force, or deal with the rural crime wave.

At the outbreak of World War I in August 1914, Kitchener was

Overleaf, Australian forces camped in the shadow of the Great Pyramid at Giza during World War I.

"H.M.S. 'Irresistible,'" one of a series of 10 "Egyptian Sketches" by artist Lance Thackery issued by John Player & Sons with Player's Navy Cut Cigarettes, ca. 1915.

"Preparing for Action" is the title of this card in the Player's Navy Cut Cigarettes' "Egyptian Scenes" series. It depicts a British military dandy of Cairo's foreign community preparing for an evening out at the time of WWI.

recalled to the U.K. as secretary for war. His three years in Egypt had at least been quiet, as the British government had wanted, but that would probably not have lasted had it not been for the intervention of the World War.

Throughout World War I, Egypt was in the strange position of being neutral but occupied by a belligerent power. As ever, Britain's chief concern was the Suez Canal. At the outbreak of hostilities, Britain was unaware of a secret alliance between Germany and Turkey, but the future status of Egypt needed to be defined. Worried by the khedive's pro-Ottoman leanings, the British government deposed him while he was on a trip to Constantinople. His uncle, Hussein Kamel (a son of Ismail Pasha), was appointed as sultan. On December 18th, 1914, Egypt was declared a British Protectorate, under which Britain would have "exclusive responsibility" for the defense of Egypt. In January 1916 the presence of large numbers of Turkish troops in the Sinai signaled an imminent attack on the Suez Canal, the defences of which were far from satisfactory. The Ottomans were hoping for an insurrection in Cairo led by Kamil el Wardani. Victory hung in the balance; as a result of the undercover intelligence work of David Todros and Ramses Emerson, the insurrection did not take place and the attack on the Canal failed.

In that same year, the British decided to clear the Turks out of the Sinai once and for all. They succeeded in pushing them back across the Egyptian border, and in December 1916 Turkish forces withdrew to the heavily fortified city of Gaza. Two British attacks under General Murray failed. In the summer of 1917, General Allenby replaced General Murray, and the third assault on Gaza was successful. Allenby then swept on to enter Jerusalem in December of 1917, which essentially ended the campaign in Palestine. While the part played by intelligence in this campaign has never been wholly determined due to the Official Secrets Act, the unsubstantiated hints in Amelia's journal are no doubt correct.

THE LIFE OF AN ANGLO-EGYPTIAN OFFICIAL

Egypt was a fine career for many Europeans, salary and rank being higher than for most Egyptians. There were Westerners from 20 countries, including the United States, in all capacities, government, engineering projects, military, including even the maintenance of the khedive's yachts.

There was a sense of mission among Anglo-Egyptians, and much impressive work was done in the early years of the occupation. However, many officials were preoccupied with their own career status and also believed that it was impossible to convert Egyptians into the Western way of thinking and acting. Egypt was seen as a useful training ground by ambitious young officials, the steppingstone to a distinguished career or influential posts elsewhere.

Some young men became very homesick at first, such as

Ronald Storrs, who was oriental secretary under Gorst. Most could not speak Arabic, so they felt cut off from the Egyptians. The cities were crowded, dirty, unhygienic, and dusty. All officials became ill at some time or other with sore throats, colds, bronchitis, gastric ailments, etc. With promotion and a greater feeling of confidence and commitment, Storr's attitude improved. As he became familiar with urban Egypt, he concluded that *"in the ordinary give and take of life there is in the world no more agreeable, courteous or entertaining race."*

For Anglo-Egyptian officials, their administrative duties followed the Egyptian pattern: office hours 8 a.m. -1 p.m. Interviews, meetings, dealing with complaints, etc., were the normal bureaucratic routine, entertainingly described by Edward Cecil in his *The Leisure of an Egyptian Official*. It was different for provincial inspectors and officials of the Public Works Department: for example, William Willcocks, the engineer and designer of the Aswan Dam, traveled all over Upper and Lower Egypt, winter and summer, working from 6 a.m. to 6 p.m. at irrigation sites, often in very spartan conditions. This was a much more rigorous life than in Cairo or Alexandria. But such men as Willcocks and Colin Scott-Moncrieff, another skilled engineer, and many others were usually more in touch with Egyptians and spoke Arabic well.

Until the creation of the Anglo-Egyptian civil service which regularized recruitment, each department employed Englishmen when required. The Ministry of Public Instruction was often the first step. Young men taught for a few years, then went on to another department, for example, Joseph "Bimbashi" MacPherson, who arrived in Cairo in 1902, worked first as a teacher and later became head of the secret police. Unfortunately education suffered from this system, and instructors were also discouraged from becoming too friendly with Egyptians. Some had no experience for the department into which they went, such as Sir Edward Cecil, who had a military background but joined the Finance Department.

Englishmen came to Egypt for a variety of reasons, though the usual were recognition, approval, and advancement. Egypt was a country for a young man with a sense of adventure. Not many intended to stay long, some stayed longer than they would have liked, but a few found contentment and stayed a lifetime, e.g. Joseph MacPherson and Thomas Russell, who each stayed 44 years. Russell came out to Egypt in 1902 to take up a post in the Ministry of the Interior, worked with the Egyptian police, and stayed in Egypt until 1946. He was especially linked with the crackdown on the drugs trade in Alexandria, where drugs were smuggled into the country. In 1914 Russell was appointed assistant commandant of police in Cairo.

Before the occupation, social life for most Europeans was confined to the large hotels in Alexandria and Cairo, such as Shepheard's. By 1900 much had changed. Many Europeans came for five months in the winter, from November to March, "the season." Cook's tours in-

NOT SO DUSTY.

Nefret Forth she's not! This Player's "Egyptian Sketch" titled "Not so Dusty," depicts a young miss of the Anglo-Egyptian community having her shoes dusted by "The diminutive Arab boy.... With his grinning welcome for every dusty boot or shoe that presents itself at the hotel entrance."

FOR THE GIRL HE LEFT BEHIND HIM.

The back-of-the-card text of this Player's "Egyptian Sketch" reads: "Tommy is very fond of doing a deal with the native, and if he never gets the better of the bargain, he generally thinks he does...."

Thomas Russell Pasha.

The 2nd Lady Cromer, in 1905.

creased accessibility of the ancient monuments. More hotels and a new Shepheard's were built; a contemporary American consul even commented that *"to the ordinary English tourist the name of Shepheard's is even more famous than that of Cheops or Chephren"* (builders of the two largest pyramids at Giza). Europeans could imagine, in such large hotels, that they had never left home.

As working hours in government offices ended at 1 p.m., there was plenty of time for sporting activities. The Gezira Club was founded in 1882 on land provided by Tewfik Pasha for the Agency. Amenities included a race course, 18-hole golf course, polo lawn, and tennis courts. The clubhouse was in the English style, and was surrounded by extensive flower beds. Membership consisted predominantly of foreign residents and wealthy Egyptians.

There were several clubs in Cairo modeled on the gentlemen's clubs in London, the most popular being the Turf Club, which was founded in the early 1890s and occupied the building which had originally been the Agency in downtown Cairo. Many civil servants went there almost every day, as meals were inexpensive, and most junior officials were on low salaries (Edward Cecil always had his breakfast there). Undoubtably this reliability of "public" appearance induced Ramses to choose the Turf Club as the setting for his alibi when he was playing another role for intelligence in 1914-15. Members also talked shop over drinks before dinner, and the club became a "refuge" for British officials, who could meet and talk with their own country-men of like mind.

There was also a good deal of entertaining at the Agency. Until his health declined, Cromer invited his staff to lunch most days of the week. The first Lady Cromer was a foil to her husband's personality with her grace and charm. She died in 1898 and Cromer remarried in 1902. His second wife, Catherine, was much younger than he, but a good official hostess. It was she who planted the oak tree in the front garden.

British officials were encouraged, especially by Cromer, to take annual leave in the summer and return to England for a break, which was thought beneficial for psychological reasons, as well as for health. Not all went, and in the summer the Agency moved to Alexandria, to a villa near the sea with a lovely garden, where cool breezes made all the difference. The khedive and his family also spent the summer at Alexandria, in Ras el Tin Palace. There was a large and somewhat volatile foreign community in the Mediterranean city, consisting mostly of Greeks, Italians, and British.

An official's income and government ranking also dictated his standard of living. Most salaries, though modest, were adequate enough for even low-ranking officials to afford a servant, which emphasized the oriental "flavor of life." It was equally difficult with or without a family. Edward Cecil's wife preferred England, so he had to maintain two households, and only saw his children once a year in the summer. He was not very good at managing his own money, which is ironic, considering that he later became a financial adviser with responsibility for the money of an entire country.

By 1900 the quality of European social life was established, and it effectively separated European from Egyptian. Once a new recruit was drawn into this close-knit society, it was very difficult to mix with Egyptians, and few Englishmen tried to do so. Some, however, found their own personal rewards, such as MacPherson, who quietly deplored *"the insular British set."* Russell was fascinated by desert life and the Bedouin; Willcocks, the irrigation engineer, became interested in popular folklore; and Harry Boyle, Cromer's oriental secretary for 24 years, admitted that he had gained much from his experiences of Eastern society. These men, like the Emerson family themselves, were exceptions. Some officials used the opportunity to study the pharaonic civilization, but most were not interested in Egypt's Islamic heritage, as Islamic culture was too close to current events.

On the other hand, there was no concerted effort to impose English culture on the Egyptians. It was order and justice that the British brought to Egypt, unlike the French, where French culture predominated among the elite. Thus, the vast majority of Egyptians never lost their national identity, which rapidly reasserted itself when the country became independent. Mrs. Emerson, while clearly deploring some of the errors committed by her countrymen, was *"proud to be a Briton,"* and certainly recognized their positive contributions.

Jocelyn Gohary

Lord Edward Cecil.

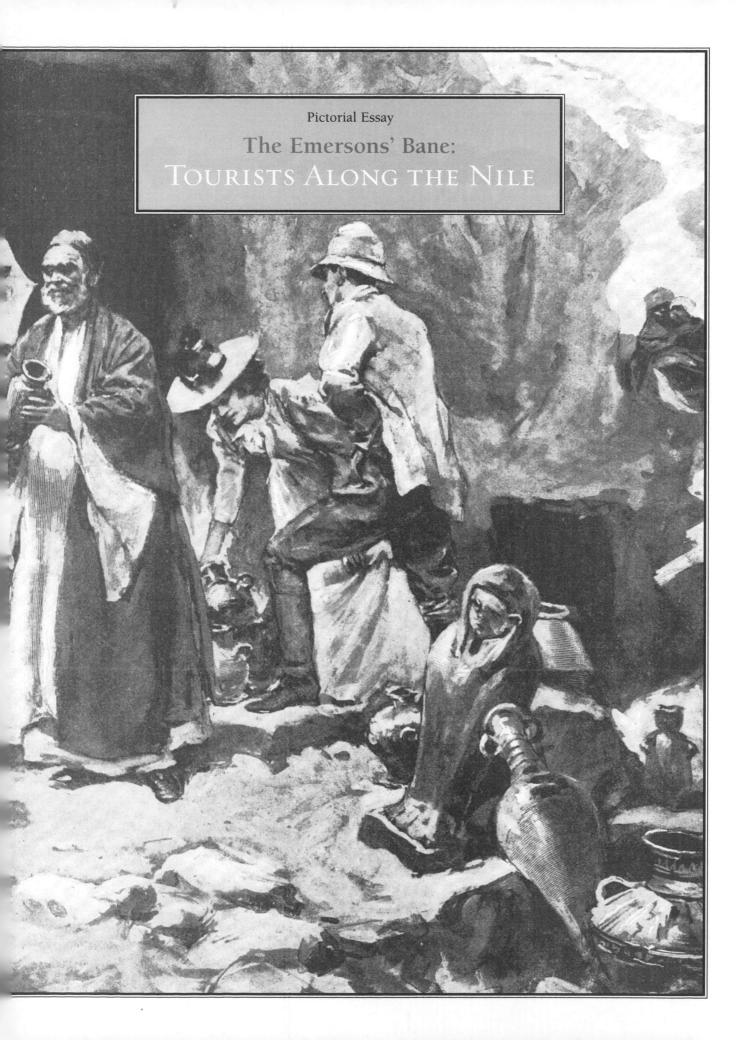

Pictorial Essay

The Emersons' Bane:

TOURISTS ALONG THE NILE

Above, the tourist's first view of Egypt: the harbor at Alexandria. Left, the essential guide: a dragoman. Below & opposite, top, the first adventure: climbing the Great Pyramid of Giza. Opposite, bottom, the second adventure: exploring the markets of Cairo.

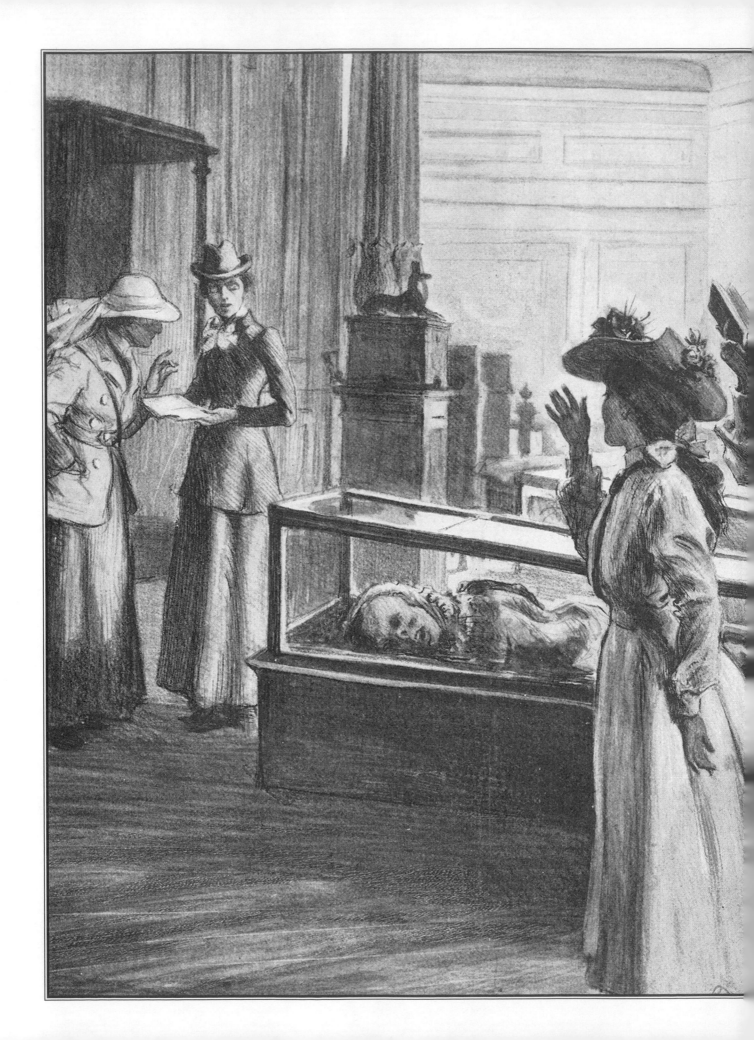

Preceding 2 pages, a visit to the Giza Museum; Left, donkey boys, the tourist taxis of Amelia's day; Above, mounted & ready for a picnic outing at the pyramids; Opposite, top, seeking bargains in the bazaars of Cairo; Opposite, bottom, stalwart mounts, stoic riders.

Counterclockwise this page: Tourist caravan; Shopping for a dahabiya; All aboard; Foraging ashore; & relaxing under the awning; Opposite, top, antikas dealer lying in wait; Bottom, posing amid the ruins.

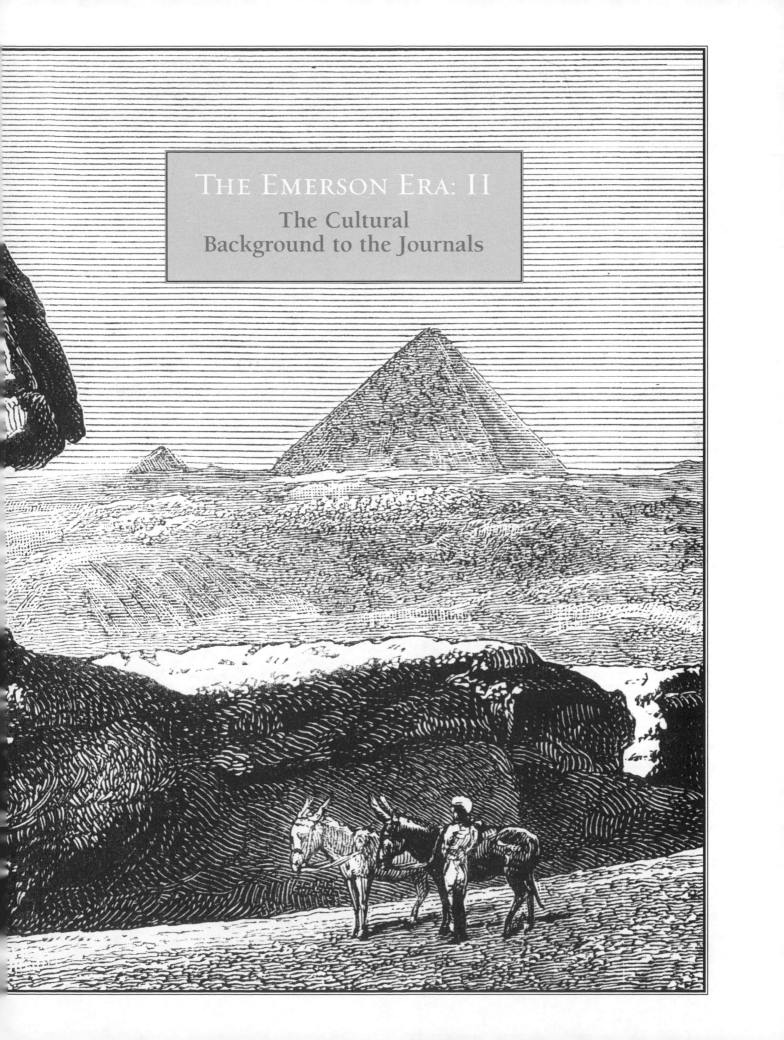

THE EMERSON ERA: II

The Cultural Background to the Journals

AN EXPERT ANALYSIS OF THE PRINCIPLES OF ISLAM
As Encountered by the Emersons

I slam means to surrender or submit to the will of Allah (God). The followers of the religion are called Muslims (Moslems), those who surrender to the will of Allah. Islam has been the predominant religion in Egypt since before the 14th Century, followed by Coptic Christianity — with other forms of Christianity and Judaism also having modern-day Egyptian adherents. Amelia Peabody's first dragoman, Michael Bedawee, was a Copt, but after her union with Radcliffe Emerson most of her servants in Egypt were Muslims.

Islam is the youngest of the monotheistic religions, and has much in common with Judaism and Christianity. It was revealed in Arabia to the prophet Muhammed in approximately AD 610. At that time Arabia was predominantly polytheistic, but included followers of Judaism and Christianity as well. According to the tenets of Islam, the angel Gabriel appeared to Muhammed and informed him that he had been selected as a messenger or apostle of God, a prophet. Over the next 20 years or so, until his death, Muhammed claimed he was the recipient of direct revelations from God. These ultimately were written down and collected together in AD 650 as the holy book known as the Quran (Koran). Muslims believe that the Quran has remained intact and uncorrupted from that time to the present, and as such, is the word of God alone. Muhammed taught that his visions and revelations had to be shared with the Arabs and others in order to lead mankind to God, and this prompted the spread of Islam beyond Arabia and throughout the Near East, Africa, and afar.

The Quran is written in Arabic. It consists of *surahs* or chapters that pertain to both religious and social life, and it makes frequent references to the Old Testament. In fact, many tenets that are set down in the latter — such as the Ten Commandments — are also integral to Islam. Muslims believe that the will of Allah was revealed to many prophets, and that the Torah, the Psalms, and the Gospels of the New Testament are all holy scriptures expressing the word of God. Muslims also acknowledge all the prophets of both the Old and New Testaments. A significant difference between Muslims and Christians, however, is that, in Islam, Jesus is believed to be a great prophet but is not regarded as the Son of God. This is what prompted Prof. Em-

Detail of the title page of a 14th Century manuscript of the Quran.

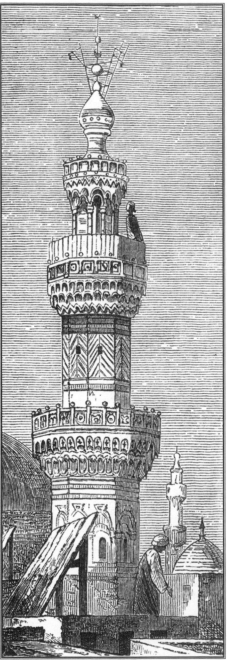

The call to prayer by muezzins *from the minarets or towers of mosques.*

erson to tetchily inform Reverend Archibald Sayce during one of their gatherings at Shepheard's that Muslims and Christians are not so disparate, as they have the same God and the same prophets.

There are five basic pillars of Islam that every Muslim is supposed to follow as closely as possible. The most important is the *shahaddah*, or profession of faith: there is no god but God; Muhammed is the prophet of God. Muhammed is regarded as the last of the line of prophets sent by God. As Emerson recited half of the *shahaddah* during the confrontation with the holy man at the steps of the Baskerville tomb, he came very close to becoming a Muslim!

The second pillar is prayer, *salat*. Muslims are expected to pray five times a day. The call to prayer, the *adhan*, is recited by a *muezzin* (one who calls to prayer) from the minaret of a mosque. In fact, the sonorous voices of the *muezzins* drifting across the city, each a bit different from the other, gave Walter "Ramses" Emerson the crucial clue in the search for his mother's kidnapper in 1895. The first prayer is performed before sunrise, the second just after noon, the third later in the afternoon, the fourth immediately after sunset, and the fifth at night. One can pray in a congregation in a mosque, or individually, regardless of where one is. In mosques the prayer is led by an *imam*, or leader. In Islam there is no formal clergy per se, just learned and holy men who have studied the Quran, the sayings of the prophets (*hadith*), and some theology. They are called, variously, *sheikhs*, *imams*, and *mullahs*.

The third pillar is the *zakat*. This is an obligatory tax to be paid by all Muslims on money and goods. The amounts vary depending on what is being taxed and one's wealth. It is voluntary and can be disbursed by the individual or through a local mosque. *Zakat* is primarily used for providing food, education, and healthcare for the poor.

The fourth pillar is fasting. This occurs during the month of Ramadan, which is the ninth month in the Muslim lunar calendar. It is thus, like the Christian Easter, a "floating" festival, not tied to a spe-

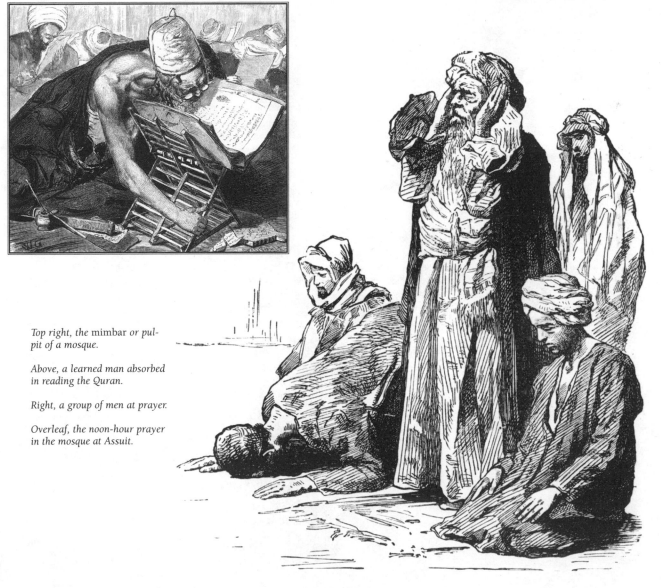

Top right, the mimbar *or pulpit of a mosque.*

Above, a learned man absorbed in reading the Quran.

Right, a group of men at prayer.

Overleaf, the noon-hour prayer in the mosque at Assuit.

cific date of the modern Western calendar. From sunrise to sunset, Muslims are not allowed to eat, drink, or smoke. Ramadan is supposed to be the month when the Quran was revealed to the prophet Muhammed. The fasting not only commemorates the revelation of the holy book, but is also supposed to remind the wealthy of what it is to endure hardship. The end of Ramadan is marked by a festival, the *Eid al Fitr* or Little Bairam.

The fifth and final pillar is the *Hajj*, or pilgrimage to Mecca. This pilgrimage should be made once in a lifetime, if one can afford it. It takes place in the month of *Dhu al-Hijjah*. The pilgrimage consists of going to Mecca to visit various sacred sites and carrying out different rituals there. The Big Bairam is celebrated at the end of the *Hajj* and commemorates Abraham's not having to sacrifice his son to God. Part of the celebrations for the *Eid al Adha* include the slaughter of a sheep in memory of this event, and the distribution of the meat to the poor.

Islamic belief and laws (*Shariah*) touch almost all aspects of life, including marriage, inheritance, commercial dealings, morality, food, and drink. The food taboos of Islam closely follow those outlined in Deuteronomy, with few variations. There are strong proscriptions against consuming pork and carrion. Alcohol is also prohibited, although prohibited is not always interpreted as forbidden, as was abundantly evident when the crew spent an evening carousing on the *dahabiya* during Amelia's first voyage to Egypt; the Quran warns most specifically against over-indulgence rather than abstinence.

Family life and marriage are encouraged by Islam. Legally, Muslim men are allowed four wives at a time; however, they may do this only if the co-wives agree, and all four are treated equally in all ways. If not, the wives can sue for divorce, depending on the grounds of the inequality. Polygamy is now rare in Egypt; even during the Emersons' time it was irregularly practiced, and then not by the poorer peasantry. The roots of polygamy in Islam date to its early history. It was a practice that was common in pre-Muslim Arabia, and became expedient in Islamic times when the number of women outstripped the number of available men.

Muslim men are allowed to marry non-Muslims, as long as the women are of "the Book," i.e. either Jews or Christians. The women can continue to follow their own faith, although conversion is preferable. However, it is forbidden for a Muslim woman to marry a non-Muslim man. For the marriage to be recognized, the man would have to convert to Islam, and even so, the cultural taboos against this are great. Thus, from the point of view of David's grandfather, Abdullah, his daughter's marriage to a Christian Egyptian violated a basic principle of their faith. Since David's father was a Copt (though as Abdullah declared, *"He was nothing. Even Christians are People of the Book, but he gave himself up to drunkenness and cursing God"*), David's marriage to Lia Emerson presented no religious obstacles, though it

Opposite, students & scholars study the Quran in the Mosque of El Azhar; Above, minaret of the Mosque of Kayt Bey, Cairo.

107

Until the early 20th Century, a face veil was a part of the Muslim Egyptian woman's apparel, always worn when she appeared in public. The late-19th Century photograph above shows an upper-middle-class matron of Cairo wearing a veil & metallic accessory in vogue at the time. Elite-status Muslim ladies of the same period found less-obscuring solutions to the veiling practice, as seen in the engraving above right.

presented plenty of others (Peters 1996:88). Marriage between Bertie Jones and Jumana, on the other hand, would have posed a serious problem, though no journal has as yet come to light which details such a union.

During the Emersons' time in Egypt, Muslim women had many privileges not enjoyed by their western counterparts, and, at the same time, several limitations not shared by contemporary western women. Some of the rules and regulations observed by the women and society were more a result of Egyptian society than of the Islamic religion, and were often shared by Egyptian Christians and Jews. Like their western counterparts (with the exception of the Emerson family, among others), Egyptian women were regarded as subservient to men. This did not always affect their behavior in private, although in public they were supposed to defer to male family members. However, Muslim women had the right to divorce, depending on the circumstances. Unlike their European counterparts, they could own and dispose of property independently of their husbands. They were, however, more sequestered than western women (some Copts and Jews also shared in this), and many wore the veil. These were obstacles that kept them from being educated or employed in anything other than traditional female jobs, such as domestic employment or prostitution, something that had started to change in Europe at the end of the 19th

Century. In villages the veil always covered the head and body, and oftentimes — especially with young women — the face. Veiling the face was the norm among wealthier women, especially in cities. In the early 20th Century, women protested against the veil and removed it very publicly in a train station, led by Hoda Sharawy, one of Egypt's first feminists. Not all women responded to unveiling, but eventually it became acceptable for women to walk unveiled in public. This did not really affect the rural population until much more recently. Certainly the veil was a boon to Amelia when she was in disguise.

In Egypt, other religious customs, such as those associated with death and burial, are basically Islamic, but with unique Egyptian additions. Prompt burial (due to the climate) is prescribed by Islam, but the elaborate ululations that accompany death and funerals are more specific to Egypt than to the entire Muslim world. Throughout the Islamic world there are variations in ritual practices that are a result of indigenous culture rather than religion.

Islamic mysticism, Sufism, no longer plays a mainstream role in the religion or culture. However, at one time it had many followers, especially in Egypt. Sufism is a term derived from the Arabic word for the wool out of which the Sufis' garments were made. Sufis search for the truth of divine love and knowledge through a direct personal experience of God. There are various branches of Sufism, including the Senoussi, who figured so prominently during the Emersons' years in Egypt spanning World War I. All Sufis try to understand the nature of God and experience the presence of divine wisdom and love

Above, the Mosque of El Amr &, below, the Mosque of El Azhar, both in Cairo.

through diverse means such as chanting and whirling. However, Sufis did not eschew politics; they were involved in different political movements, especially during the late-19th and early-20th centuries. Many of the Dervishes of Cairo, friends of Ramses whom he frequently impersonated, were Sufis who were involved in political activities.

Having spent much of his childhood in Egypt — under the influence of a father who was interested in and conversant with Islamic tradition — Ramses had obviously studied the Quran and respected the faith of his Egyptian friends. Unlike her contemporaries, Amelia also had respect for the Islamic faith, though her traditional Christian upbringing often prevented complete objectivity. While Emerson, a confirmed atheist, sanguinely regarded Islam as he did all forms of religion — *"it is as good as any other religion"* — Amelia saw the differences between Abdullah's faith and hers, as is evident in her comment, *"My God certainly hadn't said anything to me about it."* With Abdullah's death and the onset of her dreams about Abdullah, Amelia became more spiritual and less traditional. As she laid the tiny figures of the ancient gods on Abdullah's grave with the explanation, *"who can say what eternal truths are preserved in the mysteries of the ancient faith,"* one might wonder if she had studied Sufism.

Salima Ikram

Muslim Mystics: The Dervishes

Always fascinating to late 19th- and early 20th-Century European & American visitors to Egypt — and to readers of the illustrated press at home — were the sects which practiced Islamic mysticism, or Sufism, otherwise known as Dervishes, of which there were two basic groups, the Howlers and the Whirlers. By means of rhythmic screeching, fantastic gestures and whip-like body movement, or by spinning rapidly in circles to the accompaniment of music, the Dervishes sought to attain an ecstatic direct communication with Allah. Others would pierce their cheeks, lips and tongues for the same purpose. The Whirling Dervishes were recognizable by their gray felt hats that looked like overly tall *fezes*.

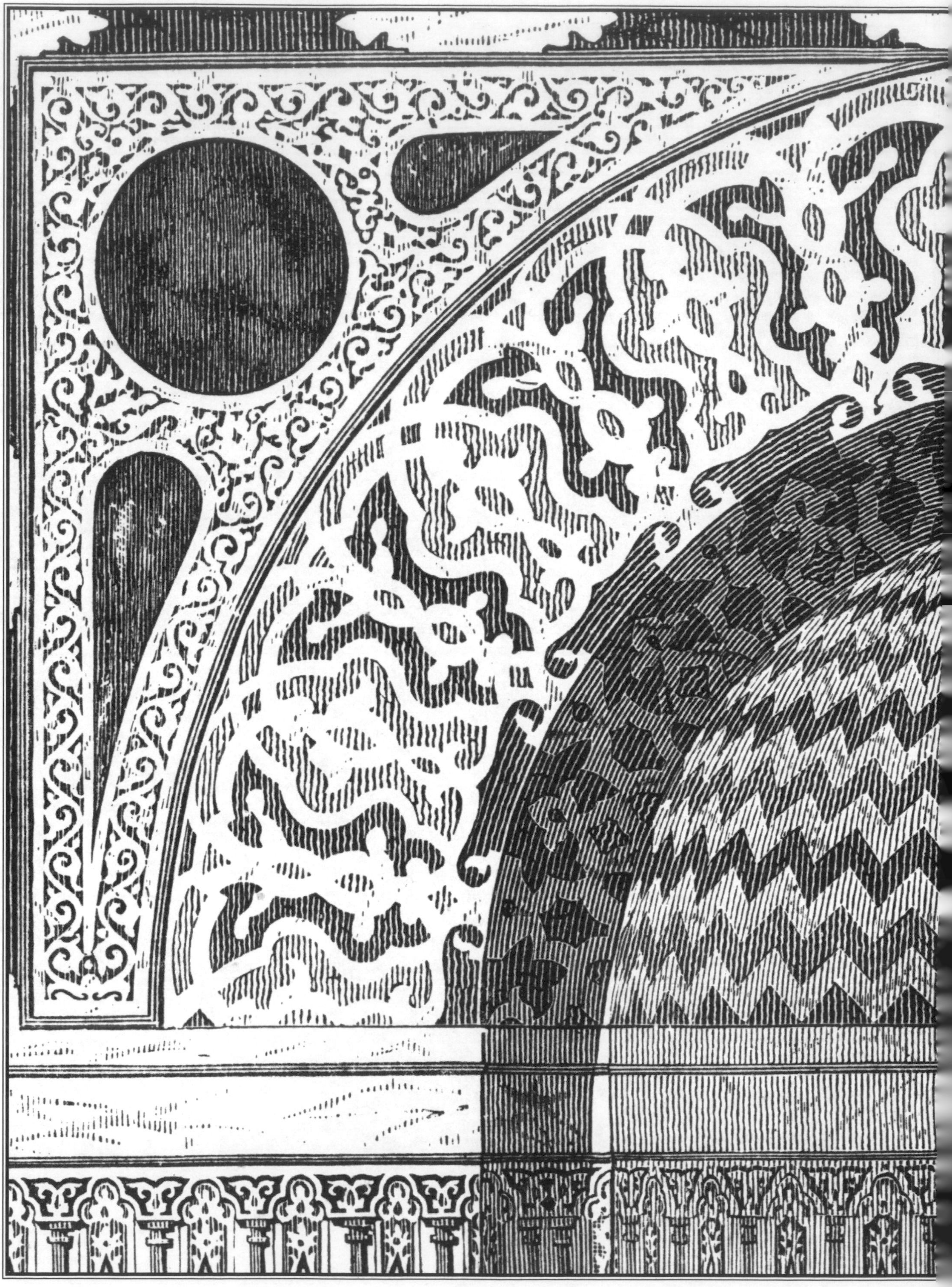

Pictorial Essay

THE ART &
ARCHITECTURE
OF ISLAM

The principal & most distinctive architectural structure of the Islamic world is the mosque, of which Cairo boasts many of the finest examples, such as: Opposite, the Mosque of Ezbek; Above, the Mosque of Hasan; & Right, the Mosque & Tomb of Kayt Bey. Below is a typical prayer niche, of which every mosque has one or more.

Because figurative representation is proscribed by the Quran, Muslim artists devised decorative motifs based on caligraphic, curvilinear, geometric & floral forms, several examples of which are seen here.

Cairo's domestic architecture of the Arab elite classes during the Emersons' years in Egypt was characterized by street-fronted, large, multi-storied structures featuring an interior open-air courtyard (examples above, below & opposite), with the characteristic mashrabiyah or projecting lattice-screened windows (left & opposite).

The interiors of older upper-class Egyptian urban houses of the Emerson era were spacious & high-ceilinged, & included separate quarters for the women of the household, called the harim (harem), as seen opposite & at right. Originally minimally furnished, except for divans & cushions & small moveable tables (above & below), by Victorian & Edwardian times the salons of "modern" Cairene houses were cluttered with furniture (examples at top in two 1905 photos). Many high-status English & American homes of this same period boasted an "Arab corner" furnished with divans, cushions, & other orientalizing decor & carpets.

"LESSER BREEDS WITHOUT THE LAW"

An Insightful Diatribe on the Victorian Attitude Towards Other Cultures & Peoples

God of our fathers, known of old,
Lord of our far-flung battle line,
Beneath whose awful Hand we hold
Dominion over palm and pine —
Lord God of Hosts, be with us yet,
Lest we forget — lest we forget!

If, drunk with sight of power, we loose
Wild tongues that have not Thee in awe,
Such boastings as the Gentiles use,
Or lesser breeds without the Law —
Lord God of hosts, be with us yet,
Lest we forget -— lest we forget!

Rudyard Kipling's poem, "Recessional," is considered the quintessential expression of imperialism. In his day Britain did hold dominion over palm and pine. From Canada to India and points in between, the world map was blotched with the pink that indicated British colonies and possessions.

It would be unfair to judge Kipling and his peers out of the context of their times. Books and articles dating between 1884 and 1917, the period covered by Mrs. Emerson's published journals, express an assumption held not only by Englishmen but by Americans and Western Europeans: the innate superiority of the "white man" and his right to rule over everyone else. Assumption is perhaps too weak a word for this viewpoint; it was an article of faith, an axiom, seldom questioned or challenged. It was in the Bible, after all. The sons of Ham were condemned by God to toil for others.

"The lesser breeds without the law" included every breed that didn't have the good fortune to be born British, or at least Anglo-Saxon. Sometimes the French were grudgingly admitted into the cat-

"Thank you, but we'd prefer to walk."

Where is a donkey-boy when you actually want one?

egory of the elect, but Italians were shifty and Russians were sinister and Jews were mercenary and orientals were inscrutable and besides, they had no morals. As for "Negroes" or "colored"— the words used by well-bred persons — they were depicted as childish, cowardly, and stupid. The terms were applied not only to Africans of all shades but to Arabs and inhabitants of the sub-continent of India. Egyptians were dark-skinned, African, and oriental. They had all ways to lose.

These views are exemplified in the quotations from Percival Peabody's book, which Peters used as chapter headings for *The Falcon at the Portal*, and, as she indicated in its Preface, Percy lifted several of them from contemporary memoirs. Plagiarism was the least of his sins, and naive readers might suppose that only thoroughgoing villains held such views. They would be wrong.

Men like Lord Edward Cecil, who served in Egypt for many years as a soldier and official, were not ignorant or uneducated or villainous. Cecil was a member of one of England's oldest aristocratic families, a gentleman, and a soldier. His memoirs, *The Leisure of an*

124

Egyptian Official, is one of the wittiest and most entertaining of such books. (It is of course easier to be witty when one is being rude.) He and the others of his set, who are often mentioned by Mrs. Emerson as exemplifying the Anglo-Egyptian society of her day, made fun of everyone they held to be their social inferiors, but they were particularly smarmy about the Egyptians. Cecil's comments about the Egyptians he was forced to associate with in the course of his work include words like dirty, obsequious, and dishonest. He did not mingle with them socially and made no effort to understand their point of view or their culture.

"*It is ridiculous to apply western democratic notions to a people so brutish, so insensitive, so mentally deficient as the Egyptians,*" wrote Ethel Smyth, a suffragist friend of Emmeline Pankhurst (who spent one winter season in Cairo) (Mansfield 1971:314). What choice did the superior Anglo-Saxon have, then, but to protect and rule these ignorant people? It was the intellectual justification for empire, and it pervaded every form of thought, memoirs and biographies, poems and novels, history, anthropology, and archaeology. Lawrence "of Arabia" admired and romanticized the Arabs; as for the Egyptians, in a private letter he repeated the comment he made to Amelia: "*The Egyptian people are horribly ugly, very dirty, dull, low-spirited...frenetic and querulous, foul-mouthed, and fawning*" (Wilson 1990:100).

Lawrence was an imperialist, like his mentor, David George Hogarth, a well-known archaeologist. Archaeology (as distinct from classical studies) and anthropology were relatively new disciplines, so perhaps it shouldn't surprise us to find them permeated with the same "white man's burden" mentality. The "primitive" cultures studied by anthropologists were by definition inferior to western civilization. It was a little more difficult to explain how the magnificent remains of ancient Egypt could have been created by dirty, ugly, mentally deficient people, but Victorian scholars got round that one by an ingenious leap of logic. Since all worthwhile civilizations were the products of Mediterranean or Aryan "races," modern Egyptians must have been a different and degenerate group from their predecessors. Egyptologists of the period flatly denied that ancient Egyptian culture could have been related in any way to African sources.

Kipling's views were not so simplistic as these, nor as narrow as some modern critics have claimed. He spent his formative years in India, and his novels and short stories treat his Indian characters "*with the understanding of love*" (Elliot 1943:26). The same thing is true of Rider Haggard, who lived and worked for many years in Africa. In one of his non-fiction books about the Zulus he wrote: "*I could never discern a superiority so great in ourselves as to authorize us, by divine right as it were, to destroy the colored man and take his lands*" (Higgins 1981:122). One of his most admirable characters is Umbopa, the exiled prince of the "black" kingdom where King Solomon's Mines were located. But Umbopa tamely submits to the role of servant to the

An English Lady of Alexandria & her black-African attendant.

"It is a quaint and interesting sight to see one of these little ebony cherubs in the arms of an Anglo-Saxon beauty. 'Blonde and Brunette' were never better brought together."
Augustus Hoppin
On the Nile, 1874

"Said England unto Pharaoh — 'I must make a man of you that will stand upon his feet and play the game.'" *Rudyard Kipling,* Five Nations. *From "Egyptian Sketches" card of Player's Navy Cut Cigarettes, 1915.*

Assault of the donkey-boys.

Englishmen, and another character in the same book expresses a sentiment with which Haggard clearly agrees: *"The sun cannot mate with the darkness or the black with the white"* (Haggard 1994:194).

Egyptologists were not exempt from bigotry — though they would not have called it that. Archaeologist William Flinders Petrie appears to have been on excellent terms with his workmen, and was known for his fair treatment of them, although his custom of paying fair market value for all valuable objects discovered was simple common sense; his men had no reason to risk the penalties for theft when they could get the same price from Petrie. *"As far as I have had to do with natives, I find that, though desperate beggars to strangers, if they once find you perfectly firm and yet kindly and jocular, they immediately settle down as good friends and never bother you again. I am simply disgusted with the brutal tones I have seen adopted toward them by travellers"* (Petrie 1932:29).

Petrie would not have recognized the implicit condescension in that sentence. He thought of himself as fair and reasonable, and compared to others of his generation, he was. But according to him, *"Every fellah in my work who has been taught to read and write has lost his wits, and is the butt of all his comrades for his stupidity. It needs generations of habit to enable English children to pick up reading without being taught"* (Petrie 1932:111). The men from the village of Quft were trained in archaeological method by Petrie, and became a body of workmen in great demand by archaeologists throughout Egypt, but Petrie apparently did not notice the contradiction between the accomplishments of his skilled workmen and his belief that they were incapable of acquiring the mystical western art of literacy.

Amelia Peabody Emerson was a woman of her time, and although she was exceptional in many ways, her opinions were inevitably influenced by the prejudices of the Victorian period. In the earlier volumes of the journals, we find many of the stereotypes: the hot-blooded Latin, the sinister Russian, the dirty, ignorant Egyptians, who didn't wash their children or their donkeys. Even Abdullah, whom she came to admire and respect, is initially depicted somewhat contemptuously. And yet, even on her first trip to Egypt, she felt a thrill at hearing Emerson's passionate defense of the people among whom he had chosen to spend his working life. *"For centuries these people were oppressed by a vicious, cruel despotism. They are riddled by disease, poverty and ignorance, but through no fault of their own"* (Peters 1975:43).

Unlike some of her contemporaries, Amelia was not entirely close-minded. Quite often she was not aware of how her viewpoint had changed — or was unwilling to admit that it had — but change it unquesionably did. The Emersons' visit to the Lost Oasis affected her more than she realized at the time. This strange culture, a blend of ancient Egyptian, ancient Nubian, and local populations, was in a sense a microcosm of the world at large — a culture in which the

darker-skinned indigenes were despised and enslaved by the ruling class. Amelia's chivalrous, romantic instincts were immediately aroused by this injustice; she yearned to raise the flag of freedom and lead a slave revolt! She was also greatly impressed by young Prince Tarek, the descendant of Nubian kings, who had every princely attribute — intelligence, selflessness, chivalry, good looks (Amelia was not impervious to such things). Tarek was in love with his foster sister, Nefret, but was willing to sacrifice his desires and even his life to see her returned to her own people. One of the turning points in Amelia's development came when Tarek quoted from one of Rider Haggard's novels: *"The sun cannot mate with the darkness or the black with the white,"* and she replied with a curt *"Don't talk nonsense."* She still had

"She waddled towards our boat as we anchored, and held out her joggly hand for the inevitable 'backshish.' Black, greasy, and repulsive, she was in a fit state for the oilpress. That woman would have furnished enough light for the whole African continent."

Augustus Hoppin
On the Nile, 1874

127

a long way to go, though. Tarek had not proposed marrying into the Emerson family.

One of the greatest influences in Amelia's life was, of course, her husband. Her son's caustic comment, *"Father despises everyone quite indiscriminately and without prejudice,"* may hold a germ of the truth. Emerson was not "tolerant"; even that word smacks slightly of condescension. He was completely indifferent to characteristics he considered unimportant, and the only characteristics that mattered to him were competence, loyalty, and honesty. There are, in every country and every era, individuals who reject the mores of their culture. Emerson was one of them. He never lectured his wife or anyone else; it would not have occured to him that the subject was worthy of debate. He treated everyone the same — servant and master, Egyptian and Englishman. In other words, he yelled at them when he lost his temper and apologized when he realized he was wrong.

It is not surprising that Ramses should have come closest to modern notions of political correctness. He never attended a public school, where he would have been exposed to the more pernicious forms of social and racial bigotry, and he had very little to do with young people of his own class. He must have been strongly influenced by his father, whom he admired enormously. But it is unlikely that he gave the matter much conscious thought until he became acquainted with David Todros, Abdullah's grandson, whom the Emersons found making fake antiquities for a brutal employer. David was a "pure-bred" Egyptian, to use Amelia's term. Respecting David's talent and intelligence, returning his affection, Ramses became increasingly sensitive about the treatment his friend received from outsiders. We see this demonstrated when Colonel Bellingham, the Southern aristocrat, ignored David *"as if he were a piece of furniture."* It was impossible for Bellingham to regard David, a member of one of the "colored races," as a social equal, but he was only slightly more prejudiced than his contemporaries in England, Europe, and America.

Amelia leaped to David's defense with Bellingham, but a few years later, in the next volume of her journals, it is clear that she had not overcome the preconceptions of her class and nation. Several of her conversations with Katherine Vandergelt are illuminating. Katherine, a kind-hearted and sensitive woman, would never have dreamed of treating David discourteously, but when she saw him with a young English girl she remarked, *"What responsible mama would allow her daughter to become seriously involved with him?"* Amelia's only response was, *"She needn't have been so rude about it."* There was an invisible barrier in her mind still, a barrier most of her contemporaries would have found it impossible to pass.

We should not have been surprised, therefore (the editor of the journals certainly was not), that when Amelia learned that David and her niece Lia were in love, her opposition to their marriage was instantaneous and unthinking. Lia's parents — who were also kindly,

"Dry Footing."

"Me good Arab."

well-bred people — felt the same. When pressed, Amelia was unable to produce an explanation. David was well-educated, intelligent, talented, and a gentleman in every sense of the word. But he was an Egyptian.

Amelia's reaction to poor David's announcement was the last demonstration of the prejudices that had been part of her thinking since childhood. As she lay awake that night examining her motives and trying to defend them to herself, one can sense her confusion and distress. Abdullah's sudden, violent death was the catalyst, not the cause, of her final change of mind. Her painful mental soliloquy as she sat alone recalling her memories of him is typical of the mental clarity that sometimes follows a terrible shock. It was not only Abdullah she had come to love and respect, but the others of his family, who had shown her the affection she never received from her flesh and blood, and who had proved, over and over again, that they were as intelligent, as capable of learning, and as honorable as any of her fellow countrymen.

Amelia had the honesty to face her prejudices and the courage to admit she was wrong. And, being Amelia, once she had seen the truth she calmly denied that she had ever been wrong. We may allow her that little touch of vanity; she had gone farther than most people could, and can, do.

Barbara Mertz

Below, posing with the "locals" near Aswan.

UPSTAIRS, DOWNSTAIRS

A Skillful Overview of
Victorian Servants & Their Duties

W hile much of the action in Amelia Peabody Emerson's journals took place on digs in Egypt, enough happened at home in Britain that *"pas devant les domestiques"* ("not in front of the servants") became a familiar refrain from Amelia (usually directed at Emerson). Through the meticulous records Amelia kept of her conversations with Emerson and with the household staff, the modern reader is given an intriguing glimpse into the mysterious world of the servant in Victorian England.

The Victorian and Edwardian eras were a heyday for servants. During that time, employment as a servant was considered one of the better opportunities available to the working classes. For those wishing to employ servants, labor was plentiful and cheap. By 1891 one out of every three women between the ages of 15 and 20 was employed as a servant.

Duties of Servants

Employing servants was not simply an ostentatious display of wealth. In the days before central heating and plumbing, servants were needed to keep a middle- or upper-class household functioning.

The butler was expected to answer the door and to distinguish between the gentlefolk and everyone else. Both the Emersons' butlers were skilled at such distinctions: Wilkins immediately spotted Miss Minton as being worthy of the parlor, even if she was a journalist, whereas Gargery "stood in the dining room" the lower-class antiquities collector, Renfrew, regardless of his wealth. In addition, the butler was expected to assist at meals, pouring beverages and passing dishes. During meals, when he was not serving, he was expected to stand behind the chair of the master of the house. The Emersons did not encourage strict adherence to these rules, which made Wilkins extremely uncomfortable. Gargery, on the other hand, flourished in the relaxed environment, and as a result he went to work for the Emersons at Amarna House, while Wilkins went to Evelyn and Walter Emerson at Chalfont.

The housekeeper was the second-in-command in household management, just underneath the mistress of the house. She was responsible for overseeing the servants to ensure that they were per-

forming, not shirking, their duties. In addition, the housekeeper was responsible for keeping the household accounts and ordering goods from tradesmen. She was responsible for ensuring that the household linens were in good repair, and that the furniture was well polished. One of her most daunting tasks was overseeing the massive top-to-bottom house cleaning that took place in the spring. It was lucky for Amelia that she had such a dependable housekeeper in Rose, since she was not inclined to supervise such activities.

The responsibilities of the footman depended on the household itself and how many other servants were employed by the family. Generally, his duties included polishing the silver, cleaning cutlery, polishing shoes and boots (unless the household employed a boot boy, which does not seem to have been the case with the Emersons), cleaning and refilling oil lamps, setting the table for meals,

and assisting the butler in serving dinner. Furthermore, the footman might be expected to assist the valet with brushing the master's clothes and seeing that the master's dressing room was in order. Since the footman frequently accompanied the family when they went out, it was an important part of his duties just to look good. Employers often chose footmen for their looks, their height, and their shapely calves. Some footmen even purchased "falsies" to make their calves appear more attractive. As usual, the Emersons do not appear to have conformed to the unwritten rules of selection, instead choosing their footmen on the basis of their general amiability, as well as the skill they demonstrated in handling an attack — a regular hazard of duty in the Emerson household.

Like those of the footman, the duties of a housemaid depended on the size of the establishment where she was employed. In a household with multiple housemaids, there was usually an upper- and an under-housemaid. The upper-housemaid was responsible for dusting and cleaning ornaments, furniture, curtains, plants, and flowers. The under-housemaid usually had the heavier housework, which included sweeping carpets, polishing and cleaning grates, carrying coal and laying fires, and carrying hot water for baths (a situation of which Emerson never approved; he often attempted to carry their loads). The housemaid had a variety of duties that kept her busy all day long, and her day would begin early, at five or six a.m., and not end until the bedchambers were prepared for the night.

The cook was the head of the kitchen, often assisted by a kitchen maid and a scullery maid. The cook usually rose at six to start breakfast preparations. Sometimes she had her morning cup of tea in bed, delivered by the kitchen maid. This was probably the only bit of luxury she enjoyed all day, as the rest of the day was devoted to meal preparations for the family. Frequently, the servants did not eat what the family ate (a practice which often saved the employer money), so the cook had to plan two separate menus. The Emersons did not require separate menus; nonetheless, all was not harmonious in the kitchen at Amarna House. The Emersons often kept erratic hours requiring a meal to be kept warm for hours at a time without drying or burning it. However, Amelia did not dictate menus to the cook, which allowed a certain amount of creative autonomy not unlike that of running a restaurant, so that a smart cook could plan the menu in anticipation of such complications.

The kitchen maid was expected to rise at five a.m. to clean and polish the stove and light a fire. During the day, she assisted the cook by pre-paring vegetables, sauces, and gravies, or carrying out other tasks under the cook's direction.

The scullery maid was at the beck and call of both the cook and the kitchen maid, pitching in wherever needed. Her main responsibility was the cleaning of the cookware.

"She is no better than she should be."
Rose

Servants self-segregated into two classes: upper servants and under servants. The upper servants included the butler, valet, lady's maid, and housekeeper. These servants ranked higher than the under servants, whose group included the parlormaid, footmen, housemaids, the cook, kitchenmaid, scullery maid, and boot boy. The housekeeper frequently had her own parlor, where the upper servants would assemble for meals, served by a housemaid. When all the servants dined together, the table would be presided over by the butler at one end and the housekeeper at the other.

Servants were not only particular about their own pecking order, but about what duties they might be asked to perform. Each servant knew exactly what his or her own duties were, and could be highly offended if asked to perform tasks which fell outside the realm of this area. For example, a footman would be highly insulted if asked to carry coal to an upstairs room (the housemaid's job). The Emersons often disregarded this pecking order, much to the dismay of a few of their transient servants; as Amelia noted, *"Wilkins [the butler] totters when asked to do something outside his duties."* Their footmen were expected to do the heavy lifting normally assigned to the housemaid. Accustomed to a household in which such definitions of rank were not emphasized, Ramses was unaware of *"the definitions of comparative duties and relative social status dependent thereon..."* (Peters 1992: 290). However, this very strict adherence to the division of household tasks allowed Ramses, Evelyn, and Rose to unmask a spy at Chalfont Castle. As Ramses explained in a letter to his parents dated 1898, Rose was incensed that Ellis, the new lady's maid, had been in Ramses's room, which was Rose's responsibility. This caused Ramses, Evelyn, and Rose to suspect that Ellis was a spy and set up a trap for her. Part of the plan to expose Ellis involved asking her to take on duties of other servants — in this case tidying the library. Ramses wrote:

"The amiability with which she agreed to take on the task of tidying the library was the final proof of her villainy. According to Rose and Aunt Evelyn, a proper lady's maid would have given notice rather than accept such a demeaning task" (Peters 1992: 290).

The Rewards of Service

The lot of servants was not all work and no play. Most servants were given one half-day off every two weeks. Time off was gradually expanded to include one day off each month, a half-day on Sunday, and an evening out during the week. Some generous employers also allowed their servants a two-week holiday. Here again the Emersons treated their servants unconventionally: family emergencies or family commitments took precedence over the plans of the Emersons. While John would have been helpful in their travels, Emerson pointed out that John could not travel when he had just started a family of his own, a consideration few employers would have contemplated.

In addition, the practice of "board wages" allowed servants to remain as a skeleton staff in a house which was not occupied. In families who owned more than one home, board wages would be crucial to a servant's employment. A family moving from one house to another could choose to relieve servants of their service and close up a house in order to avoid the cost of maintaining more than one home at a time. Or they could move their entire staff to the new home. In the Emersons' case over half of their year was spent in Egypt. The Emersons employed a full staff that lived at Amarna House regardless of their presence. During this time their servants, while still responsible for the general upkeep of the household, had a tremendous amount of free time.

Perhaps most telling of the unusual relationship the Emersons had established with their servants was David and Lia's wedding, where the servants were also their guests at the gathering, "mingling with their masters" and in Gargery's case dancing with his mistress (Peters 1999:33, 35).

"Pas Devant Les Domestiques"
Amelia Peabody Emerson

Servants' daily lives were governed by a number of rules, which were thoughtfully written down for them and published in pamphlets. The rule that was generally emphasized was the need for servants to go about their duties quietly and unobtrusively. Other rules for servants, from the pamphlet, *Rules for Servants in Good Families*, published during the Victorian era, included:

Noisiness is considered bad manners.

Never sing or whistle at your work where family would be likely to hear you.

Do not knock before entering a room.

Do not smile at droll stories told in your presence, or seem, in any way, to notice, or enter into the family conversation, or talk at the table; or with visitors.

When you have to carry letters or small parcels to the family or visitors, do so upon a small silver tray or salver.

If obliged to take anything in hand, or to lift it off the salver, do not give it to the person to whom it belongs, but lay it down on the table nearest him or her.

Servants were expected to make themselves invisible. Chores such as cleaning hearths, laying fires, or setting the table had to be completed before the master or mistress entered the room. Although the butler and footman might serve a family during dinner, they were not to be directly addressed unless the subject was about the serving of the meal. Emerson constantly broke this rule, usually including the butler in the general dinner conversation. Wilkins, a very proper butler, could not be induced to say anything other than *"I really could not say, sir"* (Peters 1988:131). However, Gargery, described by Amelia as a "romantic" butler, was quickly induced by Emerson to join in the conversation.

"You are the one who is always telling me not to discuss serious matters before the servants," Emerson retorted. "Another nonsensical rule, I have always thought. Gargery here is just as interested in serious conversation as any other man. Isn't that right, Gargery?" (Peters 1988:107).

As in many other aspects of his life, Emerson knew what society dictated in terms of treatment of servants; he simply dismissed society's dictates and opinions as nonsensical and baseless. As Amelia explained, *"Emerson has absolutely no notion of how to get on with servants. He treats them like social equals, which is extremely trying for them"* (Peters 1999). Emerson believed that servants had as much to offer as anyone else, if only they were

given the chance. His faith in servants was usually rewarded:

"Really, Emerson, do you think it advisable to take Gargery into your confidence as you do? I am sure Evelyn won't like it if her butler joins the conversation at the dinner table."

"Well, but Gargery is not like Wilkins... Gargery made a useful suggestion" (Peters 1988:131).

Emerson was not above using the conventions to suit his own purposes, however. If there was an issue he did not want to discuss with Amelia, he tried to use the "don't speak in front of the servants" rule to avoid the subject. He was usually not successful.

Amelia tried to be more conventional in her treatment of servants, although she, too, ignored the dictates of society when it suited her. As she elucidated, *"A butler who wields a cudgel as handily as he carves a roast is entitled to certain privileges"* (Peters 1999:23). An example of Amelia's more conventional behavior towards servants is the rigorous amount of time she spent working with servants such as John, the footman, to correct their diction:

"Ow, Madam, Oi tried me best, indeed Oi did. . ." *". . .Watch your vowels . . . . Five years of my training ought to have eradicated all traces of your past"* (Peters 1985:76).

One of the benefits of having better diction was that it improved a servant's prospects for future employment. However, employer efforts to improve a servant's diction did not always arise out of altruistic motives. The manners and speaking patterns of servants reflected on their employer — a well-spoken, well-mannered servant indicated a well-spoken, well-mannered family.

The fiction that servants were invisible, or at least deaf and blind to anything except their work, led to a certain lack of privacy for the family. Indeed, an exchange between Amelia and Emerson illustrates this quite well:

"My darling Peabody..."

With a pang I cannot describe, I freed myself gently but firmly. "We are not alone, Emerson."

"Is that cursed — er — that girl here again?" Emerson exclaimed (Peters 1988:184).

However, the Emersons were unusual among their contemporaries in that they insisted

servants knock before entering:

Our servants are trained to knock before entering. This custom confirms the suspicions of our country neighbours that we are uncouth eccentrics, but I see no reason why the well-to-do should lack the privacy poor people enjoy.... One knock is allowed. If there is no response the servant goes quietly away (Peters 1985:7).

Servants had many opportunities to become privy to confidential details in the family's life. These details were gossiped over in the servants' hall and passed along to servants of other households. Employers were supposed to be above listening to servants' gossip, but many idle mistresses could not pass up a juicy tidbit when offered by an indiscreet servant. Amelia's recollection of a statement by Lady Bassington summed up the situation:

"They are frightful gossips you know. I suppose they have nothing better to do. By the by, my dear, have you heard the latest about Miss Harris and the groom?" (Peters 1985:11).

Unlike the Emersons' household where servants were treated with respect and generosity, many servants were treated as inferior beings, of low intelligence and lacking in feelings. For example, if a mistress did not like a particular servant's name, she would simply call the servant by a name she liked better. When houses were remodeled to accommodate gas or electric lights, or indoor plumbing, the servants' quarters were frequently not included in the renovation. While the family enjoyed light with the turn of a knob, servants had to rely on candles. Although the Victorian era was one in which many time-saving devices were invented in order to assist with housekeeping, most employers did not consider purchasing these items owing to the cheapness of servant labor. The common line of thought was that all the chores got done the old-fashioned way; what need was there for pampering the servants with newfangled devices? It would only encourage them to be idle.

Alas, as the Emersons could have pointed out to their contemporaries, the glory of servitude could not last forever. Legislation passed during the Victorian era had improved working conditions and pay at factories and mines, and in subsequent

years there were more opportunities for employment in shops and offices. During this same time period, both the working conditions and the pay for servants remained stagnant. For example, a housemaid in a middle-class home might have a 17-hour day, while a factory worker would only have a 10-hour day. The advent of World War I also caused a decline in the servant pool, as the young men went off to fight and the young women took jobs in factories to support the war effort. As the number of people willing to work as servants gradually declined during the post-war years, desperate employers were forced to purchase the labor-saving equipment (such as the new vacuum cleaners, gas stoves, and washing machines), offer higher salaries, and provide more days off in order to attract servants. What had been a vibrant segment of the British economy was, by the 1930s, a mere shadow of its former glory. Fortunately, the Emersons never had to contend with this predicament since their attitude toward and treatment of their servants had been such that they had won their loyalty and hearts.

Margareta Knauff

FROM PARLOR TO PYRAMID

A Scholarly Study of Amelia Peabody Emerson & the Women's Movement

"Pray do not detain me, my dear Emerson," I replied. "I am on my way to chain myself to the railings at Number Ten Downing Street, and I am already late."

"Chain yourself," Emerson repeated. "May I ask why?"

"It was my idea," I explained modestly. "During some earlier demonstrations, the lady suffragists have been picked up and carried away by large policemen, thus effectively ending the demonstration. This will not be easily accomplished if the ladies are firmly fastened to an immovable object such as an iron railing.... I am hoping to be thrown into the Black Maria and perhaps handcuffed" (Peters 1998:5-7).

Readers of the works of Amelia Peabody Emerson might wonder if such swashbuckling enterprise was unique to this redoubtable Egyptologist. But she had many sisters in the women's struggle for the vote and equal protection under the law, efforts to enter the professions, and attempts to ameliorate societal evils, such as prostitution, in the late 19th and early 20th centuries. Her insistence on equal treatment and her steadfast opposition to sexism echoed other women's demands of the time, although it was a cry only beginning to be heard in the country where she chose to work, Egypt.

Amelia's background, while unusual, was not inconsistent with that of other progressive women of her time. Raised by an absent-minded, scholarly father without interference from five indifferent and pompous elder brothers, Amelia learned to be self-reliant and run her father's household on her own (*"bully the baker and badger the butcher,"* in her words). Similarly, Amelia's contemporary, the African explorer Mary Kingsley, was born into a distinguished family of eccentric intellectuals and was largely self-educated except for German tutelage, so she could assist her father with his German translations. While in Africa, Kingsley whomped inquisitive crocodiles, Amelia-like, on the nose with her parasol.

Thus, Amelia's rescue of the ailing Evelyn Barton Forbes from the streets of Cairo and her decision to take charge at Amarna when archaeologist Radcliffe Emerson fell ill and Walter Emerson was un-

A March 1906 photograph published in the Daily Mirror *of suffragists being arrested outside 10 Downing Street in London.*

138

Women on the march.

able to cope was second nature to her (*"I had Walter thoroughly under control....He would not have argued with me if I had proposed jumping off a pyramid"* (Peters 1975:106). Despite Emerson's teasing declaration that he just wanted to marry Amelia for her money, in an admission of equality he called her "Peabody," as he would have another man. Amelia's acquisition of a tool belt demonstrated her determination to do things on her own. While Emerson claimed, "[Amelia] *jangled like a chained prisoner when* [she] *walked,"* he later declared his gratitude for her tool belt when they were trapped in the subterranean chamber of a pyramid (Peters 1985:96, 265). Even Amelia's assumption of trousers — albeit loose and flowing — as part of her working costume was a political statement, mirroring Amelia Bloomer's lampooned efforts to revolutionize women's dress and so release them from the confinement of corset and bustle, both loathsome accessories to the free-wheeling Amelia. Through her personality, background, and family situation,

her sympathies thus would have rested squarely with the women's movement.

Nor were her adventurous and intellectual aspirations uncommon in her desire to excavate in Egypt (described colorfully by Amelia as *"the bright flame of Egyptological fervor was kindled in my bosom"*) and produce published work (Peters 1986: 5). During the Emersons' 1898-99 season, Amelia mentioned *"two ladies who had excavated the temple of Mut at Karnak"*; the most likely candidates are Margaret Benson (sister of archaeology enthusiast and novelist E.F. Benson) and Janet A. Gourlay, who excavated together and later coauthored *The Temple of Mut in Asher* (1899). Kate Griffith, wife of Egyptologist F.L. Griffith, excavated with archaeologist — and Emerson rival — William Flinders Petrie. Amelia B. Edwards was a best-selling novelist when she traveled to Egypt in 1873, a journey that changed her life and inspired her change of vocation to the study of ancient Egypt. Her female companion, L., who doctored the locals, was dubbed the "Hakim Sitt" (similar to Amelia's Arabic name "Sitt Hakim" — Lady Doctor). Edwards' trip resulted in the book *A Thousand Miles up the Nile* (1877) which was reprinted several times in her lifetime and still can be read today in more recent editions. Edwards later cofounded the Egypt Exploration Fund, which supported Petrie's work, and endowed a chair in Egyptology at University College, London, that went to Petrie.

"How far are we, even now, from the emancipation we deserve?" wondered Amelia in 1896 (Peters 1988:1). She had considerable reason to wonder; the status of women was far from ideal. At the time Amelia wrote those words, British women did not have full access to the professions except for low-paid teaching positions; young working women often were harassed by men in public; wives could not obtain a divorce without proving adultery, cruelty, and desertion; and the age of consent had been raised from 13 to 16 — hardly a restraint on early marriage, numerous pregnancies without recourse to birth control, and prostitution.

Most of all, British women could not vote. Although much suffrage activity was curtailed by the outbreak of the Boer War, there were some late-19th Century suffrage efforts, such as the Women's Liberal Federation (1886), Liberal Women's Suffrage Society (1887), and the Women's Emancipation Union (1892). The Women's Co-operative Guild (1883), composed of working-class women, had 14,000 members by the early 1900s (Rubenstein 1986: xiv). The Women's Trade Union League (1874) and Women's Industrial Council (1894) lobbied for suffrage, improved workplace conditions, and equal pay for equal work. In 1897 a number of smaller suffrage groups reformed into the National Union of Women's Suffrage Societies (NUWSS), led by Millicent Garrett Fawcett. Several journals promoted women's suffrage, such as *The Woman's Herald* (later renamed *The Woman's Signal*), the *Woman's Gazette,* and the *Quarterly Review of the Women's National Liberal Association* (Shiman 1992: 125-126). The government's view of women's suffrage could be summed up by the words of a future member of Parliament and prime minister, Winston Churchill.

A member of the W.S.P.U., ca. 1907.

Women's suffrage, he claimed, was *"contrary to natural law and the practice of civilized states."* Wives were, he said, *"adequately represented by their husbands,"* and unmarried women would support *"every kind of hysterical fad"* (Manchester 1983: 245).

The Illustrated London News *depiction of window-smashing suffragettes.*

The entrenched opposition came not only from men, but from women. Wrote an incensed Queen Victoria in 1870:

"The Queen is most anxious to enlist everyone who can speak or write to join in checking this mad, wicked folly of 'Woman's Rights,' with all its attendant horrors, on which her poor feeble sex is bent, forgetting every sense of womanly feeling and propriety.... It is a subject which makes the Queen so furious that she cannot contain herself. God created men and women different — then let them remain each in their own position.... Woman would become the most hateful, heartless, and disgusting of human beings were she allowed to unsex herself; and where would be the protection which man was intended to give the weaker sex?" (Strachey 1921:409-410).

Amelia's reaction to Victoria's sexist view was predictable: "Honesty compels me to note that

her gracious Majesty's ignorant remarks about the sex she adorned did nothing to raise it from the low esteem in which it was held" (Peters 1988:1). The so-called "Anti-movement" included the Anti-Suffrage League, which was founded in 1908 with Lady Jersey as chairman, and Middle Eastern explorer Gertrude Bell as honorary secretary. Its first president, the popular novelist Mary Humphrey Ward, wrote in *The Times* of February 27, 1909:

"Women's suffrage is a more dangerous leap in the dark than it was in the 1860s because of the vast growth of the Empire, the immense increase of England's imperial responsibilities, and therewith the increased complexity and risk of the problems which lie before our statesmen — constitutional, legal, financial, military, international problems — problems of men, only to be solved by the labour and special knowledge of men, and where the men who bear the burden ought to be left unhampered by the political inexperience of women."

Anti-suffragists like Ward believed women's brains were smaller than men's, thus making them incapable of governing, and that woman's rightful place was in the home. They were shocked at the violent campaign of Emmeline Pankhurst and her Woman's Social and Political Union (WSPU), in operation since 1903 and ignored by the public until Pankhurst and her colleagues adopted more militant tactics.

While Amelia's commitments in Egypt precluded an active role in the suffrage movement upon her return to England, her involvement with the high-profile, forthright Pankhursts was logical (related in her journal dated 1906-07). Their campaign of public disruption — throwing bricks through shop windows, noisy demonstrations, dramatic arrests, and the like — would have suited Amelia's temperament, and Emmeline Pankhurst and her three daughters had a wide ranging influence and received more media attention (and censure) than the more conservative NUWSS. Daughter Christabel, who held a first-class law degree, was a principal leader of the WSPU. Daughter Sylvia, an artist, worked with working-class women in London's East End. Daughter Adela participated in the suf-

Principals in the British Suffrage Movement were Emmeline Pankhurst (at left, being arrested in 1914) & her daughters, Sylvia (top) & Cristabel (above).

frage and anti-war movements in Australia. The Pankhurst-trained American Alice Paul founded the U.S. Woman's Party, endured imprisonment and force feeding in the American women's struggle for the vote, and wrote the Equal Rights Amendment.

The suffragists suspended their campaign for the vote during World War I to assist with Great Britain's war effort and thus, in their view, prove their claim to equal citizenship (with the exception of Sylvia Pankhurst, who publicly opposed her mother and sister Christabel). Their effort paid off in 1918, when a limited franchise to women over age 30 was granted. British women achieved full parity with male voters in 1928.

In an effort to apply lessons learned to the next generation, Amelia insisted on her ward Nefret's retention of her grandfather's legacy in her own name (benefiting from the Married Women's

Property Acts of 1882 and 1883, which gave British women the right to hold property in their own name; they were rooted in the experience of novelist Caroline Norton, whose physically abusive husband garnisheed her earnings and kept her children from her). Perhaps Amelia also was mindful of Evelyn's near loss of her inheritance to her cousin, and her own battles with her brothers over her father's will, related in her first journal of record.

With an even more eccentric past than Amelia, as a high priestess of a lost civilization, Nefret excelled at archery and reached beyond Amelia's amateur doctoring to undergo formal medical studies, despite society's considerable opposition. When Dr. Hannah Longshore set up her Philadelphia practice in 1851, a pharmacist initially would not sell her drugs, declaring, *"You are out of your sphere! Go home and darn your husband's stockings! Housekeeping is the business for women"* (Bonner 1992:7).

Nefret's struggles for recognition and legitimacy as a female physician were experienced by physicians Elizabeth and Emily Blackwell in the United States, and Elizabeth Garrett Anderson, sister of suffrage leader Millicent Garrett Fawcett, in England. After a long fight to enter and graduate from medical school, the Blackwells, suspected of being abortionists, were denied employment. Like Nefret's establishment of a Cairo clinic for women, the Blackwell sisters opened the New York Infirmary for Women and Children in 1856 to treat indigent women. Elizabeth Blackwell emigrated to England and worked to further women's medical education there.

Encouraged to pursue medicine by Elizabeth Blackwell, Garrett Anderson was the first female M.D. at the Sorbonne, after years of slammed doors in her native country. She *"knew what it was 'to be sneered at as a woman by a stupid fool of a man,' and to endure the insult behind the mask of a calm face"* (Manton 1965:155). She was instrumental in the founding of the London School of Medicine for Women in 1874 and later saw her daughter, Louisa, also a physician, off to France to serve in the Women's Hospital Corps during World War I. Amelia remarked that Nefret's education was due to *"the help of the dedicated ladies who had founded a woman's medical college in London,"* most likely a reference to the London School of Medicine for Women (Peters 1998:17). Nefret's residence in England for medical studies is understandable —there was no training available for female physicians in Cairo until 1913, although some training existed for female midwives (Tucker 1985:122) — yet Amelia noted that Nefret faced a more receptive climate for female physicians in France or Switzerland (Peters 1998:17).

Nefret's medical services to Cairene prostitutes had its precedent in Amelia's confrontation with Ayesha, Emerson's former lover, who operated an opium den and had been disfigured, probably by a former client (Peters 1988:159). Although Ayesha had clearly moved up in the world, with her swank Park Lane address, her curious behavior to Amelia — half defiant, half degraded — reflected contemporary contempt for prostitutes as outcasts, although many were forced into it through abandonment by their husbands. Amelia's compassion and offer to relocate the astonished woman to the country contrasted starkly with the treatment of prostitutes at the time.

In British-controlled Victorian Egypt, prostitution was legal and taxed. While the law mandated regular medical exams and valid health certificates for prostitutes in brothels operated by Egyptians, it turned a blind eye to those operated and patronized by Europeans in the European Red Blind District, and to the abysmal conditions in which the women were kept, as demonstrated by one chilling account that described *"painted harlots sitting like beasts of prey behind the iron grilles of their ground-floor brothels"* (Tucker 1985:153). These circumstances could not help but foster a flourishing "white slave" traffic.

"What frees women is the distance of men."
—Egyptian proverb

The prostitutes' situation was only one example of the less-than-desirable conditions for Egyptian women. While the Quran acknowledged women's right to own and control property, receive a legacy, and keep their own name after marriage, their subservient role in marriage and the right of their husbands to practice polygamy kept them on an unequal footing with men.

During Amelia's time there were some stirrings of Egyptian feminist thought, although the confinement of Egyptian women to the home and their low rate of literacy (estimated at less than one percent) could not have aided the cause (Fokkena 1995:1). Amelia noted the existence of several periodicals that addressed women's issues (Peters 1998: 84). Some of these had female editors, including *al-Fatah* (The Young Woman, 1892-1893); *al-Firdaus* (Paradise, 1896-1898); *Anis al-Tadis* (The Intimate Companion, 1898-1908); and *al-'A'ila* (The Family, 1899-1907) (Baron 1994:16-21).

The groundbreaking *Tahrir al-mar'a* (The Liberation of Women) by Qasim Amin was published in 1899, followed by *Al-Mar'a al Jadida* (The New Woman) in 1900. These two works stimulated heated public debate on women's rights, since the male Amin was a prominent lawyer and supreme court judge. *"From the time of her birth to the time of her death a woman is a slave because she does not live by or for herself,"* he wrote in *The New Woman*. *"Instead, she lives through and for the man"* (Amin 2000:132). Influenced by his four years in France, where he admired the freedom of French women, Amin linked the inferior status of Egyptian women to Egypt's lack of development into a truly advanced nation. *"Any country concerned with its interests,"* he wrote in *The Liberation of Women*, *"should be concerned with the structure of its families, for the family is the foundation of a country. Consequently, since the mother is the foundation of the family, her intellectual development or underdevelopment becomes the primary factor in determining the development or underdevelopment of the country"* (Amin 2000:72).

Amin called for education, remunerated employment for women, and revamped marriage and divorce laws. He denounced the practices of veiling and seclusion of women. For the professions, he named teaching and medicine as the top priorities for Egyptian women — teaching so they could edu-cate their children, medicine so that women could be properly treated without offending Islamic doctrine. He endorsed physical fitness for women and displayed a remarkable empathy for mothers. *"The pain and hardship of just one childbirth may well be more than the pain a man suffers throughout his whole life,"* he noted (Amin 2000: 180).

While many of Amin's recommendations relate to improving women in their traditional positions as wives and mothers, he did recognize women's humanity, list some of the contributions of Western women to civilization as evidence that liberated Egyptian women could make similar contributions, and point out the prominent roles of the Prophet Mohammed's wife, Aisha, and the mothers and wives of his followers.

For his views, Amin was attacked in the press and by the palace, although his pro-Western sentiments in a time of nationalistic fervor also may have been a contributing factor. But he succeeded in moving the issue of Egyptian women's emancipation to center stage in the national consciousness.

"...The wrongs of my oppressed sisters must always awaken a flame of indignation in my bosom" (Peters 1988:1).

Throughout her life, Amelia Peabody Emerson remained steadfast in the feminist principles propounded in all of her published work. Her small-but-unsung role in the British suffrage movement; her dedication to the preservation of the past and her writing, including her books of Egyptian fairy tales; her encouragement of her ward to enter the medical profession; her compassion for the former prostitute Ayesha; and her opposition to sexism all indicate her commitment. She had many sisters working on parallel lines in the fight for equal rights and opportunity, and their remarkable energy and achievements in the face of bedrock opposition have left us with an enormous, and humbling, legacy.

Elizabeth Foxwell

A SPECIALIZED INDULGENCE

Amelia Peabody Emerson & the Evolution of Fashion, 1884-1915

In the second half of the l9th Century, changes began to take place in the attitudes of Western upper- and middle-class women that were reflected in their choices of clothing. Many of them began to seek satisfaction in a larger sphere than the domestic one to which they had been consigned. Some were outspoken in their advocacy of radical ideas; others quietly made changes in their own lives, from participation in sports to entry into the business world. From Britain and America there arose a challenge to the French dominance of fashion, in the development of tailored styles more suitable to an active life than the highly feminine designs coming from France. While many English ladies were content with a pampered, conventional life and the attendant decorative but restrictive clothing, the nation produced enough independent-minded women to give rise to caricatures in Europe that represented them as overbearing, indecorous, and, indeed, shockingly masculine. The drain of men needed to maintain the Empire may have contributed to the necessity for greater independence on the part of British women, some of whom, like Amelia P. Emerson, intrepidly set out to conquer it on their own.

The social alterations that would forever affect how women viewed themselves and how they dressed occurred over several decades covering the end of the 19th Century and the beginning of the 20th. Progress was often slow, but history was on the side of the reformers. This is the precise period covered by the journals of Amelia P. Emerson that have been published to date. Her interest in fashion and personal choices provide a valuable insight into the evolution that was taking place.

In the earliest of Mrs. Emerson's journals (1884-85), she initially appeared to be an outwardly conventional, upper middle-class woman, one who had accepted the prevailing ideal of beauty, and, considering herself to be unattractive, dressed the part of a dowdy spinster. In her dark, severely cut outfits, she could almost be the model for the Continental caricatures, and she professed a lack of interest in anything so frivolous as fashion. Her attitude soon underwent a radical reversal. As her horizons expanded, the admiration of Emerson and the promptings of Evelyn broadened her understanding

Opposite, a fashionable lady of 1893 attired in a full-sleeved woolen cloak trimmed in velvet & embroidered with beads.

A bustled ensemble of 1884.

of beauty and awakened in Amelia an interest in dress as a window into personality, a useful accomplishment for the detectivally inclined.

In examining Mrs. Emerson's personal approach to the fashions of her time, a valuable source has come to light among the Emerson family papers. Investigation of a closet stacked with cartons full of household accounts, tradesmen's invoices, and miscellaneous memoranda has turned up several shoeboxes stuffed with items pertaining to the family wardrobe. Receipts for crimson satin indicate that Mrs. Emerson ordered an update of her favorite evening gown every two or three years, despite the fact that Emerson rarely noticed the difference. It is hardly surprising for readers of Mrs. Emerson's memoirs to learn that the expenditure for masculine accessories might be considered inordinately high. Plain studs and shirt buttons were acquired from wholesalers by the gross. Shirts by the dozen, two or three lots at a time, were ordered twice a year, before and after the excavation season. Conversely, the outlay for (male) nightclothes was virtually nonexistent.

Of particular interest to students of costume are notes to Mrs. Emerson from her personal dressmaker, who outfitted her from the early 1880s until retiring at the end of the Great War. Mrs. Emerson seems to have favored this lady rather than patronizing any of the fashionable couturieres of her day. While it may have been from habit, it seems probable that Amelia preferred to give her custom to a person who would follow her directives rather than attempt to impose a style on her. The identity of this lady is as yet unknown. In contrast to the formal script on her bills and in the body of her notes, the signature is a highly individualistic but illegible scrawl, consisting of initials and a flourish. TJR? FLP? It is hoped that further research will supply an answer and perhaps even Mrs. Emerson's half of the correspondence. While a number of the existing notes simply set times for fittings or accompany a completed order, a few do provide an insight into the evolving style of a trendsetting woman. The first of these dates from shortly before Amelia left for her first, momentous trip to the East.

Wednesday, 13 August, 1884
Dear Miss Peabody,

In response to the instructions you sent with your recent order, I am making up your gowns using only a small cushion for the tournure. I understand that it will be convenient for traveling and take little space in your trunks, but I do believe you should consider including a full cage bustle as well. A short version is perfectly suitable for a walking costume, but visiting and evening gowns truly demand greater support to be au courant. The latest styles are even fuller behind than last year.

I have received the package containing 12-1/2 yards of slate blue India cloth and wish to confirm that you do, in fact, wish to have it made up as a dress in the "Rational" style, similar to that of Lady Archibald Campbell at the recent Exhibition, with a divided skirt. Such a garment is described in "The Tailor and Cutter" and I do not believe that it will be offensive to womanly modesty if the cut is of sufficient fullness to disguise the division.

I have just come across a 20 yard length of Belgian bobbin lace that would be quite suitable for ruffles on your grey satin evening gown, perhaps below the tablier or edging the drapery at the back. The lace would make a charming contrast to the beaded braid that you sent to trim the bodice. I can baste it into place to show you when you come by for your fitting.

Everything should be ready by next Tuesday, if that will be suitable to you.
Very respectfully yours,

As is apparent from the first memoir, Miss Peabody's preferences prevailed; the evidence of the bill shows that the gray gown was completed without lace or ruffles, and with only a minimal bustle. The new Mrs. Emerson's tastes were to change dramatically by the following year. Marriage and a stimulating career piqued her interest in clothes and an even deeper desire to shape her apparel to her own ends. Like many women of her time, she was torn between modishness and practicality.

In approaching Mrs. Emerson's wardrobe, it makes sense to start, as a lady must, from the inside. Her choices of underclothing reflect the same dichotomy as her more visible attire. One school of

A striped-silk "visiting dress" of 1889.

*An 1894 bicycling costume
with Turkish trousers.*

thought in the 19th Century embraced the idea that wool next to the body was especially healthy, and in the 1880s turned to the unbecoming but functional styles promoted by Dr. Jaeger. Amelia's initial enthusiasm for these utilitarian garments lasted only until Evelyn introduced her to more feminine styles in Rome. Thereafter, she appears to have remained faithful to lace-trimmed white batiste. Although the 1890s and the new century saw an increasing acceptance of provocative underclothes in colored silks, no record of any such purchases has been found among the Emerson papers so far. It seems likely that confections such as those displayed in the private salon of Maison Lucile would have struck Mrs. Emerson as excessively racy. Whether Emerson would have agreed or not can only be speculation, since he would surely have found it too embarrassing to visit such an establishment. While the same cannot be said of Ramses, he would never have ventured to present his mother with such a gift, and Nefret's personal bills were not found with the other family papers.

Despite her affection for dainty muslin, Amelia retained for years her belief in the healthful properties of wool in the form of the flannel belt. If negative evidence can be considered, it seems likely that she abandoned the belts by the turn of the century. No references after that date have been found in the volumes of her memoirs published so far. Several factors could be responsible. New dress styles were demanding a cleaner line requiring fewer undergarments, but it is probable that Mrs. Emerson was influenced more by personal reasons. Not only did her husband and son thrive without them, but the arrival of Nefret in the household in 1898 may have been the final factor. She had clearly grown to robust adolescence clad only in flimsy, unconfining attire and was not afraid to express her opinions of "civilized" conventions that she considered absurd.

Nefret may also have helped to eliminate the last traces of the corset from Mrs. Emerson's wardrobe. It is evident that, while she disliked corsets, Amelia was conventional enough to wear them, at least on occasion, through the mid 1890s. She avoided extreme tight-lacing, but admitted that some stylish clothes did not set properly without such a foundation. Receipts from Mme. Louise,

Corsetiere, indicate that she favored lightweight tulle models with minimal boning, as advertised for ladies traveling to hot climates, before joining her emancipated sisters who dispensed with them altogether. Fashion finally followed suit, with designer Paul Poiret proclaiming the "banishment" of the corset around 1908, although in practice it lingered on in modified form for years.

Mrs. Emerson's most famous corset, produced to her specifications in the spring of 1896, was one which she abandoned after only a few wearings. Despite her hope to have devised an inconspicuous addition to her useful belt of tools, the file- and weapon-laden corset proved not only distressingly uncomfortable, but too inaccessible in an emergency. What if she were to find herself facing a crisis in mixed company, during daylight? It is safe to suspect that she thought of it with regret, years later, during her disastrous visit to Sethos, the "Count de Sevigny," when she could have made good use of the tools it concealed.

At the end of the 1880s, the heavy, upholstered look that had been in vogue for the past 20 years was finally superseded by a new, less cluttered line. The bustle disappeared almost overnight, no doubt gratefully consigned to the attic or rubbish heap by women who had taken up the latest craze, sports. New bicycle designs made this an enormously popular form of exercise, but middle- and upper-class women had also abandoned their embroidery hoops for tennis courts, golf courses, and other outdoor activities. Increasing numbers were finding jobs in offices, as refinements in the typewriter obviated the need for Bob Crachit-like scriveners, and the machines were seen as acceptable for ladies.

The most popular elements of the new look were the separate blouse and skirt. The skirt fitted smoothly over the hips before flaring out to a full hem, and was tailored with a minimum of ornament. Blouses could be severely tailored or elaborately fussy, providing unprecedented versatility and a chance to combine formerly contradictory elements. With a few simple changes of blouse and accessories, or the addition of a jacket, a woman could appear either businesslike or frivolous. The Emerson accounts show that Amelia welcomed the new styles, which were a variation on ideas with which she had been experimenting during her first few excavation seasons.

It was her innovative excavation attire for which Mrs. Emerson was most noted in the world of fashion. She continued revising her working clothes from her initial visit to Egypt in 1885 until the end of the century, by which time she had developed a style that was so modern and practical that variations of it are common a century later.

Her first "rational" dress proved unsatisfactory for work in Egypt, although she did keep a divided skirt or two in her wardrobe through the mid-'90s, to use in England when Turkish trousers would be inappropriate. By this time so many variations on the outfit were being marketed as cycling attire that it was no longer seen as outlandish. It was about one of these ensembles that Miss Minton commented favorably in 1896. Amelia began experimenting with bloomers for the 1885-86 season, her first as a working archaeologist. She made a few revisions the following year, primarily to accommodate the early stages of her pregnancy, and in the fall of the 1887 she ordered a colorful collection of the costumes that would become so closely associated with her: Turkish trousers and jacket, blouse and tie, to be worn with high boots and a broad-brimmed hat or pith helmet.

While satisfied with her working clothes, Amelia ordered no more until late in 1892. Because the Emersons remained in England during Ramses's early years, they were caught unprepared when they received the irresistible appeal from Lady Baskerville. It appears that, for that unexpected season, Amelia resorted to adapting outfits already in her wardrobe, causing some consternation for her dressmaker at a busy time of the year.

13 December, 1892
10:30 a.m.
Dear Mrs. Emerson,

In acknowledgement of your urgent request to alter the three walking suits you sent over, I am afraid that the fabric in the skirts cannot practically be recut into Turkish trousers of an acceptable fullness. May I suggest making new trousers out of a fabric complementary to the jackets, which can be trimmed with the same, perhaps on the reverse, or the cuffs? In this way, the jacket can do double service for you, with the skirt

The hourglass figure fashionable in the late '90s.

for ordinary wear and trousers for your "dig."

In view of your intended departure on Saturday,* I will need a reply from you by return post in order to obtain the necessary fabric this afternoon. I am assuming that you will require only a single pair of trousers for each jacket. I realize that your expedition has arisen unexpectedly, but on such short notice, so near the holiday season, I cannot promise any more.

If this is satisfactory, I will make every effort to deliver to you on Friday morning.
Yours, in haste,

(*The Emersons did not leave until after Christmas, with the result that Amelia was able to squeeze an extra pair of trousers out of her dressmaker, in addition to the three delivered on the 16th.)

In the following years, Amelia maintained a standing order for half a dozen new excavation outfits each year. A few were able to serve for more than one season, but most suffered sufficient damage from sun, sand, and bat guano that it was easier to replace than repair. The basic style remained the same until 1898, when she made her "bold stride" into masculine-styled trousers, and never looked back. That year Amelia and Emerson left for Egypt exceptionally early and on short notice, once again causing difficulties for her faithful dressmaker, who was experimenting with the new designs that Amelia had requested.

Friday, 14 October, 1898
Dear Mrs. Emerson,

Since you have advanced the date of your departure this year, I regret that it will be impossible to complete all six of your excavation suits in the new style, and your crimson gown as well. I have finished three jackets and four pair of trousers which I am sending at this time. You did request a great many pockets, which require careful setting and cannot be done in haste. I have included those you asked for set into the seat of the trousers, although I will venture to caution you against using them for anything bulky. Such a close fit allows for less concealment than your former style of bloomer, and I am sure you will want to avoid the appearance of unsightly lumps about your person. Even when covered by the skirts of your jacket, bulging back pockets could almost suggest a return

of the bustle.

I should have your gown completed early next week. There is a great deal of beading left to do, but I will send it on as soon as possible. As to the remainder of your order, do you wish to cancel or shall I make it up and, if so, will you want it sent to your address here or shipped to Cairo?

With sincere regrets and best wishes for a successful season. I remain
Yours, etc.

No discussion of Amelia's excavation attire would be complete without considering her accessories. During her years in the field and on the detective trail, Mrs. Emerson was continually expanding and refining her collection of useful accoutrements and trying to find practical ways to carry them. In her day, the oversized handbag was not yet a staple of women's wardrobes and, in any case, would have been impractical on the dig or when she needed the unimpeded use of both arms. Her well-known belt of tools was a highly successful innovation, but it did have its drawbacks. As she came up with more and more indispensable gadgets, the belt grew heavier and noisier, leading to her passion for pockets. By the second half of the 19-teens, newly full skirts even allowed her to have them set into the seams of her evening gowns.

Mrs. Emerson's need to carry concealed weapons led her to experiment not only with the quickly discarded corset but with hair and hat pins as well, the latter suggested by her experience with Lady Baskerville. A pair of enameled, Art Nouveau hair combs with five-inch strong steel teeth, known to have belonged to Mrs. Emerson about 1900, may well have been designed to subdue more than her unruly coiffure. The parasol was an accessory which Amelia found so essential that she continued to carry one long after they had ceased to be a common element of a well-dressed lady's furnishings.

Mrs. Emerson obtained hers from two sources. Her everyday black ones with the reinforced shafts came from an unknown firm in Cairo (the receipts must have been kept in Egypt and are presumed lost.) Her more decorative ones, however, were ordered from the London firm of Brigg and Sons, whose umbrellas and parasols could be equipped with a number of innovations to suit their customers. Mrs. Emerson had other provisions for her flask, pencil, and torch, all of which were available in umbrella handles; but even before Emerson presented her with the concealed sword Amelia had considered the idea of hiding a weapon in the grip. It is not known whether the pepper sprinkler for "stopping dog fights" was suggested by her to the manufacturer, or whether she was attracted to an existing model that was advertised in the early 1900s, but a receipt for one (with a crimson satin cover) is among her papers. Although there is, as yet, no published record of its use, Mrs. Emerson's purchase dates from a period in which there are a number of gaps in the journals, and some incident may yet come to light.

Fashion in the early 20th Century continued its slow progress towards comfort and practicality as designers faced competing demands from progressive and conservative attitudes towards women. The heavily corseted hourglass figure was gradually supplanted by a straighter and fuller-waisted "natural" look. This was accompanied, from about 1909, by the narrow and confining hobble skirt, posing a dilemma for fashion-conscious but active women and leading to some creative modifications by their dressmakers. Amelia was no exception.

Friday, 19 April, 1910
Dear Mrs. Emerson,

I have received your note and must admit that I am in complete agreement with you about the latest styles. They are fresh and charming to the eye, but skirts with scarcely a yard and a half around the hem do make it difficult to walk freely. Last week my little spaniel started to chase after a squirrel while I was walking her on her lead, and I was afraid that I might be pulled right over. Since then, I have been studying the patterns and I believe that I can see several ways in which it should be possible to maintain the slim line without completely sacrificing mobility.

For a day dress, I would suggest deep pleats, to be set into the seams from the knees to the hem; they might be fitted out with buttons to permit them to be closed when the extra fullness is not necessary. In different skirts these pleats could be incorporated at the sides, or placed in the side front or back to provide variety. Another possibility is a skirt that wraps over

itself, if the crosspiece is sufficiently wide to conceal the opening even while walking. I even believe it would be feasible to leave a long open slit in a skirt, with a decorative panel to cover it. The slit might be filled in with a godet to prevent accidental exposure of the lower limbs, but I believe that this expedient may serve elegantly for your new evening gown.

You will be pleased, I think, with the latest colours from Paris that are being shown this season. They are very brilliant, with extraordinary combinations that are, I understand, Oriental in inspiration, so perhaps already familiar to you. I feel sure that you will find them flattering. If it will suit you to come by next week, I have some swatches for your consideration, and you can decide on the details of your skirts. Very sincerely yours,

Evidence from the receipts indicates that Mrs. Emerson felt obliged to forgo vivid tones in her spring order that year. The death of Edward VII on May 6 sobered the nation and led her to select a deep burgundy for the evening gown instead of her favorite crimson, but the following year she felt free to select a rainbow of fashionable colors.

Amelia made her compromises with fashion during the dominance of the hobble skirt, which was fortunately short-lived. Whether the influential designers actually heeded the complaints of their customers or simply felt that a change of silhouette would increase their bottom lines, hints of fuller skirts to come were heard in the summer of 1914. What came instead was the outbreak of war. Paris remained a center for fashion inspiration, but production was curtailed, and throughout Europe women grappled with the moral issue of what place fashion should take during a time of crisis. Having been in Egypt and away from the issues gripping the home front, Mrs. Emerson was brought up to date by her dressmaker, whom she contacted shortly after her return.

Wednesday, 3 March, 1915
Dear Mrs. Emerson,

I was a bit surprised to hear from you so early this year, but am very happy to know that you have returned safely from Egypt. We heard how the Turks were driven off from the Canal, and I naturally thought of you and your family. How frightening that must have been, to know that the enemy was so close at hand! We thank God here for the safety of the Channel, which keeps the Hun from ravaging us as he has the poor Belgians and French. I pray that our soldiers will soon drive back the enemy there, as they did in Egypt, so we can be at peace again.

Business has been very slow. Some people consider it improper to think of Fashion when we are at war, so many seamstresses have been thrown out of work. I have tried to give employment to a few of them, so your order will be most welcome.

You will be pleased to know that the new styles have skirts that are much fuller than in the past few years, and shorter as well. They should be much more comfortable, and I am sure you will wish to order sev-

eral. There are those who say that it is unpatriotic for ladies to wear wider skirts when we should be giving All to our brave soldiers, but in truth, what use would they have for flowered muslin or crepe-de-chine? The new full skirts will not only make it easier for us women to take our part, unhampered, in the War Effort, they will help to keep up the spirits of everyone on the Home Front and cheer the hearts of our boys when they return. Making them will provide work for many women whose husbands and fathers are fighting or lost, perhaps saving them from destitution. I personally believe that it would be unpatriotic for those who can afford it not to order new frocks. We must all do what we can!

Excuse me, I fear that I have been carried away, but I feel sure that you will understand. We women must work together to help our country. It will be quite convenient to meet with you on Monday to settle the details of your order. Until then, I am, sincerely Yours,

A "military" day frock of 1915.

The war years essentially completed the revolution in women's fashion that had begun decades before. Garments lost much of the purely ornamental trimming that had encrusted dresses of similar design and came to rely on differences in cut to make their statements. Clothes became looser, more functional and easier to wear. No longer did elaborate gowns with inaccessible fasteners require the assistance of a maid — or someone else — which may have brought mixed feelings to the Emersons. During the war, some women had found trousers and overalls to be the most practical attire for work that they had taken over from the absent men, and although it would be some years before pants became acceptable for everyday wear, they were no longer regarded as freakish or unnatural.

Trendsetting women like Amelia were at the forefront of the change. In her later years, as she took tea in her comfortable lounging pajamas or supervised other trouser-clad women at the dig, she could reflect with satisfaction, and, perhaps, a measure of surprise, at how different life had become since she dared to order an unconventional outfit and set off to meet her destiny.

Florence Rutherford

SEEN BUT NOT HEARD

A Sympathetic Scrutiny of the Victorian Philosophy of Childrearing

The journals of Mrs. Amelia Peabody Emerson offer a tantalizing glimpse of childhood during the Victorian period, as Walter "Ramses" Emerson developed from a baby into a man. However, they also make it clear that Amelia and Emerson were not typical Victorian parents.

Childhood experiences in the Victorian period varied depending not only into which social class the child was born but also upon its gender. For the lower classes, carefree childhood days were brief, if they existed at all. At five years of age, children frequently began to work outside the home, in factories or mines. The horrible conditions under which they worked — 12- to 14-hour days, without even minimal safety regulations or rest periods — eventually aroused the conscience of the British nation. During the latter half of the 19th Century the laws were changed to prevent children under 10 from working in mines, mills, and factories. However, very young children continued to be employed as chimney sweeps and match sellers, or worked at home making matchboxes, nails, ribbons, and the like. These were the legal professions. The pinch of poverty often forced children into a life of crime as beggars, pickpockets, or thieves. It was not hard to see why children would turn to crime. A good thief could have a better income without having to work as hard.

Ramses was aware of the situation of the less fortunate and used it — somewhat cold-bloodedly, one might claim. As a child he employed the disguise of a beggar to great effect, even fooling his parents. The only problem was that this disguise attracted the unwanted attention of police constables.

The lives of upper- and middle-class children were more restricted than those of poor children, as Ramses discovered when he disguised himself as an upper-class girl: "*The only way I could get about as a girl was to attach myself to some adult, and that was not satisfactory, for the adult in question, unless extremely preoccupied, very often was the first to notice I was unattended and would inquire what had happened to my nurse*" (Peters 1988:283).

In many such households children were raised by servants, sometimes seeing their parents for only a brief period each day. Even then, "seen but not heard" was the rule; they were expected to speak only when they were spoken to, to obey orders without whining or

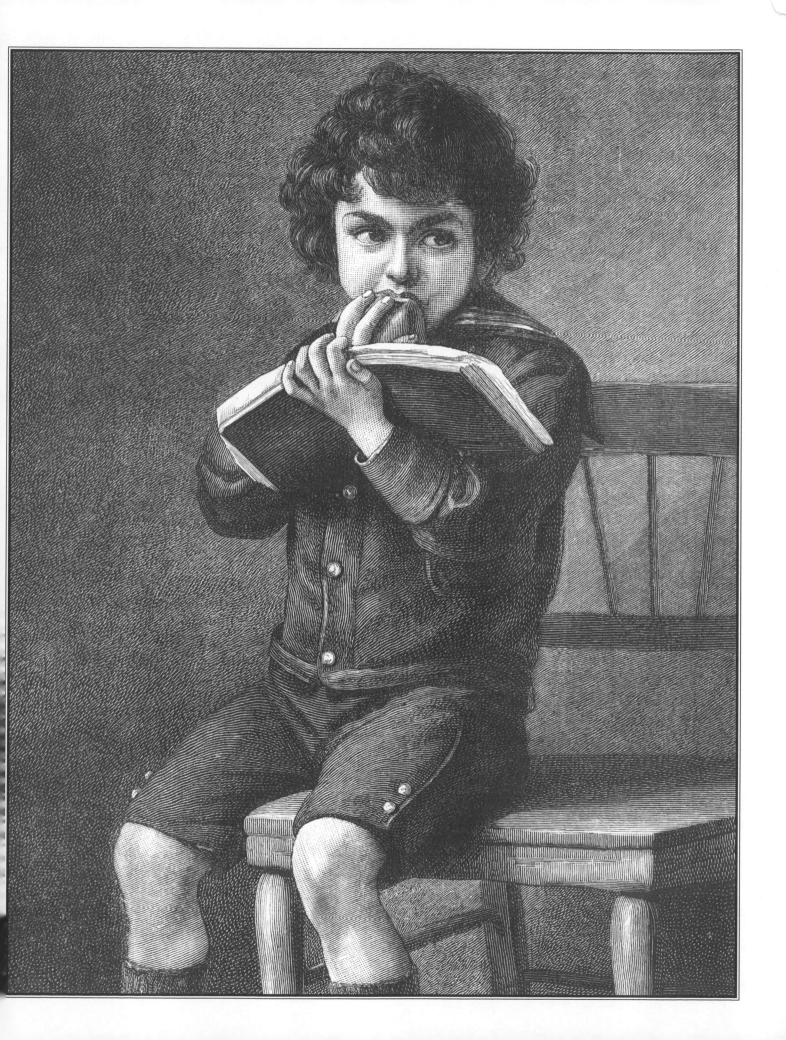

complaint, and to exhibit perfect manners. They spent most of their time in their own parts of the house — the night nursery, where they slept, or the day nursery or schoolroom. Wealthy households supplied nurserymaids for younger children and tutors and governesses for older children, and the "dear old nanny" was a fixture in such homes. Loving nannies were fondly remembered by many men and women, perhaps because they had received very little affection from their parents.

In some cases the only time children saw their parents was when they were to receive punishment, which was often of a severe nature. In a day and age when the axiom "spare the rod and spoil the child" was widely practiced, the Emersons were unusual in that they did not believe in corporal punishment for children. As Amelia explained to her nephew, *"No one is flogged or beaten in this house, Percy — not people, not animals, not even children"* (Peters 1988:61). Percy, more used to the conventional formula of child-rearing, appeared shocked at this statement, which caused Amelia to become *"all the more determined to demonstrate the superiority of our methods of child-rearing over those of his parents"* (Peters 1988:61). One cannot help but suspect, however, that Percy was seldom punished by his doting father.

Ramses's usual punishments were along the lines of receiving a lecture, being confined to his room, or being prohibited sweets. In the case of "extreme provocation," such as when he had crawled into an unstable chamber in a queen's pyramid in order to copy inscriptions for his Egyptian Grammar, his mother was tempted to go beyond verbal chastisement: *"I gave Ramses a push. He said later that I had struck him, but that is not correct. I simply pushed him in order to hasten his progress"* (Peters 1986:173).

Amelia and Emerson were also atypical parents in that both took a great deal of interest in their son's education and upbringing. As parents they were open and accessible to Ramses, not distant creatures more to be feared than loved. Emerson's treatment of his young son was affectionate if somewhat unorthodox: *"Emerson was, from the first, quite besotted with the creature. He took it for long walks and read to it by the hour, not only from* Peter Rabbit *and other childhood tales, but from excavation reports and his own* History of Ancient Egypt...." (Peters 1981:8).

There were a number of reasons why Amelia found it more difficult to express her feelings. As a Victorian mother, she honestly believed that too much praise was bad for a child. Her own upbringing undoubtedly affected her — her mother deceased, her father remote and cold. It is also possible that she was jealous of Emerson's fondness for the boy, and of Ramses's linguistic talents, which she lacked. Except for one outburst, when an injury to Ramses sent her into a berserker rage, she maintained her aloofness until he became a young man, with all the qualities of which any mother would be proud. As was typical of her, she turned from seeming indifference to demonstrations of affection and concern that astonished her husband and pleased her son, who had been trying all his life to win her approval. Emerson, on the other hand, found it impossible to express love and pride to an adult-male offspring. As he remarked self-consciously, *"Men don't say such things to other men"* — a typical Victorian reaction.

Although for some, early childhood could be a relatively comfortable (if, in Ramses's case, somewhat harrowing) experience, these halcyon days did not last forever. At some point a child had to leave the comfort of the nursery for the discomfort of the school room. The lower classes had managed to escape education for most of the 19th Century, but the newly socially conscious Victorians saw compulsory elementary school education as a way of instilling their morals, values, and "civilizing influence" into all social classes. The Education Act of 1870 had the grand goal of bringing *"education within the reach of every English home, aye, and within reach of those children who have no homes"* (Deary 1994:44).

Boys and girls were educated separately. Both were taught reading, writing, and arithmetic, but boys had additional classes, such as carpentry, shoemaking, and gardening. Girls had classes in housekeeping, cooking, and needlework. Most children left school at 13, although some did continue their education. School conditions could be rough, but they were generally an improvement over a 10-

hour work day.

While elementary education may have been new to the lower classes, it was nothing new to the upper classes, who for hundreds of years had been educating their sons through "public schools," preparatory schools, or private teachers. Despite the name, public schools were actually private, endowed institutions.

Daughters of the upper and middle classes were either educated at home or sent to girls' schools. Prevailing thought held that not only was education for women unnecessary, but that women were intellectually inferior, and that too much study would give them brain fever. What education was available was meant to help women idle away the hours and be decorative. If women wished to be educated and learn about the world, they had to take matters into their own hands, following the example of Amelia Peabody. Although the 1890s saw the establishment of both day and boarding schools for girls, which provided a more rigorous education, it was not equal to the education boys received. Advanced education for women was still limited, as Nefret Forth discovered when she attempted to study medicine.

Emerson frequently and vociferously expressed his opinion of the "pestilential purgatories called preparatory schools" and the British educational system in general (Peters 1981:24-25). Emerson's loathing came from first-hand experience: "You know what they were like, even the best of them; brutal discipline and legalized bullying were thought to make men out of boys" (Peters 2000: 391).

Indeed, at the public and preparatory schools violence and brutality were almost a way of life. For new students, the entire first year would be one prolonged hazing. Older boys used the slightest pretext to beat up the younger boys. Bullies stole the completed homework from weaker boys and turned it in as their own work. Frequently, younger boys would seek the protection of an older boy, in order to evade the constant round of bullying and beating.

Younger students were expected to wait on older students, in a form of institutionalized slavery. The younger students were called "fags" and the boys they served were their "masters." A fag was expected to make his master's bed, wait on him at meals, run errands, and perform other duties as he was ordered. Failure to perform duties would result in physical punishment. Besides having to serve his master, a fag might be commanded to attend to any senior boy who demanded his services. (The term fag was simply a slang word for "slave" or "servant" — no homosexual relationship was implied.)

With so many boys living in close proximity, it was no wonder that they became curious about sex. To deal with this, lectures and homilies were delivered on the evils of sex, all couched in euphemistic language, since a schoolmaster could rarely bring himself to address the matter outright. Sex was described as "a sort of disease like measles" (Gathorne-Hardy 1977:89), which only added to the confusion the boys had about the subject. Masturbation was a sin and was severely punished. The schools attempted to enforce the (mostly unattainable) Victorian idea that boys should remain chaste and untainted by sex until they were married. In fact, most young men had their first sexual experience either with an older boy or with a prostitute, since girls of their own class were supposed to remain virgin until marriage and their parents and guardians watched them closely.

In order to encourage a chaste lifestyle, Victorian schools tried to channel much of the boys' repressed sexual energy into organized games. Cricket, football (what Americans called soccer), field hockey, rugby, and other sports gave students the chance to prove their manly courage on the playing field. It was felt that participating in games, taking orders from a captain, working as a team, and making sacrifices for the good of the team not only helped to build character but prepared boys for life. Emerson did not share this opinion, referring on at least one occasion to cricket as "the most infernally illogical and pointless activity ever conceived by the human brain" (Peters 1988:47). Ramses, who was rather a solitary child, never played team sports, which did not prevent him from acquiring the desired moral values, including a willingness to sacrifice himself for a greater good.

In theory Amelia and Emerson did not agree with the Victorian prudery about sexual relations.

While this position was fine in the abstract, once a very real, eight-year-old Ramses began to make inquiries about the subject, Amelia discovered she was not as "modern" as she had believed, and managed to pass the task on to Emerson. Though a good many of Emerson's opinions were unorthodox, when it came to the "facts of life" he was at heart a Victorian gentleman; outmaneuvered and embarrassed, he reluctantly began the discussion with amoebae.

Given Emerson's opinion of institutionalized learning, it is not surprising to find that Ramses was not sent away to school. He was educated, not by tutors or governesses (most of them fled after a few days with Ramses), but by his parents. Early on, Amelia noticed his enormous talent for languages: *"Linguistically Ramses was a juvenile genius. He had mastered the hieroglyphic language of ancient Egypt before his eighth birthday; he spoke Arabic with appalling fluency (the adjective refers to certain elements of his vocabulary); and even his command of his native tongue was marked at an early age by a ponderous pomposity of style more suitable to a venerable scholar than a small boy"* (Peters 1988:3).

Such precocity, though unusual, was not unheard of. John Stuart Mill, son of the philosopher James Mill, had read all the major Greek authors — in the original — by the time he was 10. Young William Flinders Petrie's favorite light reading were heavy tomes on statistics. Ambitious parents saw to it that their children were ruthlessly stuffed with as much information as they could absorb, and more. However, it is unlikely that Ramses would have submitted to this even if his mother and father had believed in "cramming."

Despite his obvious intelligence, Amelia sometimes worried that Ramses was receiving a one-sided education: *"He* [had] *only the feeblest knowledge of the sciences, and none whatsoever of the great history of his nation"* (Peters 1986:23). She might have been relieved to learn that one of the most frequent complaints about Victorian public schools was the curriculum. It was very one-sided, with a large proportion of class time devoted to the classics: Greek and Latin. Little time was given to the sciences until the latter half of the 19th Century, when its importance could no longer be over-

looked. Indeed, the Clarendon Commission, which investigated public schools during the 1860s, declared that a student graduated *"ignorant...of geography and of the history of his own country, unacquainted with any modern language but his own, and hardly able to write English correctly"* (Gathorne-Hardy 1977:143). Despite this, the Commission endorsed the public schools as *"the chief nurseries of our statesmen...the largest share in moulding the character of an English gentleman"* (Chandros 1984:328). The importance of the public schools was not derived so much from what the students learned but rather the contacts and friends they made while there, which would serve them well in their adult life. In short, the concept of the "Old Boy Network" began with the public schools.

The journals of Amelia Peabody Emerson do include an example of an English gentleman educated in preparatory and public schools: Percy Peabody, Amelia's nephew. He knew the proper etiquette and had the necessary social graces, but he was a thoroughly unprincipled individual, a supercilious know-it-all, convinced of the inferiority of women and all "non-white" races. After Emerson and Amelia realized that Percy had spent most of his visit during the summer of 1896 lying and cheating and attempting to injure Ramses, Emerson remarked, *"That...is the pernicious public school training. The poor little brutes have to learn such tricks in order to survive"* (Peters 1988:282).

While it would be unfair to attribute Percy's villainy solely to his schooling, there is no question but that the system which produced Percy (and his uncles on the Peabody side before him) had a number of flaws. However, public schools did try to inculcate high moral standards, and there were graduates of admirable character. Besides Emerson, who survived public school with his values intact, public schools of the Victorian era also produced such men as the statesman Winston Churchill, WWII General Bernard Montgomery, and religious leader Robert Knox.

For most, graduating from school was a rite of passage that transformed them into adults, ready to enter the world of the university, the world of work, or the idle social whirl, depending on class and finances. Ramses's childhood differed dramati-

cally from that of the average Victorian child in that he had open, accessible, and eccentric (for the period) parents who took an interest in him and encouraged his natural talents. In contrast to the Victorian norm, Amelia and Emerson were active participants in his upbringing; their positive examples influenced his values and character. His childhood experience encouraged him to become an avid student of the culture, history, and language of the people of Egypt. The empathy he developed as he observed his parents' attitudes and behavior endowed him with unusual insight into another culture, an empathy which served him well in the art of disguise both as a child and an adult. At a time when the clash of cultures in British-occupied Egypt called for an extraordinary man to quell a native insurgency at a crucial moment during WWI, who but a man who possessed such unusual qualities — qualities which surely derived from his unique childhood environment — could have done the job?

Margareta Knauff

MODERN INCONVENIENCES

A Scientific Investigation of
Technological Developments in the Emerson Era

From the time of adventurer Amelia Peabody and archaeologist Radcliffe Emerson's first meeting at the Boulaq Museum in Cairo to their family's adventures during World War I, the evolution in technology affected the way in which the Emersons lived and worked. While occasionally missing the romanticism of the old ways, for the most part Amelia and Emerson quickly embraced the technological innovations sprouting up at an ever-accelerating pace as the century turned.

The Emersons often had unique requirements for both their vocation (excavating Egyptological sites) and their avocation (solving mysteries and foiling miscreants), so some developments affected them more than others. Changes in modes of transportation, the development of household appliances, and improvements in communications all came in handy at one point or another. But only two items stand out as inspiring particular affection on the part of the Emersons — one for Amelia, and one for Emerson.

> *"The most useful object imaginable."*
> Amelia Peabody Emerson, 1892

While the invention of the parasol predates the events of her first journal written in 1884, there's no denying its central role in Amelia's adventures. Its history dates back as far as 1300 BC, in places like Egypt, China, and India, where versions made of cloth or rice paper protected aristocratic personages from the ravages of the sun. In ancient Egypt sunshades had a religious connection — the goddess Nut was purported to shelter the Earth with her arched body, supported by the god Shu. People who walked under umbrellas were considered to be protected by the goddess.

Parasols became an item of high fashion in 19th Century Britain. Women who were out walking or taking a ride in a topless carriage would flirtatiously display beautifully decorated parasols. While Amelia had her share of frilly parasols to coordinate with dresses for fancy occasions, she describes her "working parasol" as being made of *"stout black bombazine with a steel shaft"* (Peters 1981:100). This came in handy for poking people who blocked her way, prodding stupefied young lovers, and on one occasion, hitting Emerson on the head. It

Engraved scene of telegraph wires in the desert, an aspect of the modernization of Egypt in the later 19th Century.

Late-19th Century parasols. Amelia would have favored the plainer model, almost centainly.

By the late 1890s, cameras could be operated by almost any competent adult &, although still somewhat cumbersome, were increasingly being used on archaeological excavations.

wasn't until a Christmas celebration in 1914, when Emerson presented Amelia with a new parasol as a present, that the accessory could be classified as deadly.

Sword canes and walking sticks date back to ancient times, most likely to Japan, where samurai warriors would carry staffs that concealed swords after carrying such weapons was declared illegal. Umbrellas with swords concealed inside them were made during the umbrella's heyday in the 19th Century; an ever-present accessory for the well-dressed man, umbrellas were built not only with concealed weapons, but also with hidden flasks for those who liked to take a surreptitious nip on a chilly evening. In most cases, the handle of a sword umbrella doubled as a sword grip, and a twist of the wrist would allow the bearer to unsheathe the blade.

Since most women were not in the habit of carrying weapons during this period, parasols with the same feature were not readily made, and would have had to have been specifically customized. Queen Victoria had a parasol that had been lined with chain mail to foil assassins; this was not as successful as she might have hoped, as the chain-mail parasol proved almost too heavy to lift.

Amelia's delight with her new and improved parasol might be considered eccentric even by the standards of the period that introduced the gadget: *"I don't know any other man who would have given his wife such a lovely gift, Emerson,"* she said upon receiving his present. Emerson replied, *"I don't know any other woman who would have been so thrilled about a sword"* (Peters 2000:135).

> *"I could drive you in the motorcar."*
> Radcliffe Emerson, 1906

When Isaac de Rivaz of Switzerland got the idea to use an internal combustion engine to power a vehicle in 1806, the vehicle only managed to travel a few meters. Less than 80 years later, automobiles were barreling down streets in major cities at speeds of up to 14 miles per hour. In 1896 Emerson read Amelia a newspaper advertisement for the Daimler Wagonette, speaking disparagingly of it and other *"modern inconveniences."* It didn't take

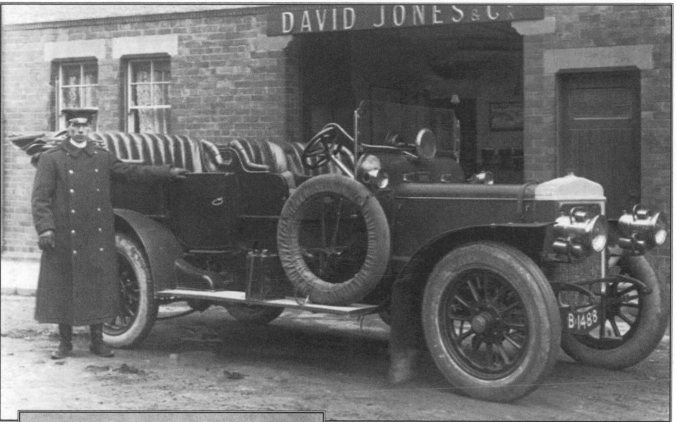

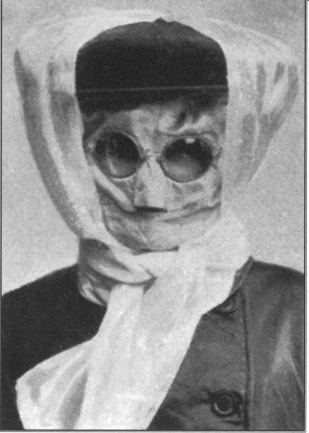

Above, a 1907 Daimler, apparently the make of motorcar owned by the Emersons. Motoring in open cars on unpaved roads necessitated special clothing to protect passengers from dust. The face mask & goggles at left resemble the ones Nefret wore (briefly) in 1906. Even pets were outfitted for the road, as at right, although it is doubtful that any of the Emerson felines would have consented to such comic attire.

him long to change his mind about automobiles, however, and only 10 years later the Emersons were in possession of their own motorcar.

While the model is not specifically stated, Ramses refers to it as "the Daimler." German-born Gottlieb Daimler designed the first four-wheel car in 1886, and founded the company that would later be known as Daimler Benz. Early cars of the 1890s were simply carriages with an engine mounted beneath the seats; headlights were lamps which had

A locomotive in Egypt, 1905; Inset, accommodations in 3rd-class coach were anything but spacious & comfortable.

to be lit prior to entering the vehicle. A few years later, in the early 1900s, cars took on a more modern look, though seating still mimicked that of coaches: vis-a-vis body types had passengers facing each other, while dos-a-dos styles placed passengers back to back.

Automobiles were a technological revolution unto themselves, with manufacturers competing to churn out newer, fancier, more efficient models. Among Daimler's competition in the late 1800s and early 1900s were familiar names like Ford, Cadillac, and Fiat, and less familiar names like Horch and Bugatti.

Drivers of these new automobiles wore goggles and sometimes helmets. As Amelia remarked, *"One glimpse of Emerson crouched over the wheel, his teeth bared in a delighted grin, his blue eyes sparkling behind his goggles, was enough to strike terror into the heart of pedestrian or driver"* (Peters 1998:6).

"Modern inconveniences."
Radcliffe Emerson, 1898

While parasols and motorcars take their turn at center stage in the journals, the Emersons encountered (and used) a number of other technological innovations throughout the course of their adventures.

THINGS TO GET ONE FROM ENGLAND TO EGYPT, OR CAIRO TO LUXOR

Steamships In addition to the motorcar, other forms of transportation were developed or reinvented during the late-19th and early-20th centuries. In 1884, during Amelia's first visit to Egypt, the *dahabiya*, a boat powered by sails (and in cases of insufficient wind, the brawn of the sailors themselves, towing with ropes from the shore) was the preferred mode of travel for tourists seeing the sights along the Nile. Within a few years, while *dahabiyas* were still available and oftentimes luxurious and well-appointed, steamers were taking over much of the travel on the Nile. Steam engines were developed in the late 1700s, and by the 1840s steamships were commonplace. Fueled by coal or wood, steam generated under high pressure in a boiler would power paddle wheels that in turn propelled the ships. Steamers were faster than their sail-powered contemporaries, but Amelia would never cease to mourn the loss of the *dahabiya*, and retained her beloved *Amelia* for use as a home base when on a dig.

Railroads Britain's love affair with railroads was evident throughout the British Empire; the development of the railroad system in Egypt was echoed in India and other parts of Africa. Railroads had been in existence since the early 1800s, but it was not until the middle part of the century that they began to take their place as a staple of transportation. Egypt's railroad expanded at the turn of the 19th Century, eventually making it the most convenient mode of travel from Cairo to Luxor. It still may have left something to be desired, as Amelia described the trip from Cairo to Assiut as *"eleven hours of heat, jolting, and dust"* (Peters 1981:70).

Bicycles For shorter trips, some people chose to go under their own steam. Bicycles are mentioned in passing throughout the journals, and were quite the fashion in Victorian England. The precursor to the bicycle, the hobby horse — invented in 1817 by German Baron Karl von Drais — had a similar shape, two wheels, but no pedals or brakes, and was powered by the long strides of the rider. In 1871 bicycles called "ordinaries" or "penny farthings" were built with oversized front wheels, allowing the rider to travel farther for each push on the pedals. As might be expected, these were difficult to get on and off, and were not particularly friendly to women in long skirts.

Amelia recounts the visit of her friend, Helen McIntosh, who called at Amarna House with her new safety bicycle, which Ramses took for an ill-fated joy ride. The safety bicycle, invented in 1887, some nine years prior to this event, was much more similar to modern bicycles, with two tires of the same size and, on women's versions, a rear guard to prevent skirts from becoming tangled in the spokes.

Zeppelins While the Emersons did not travel in one, they encountered zeppelins during the war. Zeppelins had their origins in the dirigible balloon,

Penny Farthings

invented in 1839. Hot air balloons had been around since 1783, when Etienne and Joseph Montgolfier of France developed a model that was the first to take passengers for an untethered ride. (Amelia would have mourned the loss of Marie-Madeleine Blanchard, the first professional woman balloonist, who died in 1819 when a fireworks display set her balloon on fire, causing her to crash to the ground.) But to be considered seriously for transportation, balloons would need to be able to be steered effectively; thus dirigibles were the next wave in air travel.

The dirigible's design was refined over the years, until the early 20th Century when Germany developed the "rigid airship" or zeppelin, called rigid because it was constructed of cloth stretched over a framework of metal or wood. Hydrogen gas made the craft "lighter than air." As Amelia explained, zeppelins were used to bomb cities during World War I. Ships of this kind would continue to be used until the Hindenburg disaster in 1937.

THINGS THAT ARE USEFUL ON A DIG
Even as Emerson loudly declared his disapproval of newfangled contraptions, he was quick to make use of those inventions that assisted his excavations.

Electric lights Thomas Edison invented the light bulb in 1879, but its widespread application would take another couple of decades. This was a significant development for excavators, as candles and lamps left much to be desired for lighting tombs. In an early encounter with "Miss Peabody," Emerson complained of "fools" lighting tombs with magnesium wire and lamps, which gave off a *"greasy smoke* [that] *lays a film on the reliefs"* (Peters 1975: 91). He advocated using mirrors to reflect light into tombs and pyramid passageways, much as the ancient Egyptians themselves had done. But when electric lighting became a practicable option he took advantage of it. Shepheard's, Amelia's hotel of choice when staying in Cairo, led the way with electricity in Egypt, installing its own generating plant and becoming the *"first hotel in the East to have electric lights"* (Peters 1981:53).

Flashlights Called "torches" in England, flashlights were invented about 1896. They were dependent upon two previous inventions: the battery and the light bulb. Frenchman George Leclanche is credited with inventing the first battery in 1866, but it was not until 1888, when Dr. Carl Gassner of Germany invented the first portable battery, that it became useful on a wider scale. In the meantime, Edison had invented the light bulb, and it was only a matter of time before the idea of combining the two came along.

The name "flashlight" derived from the way early models functioned — most could only sustain light for brief moments, requiring that they be "flashed" on and off. By World War I, more reliable models had been developed, many by a company called Eveready. These portable light sources made creeping around in the dark on the trail of Master Criminals a more surefooted activity.

Cameras When Amelia Peabody and Evelyn Barton Forbes encountered the Emerson brothers at Amarna, it was discovered that Evelyn was a gifted artist; naturally, she took on the role of copying tomb reliefs. In those early days, hand drawings were the best way to preserve ancient reliefs exposed to the predations of tourists and thieves. Within a few short years, however, cameras appeared on the scene and proved their indispensability alongside hand drawings in documenting these works of art. Color photography did not become popular until the 1930s, so drawings remained essential to documentation. The epigraphic techniques pioneered by Ramses Emerson use a combination of black-and-white photography and precise hand copying.

The first cameras were daguerreotypes, named for French inventor Louis Daguerre. Daguerreotypes, invented in 1839, made a direct positive image on a silver-coated plate. These were followed, and outcompeted, by cameras invented by William Henry Fox Talbot of Britain in 1841 that made a paper negative. Though early models were cumbersome and necessitated a tripod and a black drape over the photographer, portable Kodak cameras (invented by George Eastman) became widely available shortly after the turn of the century.

THINGS USEFUL FOR STAYING IN TOUCH WITH WALTER & EVELYN
Telegraph Throughout the journals Amelia men-

tions the use of telegrams: to contact distant family members, to make inquiries regarding mysterious clues and, in one case, to reassure Ramses that Bastet had returned to Amarna House safely after wandering off. The telegraph was invented in 1844 by Samuel B. Morse, and Guglielmo Marconi created a wireless version in 1895.

Telephone *"Emerson does not believe in telephones. He refuses to have them installed at Amarna House"* (Peters 1992:28). While Emerson was apparently unimpressed by Alexander Graham Bell's 1876 invention at first, apparently he capitulated before long, as Amelia indicated a phone had been installed at Amarna house by 1899. In order for the telephone to be useful, a network needed to be created and operators were necessary to man switchboards.

Boys who had worked in telegraph offices were the first telephone operators, but they mischievously crossed wires, and sometimes insulted the callers. This opened the door for young women to take on this role, as they were seen as being more responsible, a development of which Amelia would certainly have approved.

THINGS MENTIONED IN PASSING

Indoor plumbing Amelia discreetly refrained from mentioning developments in this area, except obliquely, in reference to Chalfont House in London. She mentioned Emerson's amusement with an advertisement for "the Lambeth Patent Pedestal Combination Water Closet," and while visiting Chalfont, Amelia commented on her experience with indoor plumbing: *"Like so many other modern 'conveniences,' the device that had been installed in the expectation of its producing hot water was constantly breaking down..."* (Peters 1988:168). Like many other inventions of the period, indoor plumbing and water closets — commonly known in the U.S. as toilets — were evolving and improving constantly, but as Amelia noted, early efforts weren't always reliable. Alexander Cummings received a patent in 1775 for a toilet that is a forerunner of models used today.

Gramophone While investigating the Baskerville case in 1892, Amelia commented that among the luxurious appointments in Baskerville House was a gramophone. Prolific inventor Thomas Edison is credited with inventing the phonograph; the first recording was Edison himself singing "Mary Had a Little Lamb."

"Now then — what about that whiskey and soda."
Radcliffe Emerson, 1896

The late 19th and early 20th centuries saw an explosion of inventions and new ideas, the combination of which would change daily life irrevocably. What is most striking about technology and the Emersons is that, even as the Emersons adapted to change and made use of new technology throughout their lives, the things they took most pleasure in — the wonders of ancient Egypt, family, and the inevitable mysteries and dead bodies — are essentially as timeless as a good whiskey and soda.

Lisa Speckhardt

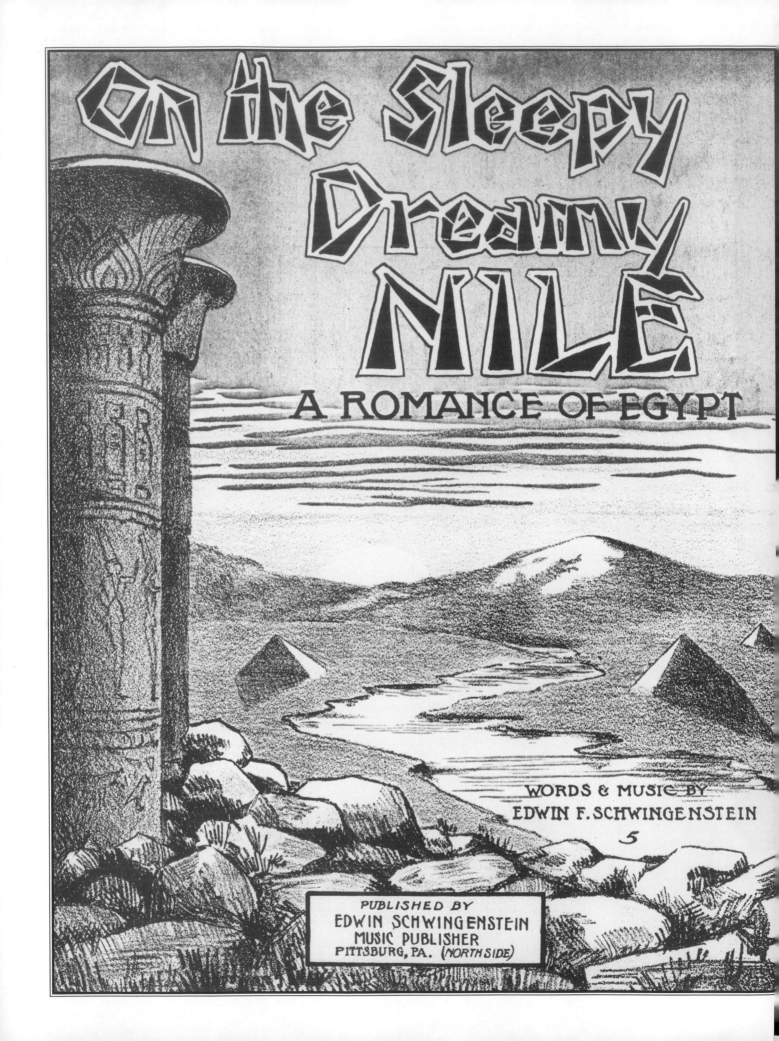

MUSICAL HERITAGE

An Adept Discussion of the Musical Repertoire of the Emerson Family

Nineteenth Century England was dismissed by its contemporaries in the European musical establishment as "Das Land ohne Musik." We need look no further than the journals of Amelia Peabody Emerson to recognize the absurdity of such a statement. Through her contemporaneous accounts at the turn of the 20th Century, we are introduced to a variety of melodies, from the Gilbert and Sullivan operettas, to sentimental and patriotic ballads, and the bawdy music of the notorious English music-halls. While a modern might believe that the Emersons were unusual in their tastes, enjoying waltzes and operas as much as ballads and satirical operettas, the sheer variety and quantity of English-composed songs mentioned in passing in the journals suggest to the reader that 19th-Century England reverberated with music which permeated the life of the ordinary Englishman. The above dismissal of England's musical life rose not from the absence of originally composed pieces but from the preponderance of music pouring forth from composers of popular music — music created especially for the ears of the common person. In a class-based society, acknowledging the worth of popular music was a "dangerously egalitarian" notion (Russell 1987:1). Little wonder then that the Emersons, who rejected the rules of class in every other part of their lives, should embrace the popular music of their time in all its forms.

In considering the evolution of Amelia Peabody Emerson's musical tastes, it is interesting to trace the music mentioned through subsequent years in her journals. That music was central to her life cannot be doubted. In her very first journal recounting her Egyptian travels she mentioned installing a pianoforte in the saloon of her *dahabiya*. Amelia was assuredly a strong-willed woman accustomed to "parasoling" her way through a crowd, but the journals also make clear that she was practical. A piano — even a pianoforte — would have been a difficult and expensive proposition had music not seemed such an integral part of her life that the absence of one was unthinkable. Indeed, the piano, a luxury item in 1840, became a familiar instrument in the English home (about one out of every 10 households owned one) as the 20th Century began. And while piano by *dahabiya* may not have been the same as a piano in an English household, Amelia was not alone in her travels with music. Margaret Orr, daughter of archaeologist Arthur Mace, described a photo from her parents' collection: *"That's my mother's Bechstein grand piano you know...it came by camel"* (Lee 1992:11). Likewise, Amelia noted that the wealthy patron and excavator Cyrus Vandergelt had outfitted his *dahabiya* with a gilded piano. Though Amelia admitted to lacking musical talent, she knew that Evelyn Barton Forbes would have learned how to play as an essential part of her proper Victorian lady upbringing — of what use this cultivation without a piano to play? And so, thanks to Amelia's foresight, Evelyn accompanied their journey down the Nile with Chopin, to their mutual pleasure.

The element of popular music enters the journals following Amelia's marriage to Emerson. Given Professor Radcliffe Emerson's disdain for class distinctions — a disdain that was to earn him some notoriety in his time — it is likely that the introduction of popular music into her life and therefore into her memoirs derived from his influence. Whatever the source of her original acquaintance, it is evident that she relished the music as much as he. In 1892 she recounted their exuberance at returning to Egypt following a five-year absence, as they joined their voices in celebration with a joyful rendering of "Champagne Charlie," a bawdy song of the early music-hall tradition:

> *From Coffee and from supper rooms,*
> *from Poplar to Pall Mall,*
> *the girls on seeing me exclaim,*
> *"O what a champagne swell!"*
> *Champagne Charlie is my name,*
> *good for any game at night, boys,*
> *who'll come and join me for a spree!*

The English music hall, originally an outgrowth of the public house, served as an outlet for the performance of a large number of the original English compositions at this time. Many of the songs of the mid- to late-1800s were designed to entertain the lower working-class of England, and the political and social commentary of the songs was as conservative as the audience to which the hall catered. Occasionally one might hear a song regarding the horrors of working-class conditions, but the concert halls were intended for entertainment, not social activism. Everything was grist for the mill, rich and poor, domestic arrangements and politics — including Gladstone's policy on Egypt and his "unforgivable betrayal" of Gordon:

> *Your policy was always too late,*
> *You would send out our troops*
> *when the mischief was done,*
> *Poor Gordon was left to his fate.*
> *How many brave heroes in Egypt were*
> *slain?*

Walter "Ramses" Emerson would have been more familiar with this form of entertainment as performance, since he visited the Alhambra Music Hall, a well-known London establishment, in order to study Alfred Jenkins, the famous magician and ventriloquist. While the early music-hall tradition — officially begun with the opening of Charles Morton's Concert House in 1849 — initially earned a less-than-stellar reputation (due to both the content of its entertainment and its drinking and carousing clientele), by the time that Ramses attended the Alhambra, the majority of the halls had cleaned up their act, accommodating average middle- and working-class sensibilities.

During Ramses's visits he may well have encountered performances of the intensely jingoistic and patriotic songs which became a feature of the halls during the Boer War and World War I. Lyrics such as,

> *Hail our Empire's Unity!*
> *Manly hearts have spread it far and wide*
> *Roaming with impunity*
> *Masters on the land and on the tide;*
>
> *For there's not a man amongst us*
> *Who would show his face again,*
> *If he did not dare or die for those at home*

and

> *I didn't like you much*
> *before you joined the army, John,*
> *But I do like you, cocky,*
> *now you've got your Khaki on*

were meant to rally the general populace into unquestioning support of Britain's imperial right and duty to spread her Empire regardless of cause or cost. When World War I persisted beyond predictions (since the opposition did not merely drop their weapons and run when given a "taste of

British steel"), sentimental songs such as,

> ... and our roads may be far apart,
> But there's one rose that dies not in Picardy,
> 'tis the rose I keep in my heart!

and the soldiers' lively chant, "It's a Long Way to Tipperary," recommended patience and — as Amelia pointed out — offered solace during the protracted war. Ramses was not alone in believing such music to be a tool of war-mongerers; but the liberal voice in matters of foreign policy was virtually shut out of the music hall, and therefore from the music written for the halls, during these years.

Ramses most certainly would not have communicated his music-hall experiences to his mother, even though they had developed fairly decent reputations by the time he attended; nonetheless, he and his mother shared in the enjoyment of several types of music, including the ritual of his bedtime song. When he was yet a child, Amelia soothed him to sleep at night with a gruesome ballad dating to the 1500s:

> There were three ra'ens sat on a tree
> Down a down, hey down a down....

The one of them said to his mate,
> "Where shall we our breakfast take?"
> "Down in yonder greene field,
> There lies a knight slain under his shield...."
> Down there comes a fallow doe,...
> She lift up his bloody head
> And kissed his wounds that were so red....

While Amelia originally offered a more conventional "lullaby" — possibly something along the lines of the romantic/tragic/historic song about Gordon and Gladstone — it is probable that Ramses insisted upon this selection, given his taste for the slightly macabre and sensational, a taste which was echoed in his reading of detective fiction/thrillers.

Amelia shared a fondness for Gilbert and Sullivan operettas with her son as well. Political and social satires, these overwhelmingly popular operettas — the result of a 15-year partnership begun in 1875 between playwright William Gilbert and composer Arthur Sullivan — could be quoted by all and sundry regardless of class. They were performed professionally by the D'Oyly Carte Opera Company at the famous Savoy Opera House, and — perhaps more importantly for their widespread appeal and perpetuity — by amateur operatic and choral societies all over England. While other English composers attempted to imitate Gilbert and Sullivan, which provided needed variety in local performances, no others garnered the same prominence or immortality in English society. As with The Bard, Gilbert and Sullivan became part of the national identity and an area of common ground for a wide variety of people from many backgrounds. It is not surprising that Ramses and Sethos adopted the parodies in Gilbert and Sullivan operettas as part of their repertoire of disguises, since both men had a similar sense of humor. Humming only a bar, Ramses immediately communicated to his mother the similarity between Sethos in disguise, *"a most intense young man, a soulful eyed young man, an ultra-poetical, super-aesthetical, out-of-the-way young man,"* and the parody of Bunthorne, the aesthete from *Patience*. At a later time, Gilbert and Sullivan's Nanki-Poo in disguise as a "wand'ring minstrel" manifested itself in Ramses' exaggerated disguise of a beggar — *"a thing of shreds and patches,"* as Nefret briefly acknowledged.

Amelia, on the other hand, unwittingly imitated Gilbert and Sullivan satire. She called to mind *The Mikado,* the moment she observed Davis's imperious assumption that Ned Ayrton and Arthur Weigall could clear KV55 in a day — *"and if your majesty says do a thing, that thing is good as done. And if it is done, why not say so"* (Peters 1998:232). Disgusted with Weigall's ineptitude in the face of such a demand, and knowing that Ayrton could not complete the task without maximum damage to the contents of the tomb, she immediately set about making certain *"that thing* [was] *good as done."* And again Amelia drew from *The Mikado* when justifying the dissolution of Lia and David's relationship to Katherine Vandergelt, *"Hearts do not break; they sting and ache...."* However, Katherine supplied the next line, *"for old love's sake, but do not die"* (Peters 1998:305). What she left unsaid was, *"Though with each breath, They long for death."* Hardly the lines to support Amelia's cause! As she admitted, Katherine *"knew* [her] *Gilbert and Sullivan better."*

Emerson, a straightforward character, employed music purely for personal enjoyment. He sang loud, with great feeling and completely out of tune, and knew the words to practically every popular song he encountered — Arab or English. His attitude was infectious, whether entreating Amelia to join him in a song about an intemperate young man, or leading his crew in the colorful Arab love song, *"When will she say to me, young man, come and let us intoxicate ourselves...."* Even during an uncertain journey into the desert people sang along and felt better when they had finished (Peters 1991:134). Indeed, when singing Arthur Sullivan's solemn *The Lost Chord* with his usual panache and dissonance,

> *I have sought, but I seek it vainly,*
> *That one lost chord divine...*
> *It may be that Death's bright Angel,*
> *Will speak in that chord again;*
> *It may be that only in heav'n,*
> *I shall hear that grand Amen,*

the occasion, despite the lyrics, remained joyful not solemn!

Impromptu after-dinner concerts with friends, such as the occasion mentioned above, were common with the Emersons, as they were with many Englishmen at this time. Especially by the turn of the century, a large portion of the English population played musical instruments — women tended to learn the piano, while many men learned the brasses and played in band concerts — and both men and women were members of competitive choirs. The music they performed included everything from classical pieces by Verdi, Handel, Rossini, and Donizetti, to well-loved hymns, and to popular love songs by English and American composers. In such a musical society, it was natural that people should enjoy music at home when not performing or competing. And, similar to the Emersons' home-grown concerts, the majority of the music they would have sung at these gatherings would have come from the love songs of the popular balladeers and composers of their day, such as Harry Lauder's "Roamin' in the Gloamin'" (Geoffrey Godwin's choice when serenading the family), Irving Berlin's "Wishing," and Victor Herbert's "Moonbeams," to name but a few that the Emersons

DAVID MONTGOMERY AND FRED. A. STONE
IN CHAS. DILLINGHAM'S PRODUCTION
The RED MILL
BOOK & LYRICS BY
HENRY BLOSSOM
MUSIC BY
VICTOR HERBERT
M. WITMARK & SONS

appreciated, according to notations in the margins of the 1911 journal. Cyrus could regularly be counted on to contribute "Kathleen Mavourneen,"

Arise in thy beauty, thou star of my night.
Mavourneen, Mavourneen,
my sad tears are falling,
To think that from Erin and thee I must part,

in honor of his wife. At the dinner hosted by the Vandergelts during which Emerson serenaded them with "The Lost Chord," Ramses and Nefret chose a duet from Victor Herbert's operetta, "The Red Mill." Herbert, a fantastically popular Irish/American composer of the early 1900s, was internationally recognized for his sentimental love songs and operettas. The song they chose, "Not that you are fair dear," was particularly fitting for their voices — tenor and soprano — not to mention as a backdrop for the ambivalence of their relationship.

It was precisely for the purpose of joining voices joyfully in song that the Emersons always held their well-loved holiday parties during the winter season in Luxor. Over the years a number of noted Egyptologists joined this annual gathering including Howard Carter, Cyrus Vandergelt, Karl Von Bork, and Clarence Fisher, and all were induced to contribute a solo or two. Amelia mentioned some of the traditional carols they sang, as well as a number of the sentimental ballads, to which Nefret played an accompaniment on the pianoforte. One can easily imagine the enthusiasm the Emersons and their friends would have brought to such Egyptologically inclined pieces as: "On the Sleepy Dreamy Nile: A Romance of Egypt," "My Sweet Egyptian Rose" from "The Bride of the Nile" and "Star Light, Star Bright" from "The Wizard of the Nile." At one point Amelia also indicated that they sang "music-hall" songs. While some of these would have been the various sentimental ballads they all appreciated, given Emerson's and Ramses's acquaintance with the broad spectrum of the music-hall repertoire, a few of them were bound to be more suggestive (especially as the evening and conviviality progressed) than those which she would have felt comfortable listing in the pages of her journal. It is likely that Clarence Fisher, to whom Amelia referred as the reserved young man who became surprisingly gregarious with bit of champagne, knew a number of the ditties that came from America's vaudeville tradition as well.

By the time of the First World War, widespread enjoyment of a comprehensive range of Western music became an indication of the blurring of the strict class lines in English society. During this same time, like many of her contemporaries, Amelia's appreciation of different forms of music had grown as her acquaintance and exposure to them had increased. This included the music of Egypt, concerning which Amelia remarked, *"modern Egyptian singing sounds strange to Western ears at first. I now found it very beautiful when it was well performed"* (Peters 1999:270). Well ahead of his time as usual, Prof. Emerson had always delighted in a variety of music regardless of the class or nationality from which it had evolved; it would be many years before this global understanding of music as a universal language would become an accepted point of view in the European musical establishment.

Kristen Whitbread

THE BEST OF WONDER

An Authoritative Analysis
of Victorian Popular Fiction

All Mrs. Emerson's readers are, of course, thoroughly familiar with the masterpieces of Western literature. One would hesitate to imply that the members of the Emerson family were less intellectual; however, the books most often mentioned in the journals fall into the category of what is today termed popular fiction.

In her day they would have been called "romances." The word had an entirely different meaning then; it was applied to Gothic mystery, detective fiction, tales of the supernatural, and swashbuckling adventure stories — "romantic" as opposed to "realistic." The line between romances and works of genuine literary merit was as distinct as it is today; the increase of literacy and the production of cheap editions of popular books had made readers of the general public, and this democratization of literature could only lead, in the minds of the critical establishment, to a fearful degeneration of taste. True art was by its very nature beyond the understanding of the common man.

The popular books and the poetry beloved by Victorians are in large-part forgotten today. I have therefore composed the following literary quiz, which will at the same time test readers' knowledge of these books and inform them.

LITERARY QUIZ

1. When Emerson was held prisoner by the sinister Schlange, the villain threatened to throw him into a deep well if there was an attempt to rescue him. *"I don't know where you get these melodramatic notions,"* was Emerson's reply. *"From some novel, I suppose."*
He was correct. What novel?

2. Seeking a way of escape from the Lost Oasis, Amelia thought it would be nice if they could increase their prestige by threatening to put out the sun — i.e., predicting a solar eclipse. Emerson's caustic response was: *"Astronomical effects don't occur so conveniently. What put such a fool notion into your head?"*
What did?

3. After Ramses had submitted to Nefret's vigorous and painful medical attentions following a knife wound in the ribs (1903), she said, *"You took it like a hero."* *"J'ai faire mieux depuis,"* Ramses answered. What does it mean and from what literary work did he borrow it?

Opposite, engraving published in the Illustrated London News *1889 serialization of H. Rider Haggard's novel,* Cleopatra.

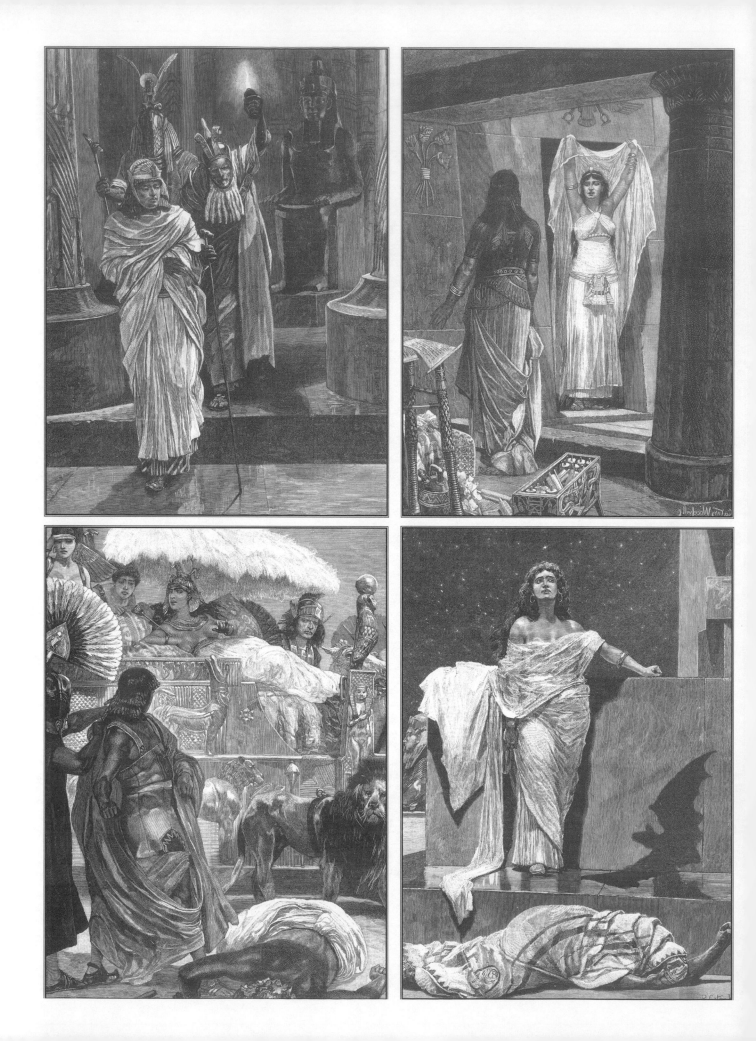

4. *"A look of sadness, a blush of shame"* spread over the face of Kevin O'Connell when Amelia scolded him for placing journalism above friendship. It spread over someone else's face in a famous poem. Name the poem and identify the blusher.

5. *"High rank involves no shame — she has an equal claim with those of humble name to be respected."* Amelia did not use quotation marks in her 1896 journal, but this is a quote. (Except for one pronoun.)

Source?

6. *"I believe you said it is a capital error to reason without sufficient evidence."* *"No, I didn't,"* said Emerson.

Who did?

7. In her attempt to disguise the identities of certain individuals who appeared in her journals, Mrs. Emerson gave them aliases drawn from her favorite reading material. Name the books in which the following originally appeared: (a) Sergeant Cuff; (b) Charles H. Holly; (c) Gargery; (d) Alan Armadale; (e) Rene d'Arcy; (f) (Karl) von Bork; (g) Charles Milverton.

8. Emerson had been carried off by the mysterious female known as the Heneshem. Amelia suspected the worst, and she wasn't thinking of torture. When she burst into the chamber where her husband lay unconscious, the veiled figure of a woman was bending over him. *"I had beheld such a scene before, through the eyes of imagination, but this was a grotesque parody of the original. My husband's ruggedly masculine features bore no resemblance to those of the golden-haired hero of the classic novel, and the shape that hovered over him would have made four of the immortal She."*

Name the book — that ought to be easy — the author and, for full credit, both names of the golden-haired hero.

9. Despite the Emersons' predilection for popular fiction, they were all familiar with *"our national poet"* Shakespeare, and quoted from him frequently. How many Shakespearean references can you remember?

Correct guesses don't count. You must know the

Above, illustration by Maurice Greiffenhagen of a scene from an early edition of H. Rider Haggard's She.

Opposite, additional steel-engraving illustrations by R.C. Woodville of scenes from Haggard's Cleopatra, *published by the* Illustrated London News *in its 1889 serialization of the novel.*

book and the context.

1. *The Prisoner of Zenda* by Anthony Hope. This romance was one of the most popular of many novels set in an imaginary Balkan kingdom. There was always a beautiful princess and a dashing young American or Englishman. In this book, the Englishman bears a startling resemblance to King Rudolf of Ruritania, who is kidnapped on the eve of his coronation by his evil brother. The Englishman takes his place, to prevent Black Michael(!) from seizing the throne and marrying the princess, while the king languishes in the dungeon of Michael's

2. *King Solomon's Mines* by H. Rider Haggard. Central Africa was still largely unknown when the book was written, but that probably does not account for certain of Haggard's fantasies. Three daring Englishmen — Captain Good of the Royal Navy, Lord Henry Curtis, and the great white hunter, Allan Quartermain — set out in search of Sir Henry's missing brother; he (the brother) has gone off into the wilds looking for the lost diamond mines of King Solomon. Along the way their caravan is joined by a mysterious "native," Umbopa. When, after many hardships, they finally reach

Opposite, another Maurice Greiffenhagen watercolor illustration of Haggard's She.

Above & right, engravings by well-known Edwardian Egyptological artist Winifred Brunton, which served as illustrations to the 1923 edition of Terrance Grey's "And in the Tomb Were Found."

castle of Zenda. It is equipped with a convenient trapdoor leading — in this case — down into the moat; and the king knows that, if an attempt at rescue is made, he will be killed and pushed through the trapdoor. Clearly "Schlange" was familiar with the novel; he even quoted one of the villain's sneering comments: *"O Woman! in our hours of ease, Uncertain, coy, and hard to please. When pain and anguish wring the brow, A ministering angel thou!"* (Incidentally, that's Alfred Lord Tennyson, another

their destination, they find the area occupied by a tribe of warlike people (who bear a certain resemblance to the Matabele) ruled by a sadistic chieftain — a usurper, who murdered the former king, his brother, and would have murdered the latter's son had not the boy been carried away by a faithful nurse....

All right, so you know who Umbopa is. His vicious uncle is hated because of his cruelties. One of them is an old tribal custom — the yearly sacrifice of the most beautiful maiden of the tribe. Captain Good has already taken a fancy to the girl who is most likely to "win" (you know these sailors), but of course no English gentleman could stand by while any maiden is cruelly sacrificed. While they are trying to figure out how to stop the ceremony, Good pulls out his almanac and exclaims (I paraphrase), *"I say, you chaps, guess what? There is an eclipse of the sun due tomorrow at exactly the same time as the ceremony! Suppose we threaten to put the sun out if they don't cease and desist."*

So they do, and it works, of course. In addition to saving the maiden and restoring the rightful king, they also find the diamond mines. Readers familiar with this work will note certain other resemblances to events recorded in Mrs. Emerson's journal of the Lost Oasis, probably because tribal customs and British reactions to them were much the same throughout the Victorian Period. This phenomenon is well known to social scientists.

3. The literal translation is *"I've done better since."* The speaker was Cyrano de Bergerac, in the eponymous play by Edmund Rostand. If you know what Cyrano and Ramses meant, give yourself an additional 10 points. If you don't, I will explain.

Cyrano was distinguished by his extraordinary swordsmanship and his very large nose. Hopelessly in love with his beautiful cousin, Roxane, he dares not confess his love because of his grotesque appearance. After an encounter with 100 swordsmen — he wins, of course — he works up courage enough to approach Roxane, only to have her tell him she is in love with a handsome young cadet in

Above & left, two watercolors by illustrator Maurice Greiffenhagen from the 1907 edition of Donald A. Mackenzie's Egyptian Myth and Legend.

This page, Evelyn Paul's early-20th Century romantic illustrations of ancient Egyptian tales.

his own regiment. Cyrano abandons his hopes with silent fortitude, and promises he will look after the young man. When Roxanne commends him on his courage in facing so many enemies he replies wryly, *"J'ai faire mieux depuis."* Ramses, who was far more passionate and romantic than anyone in his family suspected, dared not tell Nefret he loved her, because he was only 16 and she thought of him as a beloved younger brother. It required considerable self-control for a boy of that ardent age to sit still and unresponsive while she hovered over him winding bandages around his ribs and...well, read the scene.

4. "Barbara Fritchie," by Whittier. This poem was probably one of Amelia's favorites because it is about a courageous woman who dared to display the Union flag while Confederate troops marched through her hometown of Frederick, Maryland, during the American Civil War. (At least that's the way they tell it in Frederick.) Amelia quoted from it again in her 1897-98 journal. *"'Shoot if you must*

this old gray head, But spare your country's flag!' she said," is how the poem actually reads. The blusher, believe it or not, was Stonewall Jackson, who responded to Dame Barbara's challenge with a curt *"Who touches a hair of yon gray head, Dies like a dog! March on!' he said."*

They really knew how to write poetry in those days.

5. "Iolanthe" by Gilbert and Sullivan. The Emersons were extremely fond of G and S; all of them quote frequently from the operas.

6. Amelia misquoted, as she often did. However, devoted readers of Sherlock Holmes ought to have recognized one of Holmes's best known axioms, which appears in "A Scandal in Bohemia": *"It is a capital mistake to theorize before one has data."*

7. Some of these are really unfair: (a) *The Moonstone* by Wilkie Collins; (b) *She* by H. Rider Haggard; (c) *David Copperfield* by Charles Dickens; (d) *Armadale* by Wilkie Collins; (e) *The Crusaders* by H. Rider Haggard; (f) "His Last Bow" by Conan Doyle; (g) *The Hound of the Baskervilles* by Conan Doyle.

8. *She*, of course, by Rider Haggard. The final question is somewhat tricky. This is another of those novels in which a handsome young Englishman finds a beautiful woman in some imaginary kingdom — not in the Balkans, but in the other favorite location for imaginary kingdoms, Central Africa. Following clues left by a remote ancestor and handed down in his family for generations, the dashing young hero, Leo Vincey, is led to the caves of Kor, where an immortal, fantastically gorgeous, incredibly intelligent woman, "She Who Must Be Obeyed," rules over a tribe of savages. Why is she hanging out in such a nasty place? Well, it seems that 2,000 years earlier she lost her temper with Leo's ancestor, Kallikrates, because he refused to abandon his Egyptian wife and become her lover, and, in a fit of frustrated passion, she stabbed him to the heart. Remorse and grief force the penance upon her. Also, she believes in reincarnation and is convinced that Kallikrates will one day return to her in the same body if not the same mind. Leo is

his spitting image, as you may have anticipated. She's kept his original body, perfectly preserved by a mysterious process known to the ancient inhabitants of Kor. Egyptian mummies can't hold a candle to these; they look like exquisite statues, their skin color (white, of course) and shape the same. (The only problem is that they have a tendency to crumble into dust when touched.)

9. *"A pennyworth of blood to this great deal of bandages."* Emerson, *Lion in the Valley.*

"I must be cruel, only to be kind." Ramses, *He Shall Thunder.*

"Such a night as this" was made for affectionate exchanges. Amelia (who generally misquotes Shakespeare), *Lion in the Valley.*

"Bid the soldiers shoot, etc." Amelia, misquoting again, *He Shall Thunder.*

"Yet who would have thought the old man had so much blood in him?" Ramses, *The Last Camel Died at*

Two more 1889 steel-engraving illustrations from the Illustrated London News *serialization of H. Rider Haggard's* Cleopatra.

Noon.

The *"too solid flesh"* soliloquy (Hamlet) is mentioned by Emerson in *The Last Camel Died at Noon.*

(Scoring: We don't believe in standardized tests, so consider yourself well read if you get more than half the answers right. If you get them all right, you are either a genius or of questionable veracity.)

Given Amelia's encounters with ambulatory mummies, curses, and other elements of Gothic fiction, some might consider it surprising that she did not seem to have been attracted to this category of the romance. However, the heyday of this form of fiction had passed by the end of the 19th Century, though elements of it survived in writers like Bram Stoker (*Dracula*) and others (including Conan Doyle, who wrote an excellent mummy short story). My personal analysis is that Amelia despised

the helpless heroines that pervaded the Gothic novel. She preferred tales of adventure, and probably identified not with the heroines, but with the heroes.

Her favorite author seems to have been H. Rider Haggard. The youngest son of a Norfolk squire, young Rider was sent off to South Africa after he had failed to become a success at home. His experiences there served him in good stead when he began his writing career, for many of his novels have African settings. "Prolific" is certainly a valid word; he wrote 68 books, of which *King Solomon's Mines* and *She* were the most popular. They were howling best sellers, despite the sneers of certain members of the literary establishment, and Haggard had many imitators, though none were nearly as successful. The immortal She reappears in many of these out-and-out plagarisms and in several sequels and prequels written by Haggard. Another recurring character is Allan Quartermain, the great white hunter of *King Solomon's Mines*, who is featured in an eponymous novel and a number of others. The quality of Haggard's books varies, and so does their subject matter. His interest in ancient Egypt produced books like *Cleopatra* and *The Ancient Allen* (Quartermain in one of his previous incarnations as Pharaoh Shabaka). Other of his historical romances deal with the Norse sagas, ancient Mexico, the Crusades, and so on.

Another author with whom Amelia was obviously familiar is Wilkie Collins. A close friend and contemporary of Charles Dickens, Collins's best-known book is undoubtedly *The Moonstone*. It has been called "the first detective novel," and it features a memorable detective — Sergeant Cuff, whose name Amelia borrowed when describing her own encounters with a sergeant of Scotland Yard. The plot centers around the effort of a group of mysterious Indians to recover a famous gem — a diamond, despite its name — which was stolen from a statue of their god by a British adventurer. The jewel has come into the possession of his descendant, Rachel Verinder, a wealthy young heiress. During a house party at her home, the Indians appear, disguised as itinerant magicians. There wasn't much to do in those straight-laced days BT (before television), so the Indians are invited to perform. The trick — if it is a trick! — is a standard device of mystics. The Indians make use of a young boy apprentice to stare into a pool of liquid until he sees a vision of the past or future. It is called scrying or, if one is a skeptic, self-hypnosis. Amelia referred to this procedure in her journal recording her adventures at the Lost Oasis, when it was practiced on Ramses.

Later, when the great gem vanishes, the most likely suspects are not the Indians but members of the house party, including two of the men who are courting the lady. Rachel's behavior thereafter becomes very erratic; she refuses to call the police and is sullen and uncooperative when her mother does so.

Who stole the Moonstone? It would be doing the reader a disservice to disclose the solution if he or she has not read this splendid thriller.

I feel certain that, although she did not mention them, Amelia had read Collins's other books. *The Woman in White* and *No Name* would have appealed to her because of their depiction of strong, independent women. Collins was ahead of his time — very far ahead of his friend Charles Dickens, whose heroines are either vapid or wicked — in his sympathy for the unfair social and legal status of Victorian women.

Amelia had obviously read the Brontes. She recommended *Jane Eyre* and *Wuthering Heights* to the children's governess. It was in the library of her sister-in-law Evelyn, however, that Nefret came across the works of Jane Austen. Perhaps they were a little too tame for Amelia.

Though Emerson quoted from Dickens and Shakespeare (and, as we have seen, from Conan Doyle), he pretended to have little patience with "romances." It is clear, however, that he had read some of Haggard's novels.

Ramses's reading tastes were the most eclectic. Even at an early age he was fond of poetry, as witness his reference to Keat's "The Eve of St. Agnes" (to which his mother responded with a horrified "*Good Gad!*"). Amelia was deeply suspicious of poetry, which she regarded as "*too sensational for the young.*" In the case of her son she was probably right. From the delicate eroticism of Keats, he proceeded to Swinburne and Rostand. Swinburne's work was considered quite shocking in his day.

We don't know what other books were on Ramses's bookshelves, but a casual reference to Plato indicates that he was familiar with at least one of the great Greek writers. Perhaps he read them in the original, during the period when he had been invited to read classics at Oxford with Professor Wilson. He had also read *The Picture of Dorian Grey*. Its author, Oscar Wilde, was one of the aesthetes satirized by Gilbert and Sullivan in "Patience," to which Ramses and his mother referred during the suffragette demonstration upon the steps of Lord Romer's London home.

Ramses was the only member of the family who admitted to a taste for "detective stories," but it is probable that both his parents read them on the sly, despite Amelia's contemptous dismissal of the genre: "*These so-called detective stories...pretend to exhibit the strictly intellectual qualities of the protagonist. In fact, they do nothing of the sort; for in the few I have read the detective arrived at his solutions not by the inexorable progress of true reasoning but by wild guesses which turned out to be correct only because of the author's construction of the plot*" (Peters 1986: 139).

She was obviously acquainted with Ramses's favorite detective Mr. Sherlock Holmes but she must not have read him closely or she would have recognized the *soi-disant* Tobias Gregson as an imposter.

All the Emersons would have agreed with a modern critic who remarked that romances appeal to a "*fundamental human desire: that the best of wonder should be honestly and fully satisfied*" (Schlik 1994: 34). Or as Amelia put it: "*However rational the mind...it requires periods of rest, when the aery winds of fancy may ruffle the still waters of thought and encourage those softer and more spiritual musings without which no individual can be at his or her best*" (Peters 1986:139).

Barbara Michaels

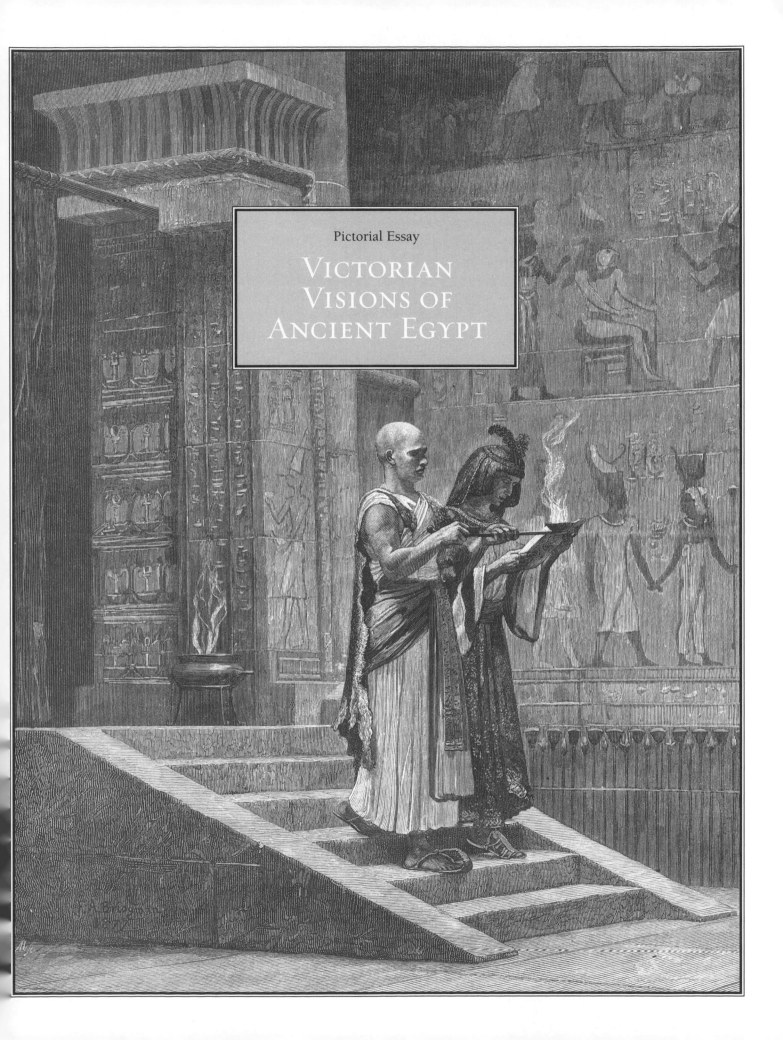

Pictorial Essay

VICTORIAN
VISIONS OF
ANCIENT EGYPT

Victorian-era artists & illustrators for the popular press were attracted to interpreting ancient Egypt in their work — a romanticized ancient Egypt of their imaginations, in large part, although some of the details they included had an artifactual basis & are relatively accurate depictions.

Dutch-Anglo painter Lawrence Alma-Tadema (1836-1912), best known for his huge ouevre of classical Greek & Roman genre scenes, also created a number of ancient Egypt-themed canvases, several of which were then engraved — more or less successfully — for reproduction in the press of the day. Four of these are shown here: A Citizen of Memphis (opposite far left); Joseph, Overseer of Pharaoh's Granaries (above); Egyptian Widow at the Time of Diocletian (next two pages); & Death of the Firstborn (top, p.194). Alma-Tadema, who was born in Holland & lived the latter part of his life in England, was noted for carefully researching the costuming, furnishings & architectural elements of his scenes. Other artists were more fanciful, as in Sacrifice to the Nile (left), Egyptian Dancing Girl (right) & The Last Honors (bottom, p. 194).

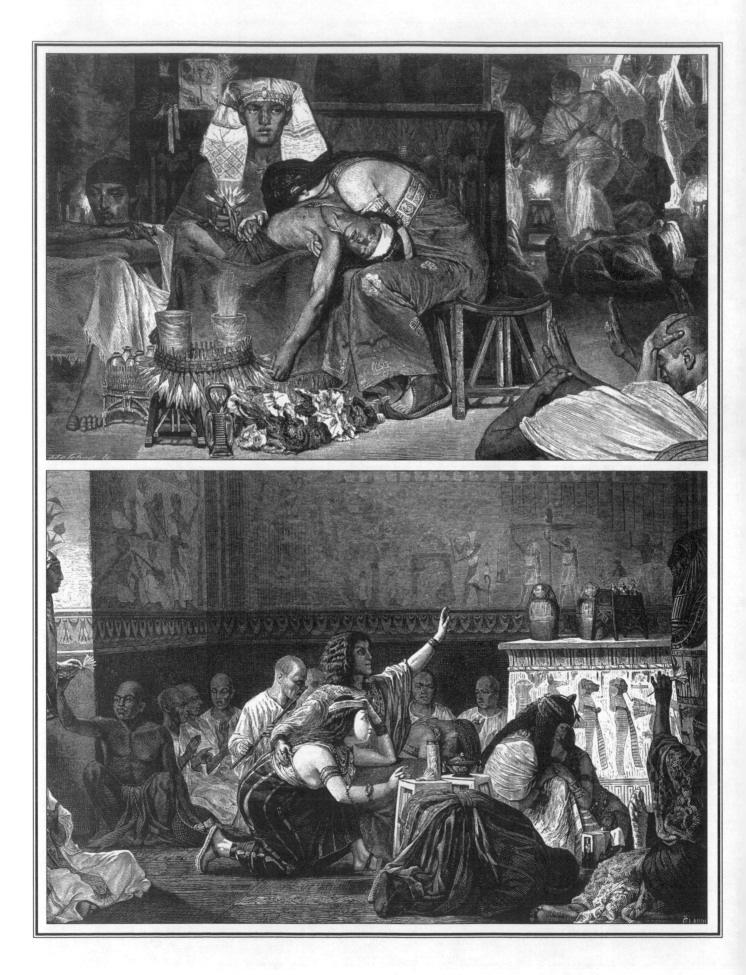

People, Places, & Things
A Handy Reference to the Journals

THE PEOPLE OF THE JOURNALS
(& a Few Animals, Too)

A

Abd el Atti Cairo antiquities dealer — *"worse than some, not so bad as others."* Most, if not all, of the antiquities dealers handled stolen property and forgeries. Abd el Atti made the mistake of getting involved with a group of people who, as Emerson could have told him, were even more dangerous than tomb robbers. He did appeal to Amelia for help, but too late.

Abd el Hamed Probably the greatest forger of antiquities Egypt has ever seen. Ostensibly his business was the production of copies for the tourist trade, but his work was good enough to deceive serious collectors, who bought his work for themselves or the museums they represented. *"It is a pity talent and moral worth don't go together"*; Abd el Hamed was a sadist and bully who mistreated his young apprentice, David Todros (q.v.), a boy of approximately Ramses's age. Abd el Hamed had three wives. In his case polygamy turned out to be an error.

The Abd er Rassuls A notorious and extremely skilled family of tomb robbers from the village of Gurneh at Luxor. Brothers Mohammed, Hussein, and Ahmed discovered the cache of royal mummies at Deir el Bahari and marketed small objects from it for years before the Service des Antiquités got onto them. The methods of interrogation employed in those days were singularly unpleasant. Mohammed finally cracked — some say there was a falling out between the brothers — and led the authorities to the hiding place. He was rewarded by being given a position with the Service. Later Mohammed found another collection of mummies at Deir el Bahari, those of the high priests of Amon.

Never let it be said the family gave up hope, however. Upon the discovery of the Tomb of Tetisheri in 1899, Hussein Abd er Rassul was on the spot to offer *"effusive congratulations"* and *"the assistance of himself and his brothers."* Amelia declined.

Abdul Waiter on Philae. Amelia notes that he was a handsome boy.

Abdul Hadi The best and slowest woodworker in Luxor. However, it was not his fault that he never completed the frame for Amelia's portrait.

Abdul Hassan A tomb robber from Gurneh; another of those dead bodies the Emersons often encountered.

Abdullah

Abdullah ibn Hassan al Wahhab The Emersons' *reis,* or foreman, for many years, he became an admired friend. He was married at least four times and had many children and grandchildren. Originally from Luxor, he lived in the village of Aziyeh near Cairo for a while and had kin in both places; many of them worked for the Emersons. His exact age is never specified, but it appears that he was in his fifties when Amelia met him in 1884. Though he had serious reservations about Amelia at first — *"what is a woman, that she should cause such trouble for us?"*— he became very attached to her, and she to him. She never told anyone what he whispered to her as he lay dying in her arms after saving her from an assassin's bullets.

Abu One of Abdullah's innumerable kinsmen; Cyrus Vandergelt's *reis.*

Achmet and its variants (**Ahmet, Achmed**) is a common name in Egypt; soubriquets were often used to distinguish one Achmet from another. We encounter the following Achmets:

Achmed. One of the Emersons' workers, another of the relatives of Abdullah, often acted as night watchman on *The Amelia*.

Achmet. Alias of David Todros when he accompanied "Ali the Rat."

Achmet, Old. Extremely ragged street vendor who stayed close to Shepheard's and knew all the latest gossip. Upon his return to Egypt each season, Emerson often sought him out.

Ahmed. The unfortunate Egyptian cook for Reggie Forthright in Gebel Barkal. Uttered the time-honored sentiment, *"The Effendi offered lots of money. What is a poor man to do?"*

Ahmed Mohammed ibn Aziz. One can only hope no such individual existed, since Emerson's impersonation of him might have got him in serious trouble.

Ahmet il Kamleh (Ahmet the Louse). User of and dealer in opium in London. "The Louse" was a particularly appropriate sobriquet for this miserable creature.

Akenidad A citizen of the Lost Oasis. One of Tarek's aides who accompanied him to England and later worked for the Emersons at Nuri.

Albert Cyrus Vandergelt's Belgian "major domo."

Alberto Posing as a drawing master, he became the lover of Evelyn Barton Forbes (q.v.), and conspired with his cousin (on his father's side), Lucas Hayes (q.v.), to rob the young woman of her inheritance. Imprisoned in Cairo after he was caught impersonating a mummy by Amelia and Emerson. Passed away some years later, *"quite peacefully, according to his cellmate."*

Albion, Joe A wealthy, unscrupulous American collector who scandalized Emerson by asking to be introduced to a few tomb robbers. He was accompanied by his wife (whose first name is never given) and his son Sebastian.

Albion, Sebastian Son of Joe (above). Despite the

Sebastian Albion

presumed advantage of graduating from Harvard, his morals were no better than those of his father. Though the Albions gave the Emersons some trouble, they were, in Emerson's opinion, an example of how *"the general quality of criminals has sadly deteriorated."*

Ali Another very common name in Egypt. Several Alis appear in the Emerson saga, including:

Ali. One of Abdullah's younger sons. Fatima's (q.v.) nephew. Attempted to learn how to "buttle" at the Emersons' Luxor home, but Fatima, unwilling to relinquish her job of attendance, did not find him suitable for the job.

Ali. Originally a stableman of the Emersons', he was eventually promoted to doorman. An excitable fellow who enjoyed drama, he got plenty of it from his employers.

Ali. A *saffragi* at Shepheard's.

Ali Hassan. A member of the notorious Abd er Rassul family, who attempted to lead Amelia astray. He failed, of course.

Ali Murad. See Murad, Ali.

Ali the Rat. One of Ramses's alter egos.

Amenishakhete A queen of Meroe, 1st Century AD, whose magnificent jewels were discovered in her pyramid by Giuseppe Ferlini (1834). Her much-later namesake was queen of the Holy Mountain when the Emersons arrived there, and the mother of Prince Nastasen (q.v.). A pleasant, good-natured lady of extreme corpulence. Obesity was a notable characteristic of Cushite queens.

Amenislo Son of Lady Batare (concubine) and Tarek's father and, therefore, one of the many brothers of Tarek (q.v.).

Amenit Princess of the City of the Holy Mountain, sister of Prince Nastasen, and one of the Handmaidens, a select group of young noblewomen who served the goddess Isis and her priestess. Amenittasherit was her full name. She became an assiduous but inconvenient assistant to Amelia, so Amelia ensured that the inconvenience was mutual.

William Amherst

Amherst, William A young Egyptologist, no relation to the distinguished patron and collector Baron Amherst. *"A fine looking young fellow, with sandy hair and neatly trimmed mustache,"* he was fresh down from Oxford where he had been reading classics. He worked for Cyrus Vandergelt (q.v.) in the Valley of the Kings and was later employed by the Emersons at Giza. Apparently he left the field after WWI.

Amin, Madame Sayidda Ostensibly Fatima's writing "teacher" in Luxor — she was, as with so many of the people Amelia encountered, more than the simple teacher and advocate for women's rights in Egypt she professed to be.

Andrews, Mrs. Emma B. Traveling companion of Theodore Davis. Certain rumors about their relationship were prevalent even at the time, though Amelia refused to countenance them — *"That is just idle gossip, Emerson, she is his cousin."* Emerson, however, did countenance them, as was evident in his

response — *"Ha."* Mrs. Andrews's unpublished journals give interesting, if uninformed, sidelights on events of the time.

Anubis

Anubis Egyptian cat belonging to Leopold Vincey, he was later adopted by the Emersons and became the progenitor of a long line of Egyptian felines. According to Abdullah, who was not a cat-fancier, he was a "servant of evil"; however, after Anubis had transferred his loyalties to Emerson, he only misbehaved with Abdullah. Cats will do that.

Applegarth, Mr. Hiram An alter ego employed by Ramses in flushing out forgeries. *"His accent was a devastatingly accurate imitation of our friend Cyrus's voice."*

Arbuthnot, Sir Reginald Assistant commissioner of Scotland Yard, involved in the Romer case. This was obviously a pseudonym since there was no assistant commissioner of Scotland Yard of that name. Amelia poked fun at him, so she may have decided to conceal his true identity.

Armadale, Alan Professional Egyptologist working for Lord Henry Baskerville (q.v.) in 1892; *"the one with the face of a woman and the heart of a man."* One of the victims of the "curse," by the time the Emersons encountered him he was dead. Buried in the English cemetery in Luxor.

Asad The *nom de guerre* of a young Egyptian nationalist who was one of El Wardani's (q.v.) aides, or thought he was. Timid, intelligent, loyal. Ramses thought well of him: *"He's afraid all the time, and yet he sticks."*

Asfur Arabian mare belonging to David, the gift of

Sheikh Bahsoor (q.v.). Her name means bird. She gave birth to the filly, Moonlight (q.v.).

Ashraf A crewman on the *Amelia*.

Aslimi Aziz Antiquities dealer in Cairo, eldest son of Abd el Atti (q.v.). Not particularly good at business, legal or otherwise, he kept getting dragged into dubious projects he would much rather have avoided.

Atiyah Cairene, Copt, servant of Lady Baskerville (q.v.), whose addiction to opium probably saved her life. This is not the sort of moral one would like to present, but there it is.

Ayesha An Egyptian woman of dubious antecedents and criminal connections, she was the owner of an opium den in London and, as Amelia discovered, only too well acquainted with Emerson.

Edward Ayrton

Ayrton, Edward English Egyptologist. He worked at Abydos, Ghurab, and Deir el Bahari before being employed by Theodore Davis (q.v.) in the Valley of the Kings, where he made a number of remarkable discoveries for his patron, including the tombs of Siptah, Queen Tausret, and Horemheb, and the strange burial in KV55. It was while he was working on the latter that he came into close contact with the Emersons, who called him "Ned." A few years later, he went to work for the Archaeological Survey of Ceylon, where he died by drowning in 1914.

Axhammer, Mrs. An elderly American lady from Des Moines, Iowa, with an impressive set of teeth and a masterful presence.

Aziz See Aslimi.

Mrs. Axhammer

Aziza A young Egyptian girl whom Emerson was unable to save from the murderous attack of her father, Habib (q.v.). Had it not been for Emerson, Habib would have been vindicated, since local custom gave a father the right to destroy a daughter who had "dishonored" him by losing her virginity.

B

Charles Baehler

Baehler, Charles A Swiss hotelier who began as headwaiter at Shepheard's Hotel, Cairo, in the 1880s and who went on to found companies that owned hotels all over Egypt. Shepheard's was always his best-loved hotel; he presided over it during its periods of greatest expansion and glory. A charming, handsome man, he was a favorite of Amelia. Her claim that they never had any trouble booking rooms at Shepheard's may have been due to his affection for her or his (justifiable) fear of Emerson's making a scene if thwarted in any way.

Sheikh Bahsoor

Bahsoor, Sheikh Mohammed A Bedouin chieftain (and long-time friend of the Emersons), he *"had the acquiline features and manly bearing of that splendid race."* Ramses and David spent one summer with him, learning *"to ride and shoot and become leaders of men..."* and, Ramses's mother feared, other things.

Major Evelyn Baring

Baring, Major (later Sir) **Evelyn** British agent and consul general of Egypt from 1883-1907. Became Lord Cromer in 1901. A former acquaintance of Mr. Peabody Senior. Amelia maintained the connection in case of necessity, but ever the social critic, she wrote, *"solid British respectability lay upon him like a coating of dust."* For a discussion of the political environment of the time, see the article herein, "A Commanding Perspective: The British in Egypt, 1884-1917" by Jocelyn Gohary.

Barnes, Edward (Ned) Young dissolute friend of Lord Liverpool the younger. He was unwillingly involved in the dastardly plot involving the British Museum in the summer of 1896, which was subsequently uncovered by Amelia, but he had sense enough to pull out before the hideous conclusion.

Barsanti, Alexandre Italian engineer/architect, self-taught archaeologist, known for his restoration and repair work. Excavated and restored the mastabas and tombs in the pyramid field of Sakkara; cleared the substructures of the Layer Pyramid and the shaft of the Northern Pyramid at Zawayet el Aryan. The Emersons completed the work of clearing the shaft in 1911-12. (For a complete report see R.A. Emerson's article in *Zeitschrift für Aegyptische Sprache*: "Im Bezug die Aufgrabungen zu Zawayet el Aryan und die Beseitigungen und Forschungen des Zwei Pyramidenunterbaues.")

Alexandre Barsanti

Barton Forbes, Evelyn Only child of the eldest son of the Earl of Ellesmere according to Amelia's first journal. (In later journals he is described as Duke of Chalfont. Presumably this is another of Amelia's inconsistent efforts to conceal Evelyn's true identity.) Amelia first met her in Rome, where she had been abandoned by her scurvy lover, and took her on as a companion. She later married Walter Emerson (q.v.) and had a number of children. She was a talented painter of Egyptian scenes, who might have had a fine career had she not been distracted by motherhood. She is best known in Egyptological circles for the plates she produced for *The Tomb of Tetisheri at Thebes*.

Bashir One of El Wardani's (q.v.) aides. He came and went. Presumably he ended up exiled or in prison after the events narrated in 1914-15.

Basima A member of Abdullah's extended family, and Sennia's (q.v.) nurserymaid. While Amelia admitted Basima spoiled Sennia, Basima was not alone in her inability to deny the child anything she demanded.

Baskerville, Lord Henry Amelia's references to him as "Sir" were obviously incorrect; no doubt she was unconsciously influenced by thoughts of another Sir Henry Baskerville (of the Devonshire branch of the family). An amateur Egyptologist whose death in 1892 under mysterious circumstances was attributed to the "Curse of the Pharaohs."

Baskerville, Lady Wife of Lord Henry (above). Originally a hospital nurse, *"a young lady of no fortune and insignificant family,"* she asked Emerson to complete the excavation of the tomb discovered by her late husband. This was a serious mistake on her part.

Baskerville, Lord Arthur Nephew and heir of Lord Henry (q.v.). *"Handsome he undoubtedly was; outstandingly intelligent he was not,"* he was extremely fortunate the Emersons chose to complete the work of his late uncle.

Lord Arthur Baskerville

Bastet A large Egyptian cat originally belonging to archaeologist Alan Armadale (q.v.), who became Ramses's constant companion and feline familiar until her lamented death many years later. It took Bastet much longer than Amelia had expected to become interested in the opposite gender (feline gender, that is), possibly because she was a highly intelligent creature who had other priorities. Eventually she became the ancestress of a long line of cats who had the same physical characteristics: big ears, a brindled tawny coat, large strong bodies.

Bayes, Mrs. Obviously an alias, but if Amelia knew her real name she never revealed it, perhaps because of the Official Secrets Act.

Bedawee, Michael Amelia's Coptic dragoman during her first expedition to Egypt in 1884. He was devoted to Evelyn and Amelia because they had saved the life of his child. His loyalty almost cost him his life. Recently discovered sources suggest he was generously rewarded by Amelia and set up a highly successful tourist agency.

Bell, Gertrude Born into a wealthy Victorian family, Bell was one of the first women to study at Oxford. She refused to settle into the social life of her class, becoming an intrepid traveler and writer of travel books. Her great love was the Middle East, where she explored areas into which few European men and no women had ventured. During WWI she became an intelligence agent in the Arab Bureau in Cairo, with Woolley and Lawrence, and after the war she played a major part in the founding of Iraq. She and Amelia shared a number of interests, including archaeology and flowery hats, but it is unlikely that they ever became friends. For one thing, Bell was vehemently anti-feminist.

Bellingham, Colonel *"His title derived from his service (Confederate) in the American Civil War."* A much-married man, his wives did not fare well.

Dolly Bellingham

Bellingham, Dolly The Colonel's daughter — spoiled, pretty, predatory. The word "nymphomaniac" was one Amelia never would have used, but she was obviously familiar with the concept.

Bellingham, Lucinda The Colonel's fourth wife, (very) deceased.

Belzoni, Giovanni Battista One of the most flamboyant of the early-19th Century adventurers and exploiters of Egyptian monuments. A former circus strongman, he made a number of great discoveries, including one of the most beautiful tombs in the Valley of the Kings, that of Seti I. He cleared the facade of the Temple of Abu Simbel of the sand that had covered it for centuries. Admittedly, he did a lot of damage, especially during his earlier excavations — however, so did the majority of his contemporaries and many of his successors.

Berengeria, Madame Claimed to have been married to Emerson in several previous incarnations, when he was Amenhotep III, Setnakhte, and other pharaohs. An alcoholic of staggering proportions (as were her physical proportions), she went about dressed in shabby imitations of ancient Egyptian costume. Her full name is never given, possibly because Amelia's descriptions of her were scurrilous verging on slanderous. Her only daughter, Mary, a beautiful young woman and talented artist, was courted by Lord Arthur Baskerville (q.v.) and Karl von Bork (q.v.), and eventually married the latter.

Bert One of three burglars, who (unfortunately for him) attempted to confiscate a forged scarab from the Amarna House study. Notable in that his experience as recorded below was *not* out of the ordinary:

> The burglar glared wildly at Emerson, bare to the waist and bulging with muscle — at Gargery and his cudgel — at Selim fingering a knife even longer than Nefret's — at assorted footmen armed with pokers, spits and cleavers — and at the giant form of Daoud advancing purposefully toward him. "It's a bleeding army!" he gurgled. "The lyin' barstard said you was some kind of professor!"

Bertha A woman of mystery, and mistress and confederate of the malevolent villain "Schlange" (q.v.). Her antecedents are unknown; the pathetic story she told Amelia was almost certainly untrue, but she was of mixed Egyptian and European blood. After Schlange's death she found a new protector, a man whose evil genius equalled hers, and became his assistant in crime. Sethos (q.v.) was the love of her life, but her passion for him turned to hatred when she realized Amelia would always be the love of *his* life. Jealousy led her to attack Amelia on sev-

eral occasions. She became a feminist in a rather unusual sense. The formation of a criminal organization for women was possibly not what Amelia had in mind when she encouraged Bertha to explore careers for women.

Blacktower, Viscount (Lord) A vile old aristocrat; Nefret's grandfather...or was he?

Bob Huskiest of the footmen at Chalfont House, the London establishment of Walter and Evelyn Emerson. He later enlisted in the service of the senior Emersons.

Bob

Boutros Ghali Pasha Served under the Gorst administration as minister of foreign affairs, minister of justice (when he presided over the Denshawai trial) and prime minister. He was assassinated in 1910 by a young Egyptian nationalist named Ibrahim el Wardani (q.v.) who considered him to be a tool of the British (which he was).

Bracegirdle-Boisdragon, Algernon The name must have been one of Amelia's more extravagant efforts to conceal an individual's real identity, since it does not appear in the records of the Egyptian Public Works Department or those of Anglo-Indian officialdom. In this case, Amelia had an excellent reason for mystification.

Breasted, James Henry American Egyptologist whose remarkable career included the founding of the Oriental Institute of the University of Chicago, with the financial aid of John D. Rockefeller. On two trips to Egypt, he copied and translated most of the known historical texts, which were published in his *Ancient Records of Egypt*. A gifted and eloquent writer, his *History of Egypt* is still a wonderful read, though it is outdated.

James Henry Breasted

Brugsch Pasha, Émile Worked for Mariette (q.v.) and Maspero (q.v.); was the man who cleared the Royal Mummies Cache at Deir el Bahari. He had a questionable reputation as a secret dealer in antiq-

Émile Brugsch Pasha

uities while he was in the employ of the Service des Antiquités. Amelia enjoyed Brugsch's first-hand account of the discovery of the Royal Cache; however she *"did not care"* for him. *"His bold stare and hard face affected me unpleasantly, as did his calloused description of the interrogation of the unfortunate Abd er Rassul brothers."*

Brugsch, Heinrich German Egyptologist, brother of Émile (above). Amelia conceded that there was nothing questionable about *his* reputation — *"a respectable and well-known scholar."*

Brunton, Guy British Egyptologist who worked with Petrie (q.v.) and others; a careful excavator and good scholar. Fought in World War I. Following service he returned to excavating, which led, among other things, to the discovery of some of the oldest-known cultures of Predynastic Upper Egypt. His wife, Winifred, was a talented artist.

Buchanan, Miss The director of the American Mission School for Egyptian Girls in Luxor. Her friendship and support lent verisimilitude to the teacher Saiyyida Hashim (q.v.) — and therefore to the cover of one of the most dangerous and despotic criminal gangs in Luxor during the early 1900s. A dedicated teacher of spotless character, it is most certain she had no idea that taking tea with Madame Hakim carried such profound implications.

Buckman, Captain Brief but helpful acquaintance of Amelia during the Emersons' expedition to the Sudan. The type of Englishman despised by Emerson, with *"prominent teeth, no chin to speak of, and a habit of tossing his head when he laughed in a high-pitched whinny."* He also lacked intelligence, as he was full of compliments for Budge.

Budge, E.A. Wallis Assistant keeper, then keeper, of Egyptian and Assyrian antiquities at the British Museum, he was notorious for his cavalier attitude toward the laws regarding the export of antiquities. Petrie called him "the Bugbear," while Emerson used words unfit for print. Breasted described him as "pudgy, logy and soggy-faced." He was prolific, publishing books about practically every aspect of archaeology, from mummies to scarabs. Few if any of them exhibit an acceptable degree of scholarship, but many are in print to this day. His autobiography, *From Nile to Tigris*, describes some of the methods he employed in acquiring antiquities for the British Museum, with a candor that can only be called shameless.

Burton, George An American Egyptologist working for the Metropolitan Museum at Luxor in 1917. An extremely disconcerting encounter with an avalanche and a corpse — only to be expected if one hobnobbed with any of the Emersons — did not put him off his stride for long. He continued working for the Met until he left the field for a more lucrative career as a film stunt man.

C

Cabot, David Of the Boston Cabots. His extraordinary good looks were his most distinctive characteristic. A Brother of the New Jerusalem and devoted acolyte of the Reverend Jones (q.v.), which was in itself evidence of minimal intelligence, as well as evidence that he took the old adage about the Cabots too much to heart.

Carnarvon, Lord (George Edward Stanhope Molyneux Herbert, 5th Earl of Carnarvon) Howard Carter's (q.v.) wealthy patron. After a serious motoring accident, he went to Egypt for his health and became fascinated by archaeology. Sponsored Carter's digs in the Valley of the Kings for many years before the great discovery of Tutankhamen. His death shortly after the finding of the tomb prompted a number of wild and foundationless stories about curses. Statistically, the people involved with the clearing of the tomb were longer-lived and healthier than the average.

Carrington, Sir Harold and **Lady** The Emersons' extremely boring neighbors in Kent. Lady Harold was unable to appreciate the "Zebwa" bone excavated from the garbage heap with which she was presented by Ramses, while her equally unimaginative husband could not comprehend Emerson's justifiable concern over the idiocy of foxhunting. Amelia admitted that some of the antagonism might have been Emerson's fault, as *"the thrashing [Emerson gave Sir Harold] was superfluous."*

Howard Carter

Carter, Howard Long-time friend of the Emersons. Best known as the discoverer of the Tomb of Tutankhamen, he had a long career in Egypt working with Petrie (q.v), Naville (q.v.), Theodore Davis (q.v.), and others. Became inspector for Upper Egypt in 1899, but resigned from the Antiquities Service after a contretemps involving a group of French tourists. Amelia's repeated assurances that *"something will*

come up" (which may well have been yet another example of her famous "forebodings") and the steadfast friendship of the entire Emerson clan undoubtedly lent him support during the long dry spell prior to his work for Lord Carnarvon. He should not be disparaged for eventually finding work with a "wealthy dilettante," as his claims to the contrary were made when he was young and impressionable, with a deep desire to emulate Professor Emerson.

Cartright, Captain Doctor who tended Emerson's bumps at Shepheard's, and then administered the usual treatment of the time for hysterics to Amelia when she yelled, *"Emerson, who am I?"*

Cartright, Major (formerly Captain) Does not appear to be related to the Cartright above. An officer and a *"flower of the Egyptian army,"* who was in British intelligence during WWI. Like certain of his colleagues, he used patriotism as an excuse for deceit and betrayal.

Cecil, Lord Edward Most prominent of the "bright young men" brought into the Egyptian Civil Service by Kitchener (q.v.). Cecil was the fourth son of the Marquess of Salisbury. He did not go to university but into the army, where he was on the staff of General Wolseley, victor of Tell el Kebir. He took part in the Sudan campaign, winning a DSO, and served with distinction in the Boer War. He then went to Egypt into an administrative post in the Finance Department. He was typical of many Anglo-Egyptians, little more than a glorified schoolmaster trying to keep his unruly but likeable pupils in order. A wit in the opinion of some, a puzzle to others, Cecil had few, if any, real friends. He had a reputation as a cynic, but was really a sad, vulnerable man separated from his family — an example of British "stiff upper lip." His memoir, *The Leisure of an Egyptian Official,* is perhaps the best written of the many personal accounts of the period, and an excellent illustration of the supercilious attitude of British officials toward Egyptians (and most other people).

Chetwode, Lt. Gen. Sir Phillip Commander of the mounted Desert Column in the Palestine campaign of 1916-17. He had a distinguished military career, becoming Baron Chetwode and Field Marshal.

Chetwode, Lt. Phillip B. The general's nephew (see above), an intelligence officer who was not so ingenuous as he appeared. His military career was not as successful as that of his uncle. Amelia would have said it served him right when he was cashiered in 1918 for inhumane treatment of Turkish prisoners of war.

Clausheimer, Caleb T. Courtly American encountered by Amelia atop the Great Pyramid. It is possible she ought to have suspected his bonafides; after all, she suspected nearly everyone else's (including Howard Carter's on one occasion).

Caleb T. Clausheimer

Clayton, Gilbert Rather like Pooh Bah, he wore several hats: Cairo representative of the Sirdar of the Sudan, and head of the hastily formed Intelligence Department during World War I. He had a distinguished career in the Egyptian service, and ended up as a Brigadier.

Conte d'Imbroglio d'Annunciata Father of Lucas Hayes (q.v.). (Obviously a false name.)

Cromer, Lord See Baring.

Inspector Cuff

Cuff, Inspector Planned to retire to Dorking and grow roses after 30 years in the Metropolitan Police. Though he had been a confirmed bachelor, he informed Amelia that she had *"shaken his belief in the advantages of the single life."* It was his admiration for her and the other members of the family that prompted him to come out of retirement to assist the younger Emersons in criminal investigations at Chalfont during the fall of 1898. That, and the fact that he had become stupefyingly bored with tending roses.

Curtin, Alice Fiancée of Johnny Emerson (q.v.) prior to the tragedy.

D

Daoud Abdullah's nephew and one of the Emersons' most reliable assistants and closest friends. Married to Kadija (q.v.). If he had other wives they are not mentioned; however, one suspects that Kadija would not have put up with this. Daoud was famous for his physical strength and for the kindness of his heart. He was also a fine storyteller; he invented and promulgated the numerous legends about the Emersons that persist even today.

Daoud the Nubian

Daoud the Nubian A suspicious servant of Reggie Forthright (q.v.), he was unsuccessful in preventing the Emersons from following his employer.

D'Arcy, Rene Purportedly a young French archaeologist, he worked at El Amarna during the 1989-90 season with the Emersons and Cyrus Vandergelt (q.v.).

Daressy, Georges French Egyptologist who excavated numerous sites in Egypt and published over

500 articles. Arranged the exhibits in the Cairo Museum after the collections were moved from Giza in 1902. Secretary General of the Antiquities Service under Lacau, he carried out the latter's duties while Lacau was doing war work in France in 1916-17.

Davies, Norman de Garis *"A promising painter of Egyptian scenes."* Worked for the Egypt Exploration Society and the Metropolitan Museum of Art. Among his numerous publications are several volumes on the El Amarna tombs, invaluable to present-day scholars because so many of the reliefs have now disappeared. Some feel that his wife, Nina, was an even better *"painter of Egyptian scenes."* She also published a number of books of reproductions of tomb paintings.

Theodore M. Davis

Davis, Theodore Wealthy American who financed excavations in the Valley of the Kings from 1903-12. The actual digging was carried out by Howard Carter (q.v.), James Quibell (q.v.), Edward Ayrton (q.v.), and others. In January of 1907, when the Emersons were also working in the Valley of the Kings, Ayrton discovered the strange burial Egyptologists call KV55, since the identity of the mummy is still being hotly debated (see Note). The confusion is due in part to the inadequacy of the excavation, which Amelia described as *"a crisis in archaeological terms,"* stating that *"Emerson was beyond outrage...and had passed into a kind of coma of disgust."* Maspero (q.v.) encouraged dilettantes like Davis (in Emerson's words, *"a pompous, arrogant ignoramus"*), who paid for his own excavations and was given antiquities in return. He was, by all accounts, a difficult man to work for; and although

he published the results of his excavations, the volumes in question cannot be considered scholarly reports. Very little is known of Davis's personal life and financial activities before Egypt; a biography is purportedly in process.

Note: While Davis's records of KV55 are incomplete, the journals of Mrs. Emerson indicate that David Todros (q.v.) illegally copied the shrine panel and door in the tomb corridor, and further suggest that there is a full photographic record of the tomb prior to its dismantling. In addition, there are obviously a number of pieces missing from the original contents of the tomb (c.f., Paul, Mr.). It is hoped that a full record may be discovered among the missing Emerson papers.

Enid Debenham

Debenham, Enid A young orphaned socialite who attracted the attentions of the villainous Prince Kalenischeff (q.v.) during her visit to Egypt in 1895, and, as a result, those of Amelia as well. Amelia succeeded in clearing Enid's name of the charge of murder and in uniting her in marriage to her second cousin, Ronald Fraser (q.v.). Enid returned to Egypt in 1903, at which point Amelia saved her floundering marriage, possibly with the assistance of Ramses. As Sethos once observed, *"It is your habit to adopt every unfortunate innocent you come across — by force if necessary."*

De Morgan, Jacques French engineer and archaeologist, he was director-general of the Antiquities Service from 1892-97, succeeding the unpopular Eugène Grébaut (q.v.) and proving himself a highly competent administrator. Among his most famous discoveries were the jewels of the 12th Dynasty princesses at Dahshur, although, as Readers of the journals know, he wasn't the original finder.

Jacques de Morgan

Amelia B. Edwards

Library. There is some speculation that, while Amelia was certainly well-versed in the classics and in various travelogues of the Victorian era, Edwards's book may have served as the initial inspiration for her first trip to the Land of the Pharaohs.

Dobell, Lt. Gen. Sir Charles Served in the Western Force against the Senussi; after their defeat he was transferred to the Eastern Force under General Chetwode (q.v.). It was he who formed the mounted troops into the famed Desert Column, and was one of the first to use motorcars for reconnaissance and combat in the Palestine campaign. It may have been one of these vehicles Emerson was able to "borrow" when the family made their cross-country trek to Gaza in 1917.

Dolly The nickname of Lia and David Todros's (q.v.) eldest son, Abdullah Walter Francis Todros, named for his great-grandfather.

E

Eberfelt, Herr German (Prussian) scholar whose name is suspiciously similar to that of Georg Ebers, see below. Given the prevalence of poseurs in Amelia's life, it is possible that this should have rung a few alarm bells.

Ebers, Georg German Egyptologist who produced numerous scholarly works and a number of popular novels, including *An Egyptian Princess*, which Amelia mentioned having read. He was the owner of a famous papyrus which bears his name.

Edwards, Amelia B. A writer of popular thrillers, she first visited Egypt in 1873-74 and became enamoured of the country and its antiquities. She helped found the Egypt Exploration Fund (later Egypt Exploration Society) and established a chair of Egyptology for William Flinders Petrie (q.v.) at the University College, London. Her *A Thousand Miles up the Nile* is a classic. An original, dog-eared edition of it has been discovered in the Emerson

El Gailani, Abd el Qadir One of the biggest smugglers and dealers in drugs, especially hashish brought from Greece to the Egyptian coast. He was finally caught by Thomas Russell (q.v.) of the Alexandria police.

Elia The intelligent, pretty 14-year-old stepdaughter of Fatima (child of her late husband's second wife). Attended school under the Emersons' auspices. She aspired to be a lady's maid to Nefret.

Ellesmere, Earl of See Hayes, Lucas Elliot.

Ellis Evelyn's maid. According to Rose (q.v.) she was, *"No better than she should be."* Her eager agreement to dust the study was a highly suspicious act since no proper lady's maid would have consented to a chore that lowered her station. For a fuller understanding of servants' duties, see herein, "Upstairs, Downstairs: A Skilllful Overview of Victorian Servants & Their Duties" by Margareta Knauff.

Emerson, Amelia (the younger) Eldest daughter of Evelyn and Walter Emerson (q.v.). She had golden curls and wide blue eyes. Insisted on being called Lia in order to avoid confusion with her aunt. Nefret Forth's confidante. Married David Todros (q.v.) and soon gave birth to their first child. Emerson feared a repeat of the family habit of reproduction, which would interfere with the travels of his talented epigrapher, David Todros.

Emerson, Amelia Peabody Like many unmarried Victorian gentlewomen, she was the devoted attendant and unpaid servant of her widowed father until his death. He repaid her loyal service by leaving her all his money, which she managed to hang onto despite the efforts of her brothers to overturn the will. She then set out on a European tour, and found her life's work in Egypt. She also found Radcliffe Emerson, whom she married after their first season at El Amarna. Amelia never received formal training in Egyptology. This was true of a good many excavators of that period, however, and her quick intelligence and long experience working with Emerson made her as qualified as most. She

Amelia Peabody Emerson, Age 3

had only one child, Walter Peabody, aka Ramses. Amelia would claim he was quite enough for any woman. She published many articles in various journals and assisted her husband in the preparation of his books. She is still noted today for her much-loved *Egyptian Fairy Tales,* which were published as an anthology, not to mention her acclaimed journals which offer both laymen and scholars intriguing insights into the Victorian, Edwardian, and WWI eras in Egypt and England, as well as

provocative details concerning the formative years of Egyptology.

Emerson, John — aka **Johnny** One of Evelyn's twins; the comedian of the family. Engaged to Alice Curtin prior to WWI. Killed in France, 1915.

Twins Johnny (l.) & Willie Emerson

Emerson, Margaret The youngest of the Evelyn-Walter clan.

Note: Amelia's references to her nieces and nephews were somewhat confused. She could not seem to keep track of their numbers, age, or sex until they reached maturity. Presumably this is because she was not much interested in young children.

Emerson, Radcliffe the younger, aka **Raddie** Eldest son of Evelyn and Walter Emerson (q.v.). Scholarly and mild mannered like his father. Went down from Oxford with honors.

Emerson, Radcliffe Archibald MA Ox., D.C.L. (Oxford), L.L.D (Edinburgh), F.B.A., FRS, FRGS, MAPS. Eldest son of Thomas Emerson of The Grange, Cornwall, and Lady Isabel Courteney, daughter of the Earl of Radcliffe. After going down from Oxford, he visited Egypt in the course of a world tour and found his métier. He had been working in the field for some years before he met Amelia Peabody in Cairo's Boulaq Museum. It would not be entirely accurate to describe him as a misogynist, for there are references to numerous "romantic" encounters in his early life; however, he was uncomfortable with women of his own class and was disinclined toward marriage until he found himself irresistibly drawn to Amelia. The numerous academic honors he received justify to some extent his wife's effusive

Radcliffe & Walter Emerson
circa 1864

description of him as *"the greatest Egyptologist of this or any other age."* He was one of the first to insist on strict methodology and accurate record-keeping. Tall, broad shoulders, black hair, sapphire-blue eyes, deep tan, bass voice. In Amelia's first journal he had a large black beard and was described as *"very hairy."* Obviously this was one of Amelia's early attempts to disguise his identity, since she never referred to this quality again and indeed implied the reverse. Publications: *The Development of the Egyptian Coffin from Predynastic Times to the End of the Twenty-Sixth Dynasty, with Particular Reference to its Reflection of Religious, Social, and Artistic Conventions; History of Ancient Egypt*, 5 v.; *The Tomb of Tetisheri at Thebes; Giza Mastabas*, 3 v., *Excavations at the City of Akhetaton; The Pyramid Temple of Snefru at Dahshur; The Pyramid Field of Nuri; Principles of Excavation*; plus numerous articles in such publications as *PSBA, JEA, ZÄS*. He declined a title from the Queen.

Ramses Emerson, 1887

Emerson, Walter The younger brother of Radcliffe Emerson, the only one who dared call him by his given name. Like his brother, he had dark hair and blue eyes; though more slightly built, he was *"nicely muscled"* according to Amelia (who noticed such things). He was gentle and mild tempered, but could fight when he had to. Trained in excavation by Emerson, his primary talents and interests were in philology. It is in this aspect that he made his name in Egyptological circles. While Frank Griffith (q.v.) is generally credited with being the pioneer in the translation of Meroitic, it is evident from the Peabody-Emerson journals that Walter was more involved in the decipherment than was previously realized. After his marriage to Evelyn Barton Forbes (q.v.), he settled down in Yorkshire with her and an ever increasing brood of children. It may well have been this distraction which kept him from receiving the full recognition in his own time that his contributions merited. In addition, he was gracious and unselfish with his information and studies. Truly, in the world of scholarly competition, he was an anomaly.

Emerson, Walter Peabody — aka **Ramses** Son of Amelia and Radcliffe. Born July, 1887. His father gave him the nickname of Ramses because as a child he was *"as swarthy as an Egyptian and as arrogant as a pharaoh."* His eccentricities are attributable, for the most part, to the fact that he was the only offspring of two decidedly eccentric parents. His father despised the English public school system (with some reason) and refused to send him to

school, so his early education was somewhat haphazard. Later he acquired degrees from Chicago and Berlin. Linguistically gifted; appallingly precocious; hideously verbose. The latter was a characteristic which can safely be attributed to his mother. Physically he strongly resembled his father, except for dark eyes that increased his resemblance to the Egyptians among whom he spent so much of his life. When he was six, his parents began taking him out to Egypt with them nearly every winter. A significant development in his life occurred when, following an encounter with Sethos, he became interested in the art of disguise. As a child he was unprepossessing (according to his mother) and irritating (according to practically everybody), but at the age of 16 he turned into a young man who was *"unfortunately attractive to women — especially strong-minded women."* After a long and decidedly arduous courtship, he married one of the most strong minded, Nefret Forth (q.v.).

Emerson, William, aka **Willie** Johnny's twin brother.

Engelbach, Reginald English engineer and archaeologist. A student of Petrie (q.v.); later in his professional career he was director of the Egyptian Museum in Cairo.

Enver Pasha Leader of the Young Turks, who took over the government of Turkey in 1913, replacing or assassinating the supporters of the old regime. Nominally he served under the Sultan, but he became absolute ruler of the country during WWI.

Erman, Adolf One of the most renowned of German Egyptologists. He specialized in philology, and started the great *Berlin Dictionary* (known to Egyptologists as the *Wörterbuch*), which is still a basic reference. He also produced classic works about literature, religion, and daily life in ancient Egypt.

Esdaile A London dealer in antiquities who sold the alleged "Todros" fake *ushebtis* to Budge (q.v.), who exhibited them in the British Museum. These have since been withdrawn from display.

Esin Sahin Pasha's (q.v.) 18-year-old daughter. Educated in England and France, she acquired strong feminist leanings and a regrettable taste for romantic novels. Though she was instrumental in saving Ramses' life, there were times when he likely wished another instrument had been used.

Eugénie, Marie-Eugénie-Ignace-Augustine Empress of France, wife of Napoleon III. She set the tone for fashion and style in the French court, at the same time that she influenced many of her husband's political decisions. A cousin of de Lesseps (the builder of the Suez Canal), she attended the opening ceremonies of the Canal and enjoyed the lavish hospitality of Khedive Ismail. Upon the collapse of the Empire she fled with her husband and son to England, where she found a sympathetic friend in Queen Victoria. She was touring in Egypt at the time of Davis's (q.v.) discovery of the Tomb of Yuya and Thuyu (1905). Visiting the site during the tomb's clearance, she reportedly seated her aged self on a 3,400-year-old chair that had once belonged to an Egyptian princess — amazingly without incident.

Ex-Empress Eugénie of France at the time of her 1905 visit to Egypt

Evans, Sir Arthur Distinguished archaeologist, the discoverer of the Minoan civilization. David Todros (q.v.) assisted him in restoring the frescoes of the Palace of Knossos in Crete while on his honeymoon in 1911.

Viscount Everly

Everly, Viscount Effete young aristocrat. It should come as no surprise to hear he was not what he implied.

F

Failani A member of a drug dealing ring in Cairo. Though no other records of him have been uncovered, we may assume he ended up in jail, since he was "fingered" by Ramses and David.

Farouk One of El Wardani's lieutenants. A handsome young man with a black heart — a man to watch, as Ramses acknowledged.

Farrar, Archdeacon Frederick William A popular and controversial theologian and speaker, he was the rector of St. Margaret's in Westminster, London when Amelia took Ramses, Percy, and Violet to hear his famous discourse on brotherly love during the summer of 1896. Despite Amelia's hopes to the contrary, his sermon had no effect whatsoever on the children.

Fatima Widow of Feisal (q.v.), Abdullah's eldest son. After her husband's death, she came to Amelia and asked for a job so that she could remain independent. Amelia was happy to assist Fatima in her quest. (Abdullah was ambivalent — on one hand Fatima should have married a second husband of his choice, on the other hand Abdullah was able to abdicate the duties of readying accomodations for the Emersons at the opening of each season — the results of which were never quite adequate by Amelia's standards.) Quietly ambitious, Fatima learned to read and write, and speak English; she became the Emersons' housekeeper in Egypt. As any woman of a lively household would recognize, Fatima was a godsend, allowing Amelia the time to concentrate on her career (when she wasn't counseling and rescuing family members). Rose petals on the bed sheets and in the washbasin were an unforeseen luxury of her service.

Fatima

Feisal Abdullah's son. Worked for the Emersons. He had two wives, one of whom gave him several children; Fatima (q.v.), his first wife, was childless. RIP 1910.

Feisal Sheikh Bahsoor's (q.v.) son, a desert Bedouin. Ramses used his persona as a cover when in Zaal's (q.v.) fortress. A note in Ramses's journal indicates that this caused some embarrassment to Feisal, which Ramses had to personally mend with Sheikh Mohammed. A daring rescue of an Englishman and escape from Zaal's fortress notwithstanding, "Prince Feisal," a devout Muslim, was discovered by Zaal's men stranded at an oasis with saddle bags full of alcohol. Word gets around in the desert.

Ferguson, Dr. Beatrice An American surgeon and gynaecologist, she joined the staff of Nefret's Cairo hospital in 1917. She was lucky to get the job, since there were few openings for women surgeons. Nefret was equally fortunate to have found her.

Ferlini, Giuseppe Italian physician who served in the Egyptian army. While at Khartoum he excavated the pyramid field of Meroe. It was he who found the fabulous jewelry of a Nubian queen at the other Cushite capital of Napata. The appearance of a strikingly similar piece of jewelry was partially responsible for Emerson's decision to work at Napata in 1898, though his excavations were interrupted by the need to search for the missing explorer Willoughby Forth (q.v.) and his wife.

Ferncliffe, Mrs. Louisa of Heatherby Hall, Bastington on Stoke The fact that such an absurd appellation was not cause for immediate suspicion demonstrates the sorry state of affairs to which the English naming process had come.

Fisher, Clarence American archaeologist who worked with Reisner (q.v.) at Giza, also in Palestine and Mesopotamia. According to Amelia he was usually rather dry in his discourse, but she observed, *"Champagne has a way of loosening people's reserve; it had a surprising effect on Clarence...."*

Fletcher Amelia's solicitor. After she inherited her father's money, Fletcher proposed marriage to her, remarking coolly, *"It was worth a try,"* after she turned him down. He was a good man of business, whose financial advice increased Amelia's fortune throughout her lifetime. It was in no small measure due to her ample and intelligent investments that Professor Emerson was able to conduct such thorough, modern excavations.

Fortescue, Mrs. Probably not her real name. She appeared in Cairo during the first year of WWI as a recent widow (her *"tragedy in black"* persona inspired undeserved respectability) and disappeared shortly thereafter, when it became clear that Amelia's suspicions of her bona fides were correct.

Forth, Nefret The putative daughter of Willoughby Forth (q.v.), eldest son of the Marquis of Blacktower (q.v.); rescued by the Emersons from the Lost Oasis where she had lived from birth till the age of 13. Their foster daughter — wealthy, beautiful, intelligent, impulsive. Nefret Forth was a truly extraordinary woman for her time. In 1991 the disclosures in Mrs. Emerson's 1897-98 journals finally confirmed what had previously only been speculation, that Forth had spent her formative years as high priestess of Isis for a lost Egyptian civilization. This must certainly explain some of her unconventional and even defiant conduct in the face of contemporary controversy and even contempt. She began medical studies as a result of her interest in mummies, and continued to pursue them, despite the difficulties women encountered at that time, until she qualified as a surgeon in 1914. Her first marriage was to Geoffrey Godwin (q.v.) and lasted only a few weeks. It is evident that, had he not died violently and deservedly, she had cause for an annulment. Her second marriage, to Ramses Emerson (q.v.), was considerably more successful. Nefret Forth established (and subsequently generously funded) the Foundation for the Exploration and Preservation of Egyptian Antiquities (FEPEA), which supported the work of a number of significant expeditions. She also founded a hospital for women (including "fallen women") in Cairo and clinics elsewhere in Egypt.

Forth, Willoughby — aka **Willy** Frustrated explorer and geographer. He always wanted to find something — the source of the Nile, the Mountains of the Moon — but was always a few months late or a few hundred miles off. He finally made his great discovery but never returned from the Western Desert. His young wife, whose name Amelia never mentioned, disappeared with him on the same expedition.

Forthright, Reginald — aka **Reggie** Nefret's cousin, son of Lord Blacktower's (q.v.) younger son. His father married a Miss Wright, and at the insistence of his wealthy father-in-law, added his wife's name to his own. Reggie had a habit of fainting...quite a lot.

> "*The camel stopped. ...the rider slid from the saddle and fell unconscious at my feet. The rider was, of course, Mr. Reginald Forthright. I had anticipated this, as I am sure the Reader must have done.*"

Framington-French, Alice A member of the English uppercrust in Cairene Society. One of the many young women who pursued Ramses and consequently delighted in tormenting Nefret.

Fraser, Donald —aka **Nemo** Young Scot who went native and took to drugs, after leaving the army in disgrace. Rescued, rehabilitated and married off (to Enid Debenham [q.v]) by Amelia. Turned to spiritualism and had to be rescued again while the Emersons were excavating in Thebes in 1903.

Fraser, Ronald Donald's evil twin (actually his younger brother). While the similarity between the two young men was uncanny, Amelia (with her usual attention to the physiological details of potential profligates) recognized that Ronald was *"slighter and softer, from his delicately cut features to his plump, manicured hands."*

Friedrich The head steward at Shepheard's during

Donald "Nemo" & Ronald Fraser

the early 1900's, who learned quickly, as did those of any intelligence, to overlook Nefret Forth's disregard for convention. If she chose to visit the Long Bar, a decidedly male domain during that time, her drink was served forthwith.

G

Gargery Butler at Chalfont House until 1896 when he transferred service to the elder Emersons at Amarna House, since it had become evident that his personality was more attuned to their lifestyle than to that of the younger Emersons. He was known to withhold the mint jelly when vexed with the family. Amelia acknowledged, *"A romantic butler is a cursed nuisance,"* but *"a butler who wields a cudgel as handily as he carves a roast is entitled to certain privileges"* — and he was absolutely devoted to all of the Emersons, with the exception of Horus (q.v.).

Gargery

El Gharbi

Gharbi, el El Gharbi was a Nubian procurer who was in complete control of the Red Blind district in Cairo before and during WWI. Nefret described the transvestite: *"sitting cross-legged in the litter like some statue of ebony and ivory, veiled and adorned. I could smell the patchouli ten yards away."* He was undoubtedly immoral, *"a vile trafficker in human flesh"* according to Emerson, but even Thomas Russell (q.v.), the assistant commandant of police, admitted that he was a kinder master than some. During WWI Russell's superior, Harvey Pasha (q.v.), attempted to close the houses of prostitution because of the heavy toll taken by venereal disease among Allied troops stationed in Cairo. Many of the women and procurers, including el Gharbi, were arrested. The Emersons had several encounters with el Gharbi during these years, and it is believed that they were partially responsible for obtaining his release and exile to his village in Upper Egypt, in return for certain favors he had done them.

Girgas, Father Originally a priest, with an impressive beard, of the church of Sitt Miriam in the Coptic village of Dronkeh near Dahshur. The Emersons encountered him during their mercifully brief excavation at Mazgunah (1894-95). A magisterial man to whom Amelia referred as *"the great (in all but the moral sense) Father Girgis."* The following season they met his successor, Father Todorus (q.v.), a mediocre substitute in every sense.

Godwin, Geoffrey *"Fair as a washed out watercolor,"* he came from a family of huntin' fishin' squires, but his abilities lay in other areas. Unfortunately,

not all of his talents were legitimate. He worked at Giza with George Reisner (q.v.) for several seasons, during which time he met the Emersons. His marriage to Nefret Forth (q.v.) was brief, and his eventual fate well-deserved.

Geoffrey Godwin

Gordon, General George English general sent to evacuate Khartoum (at the 6th Cataract in the Sudan) during the Mahdist revolt; he was unable or unwilling to do so and was killed when the city fell to the Mahdi. The expedition sent to relieve him arrived too late. Amelia referred to him as *"the gallant Gordon,"* while Emerson conferred upon him the less gracious title *"gallant nincompoop."*

Gordon, Mr. The American vice-consul in 1898, he became consul in 1906, though Amelia certainly could not have said why he deserved a promotion.

Gore, Albert An unfortunate night watchman at the British Museum. We know nothing about him except that he enjoyed an amoral existence which surely contributed to his premature demise.

Gorst, Sir Eldon In l907 he replaced Cromer (q.v.) as consular agent. Hard-working and brilliant, especially in finance, he tried to give the Egyptians in the government, including the khedive, more power, which made him extremely unpopular with his fellow officials. Though his ideals were good, his methods were ineffective; and, when he died in 1911, he was replaced by Kitchener (q.v.), who had despised him and who reversed most of his attempted reforms.

Gorst, Sylvia (No relation to Sir Eldon, above.) Another of the many young women of upper-crust English society in Cairo who pursued Ramses with the same determination that she applied to slandering Nefret. There was almost an audible collective sigh of relief from the bachelor population of Cairene society when Ramses finally announced his marriage to Nefret Forth.

Great Cat of Re, The If nurture and training have anything to do with behavior, then this stray kitten was destined for greatness the moment it was adopted by Sennia and Horus. Absolutely necessary to capitalize its title/name since Sennia insisted it was the incarnation of the original Great Cat of Re, a divinity who protected the sun god.

Grébaut, Eugène Director of the Antiquities Service, l886-92. The Service was traditionally headed by a Frenchman — a concession made by the British after they took control of all other government departments. Many directors did a good job; however, Grébaut was not popular with his contemporaries, who considered him too rigid and hidebound. While Emerson had little difficulty in obtaining *firmans* during these years, his success may have owed something to his methods of persuasion. Despite rumors to the contrary, it is doubtful whether Grébaut's decision to leave the Antiquities Service was based entirely on his experience with the Emersons.

Gregson, Tobias While he claimed to be a *"well-known private detective,"* Amelia could have saved herself a tremendous amount of trouble had she paid closer attention to Ramses's protests regarding Mr. Gregson's bona fides. However, if she had, Readers would have missed a spectacular battle.

Griffith, Captain Veterinary surgeon in charge of the camels of the Egyptian Expeditionary Force at Sanam abu Dom, he expressed *"full confidence in* [Amelia's] *veterinary skills."* Always ready to convert an attentive listener, Amelia took the opportunity to lecture Griffith on appropriate attire for excavation: *"'One of these days,' I declared, 'women will boldly usurp your trousers, Captain. That is to say, not yours in particular.' We enjoyed a hearty laugh over this."*

Griffith, Francis L. British Egyptologist and philologist. He and Walter Emerson (q.v.) were considered the foremost specialists in hieratic, demotic, and Meroitic, and enjoyed a friendly relationship of mutual admiration. As with W. Emerson, Griffith is known for his ground-breaking translations of Meroitic script. Given both their friendship and the overlap in their scholarship, it is certain that they generously shared information. While such scientific generosity is usually unheard of, their cooperation undoubtably did more to further the understanding and knowledge of the development of ancient Egyptian writing than at any time before or since.

H

Habib A handsome young waiter on the *Philae*. Amelia, it would seem, had the unique good fortune to be surrounded by handsome young men.

Habib, the villain

Habib One-eyed villain who murdered his own daughter and tried to kill Emerson. Neither action served to prolong his life.

Hakim, the Seer of Mysteries— aka **Alfred Jenkins** A talented magician of the English stage. While Amelia would not have approved, it is certain that Ramses made Alfred Jenkins's acquaintance after attending his shows and as a result further augmented his art of disguise and persuasion through emulation of Jenkins's techniques.

Hamid (from Manawat) See Hassan, Abd el Atti's son.

Hamid The Emersons' cook during the 1895-96 season.

Hamilton, Ewan, Major Corps of Engineers. Served as advisor on the defenses of the Suez Canal in 1914. This was not, however, his primary occupation.

Hamilton, Melinda — aka **Molly** The precocious niece of Major Ewan Hamilton (q.v.), she was rescued from the slope of the Great Pyramid by Ramses, who would live to regret this kindness. Her true parentage did not become known to the Emersons until after their original encounter with her. Married an elderly, rich, doting American, Mr. Throgmorton, in 1917.

Hanem, Dr. Sophia Chief physician in charge of Nefret's clinic for women in Cairo. Syrian Christian. An extremely determined woman, she earned a medical degree in Zurich, despite opposition from her family and her government.

Harsetef A young officer of the royal guards in the Lost Oasis, his life was saved by Emerson. Harsetef promised to follow the Father of Curses *"through life unto death,"* but, to Emerson's disappointment, Amelia refused to allow Harsetef and his men to return with them to England. The pipe Emerson gave him as a parting gift is cherished to this day in his family as a sacred relic.

Harvey Pasha, Lews Since 1888, this gruff old soldier had commanded first the Alexandria police and then that of Cairo. No historian questions his integrity or praises his intelligence. "Blimpish," an adjective sometimes used to describe him, refers not to his contours but to a well-known cartoon character, Colonel Blimp, who was the epitome of bull-headed ultraconservatism, complacent stupidity, and extreme jingoism. In 1917 Harvey was succeeded by Thomas Russell (q.v.).

Hashim, Madame A wealthy Syrian widow living in Luxor who held reading classes in the evenings for Egyptian women. Fatima attended her classes. Her questionable benevolence came with a price.

Hassan Another common Egyptian name. Among others Readers encounter:

Hassan, the *reis* or captain of the *Philae* during Amelia's first trip to Egypt, a Luxor man.

Hassan (junior), son of above, succeeded his father as *reis* of the restored *Philae* (newly named *Amelia*) at the opening of the 1899 season. He was prepared to deal with the Emersons' eccentricities, as his father had recounted numerous tales from his few years with the family.

Hassan, younger son of Abd el Atti (q.v.), a drug user involved in the illegal antiquities game

and therefore guaranteed an abbreviated existence.

Hassan, one of Abdullah's many sons who worked for the Emersons.

Hassan, Daoud and Kadija's son, he had the same gentle brown eyes and large smile as his father.

Hassan ibn Mahmud, resident of El Till, sidekick of Mohammed (the mayor's son, q.v.).

Hassan, Sheikh, chief of the guides for the Luxor pyramid.

Lucas Hayes ("Luigi")

Hayes, Lucas Elliot — aka **Luigi** Fourth Earl of Ellesmere (Duke of Chalfont), cousin of Evelyn Barton Forbes (q.v.). His mother was the third Earl's eldest daughter, who eloped with the Conte d'Imbroglio d'Annunciata and was cut out of his will. Lucas changed his name because his grandfather hated Italians, especially Lucas's father. Interestingly, he was never prosecuted for the part he played in attempting to strip Evelyn of her fortune, though his cousin Alberto was. Doubtless, the privileges attendant upon race and class (he was an English nobleman) influenced this decision. Of weak character, as well as chin, it is believed he succumbed to drink *"somewhere on the Continent."*

Heneshem Title of the God's Wife of Amen in the City of the Holy Mountain. A variation of the ancient Egyptian title *hemet netcher amun*. The lady who held the title when the Emersons discovered the Lost Oasis was more than they could have anticipated, in every way!

Henry One of the footmen at Chalfont House.

Hicks An unlucky British soldier who led the Egyptian army against the Mahdi and was killed with most of his men at El Obeid in 1883.

Hodgkins, Mr. The butcher in the village where Amelia grew up. Rumor had it that the best time to shop (you could get the highest-grade meat at the cheapest prices) was on Tuesday mornings, coincidentally Amelia's market day. While they wished her well, the townsfolk dearly missed Miss Peabody when she left for Egypt and a new life. Excepting, possibly, Mr. Hodgkins.

Hohensteinbauergrunewald, Baroness She was related to the Wittelsbachs (the royal house of Bavaria) and was almost as wealthy; an amateur collector of antiquities and handsome men. Ramses freed her lion cub several times (it finally ended up at the Emersons' estate in Kent).

Charles Holly

Holly, Charles A young American archaeologist whom the Emersons met during their excavations at El Amarna during the 1898-99 season. He does not appear again, nor is he present in *Who's Who in Egyptology*, which suggests that archaeology was not his true calling.

Horus One of the Emersons' tribe of Egyptian cats. Huge (20 lbs) and muscled. Owned Nefret, hated and was hated by everyone else, especially Ramses. Horus's first meeting with Sennia was cataclysmic: *"If a cat's jaw could drop, Horus's did. He stopped dead in his tracks, staring."* He eventually abandoned Nefret for Sennia, whom he would protect with his life...almost. His relationship with Gargery, Sennia's other self-appointed bodyguard, was problematic, except for a brief hiatus when Gargery believed Horus to have died in the line of duty. Unfortunately Horus revived.

Hussein, Ali Proprietor of the Naga el Tod, one of the lesser-known hotels of the West Bank, Luxor. There were a number of reasons for this, among which were the bathtub and chickens in the courtyard.

I

Ibn Rashid Emir of the Rashids, the chief rivals of the Saudis in Arabia prior to WWI. *"Only a boy... who had probably killed his first man before he was 14."*

Ibrahim A member of the Emersons' excavation crew and a relative of Abdullah (q.v.), he took his place alongside Mohammed (q.v.) as one of their most valuable carpenters by the time the excavation of Tetisheri's tomb was completed.

Insinger, Jan Herman Dutch dealer in antiquities at the turn of the century. When the Emersons returned to Egypt in 1892, they spent an evening at Shepheard's with Wilbour (q.v.) and several of his guests, including Insinger and Sayce (q.v.); this informal dinner appears to have been the inspiration for Mrs. Emerson's celebrated gatherings of archaeologists at Shepheard's at the opening of each season.

Ismail (Hebrew Ishmael) A popular name in Arab-speaking countries, since according to the Old Testament Ismail was the son of Abraham by his Egyptian hand-maiden Hagar. Unable to conceive, Sara, Abraham's wife, had urged him to take the girl. Later Sara gave birth to a son, Isaac, and convinced her husband to cast Hagar and Ismail out into the desert. There they were sheltered by God, who promised Ismail to make him a great nation. Hence, Ismail is considered their progenitor by Arabs, and the descendents of Isaac (with whom God had made his covenant) became the Israelites. None of the Ismails encountered by Amelia possessed such renown.

Ismail. Daoud's (q.v.) son — younger than Mustafa (q.v.).

Ismail Pasha, the khedive. Viceroy of Egypt from 1863 till 1879, when he abdicated in favor of his son, Tewfik. A man of extreme intelligence, charm, and ugliness, he achieved greater independence for Egypt from Turkey (along with the title of khedive); but his greatest accomplishment was the completion and opening of the Suez Canal. The extravagances attendant upon this event (and others) brought the country deeply into debt, however. Ismail was forced to appeal to Britain for relief, and this concession brought about the virtual occupation of Egypt by England.

Ismail Pasha, the Imposter. Sethos by another name, but this one didn't smell so sweet.

J

Jamad One of the stablemen at the Emersons' Luxor home.

Jamal Gardener responsible for the lush gardens at the Emersons' Luxor home.

Jamil Brother of Jumana (q.v.), nephew of Abdullah (q.v.), and the favored youngest son of Abdullah's brother, Yusuf (q.v.). Though not as intelligent as his sister, he was a shrewd young man who expected the indulgences he received as a child to attend him throughout his life. This attitude did not serve him particularly well.

Jane A maid at Chalfont House in London. Temporarily a nurserymaid to Violet Peabody (q.v.) in the summer of 1896. Only her deep affection for her employer (Evelyn) persuaded her to remain at her post following this duty.

Jenkins Constable at Scotland Yard. Served tea to Inspector Cuff (q.v.) and Amelia during their consultation. Eventually replaced his superior upon Cuff's retirement — thankfully his promotion did not depend on his ability to make tea.

Jenkins No relation to above. One of the three Egyptian Army regulars (the other two were Cartright [q.v.] and Simmons [q.v.]) who demonstrated the honorable stuff of which he was made during an encounter with Ramses at the Turf Club.

Jerry A footman in the service of Walter and Evelyn Emerson, later employed by the Peabody-Emersons.

John Footman at Amarna House. Formerly a pickpocket, he declared, *"I would give me life's blood for the professor, madam. The day he caught me trying to steal 'is watch in front of the British Museum he saved me from a life of sin and vice. I will never forget his kindness in punching me in the jaw and ordering me to accompany him...."* Very large and very young, he accompanied the Emersons to Egypt as Ramses's bodyguard during their season at Mazgunah. He wasn't particularly adept at the job (but then again, who was?). He later married one of the Emersons' housemaids and settled down in England, where he raised a rather large family. A number of his grandchildren hold prominent posts in the British government today.

John the Footman

Jones, Anna Daughter of Katherine Jones (q.v.). Adopted by Cyrus Vandergelt (q.v.) when he married her mother. Somewhat priggish and jingoistic, she did not approve of Ramses's pacifism during the War and went to work as a nurse/aid for the war effort in Egypt and in England. She did not inherit her mother's charm.

Jones, Bertram — aka **Bertie** Son of Katherine Jones (q.v.). Adopted by Cyrus Vandergelt (q.v.) after his mother's marriage. Among the first to volunteer following the outbreak of WWI in 1914, he was badly wounded in France and sent home to Egypt to recuperate. It is not surprising that he came to agree with Ramses's views on the war. As with many Egyptologists, his introduction to the Land of the Pharaohs awakened a passion which destined him for the Egyptological history books. However, additional factors were his affection for his Egyptologically inclined step-father and his attraction to Jumana (q.v.).

Jones, Charity Sister and disciple of Ezekiel Jones (q.v.), she tended him along with his other disciple, David Cabot (q.v.). Despite her sweet disposition,

"Bertie" Jones

Amelia formed a negative opinion of her: *"I suppose that one day...Charity and Brother David will be wed. They have in common not only their devotion to a madman but their invincible stupidity. Some persons cannot be rescued, even by me."*

Jones, Ezekiel, Reverend Head of the Brothers of the Holy Jerusalem mission to Dronkeh. He was unlike most Christian missionaries, who were worthy individuals (except in the opinion of Emerson who claimed it was *"rude to walk into a man's house and order him to leave off worshipping his chosen god"*). Amelia writes of Jones, a religious fanatic: *"The only living person who actually read part of the*

Rev. Ezekiel Jones

lost gospel will never tell us what it contained. He is a raving lunatic; and I have heard that he wanders the corridors of his home...dressed in a simple homespun robe, blessing his attendants. He calls himself the Messiah."

Jones, Katherine No relation to the above. Her first marriage to a drunken, abusive husband produced two children, Bertie (q.v.) and Anna (q.v.). After his death she turned to various occupations in an attempt to support her children; when the Emersons met her during the 1903-04 season, she called herself Whitney-Jones and, as a spiritualist medium, was busily bilking Ronald Fraser (q.v.) of large sums of money. Befriended and reformed by Amelia, she married Cyrus Vandergelt (q.v.) and became one of Amelia's closest friends

Jumana Sister of Jamil (q.v.), niece of Abdullah (q.v.), daughter of Abdullah's brother, Yusuf (q.v.). Eager and intelligent, she showed great promise as a field archaeologist, even at a young age. Amelia recognized her ability and intervened upon her behalf with her family so she could pursue Egyptology. She trained under both the Emersons and the Vandergelts during the early stages of her career.

Junker, Herman Austrian professor of Egyptology at Vienna. Philologist, epigrapher, and excavator. Emerson considered him an excellent scholar, and Junker expressed his regard for Emerson by asking him to continue his work at Giza after he and other German and Austrian scholars were expelled from British-controlled Egypt during WWI. His major contribution to Egyptology was the systematic excavation of part of the Giza mastaba field.

K

Kadija Wife of Daoud (q.v.). A large, silent woman of majestic proportions and dignity. Of Nubian ancestry on her mother's side, she possessed the recipe for a "magical" green ointment with astonishing healing powers — very useful to the Emersons, considering their habits.

Kalaan, Ahmed Sennia's (q.v.) mother's pimp — *"one of the most notorious...in Cairo."* He attempted to blackmail the Emersons, promising that he would keep his silence regarding Sennia's origins and sell her into slavery in exchange for their financial assistance. He sorely misjudged the Emerson family.

Kalenischeff, "Prince" Sleek black hair and mustache, bold dark eyes, monocle. His eyes were not his only bold attribute; he was one of very few men who risked life, limb, and Emerson's wrath with a *"rude encroachment"* upon Amelia's knee. His title was as apocrypal as his claim to be an Egyptologist.

Karim, Abdul — aka **The Munshi** Servant of Queen Victoria. There were a number of rude rumors (possibly originating with Emerson, though this has yet to be substantiated) about the Queen's attachment to this individual, who came into her service after the death of Prince Albert.

Karima Niece of Fatima (q.v.). Responsible for housekeeping duties upon the *dahabiyah*, as well as for the Emersons' Luxor home while Fatima visited England for the wedding of David and Lia. Not surprisingly, she did not meet Fatima's standards.

Kemit Alias of Tarek (q.v.) while working for the Emersons at Napata.

Khalifa, The (Abdullah el Taashi) Lieutenant and successor of the Mahdi (q.v.). His defeat by Kitchener (q.v.) at the battle of Omdurman (near Khartoum) signalled the end of the Mahdist revolt and the return of the Sudan to Egyptian control.

Kitchener, H.H. Sirdar of the Egyptian Army, 1890, later First Earl Kitchener. Headed relief expedition to relieve Gordon (q.v.) at Khartoum, which led to his nickname of K of K. Replaced Gorst (q.v.) as British consul general in 1911. After the outbreak of WWI, he was appointed to head the War Office in England.

Kiticas (Kyticas) Greek antiquities dealer in Cairo.

Kitty The younger Emersons' maid at Chalfont House.

Kuentz, Alain Swiss archaeologist who worked at Deir el Medina before the *firman* was given to the Emersons in 1916. Since it was they who exposed Kuentz as a foreign (i.e., non-British) agent and a would-be tomb robber, one might claim they deserved it. His fate, after being apprehended by the Emersons, is unknown. However, one must presume he paid the ultimate penalty inflicted on spies.

L

Lansing, Ambrose An American, he was a field archaeologist for the Metropolitan Museum before becoming its curator.

Lawrence, T.E. Known to the world at large as "Lawrence of Arabia," because of his habit of riding romantically about the desert in white robes.

Studied classics at Oxford, where he became interested in the Middle East, and spent several seasons excavating at Carcemish with Leonard Woolley (q.v.) and others. Before WWI he participated in a mapping survey of the Sinai. It was an open secret that the survey had military as well as archaeological motives. He spent one season working with Petrie (q.v.) in the Delta. At the outbreak of the war

Lawrence of Arabia

he joined the hastily formed intelligence service in Cairo and helped plan the Arab Revolt against the Turks in Palestine, where he later served. He and Ramses made their acquaintance during Ramses's season with Reisner (q.v.) in Palestine. His later career has been described in detail by a number of historians and biographers, and in his own classic work, *Seven Pillars of Wisdom*. (One is reminded, upon dipping into this volume, that a classic may be defined as a book everybody has heard of and nobody has read.)

Layla

Layla Third wife of Abd el Hamed (q.v.). A lady of

dubious virtue and many talents, she was attracted to Emerson, as was evident in her offer, *"If you would visit me, Father of Curses, for you I would lower the price."* Her relationship with the Emersons was never predictable — certainly not by Amelia, who actually encouraged her son to thank Layla properly for her role in saving Ramses's and David's lives. Her definition of what constituted proper thanks differed from that of Layla.

Legrain, Georges French Egyptologist. He worked at many sites in Egypt but is chiefly remembered for his excavation and conservation of the Temple of Karnak — an enormously complex and difficult job that took him many years. It was while working on the temple in 1906 that he met the Emersons and *"was particularly fascinated"* by Nefret. (Amelia ascribed his attraction, in part, to his nationality.) In 1903 he discovered a hoard of statues that had been buried in the temple courtyard — the so-called Karnak Cachette (why "cachette" is anyone's guess; there were 17,000 statues in the pit!).

Georges Legrain

Lepsius, Karl Another of the great names of Egyptology and a scholar of enormous accomplishment, perhaps his chief achievement resulted from an expedition to Egypt and the Sudan in 1842-45, when he visited every accessible site and excavated a number of tombs. The texts and reliefs he copied were printed in a series of super elephant-sized folios. *The Denkmäler*, as it is called by students, provides physical exercise as well as information; the simple act of removing a volume from the shelf requires strong muscles.

Lesseps, Ferdinand Marie de (Vicomte) French

diplomat, the designer/engineer of the Suez Canal.

Liverpool, Lord Owner of a mummy donated to the British Museum around which a chain of sinister events occurred in the summer of 1896. Allegedly killed in a *"hunting accident,"* though it is more likely his death should be attributed to the fact that he was the wealthy parent of a weak-minded, somewhat venal, dependent young man — such dependence can be fickle or even fatal. Related to *"a distinguished lady."*

Liverpool, Lord Edward — aka **Ned** Aforementioned weak-minded, somewhat venal, dependent young man, formerly Viscount Blackpool. Suffered from an unmentionable and, at that time, incurable disease.

Lord "Ned" Liverpool

Locke, Mr. and **Mrs.** The builders and owners of Mena House, an elegant hotel near the Great Pyramid at Giza. It was designed to look like an old English manor outside, but was furnished in oriental style. Amelia would hardly recognize the present-day establishment, with its extensive wings and large swimming pool, but the core of the building still remains, and the views of the pyramids from most of the rooms make it one of the world's most unique hotels.

Loret, Victor French Egyptologist and director of the Antiquities Service, 1897-99. Discovered the Valley of the Kings tombs of Thutmose III and Amonhotep II, among others there. His excavation methods were not bad for his time, but he published almost nothing and was not a popular administrator.

Lowry-Corry, Lord and **Lady** A pair of those in–

numerable, insufferably boring aristocrats with whom Emerson was afflicted, and whose company Emerson suggested Amelia did not properly discourage. Not to be confused with Somerset L.C., the Second Earl of Belmore, who visited Egypt in 1816-18 and brought back a number of antiquities.

M

Maaman First cook on the *Amelia*. Succeeded Mahmud (q.v.) as the Emersons' cook in Luxor. It is to be hoped that he did not burn the soup.

Mackay, Ernest British archaeologist who trained under Petrie (q.v.) and worked on the Theban Tombs' Survey until he joined the army in 1916. After the war he turned to Palestinian archaeology and to Indic Studies.

MacMahon, Sir Henry The first British high commissioner in Egypt, this position having replaced that of consular agent after the formal establishment of the Protectorate in 1914. Untrained in Egyptian affairs, he was usually guided by Lord Edward Cecil (q.v.) and his other high officials.

Mahdi, The Mohammed Ahmed Ibn el Sayyid Abdullah. Regarded by his followers as the reincarnation of the Prophet, he led the Mahdist or Dervish Revolt of the Sudan against Egypt in 1884; the fall of Khartoum in February 1885 forced withdrawal of English-led Egyptian troops and was the beginning of 10 years of Sudanese independence.

Mahira Yusuf's (q.v.) eldest wife, stepmother of Jamil (q.v.) and Jumana (q.v.). A withered little old lady with a vicious temper.

Mahmud (Mahmoud) Steward on the *Amelia*, as well as the Emersons' cook. Thankfully, retired after years of punishing them for their unpredictable schedule with burnt and dried-out meals. However, anyone who has spent hours preparing such meals could understand his frustration and easily imagine that the retirement may have been as much a relief to him as to the Emersons.

Mahmud ibn Rafid One of Emerson's many "dear old friends," who owned a house in Khan Yunus.

Maleneqen A Handmaiden in the city of the Lost Oasis who replaced Amenit (q.v.) when the latter was "removed" by Amelia.

Mariette, Auguste Founder and first director of Service des Antiquités, one of the great names in Egyptology in the 1800s. His methods of excavation would not meet today's standards (or those of Emerson, of course), but his contributions to the field were notable. He helped to found the National Museum at Boulaq, which was quickly filled with many of his finds. He discovered and excavated a number of monuments and sites, such as the Serapeum at Memphis, the Valley Temple of Khafre (Chephren) near the Sphinx, the statues and monuments at Tanis, the burial and jewelry of Queen Ahhotep, and the temples of Luxor and Edfu. He was instrumental in developing a world-wide conscience about the conservation, expropriation and care of antiquities.

Markham, Mrs. Seemingly engaged with Mrs. Pankhurst (q.v.) in the movement for women's rights, she had, as it appeared, other motives.

Marmaduke, Gertrude Theosophist and spiritualist medium. She *"looked like a bedraggled black crow."* Hired by Amelia to tutor Nefret and Ramses in all subjects, especially literature, she became quite taken by Nefret...and vice versa.

Marshall, Enid Temporary alias of Enid Debenham (q.v.).

Gaston Maspero

Maspero, Gaston Another great name in Egyptology, a man gifted in all aspects of the discipline. French director of the Service des Antiquités, 1881-1886, 1899-1914. He was known for his amiable disposition, but despite his fondness for Amelia, his genial temper finally cracked after years of bullying by Emerson, resulting in the latter being banned from the Valley of the Kings. He retired from the Service in 1914. The military experience of his son, Jean, a gifted papyrologist (who was killed in action in 1916), probably contributed to his own ill health and subsequent death (the same year).

Master, The The soubriquet of Sethos (q.v.) used by his henchmen.

Master Criminal See Sethos.

Matilda Tough, muscular henchwoman of Bertha (q.v.). Her antecedents and subsequent fate are unknown. Fiercely loyal to the latter, she aided her attacks on Amelia over a period of years. Matilda's subsequent career may yet be exposed in a later journal.

Maxwell, General Sir John A distinguished soldier and administrator, he commanded the Army of Occupation in Egypt from 1908-12 and was reappointed in September 1914. In 1916 he was sent to Ireland, where the nationalist movements were also giving the British trouble. He was replaced by Archibald Murray.

Mazeppa *"Charming little mare"* belonging to and beloved by the Mayor (Sheikh el Beled) of Menyat Dahshur. Borrowed (without permission) by Ramses, whose parents were then persuaded to pay an exorbitant price for its hire. Ramses gave the same name to the horse he rode at Chalfont Castle — no doubt for sentimental reasons.

Mazeppa Obviously a popular name for a horse, de Morgan's (q.v.) was also Mazeppa. It is the title of a then-popular poem by Byron, whose hero is a king's hetman of the same name; but why the Frenchman gave it to his horse is not known. Obviously the Sheikh el Beled imitated de Morgan,

since it is unlikely that he had read the English poets.

McIntosh, Helen Classical historian and headmistress of a girls' school in Kent. A trusted friend of Amelia with whom she shared common intellectual interests and a passion for women's rights and expanded opportunities. Her bicycle proved too much of a temptation for Ramses and her advice regarding Nefret was not particularly helpful. However, even good friends can make mistakes.

McKenzie, George One of the eccentric amateurs of the early days of Egyptology, to whom *"age and the passage of time* [gave] *an air of respectability not always deserved."*

Mentarit A princess of the City of the Holy Mountain; Tarek's (q.v.) sister and one of the Handmaidens.

Milverton, Charles Alias of Lord Arthur Baskerville (q.v.) in his capacity of photographer to the Baskerville expedition in 1892-93.

M.M. Minton

Helen McIntosh

Minton, M.M. (Margaret), **the Honorable** Reporter for *Morning Mirror*, granddaughter of the Dowager Duchess of Durham. In 1896 she almost suffered a hideous fate at the hands of an evil cult (in a manner even more outrageous than anything she had reported in her column in the early years of her career). As a result of her acquaintance with the Emersons (and her affection for one of them in particular), she became interested in the Middle East and courted the assignment of field correspondent during World War I. Minton earned great respect in journalistic circles as a specialist in the Middle East and its politics.

Mohammed Son of the mayor of El Till. Thin, epicene, and calculating. Fourteen years after the Emersons' first encounter with him in 1884, he had not particularly improved. Nor did his luck.

Mohammed, the carpenter

Mohammed One of Abdullah's clan, he established himself as a skilled carpenter, with a *"delicacy of touch unequaled,"* during the Emerson expeditions as early as 1894. Egyptologists owe him a debt of gratitude, for, with Ibrahim (q.v.), he was largely responsible for the careful and successful preservation and transfer of the artifacts from Tetisheri's Dra Abu el Naga cliff-tomb.

Mohammed Hamad A tomb robber of Gurneh who was not, fortunately for him, one of the gang that discovered the tomb of the three wives of Thutmose III.

Mohammed Ibrahim A lesser thug, one of many encountered by the Emersons. It is difficult to keep them straight, especially since the majority of them did not survive the encounters.

Mohassib, Mohammed One of the most respected antiquities dealers in Luxor, he had been in the trade for 30 years by 1906 and was an old acquaintance of Amelia.

Moonlight Nefret's pale gray mare. Offspring of Risha (q.v.) and Asfur (q.v.), born during the 1905-06 season.

Mubashir "The Syrian." According to Sethos (q.v.), whose henchman he had been, he was *"the best man with a knife I have ever employed."* His skill and ruthlessness did not avail him, however, against an equally skilled opponent inspired by nobler motives.

Mukhtar One of Wardani's (q.v.) lieutenants.

Murad, Ali *"A Turk with great curling mustaches,"* he was the American consular agent in Luxor in the 1880s and '90s. Though most of them were not natives of the country they represented, the consular agents had diplomatic immunity, which some used to deal in illegal antiquities. As with his peers in the trade, Murad's encounter with the Emersons proved painful: "[Emerson] *bade him a pleasant good evening. There was no response from the antiquities dealer. He appeared to be unaware of the fact that hot wax was dripping onto his hand."*

Murch, Chauncey American missionary at Luxor, collector, and dealer in antiquities.

Murdle Constable, an aquaintance of Ramses, caught in the affray during the suffragette demonstration on the steps of Lord Romer's (q.v.) London home.

Murtek Royal councillor, high priest of Isis, first prophet of Osiris in the City of the Holy Mountain. He was the uncle of the two warring princes and a plotter of Machiavellian skill.

Musa Oiled and muscular servant of El Gharbi (q.v.).

Mustafa Daoud's (q.v.) second son.

Mustafa One of the henchmen of Sethos (q.v.). He and a confederate bore the brunt of Amelia's berserker rage as recorded in her 1894-95 journal. Notes in the margin of that journal — most assuredly added at a later date — indicate that Sethos allowed Mustafa to retire (something he rarely did) following this incident, as he *"startled easily everafter"* — not a useful trait in a criminal.

Mustapha abd Rabu Sheikh who *"lacked the dignity one associates with that title,"* and one of Emerson's numerous acquaintances prior to his marriage. He helped them find housing in Gebel Barkal when they arrived to excavate at Napata.

N

Najia A young Egyptian girl, niece of Mohammed Hammad of Gurneh (q.v.). The willing but unwitting accomplice of Jamil (q.v.), she lost to him *"a woman's priceless jewel"* and might have suffered the unpleasant consequences had not Amelia and Nefret conspired to hide her "shame."

Narmer The dog rescued by Nefret in 1911, he became their Luxor watchdog. *"He had a perfectly astounding voice for a dog his size; one was reminded of blasted heaths and spectral hounds."*

Nasir the Steward Steward on the *Amelia*. A fresh-faced boy who kept dropping things, especially when Nefret was present.

Nastasen Nemarah Prince of the City of the Holy Mountain. Named after his ancestor, a pharaoh of Cush, ca. 336 BC, whose pyramid at Napata was discovered by the Emersons in 1897. They nicknamed the prince "Nasty," which neatly summed up his personality.

Edouard Naville

Naville, Edouard Swiss archaeologist and biblical scholar, excavated temples of Deir el Bahari for the Egypt Exploration Fund. He preferred big temples to the nitpicking kind of archaeology practiced by Emerson and Petrie (q.v.). He was a good-hearted man, and despite the fact that he had been rudely accosted by Emerson only days before, he was one of the first to offer his crew to help search for Emerson when he was kidnapped in the fall of 1898.

Nazir the Guide Extremely popular Egyptian guide with Cook's tours. Graduated from the P.T. Barnum give-them-what-they-want/there's-a-sucker-born-every-minute school of philosophy; his reputation

for leading the most satisfied and misinformed tour groups became legendary.

Nemo, Donald See Donald Fraser.

Neville, Mr. Young Egyptologist, specializing in philology. Not to be confused with Naville (above), who continued in the profession.

Percy Newberry

Newberry, Percy British Egyptologist who worked with a number of excavators including Petrie (q.v.), Margaret Benson, Theodore Davis (q.v.), and Lord Amherst. Carried out a thorough survey of the Theban Necropolis. A friend of the Emersons and occasional attendant of their soirees.

Newcombe, Stewart He was a captain of the Royal Engineers when he joined Lawrence (q.v.) and Woolley (q.v.) in their survey of the Wilderness of Zin (the Negev), completing the Survey of Western Palestine for the Palestine Exploration Fund (and the British War Office). When war broke out, he became a member of the British intelligence service in Cairo.

Nordstrom, Miss — aka **Nordie** An unfortunate governess of Melinda Hamilton (q.v.).

Nuri Said A "disgusting" and "old" man according to Jumana, whose hand he had sought in marriage. He may actually have been as elderly as 40.

O

O'Connell, Kevin. Star reporter for the *Daily Yell*, a London newspaper during the late 1800s and early 1900s. The *"brash young Irishman"* first posed impertinent questions to the Emersons in 1892,

Kevin O'Connell

hurst (q.v.), and suffragette. One of Ramses's numerous admirers.

Pankhurst, Emmeline Founder of the Women's Political and Social Union (WPSU), which was to become one of the most militant of the organizations demanding votes for women. It is a wonder that the incident involving Sethos and the robbery of Lord Romer's home did not permanently mar the reputation of the WPSU. Of course, it could be argued that this reputation, in a society that denied the concept of women's rights, really had nowhere else to go. Her daughters, Christabel (q.v.) and Sylvia, were also suffragists.

Emmeline Pankhurst

whereupon Emerson kicked him down the stairs of Shepheard's Hotel. For years Emerson regarded the young man as no more than an infernal nuisance, though it is obvious from the journals that Amelia did not share this initial loathing. Likewise, Kevin was of considerable assistance to her in several cases. Through their acquaintance Kevin claimed authority on ancient Egyptian curses, which he used to great advantage in the early part of his career. He never gained the stature of his colleague, Margaret Minton (q.v.), as he was keen on reporting the more fantastic stories in Egyptology. However, it was precisely his fascination with the bizarre that led him to pursue the Emersons — Emerson *"makes such splendid copy"* — and the information in his columns (for he followed the Emersons' activities minutely, even when not on the scene) have aided in verifying many of the journals' more outrageous claims, especially when he used external witnesses. O'Connell's name (and that of his wife) appear on the guest lists for a number of the Emersons' private events, including the children's weddings, which suggests that Emerson and O'Connell became friends, or at least declared a truce, in later years.

Oldacre, Jonas Assistant keeper of Egyptian and Assyrian antiquities at the British Museum, he was an effete snob who met the fate he deserved.

Omar Antiquities dealer in Luxor.

O'Neill, James Well-known actor of stage and early films, and father of the playwright Eugene O'Neill.

P

Pankhurst, Cristabel Daughter of Emmeline Pank-

Paul, Mr. Prior to the publication of Mrs. Emerson's 1906-07 journal this mysterious photographer is mentioned only in the Theodore Davis (q.v.) records which describe the excavation of KV55 in that same season. Nothing remains of Paul's photographs, save the few plates published by Davis in

Mr. Paul

his volume on the tomb. Mrs. Emerson's journal makes the sensational announcement that the elusive Mr. Paul was none other than her arch-nemesis Sethos, the Master Criminal, who took advantage of Davis's carelessness to remove many of the most valuable antiquities during his brief but productive (from his point of view) tenure in the tomb. He was apparently assisted by Sir Edward Washington (q.v.) who was a more skilled photographer and his chief lieutenant. There is some hope that further records, photographic and antiquarian, may be discovered in the private, rather guarded estate of the Emerson heirs.

Peabody, Amelia See Emerson, Amelia

Peabody, Elizabeth Wife of James Peabody (q.v.). Amelia discovered her unattractive sister-in-law *"squatting like a toad in her house; she had dismissed all the servants except for a single overworked housemaid, ...[and was] in the drawing room with a novel and a box of chocolates."*

Note: It should be pointed out here that the novel and box of chocolates were not, in fact, evidence of her criminality, but rather of her mendacity and self-indulgence, as she had foisted her children upon the Emersons on the pretense of poor mental health.

Peabody, Henry One of Amelia's disagreeable older brothers, he *"succumbed to a digestive disease.... The rumor whispered about by her loving sisters-in-law that he had been poisoned by his long suffering wife was probably false, though I would certainly not have blamed her if she had done it."*

Peabody, James Amelia's eldest brother. After the death of their father he and his brothers attempted to invalidate the senior Peabody's will, since the latter had left all his money to Amelia. Relations continued to be strained until the summer of 1896, when he persuaded Amelia and Emerson to take temporary charge of his children, Percy (q.v.) and Violet (q.v.), after which they collapsed completely.

Peabody, Percival — aka **Percy** Son of James and Elizabeth. *"A sly unprincipled child,"* his attempts (aided and abetted by his sister) to get Ramses in trouble (or worse) during the fateful summer of 1896 almost succeeded. In 1911 he joined the Egyptian army and self-published his memoir, *A Captive of the Arabs*, which recounted his escapades of the previous summer. Originally regarded as a

minor classic in the jingoistic Cairene society, it was soon realized that the preponderance of it had been plagiarized; thereafter it was relegated to obscurity. Percy became the bitter enemy of the entire Emerson clan, most particularly of Ramses. Percy's hatred of his cousin undoubtedly stemmed from envy and resentment of an individual who had all the qualities he lacked. It is difficult to say anything good about Percy, as he had absolutely no redeeming characteristics.

Percy & Violet Peabody

Peabody, William Another of Amelia's objectionable older brothers. Readers learn only that, upon goading his little sister into climbing an apple tree, he fell from the branches and broke his arm (while Amelia sat unharmed in the tree). It is difficult to say whether one should learn from this that Amelia lived in the shadow of serendipity, or that those around her should have been particularly vigilant. (Not that she ever admitted that she had pushed him.)

Peabody, Violet Daughter of James and Elizabeth Peabody (q.v.), sister of Percy. Characteristic speech at a young age: *"Dead, oh, dead!"* Distinguishing characteristic: eating, especially sweets. Amelia obviously detested her, but there are no references to her in later journals. Should the missing Emerson papers ever turn up, we may discover what happened to her.

Pesaker Royal vizier and high priest of Aminreh in the City of the Holy Mountain. He wore a perpetual scowl, which certainly intensified as the Emersons lent a hand in the political upheavals of the palace.

Petrie, (Lady) **Hilda Mary Isabel** British Egyptologist. Wife of William Flinders Petrie (q.v.), she assisted in his excavations, particularly in the detailed measuring and drawing, fundraising and administrating of each site. In addition she published two works of her own which dealt with her excavation at Saqqara. An independent woman, she and Amelia had many characteristics in common, which is probably why they did not get on. This may also be due to the admitted Egyptological rivalry between their husbands, to whom the women were devoted.

Sir Flinders Petrie

Petrie, (Sir) **William Matthew Flinders** British Egyptologist. Self-taught and brilliant, his contributions to the field were enormous. One of the first (Emerson was the other) to insist on strict methodology and the examination of every small fragment, he despised archaeologists who tore through a site looking only for major objects. Investigated numerous sites in Egypt and published his finds with remarkable promptness. Primarily an excavator, he also wrote a *History of Egypt*. Outspoken and critical, he parted company with the Egypt Exploration Fund and started the British School of Archaeology.

Petrie's eccentricities have become the stuff of legend; one of them was his habit of eating half-rotten food, which never affected him in the slightest, but which gave many of his assistants violent stomach trouble. He and Emerson were (more or less) friendly rivals. Petrie lived to the advanced age of 89.

Pettigrew, Mr. and **Mrs. Hector** He was an official of the Ministry of Public Works and one of the loudest patriots in Cairo; like many married couples, they resembled one another to an alarming degree — in this case being stout, red-faced, and rude.

Philippides Director of the Cairo Political CID before and during WWI, he served directly under Harvey Pasha (q.v.). Apparently everyone except his complacent boss knew he was venal and unjust; but, because he was a favorite of Harvey's, it was some years before he was finally brought to justice.

Piero Amelia's Italian guide in Rome during her travels in 1884. Not the first nor the last to discover (to his chagrin and disappointment) that there was more to Miss Peabody than met the eye.

Pinckney, Lieutenant An innocent (and rather stupid) young subaltern in Cairo during WWI.

Pritchett, Miss Amelia's companion during her first travels in 1884, until, *"like the weak-minded female she was,"* she took the typhoid in Rome.

Q

Queenie Cyrus Vandergelt's (q.v.) mare.

Quibell, James F. A student of Petrie's (q.v.), later with the Service des Antiquités, and subsequently keeper of the Cairo Museum and secretary-general of the Service. He was working at Saqqara when he staggered into the Emersons' camp at Mazghuna asking for ipecacuanha for himself and the young ladies. He later married one of them, Annie Pirie, who published several popular books about Egypt. As per her usual foresight in such matters (and despite never having met Miss Pirie), Amelia realized as soon as Quibell turned up that a marriage between the two was imminent.

Note: While the editor of the original volumes has observed that some of these prescient comments are penciled in the margins of Amelia's journals, it is doubtful that Amelia would have added such details later simply to prove her insight.

James F. Quibell

R

Ramsay, Major Subordinate of Sir Eldon Gorst (q.v.), Amelia described him as one of the *"least intelligent and most unsympathetic."* She had *"taken the opportunity to correct some of his ill-informed positions on the subject of women"* at a social gathering, and Emerson responded to the major's rudeness with *"something about punching someone in the jaw. It was only one of Emerson's little jokes but Major Ramsay had no sense of humor."* He was not particularly helpful when Amelia sought assistance from the office of the constabulary in Cairo.

Ramses See Emerson, Walter Peabody.

Rashad One of Wardani's (q.v.) more ambitious aides, it was probably lucky for him that Wardani was not the man he seemed to be.

George A. Reisner

Rashida Sennia's (q.v.) child-prostitute mother. Caught in the web of intrigue initiated by an obscure English traitor during WWI, she was horribly murdered when Sennia was but a toddler.

Reisner, George A. One of the most distinguished American Egyptologists, first encountered by the Emersons during their 1898-99 season at El Amarna, while he was serving on the International Catalogue Commission of the Cairo Museum; excavated at Giza, Nubia, and Samaria in Palestine, among other sites. Ramses worked with him for a season at Samaria in 1913 and was offered a position on his Giza staff, which he declined. Curator of the Museum of Fine Arts in Boston, professor of Egyptology at Harvard.

Renfrew London collector and dealer in antiquities. Suffered the indignity of being *"stood in the dining room"* by Gargery (q.v.), though he did not seem to notice the insult.

Reynolds, Jack American student of archaeology. Worked with Reisner (q.v.) at Giza. Acquainted with Ramses through Reisner. Fond of firearms, opium, and alcohol — none of which have ever been a recipe for success.

Maude Reynolds

Reynolds, Maude Sister of Jack Reynolds (q.v.). Talented amateur artist — she committed her craft to the wrong purpose for the wrong people and suffered the unpleasant consequences. Laid to rest in a Protestant cemetery in Old Cairo.

Riccetti, Giovanni The Austrian consular agent; resembled the hippo-goddess Tausert — his face *"heavy rather than fat, especially around the clean-*

shaven jaws and chin," which *"protruded like the muzzle of an animal...."* He made a name for himself by marketing loot from the Royal Mummies Cache at Deir el Bahari. At one time in control of the illicit antiquities market in Upper Egypt, he was supplanted by Sethos (q.v.). Attempting to regain control after the presumed death of Sethos, he made the fatal mistake of annoying Amelia and Emerson by kidnapping Ramses.

Risha Silver-gray stallion whose name means "Feather," a gift to Ramses from Sheikh Bahsoor (q.v.) during his 16th summer.

Romer, (Lord) **Geoffrey** One of the most vocal opponents of the women's suffrage movement and a collector of Egyptian antiquities. It undoubtedly gave Amelia some satisfaction when he was robbed, tied up, and left in his underwear by Sethos.

Rose Originally one of the Emersons' housemaids in Kent, eventually became their parlour maid, and then assumed responsibilty for the entire household. Took a shine to and charge of Ramses — no one else would do it, in any case. Rose became very protective of the boy and was rather hurt when Ramses transferred his attentions (and mummified mice) to Nefret Forth (q.v.).

Rose

Rundle General in charge of the Egyptian Expeditionary Force at Sam abu Dom in Nubia— *"an amiable man but his conversational efforts did not tax [Amelia] unduly."*

Russell, Thomas (later Sir Thomas Russell Pasha) Known for his uncompromising honesty and dogged pursuit of criminals, Russell became a legend in the annals of the Egyptian police. His career began in Alexandria in 1902. Transferred to Cairo as assistant commandant, he succeeded Harvey Pasha (q.v.) in 1917 and served in that capacity until his retirement. A keen sportsman, he enjoyed hunting, and racing his camel. Amelia respected his abilities, but resented his attempts to *"turn Ramses into a policeman."* In her usual nonchalant disregard for accuracy, she sometimes referred to him as assistant "commissioner" rather than commandant.

Rutherfords, The One of those couples with whom Amelia occasionally dined at Shepheard's (for the gossip), and whose company Emerson barely tolerated.

S

Sahin Bey (later Pasha) "The Turk." Head of the Turkish Secret Service during WWI. An aristocrat and a man of honor, insofar as the traditions of the service allowed — recognized and appreciated an opponent of integrity, namely Ramses, but not to such an extent that he forgot his own allegiance.

St. Simon, Lord St. John — aka **Jack** Canterbury's youngest son, friend (and *eminence grise*) of young Lord Liverpool (q.v.). Following his fateful meeting in 1896 with Amelia Peabody Emerson, Lord St. Simon became renowned for his altruism and humanitarianism. In the fall of 1896 he established several institutions for the education of orphaned girls. Unusually for their time, the instruction in these establishments was noted for cultivating fortitude and independence, and insisting upon the rigorous application of intelligence. Upon his death he left his entire estate to charitable causes.

Saiyid (Sayid) A dragoman, *"one of the ugliest human beings...as persistent as a fly,"* as well as *"one of the most notorious cowards in Luxor."* A good man from whom to extract information, as he managed to get around.

Saleh Ibrahim One of Sennia's (q.v.) kidnappers. Murdered with his faithful dog, for losing his captives, thanks to Amelia, Emerson, Gargery, and Horus.

Salisbury, Lord The fourth marquis, elder brother of Lord Edward Cecil (q.v.), who served in the British cabinet and the House of Lords. His father, the third marquis, was foreign minister several times.

Sayid A member of the Emersons' crew.

Sayyid Ahmed The Sherif el-Senussi, chief of the Senussis. This sect originated as a religious reform movement, a return to the purity of Islam. They joined forces with the Central Powers against Italy and its ally Britian after the Italians invaded their homeland of Libya, due west of Egypt.

Sayyida Amin Head of a women's school in Luxor.

Sayce, Reverend Archibald Assyriologist, who also worked in Egypt and spent winters there on his *dahabiya* the *Istar*. He was a close friend of Charles Wilbour (q.v.). Unfortunately, Emerson never could let pass a chance to needle him about his religious beliefs and his errors in scholarship, and since he almost always accepted Amelia's invitations to dinner, their relationship was a bit strained.

Rev. Archibald Sayce

Schadenfreude, Sigismund A well-known Viennese specialist in mental disorders. Whatever the reason he was drawn to the field, his name, oddly enough, means "enjoying the fear of others."

Schiaparelli, Ernesto Italian Egyptologist, director of the Museo Egizio in Turin. Excavated a number of important sites in Egypt, including the tombs of Queen Nefertari, princes Khaemwese and Amenherkhepshef (sons of Ramses III), and the Temple of Hathor at Deir el Medina. Reproduced a number of funerary papyri, as well as the *Book of the Dead*, in a 3-volume folio. His most astonishing find, in 1906, the completely intact tomb of the architect Kha and his wife, Merit, at Deir el Medina, was undoubtably the purpose of Emerson's visit to the Turin museum in 1911. Not only had Schiaparelli

been allowed by Maspero (q.v.) to remove the entire contents of the tomb (except for a single lamp) to Turin, he did not publish anything until 21 years after the discovery. It is a wonder that Emerson waited five years before interrogating his colleague on the particulars of the burial. (Schiaparelli's lack of meticulous detail in his elephant-folio report on the discovery would have infuriated Emerson in any case.)

Ernesto Schiaparelli

Schlange Villainous captor of Emerson during their 1898-99 season at El Amarna. Obviously an alias. (The word means snake in German.)

Schliemann, Heinrich German archaeologist who excavated at Mycenae and the site of Hissarlik, which he was to identify as Troy. Perhaps best known for his discovery of the "Gold of Troy."

Schmidt, Herr Young associate of Herr Eberfelt (q.v.), or so the Emersons believed, who rescued Amelia from abduction.

Scudder, Dutton Colonel Bellingham's (q.v.) secretary. He eloped with, or made off with, Bellingham's fourth wife.

Sekhmet One of Bastet's (q.v.) daughters, inappropriately named for the ancient Egyptian lion-headed goddess of war. Originally intended by Nefret and Amelia as a replacement for Bastet. Ramses presented this completely undiscriminating, easygoing cat to the Vandergelts, whereafter she lived in The Castle in her own room *"furnished with cat beds, cat toys, and cat dishes. Many human beings do not enjoy quarters as comfortable."*

Selim Abdullah's (q.v.) youngest son. A handsome

and exuberant lad of 14 in 1894, he later replaced his father as *reis* of the Emersons' excavations. An extremely talented excavator and administrator in his own right. Mechanically inclined, intelligent and serious, he proved an important ally in many adventures — archaeological and criminal. He had two wives, both of whom he taught to waltz.

Sennia The child of Percival Peabody (q.v.) and Rashida (an unfortunate young prostitute, q.v.), Sennia came into the Emersons' lives when she was approximately two years of age and was the innocent cause of considerable unhappiness to various persons. Amelia's strong sense of responsibility and the affection felt for the child by all members of the family led to Sennia being adopted by them. An intelligent and rather assertive child, she captured their hearts and much of their attention.

Seshat Granddaughter of Bastet (q.v). Adopted by Ramses in 1915 — though there is no suggestion that she ever truly took the place of her grandmother.

Sethos — aka **The Master Criminal** (various other aliases) A genius of crime and master of disguise, dreaded head of the illegal antiquities racket in Egypt. First encountered by the Emersons in 1894-95, when he was masquerading as Father Girgas (q.v.), a Coptic priest, and trying to rob the Dahshur tombs. He reappeared a year later as several other people, before revealing himself to Amelia and declaring his undying passion for her. He promised thereafter never to interfere with her again but popped up periodically (always in disguise) in order to rescue her from other enemies (his enemies or hers). He spoke Arabic and various European languages, but Amelia became convinced that he was an Englishman. Tall, well built, with *"strange chameleon eyes"* that could appear black, brown, or gray. The Emersons did not discover his true identity until the events narrated in *He Shall Thunder in the Sky*. It came as a considerable shock, as did his habit of dramatic demises. *"'We saw him die, Emerson.' 'I wouldn't put it past him to survive solely in order to annoy ME,' Emerson declared."*

Sevigny, Count de French widower three times over, of whom Nefret wrote, *"he stalks about like a stage villain, swirling his black cape and ogling women through his monocle."* Nefret rightly suspected his truthfulness and authenticity.

Shelmadine, Leopold Abdullah — aka **Mr. Saleh** Anglo-Egyptian clerk employed in the Interior Ministry. Claimed to be the High Priest Heriamon, reincarnated throughout history to protect the tomb of his queen — Tetisheri. Then again, he may simply have been a member of one of two rival criminal gangs, who preferred the Emersons on his side. It made little difference to him in the end.

Simmons A minor official in the Finance Department in Cairo and a member of Pharaoh's Foot, a volunteer troop viewed with contempt by the regular army, he didn't know how to fight like a gentleman, or otherwise.

Singh, Dalip A Punjabi, one of the Indian troopers defending the Suez Canal in 1915, at which time he and Ramses met, to their mutual satisfaction. The Indian troops were "first-rate fighting men" — led, of course, by British officers.

Sitt Hakim The Egyptian nickname for Amelia, means Lady Doctor.

Skuggins Constable in London. An acqaintance of Ramses who attempted to seize Amelia during the infamous suffragist demonstration at Lord Romer's, and ended up tripping over Ramses' well-placed foot. Ramses was not, after all, a violent man.

Slatin, Rudolf Carl von An Austrian military adventurer who served with the Egyptian army and as governor of Darfur during the Mahdist rebellion. Forced by overwhelming odds to surrender, he was kept prisoner under horrifying conditions for 11 years, before he escaped and played a leading role in the retaking of the Sudan. Was given the titles of bey and pasha. The Emersons met him during their season at Nuri, at which time he had completely recuperated from his ordeal and was organizing his troops for the struggle.

Joseph Lindon Smith

Smith, Joseph Lindon American artist and traveler who copied antiquities in Central America and Greece, as well as in Egypt. Worked with Davis (q.v.), Reisner (q.v.), and Quibell (q.v.). He was affectionately called "Uncle Joe" and was known for his good humor as well as his talent. Painted some of the objects from Davis's tomb, KV55.

Smith, Mr. The unimaginative *"nom d'espionnage"* of A. Bracegirdle-Boisdragon (q.v.).

Smythe Amelia's personal maid; after several years of attempting to shape an unobliging Amelia into the proper (as she saw it) mistress, she left the Emersons' service for that of Lady Harold. One must assume she realized her mistake after the fact.

Socrates Ink-speckled bust of the Greek philosopher. Deserves mention as a result of the continual indignities it suffered in the name of scholarship. Met a violent end when shattered with a bullet during a break-in in 1911. From the hemlock it was all downhill.

Soleiman Hassan Hired by the Albions (q.v.) as their *reis*, he was let go before he began.

Solimen Hamed Son of the great forger Abd el Hamed (q.v.), attacked Nefret disguised as David Todros (q.v.). Managed to flee to foreign parts before Emerson caught up with him.

T

Tabirka Half-brother of Tarek (q.v.), son of Tarek's father by his favorite concubine. Died in the attempt to bring the Emersons to Nubia and is buried on the grounds of Amarna House under a nice little pyramid.

Tarekenidal Meraset —aka **Tarek** Prince of the City of the Holy Mountain. The Emersons greatly admired this fine young man, who risked himself and his throne in order to return his foster sister, Nefret, to her family. They were instrumental in helping him to win his crown, and to this very day there is a monument to them in the main square of the City. It has been admired by many connoisseurs of Cushite art, though in Amelia's opinion Ramses is too prominently featured.

Tasherit A goat. Rescued by Nefret from the face of a cliff, of course. Did quite well for herself, as goats go.

Todoros, Father The real priest of Dronkeh and a disappointment to Amelia. Amiably corruptible.

Todros, David The grandson of the Emersons' foreman, Abdullah (q.v.). Abdullah's beloved daughter infuriated him by running off and marrying Michael Todros, a Copt (Christian Egyptian). When she died in childbirth, Abdullah tried to get the boy but did not succeed; David's embittered father had turned him against the rest of the family. Recognizing the boy's artistic talents, the best forger in Gurneh, Abd el Hamed (q.v.), took him for an apprentice. The Emersons rescued him from his abusive employer, and he was virtually adopted by Walter and Evelyn Emerson. He became Ramses's "blood brother" and best friend. A talented artist, he was one of the first Egyptians to be trained in archaeology. He made a name for himself as a sculptor as well. Married Lia, daughter of Walter and Evelyn, in 1911.

David Todros

Tollington, Booghis Tucker Alias of Dutton Scudder (q.v.).

Tom Footman at Chalfont House.

Travers Amelia's maid — a woman with a *"round cheery face and the soul of a dried up spinster,"* she was sent home at the beginning of Amelia's first travels abroad (presumably she was fired, since she never showed up again).

V

Vandergelt, Cyrus. Scion of a wealthy New York family, he did not succumb to the temptations of idleness and dissipation that often afflict young

Cyrus Vandergelt

Von Bork, Karl Young German philologist; he worked on the Baskerville excavations, with Sethe in Berlin, the Damascus expedition, and with Junker (q.v.) in the Western Cemetery at Giza. The prime suspect during the Baskerville excavations, also during the Emersons' later El Amarna excavations in 1898, and again during their excavations at Zawaiyet el Aryan. His lot in life seems to have been to be the unwitting suspect in a number of crimes the Emersons encountered — always in the right place at the wrong time or vice versa.

Karl von Bork

men born rich, but graduated with honors from Yale and then proceeded to build the money he had inherited into a large fortune, by brilliantly investing in railroads, mines, and publishing. He was then able to devote his formidable energy, intelligence and money to the pursuit of Egyptology, in which he had been interested since his college days. Though he had never been west of the Mississippi or south of the Mason Dixon line, he affected a vaguely Texan drawl, presumably because it amused him to do so. His first encounter with the Emersons occurred during the Baskerville case. Though an admirer, in the most respectable sense, of female loveliness, he was unlucky in love until he met Katherine Jones (q.v.), whom he married (with Amelia's encouragement) in 1905.

Villiers, Madame A frightful gossip in Cairene society during WWI. Regarded Ramses as a potential match for her unmarried daughter, hopeless cause though it was, and therefore was disgustingly obsequious to Amelia prior to Ramses's marriage to Nefret. Some of the most harmful rumors which circulated regarding the Emerson family during the war have been traced to a number of letters she wrote immediately following Ramses's marriage.

Villiers, Celestine Daughter of above. Amelia considered her plain. This had less to do with her face than with her personality — she had none of the spite of her mother, but then none of her imagination, either.

Vincey, Leopold A disgraced archaeologist, he attempted to profit from his excavations in Turkey, behind his patron's back. Not a nice man, even if he did like cats.

Von Bork, Mary *nee Berengeria* Talented artist, wife of Karl, mother of four. She spent much of her life in Egypt on digs with her husband; unfortunately she was susceptible to a number of ailments which interfered with his excavations. She spent several years in Germany recuperating and raising the children, but returned to Egypt when it appeared that her husband did not manage well out of her presence.

Von Kressenstein, Kress Brilliant German general. Chief of staff to Jemal Pasha, who was commander in chief of the Turkish army in Syria. Directed the attack on the Suez Canal in 1915, which might well have succeeded but for the undercover work of Ramses and David Todros. Kressenstein has been called the Rommel of the First World War.

W

Wallingford, Dr. Retired Englishman in practice in Luxor. This may be Amelia's pseudonym for Dr. Willoughby (q.v.), whom the family used regularly.

Wardani, Ibrahim el A young Egyptian nationalist who assassinated the Coptic prime minister, Boutros Ghali Pasha (q.v.), whom he considered too moderate. Boutros Ghali's participation in the trial of the Denshawai "rioters" particularly infuriated the Nationalists. Ibrahim was tried and executed for the crime, but became a national hero.

Wardani, Kamil el Charismatic leader of the Young Egypt party, Wardani was not his real name; he took it as a gesture of respect for a martyr of the cause, Ibrahim el Wardani (q.v.), who assassinated Prine Minister Boutros Ghali (q.v.) for being too soft on the Brits.

Washington, (Sir) Edward A photographer, he was introduced to archaeological photography during the Newberry (q.v.) and Spiegelburg Northampton expedition in 1898-99. One of the members of a distinguished English family from Northampton-shire that included the first American President. Charming, mellow baritone, attractive — *"the good ladies of Cairo's European society had had a great deal to say about Sir Edward Washington."* It was his real name, but it is unlikely that his parents knew his real occupation — that of chief aide and lieutenant to Sethos. He served with distinction in France during WWI.

Arthur Weigall

with a charming literary style, he wrote a number of popular books after he left Egyptology. Unfortunately, as with so many of his colleagues in the field, Emerson could not *"stand the fellow."* Nonetheless, personal feelings aside, he saved Weigall from a small avalanche during the clearing of KV55. Amelia may have echoed Weigall's sentiments when she pointed out, *"Perhaps you need not have pushed him quite so hard, Emerson."* However, he rightly responded, *"There was no time to calculate, Peabody. Do you suppose I would deliberately set out to injure an official of the Antiquities Service?"*

Sir Edward Washington

Watson, Mrs. A widowed cousin of Evelyn Barton Forbes (q.v.), she assumed the role of housekeeper at Chalfont House in London. As with all of Evelyn's servants, she was absolutely devoted to her mistress.

Weigall, Arthur Worked with Petrie (q.v.); joined the Antiquities Service in 1905 and replaced Carter (q.v.) as inspector for Upper Egypt. He is credited with making the Valley of the Kings more accessible to tourists and protecting the tombs. Gifted

Hortense Weigall

Weigall, Hortense Wife of above. Following the incident detailed above, she did not respond to Amelia's gestures of friendship.

Wentworth, Mr. Decrepit vicar of St. Winifred's in Kent — presented congregationists with many-a-soothing Sunday.

Whiteside, Ida Assistant to Miss Buchanan (q.v.) of the Mission School in Luxor.

Whitney-Jones Alias of Katherine Jones (q.v.).

Wilberforce American politician and dilettante Egyptologist. One of Amelia's slapdash efforts to disguise the identity of a real individual, she was clearly referring to Wilbour (q.v.).

Charles Wilbour

Wilbour, Charles American businessman who studied Egyptology in America, Paris, and Berlin. After becoming involved with the notorious Tweed Ring in New York, he left the U.S. and spent winters in Egypt on his *dahabiyah*, the *Seven Hathors*. Named Abd er Dign by the Arabs because of his *"magnificent white beard...white as the finest cotton, it sweeps down to the center of his waistcoat and frames a face both benevolent and highly intelligent."* He was known for his scholarly insights, which he shared generously with colleagues. A regular at the gathering of friends and colleagues Amelia arranged at the opening of every season. Except for a single article, the only book to appear under his name is a collection of letters he wrote, published posthumously. It gives fascinating information about the Egypt of his day.

Wilkins Originally the elder Emersons' butler — a man of indeterminate age, *"he totters and mumbles when he has to do something of which he disapproves like an aged man on the verge of collapse, yet I have seen him move with the celerity of a man of twenty-five."* By 1899 he had exchanged service with Gargery (q.v.) and buttled for the younger Emersons instead. With the notable exception of the season Ramses, Nefret, and the lion stayed at Chalfont,

this was a much more satisfactory arrangement for everyone involved.

Wilkins

William A coachman of the younger Emersons and one of Nefret's many admirers.

Willoughby, Dr. English physician, resided in Luxor. Treated the Emerson family during their numerous crises, until Nefret was trained as a physician and assumed this role. Dr. Willoughby's family recently sent the editor of the journals several copies of bills for service dated in the years after Nefret qualified as a physician. They all bear Emerson's name. It is an intriguing insight into the archaeologist that he was never fully comfortable being examined by his daughter-in-law. Then again, he was never fully comfortable being examined by his wife either, with or without scalpel in hand.

Wilson, Eustace Budge's (q.v.) short-lived assistant at the British Museum (1896). Took his Egyptological studies to a new level altogether.

Dr. Willoughby

Wingate, Sir Reginald Governor general of the Sudan under Cromer (q.v.), he succeeded MacMahon (q.v.) as high commissioner in 1916, and served in that capacity until the end of WWI.

Woolley, Leonard Known primarily for his excavations of Ur in Mesopotamia, he worked in Egypt as well, and with T.E. Lawrence (q.v.) carried out a survey of the Empty Quarter which was of considerable use to the War Office. During WWI worked in the intelligence department of the Arab Bureau in Cairo.

Y

Yussuf One of Abdullah's (q.v.) sons.

Yusuf Father of Jamil (q.v.) and Jumana (q.v.) and brother of Abdullah (q.v.). Not the man his brother was.

Yusuf

Yusuf An old acquaintance at Gebel Barkal — helped to procure workers for their excavations in the pyramid field of Nuri.

Yusuf Mahmud Second-rate antiquities dealer and crook — inspired accolades such as, *"he would cheat his own mother, but he is no killer."* Unfortunately, this code of conduct did not hinder his untimely and rather horrible demise.

Z

Zaal A notorious Egyptian *"bandit in the old style, preying on Arab and European alike."* He and his scruffy followers adopted an old Crusader's castle as their headquarters and stronghold for their nefarious activities. One of those activities included holding Percival Peabody (q.v.) for ransom, from which derived Percy's imaginative memoir of the experience, *A Captive of the Arabs*, 1911.

(*Note: The reader may be interested to learn the source of many of the illustrations in this section. While the Emerson family albums are missing, fortunately a handful of random photographs and sketches have been found in the current Emerson papers. Some appear to have been pen and ink studies by David Todros; a number of the photographs indicate they were the work of David or Nefret. The photos of the Master Criminal come from the papers of Sethos himself, as he kept a complete photographic record of each of his disguises. The editors have chosen not to include the cryptic notes on the back of each photo as they would not serve to enlighten the reader. The portraits of individuals known to history are from archival sources, of course.*)

An Upper Egyptian village.

The facade of the Temple of Seti I at Abydos; Inset, relief detail in the temple of King Seti offering to a god.

UP & DOWN THE NILE
(& Other Places, As Well)

A

Abbasia Quarter Area east of Cairo proper. In Amelia's time there wasn't much there except the Egyptian army barracks and an insane asylum.

Abu Roash Part of the Memphite cemeteries, a few miles north of Giza. The pyramid was started by Djedefre, son of Khufu. It was never finished. The Emersons never worked there.

Abu Simbel Site of the rock-cut temples built by Ramses II for himself and his chief wife, Nefertari. (His is, of course, much larger than hers.) Located in Nubia, 174 miles south of Aswan, they were, like innumerable other archaeological sites, threatened by the building of the second Aswan Dam. A huge international effort resulted in the temples being literally cut out of the rock and moved to a location above the rising waters of the newly formed lake. The Emersons were fortunate enough to see them in their original location, and (as a result of Amelia's careful calculations) on one of the two days each year when the rising sun shone straight into the sanctuary. Ramses's supercilious criticism of the temple betrays his classical prejudices; what it lacks in symmetry it gains in size and impressiveness.

Abusir Once an important ancient cemetery south of Giza. The royal pyramids of the 5th Dynasty were smaller and less well built than the 4th Dynasty Giza pyramids. Some interesting material, including statues, papyri and fragments of beautiful reliefs, were found when the funerary temples were excavated.

Abydos An ancient site 55 miles north of Luxor, it was revered as the burial place of the god Osiris. The monarchs of the 1st Dynasty were buried there — or erected cenotaphs there, the question is still being debated — and later kings continued to honor it. The beautiful temples of Seti I of the 19th Dynasty are still fairly well preserved. The Emersons worked there briefly in the spring of 1899, discovering a stela that provided a clue to their eventual discovery of the Tomb of Tetisheri.

Alexandria City on the Mediterranean, founded by — who else? — Alexander the Great. It is thus a modern upstart in Egyptian terms, hence of little interest to the Emersons. Alexander's tomb is supposed to be there, but it has never been found. In recent years the remains of the Ptolemaic city have been discovered under the waters of the harbor. Before the days of air travel, visitors to Egypt arrived by boat at Alexandria or Port Said, depending on which shipping line they favored.

Rock-cut colossus of Ramses II fronting Abu Simbel's Great Temple.

Amarna, El Midway between Cairo and Luxor the cliffs of the eastern desert draw back to form a roughly semi-circular plain approximately seven miles long and three miles wide. Here lie the ruins

of the city of the heretic pharaoh, Akhenaton; in the cliffs framing the plain are the tombs of the nobles of Akhenaton's court. The king's own tomb was excavated in a remote wadi several miles distant. The name, as Amelia informed us, is a misnomer; the ancient name of the place was Akhetaten, the Horizon of the Sun Disc. Three villages occupied the place in Amelia's day: El Till, Amarah and Haggi Kandil. After their first romantic encounter in Cairo, Emerson and Amelia met again while he was excavating part of the extensive city site and living in one of the tombs. The days spent there confirmed Amelia's passion for Egyptology and for Emerson; they were married shortly after the triumphant conclusion of their first criminal case, which involved a perambulating mummy. A number of individuals and groups have excavated at El Amarna, including Flinders Petrie (he hit practically every site in Egypt); the Deutsche Orient Gesellschaft, which discovered the beautiful head of Nefertiti; and, most recently and currently, the Egypt Exploration Society. The city was abandoned soon after the death of its founder.

Amarna House The Emersons' home in Kent. Emerson and Amelia took it for a year, after they decided to remain in England while Ramses was an infant; they finally purchased the house on its current 250 acres in 1889. Amelia described it as a *"manor house in the Queen Anne style, of mellow red brick, with eight principal bedrooms, four major reception rooms, and the usual offices."* (This word does not refer to offices in the modern sense, but to the kitchen, servants' quarters, butler's pantry, and so on.)

Arish, El The Egyptian town near the border of Palestine; it lies near the mouth of the Wadi el Arish, which Emerson considered a reasonable detour for motorcars. His wife disagreed.

Asasif The area on the west bank at Luxor, between the cultivation and Deir el Bahari. Rich in tombs.

Assiut A city in Middle Egypt. In ancient times it was the starting point for caravans going to the desert oases, and an important commercial center. At the end of the 19th Century AD, the British built a barrage to regulate the flow of the Nile; locks provided passage for boats and a bridge crossed the river here, one of few such conveniences between Cairo and Luxor.

Aswan (Assuan) A city near the First Cataract (and present dam). There is not much left of pharaonic monuments on the east bank, except the quarry, which supplied the prized red granite for obelisks and other monuments. On the west bank are the tombs of nobles of the Old and Middle kingdoms, including those of the caravan leaders of whom Amelia spoke so admiringly in her 1897 journal, *Last Camel*. In pharaonic times the present site of Aswan was the market for the Egyptian city, which was located on Elephantine Island. Its ancient name was Abu, elephant; the huge rounded black granite rocks marking the Nile at this point do resemble the hindquarters of these animals. There are several re-located temples near Aswan, rescued from the rising waters after the construction of the second dam. See Philae.

Atiyeh A village on the west bank, a few miles south of Giza, which was formerly known as Aziyeh until 1914, when it changed its name for reasons which have never been satisfactorily explained. The northern branch of Abdullah's family settled there.

Azhar, El (Al) A mosque of the Fatimite period in Cairo, which was converted into a university in 988 AD, making it the world's oldest institution of higher learning. In addition to theology and a study of the Koran, students took courses in rhetoric, algebra, grammar, logic, and poetry.

Aziyeh See Atiyeh.

B

Babylon An area now part of Cairo, which was in ancient times a kind of suburb of Heliopolis. The Greeks called it Babylon — probably a corruption of an Egyptian name. Under the Romans it became the headquarters for one of the legions stationed in Egypt.

Bahariya One of the five oases in the Western desert. Except for Siwa, it is the northernmost. In Amelia's time a caravan from the Nile took between four to five days to make the journey, though there wasn't much reason to go there. In the 1990s Bahariya hit the archaeological headlines with the discovery of Roman-era tombs stuffed with mummies, but it is unlikely that the Emersons would have been impressed by such late material.

Bassam's Emerson's favorite restaurant near the Khan el Khalili. The only menu was Bassam's apron. A man of many parts, he acted as cook, bouncer, and waiter.

Beersheba Known from scripture as the southernmost town of the Israelites (hence the expression for all of Israel— "from Dan to Beersheba" — Dan being the northernmost town of the Israelites). It was a prosperous market town in Roman times. In 1917 it was invested by British troops as part of the third battle for Gaza.

Beni Hassan Approximately 170 miles south of Cairo on the east bank. There are monuments of various periods here, but the ones most visited are the rock-cut tombs of the princes of the Middle Kingdom, which display vivid painted reliefs showing scenes of daily life. Owing to the depredations of visitors, tomb robbers, and archaeologists, many

The rock-cut tombs of Beni Hassan.

The harbor at Boulaq.

of them have decayed even more since Amelia's time.

Bitter Lakes Two basins now forming part of the Suez Canal. Before they were connected to the Mediterranean, they were salt-encrusted and nearly dry.

Boulaq (Bulaq, Boulak) Now a northern district of the teeming city of Cairo, it was in Amelia's early days a suburb, the site of the first museum of Egyptian antiquities, and the place where tourists went to hire *dahabiyas*.

C

Cairo Located on the east bank of the Nile opposite the Giza Plateau and separated from the Arabian Desert by the Mokattam Hills, it has been the site of Egypt's capital since the time of the Arab conquests in 641 AD, though the city proper was not established until the 12th Century under the Fatimids. Called the "Gateway to the East," Cairo witnessed a confluence of cultures (Arab, African, Turk, Greek, Roman, English, German) and religions (Islam and Christianity); as a result, the city endured continual conflict throughout its history. During Amelia's time Cairo, always a bustling city, enjoyed rapid economic expansion thanks to the opening of the Suez Canal, which increased trade access.

"Castle, the" Cyrus Vandergelt's palatial home on the west bank at Luxor, near the entrance to the Valley of the Kings. Its turrets and towers and balconies were inspired by Crusaders' castles, of which there were a number in the Middle East. Its formal name was "House of the Doors of the Kings," but Egyptians called it "Castle of the Americani," and most Europeans simply referred to it as "Vandergelt's place." It is now the headquarters of the Foundation for the Exploration and Preservation of Egyptian Antiquities (FEPEA).

Cemetery of the Monkeys See Gabbanat el Qirud.

Chalfont Castle The ancient seat of the Dukes of

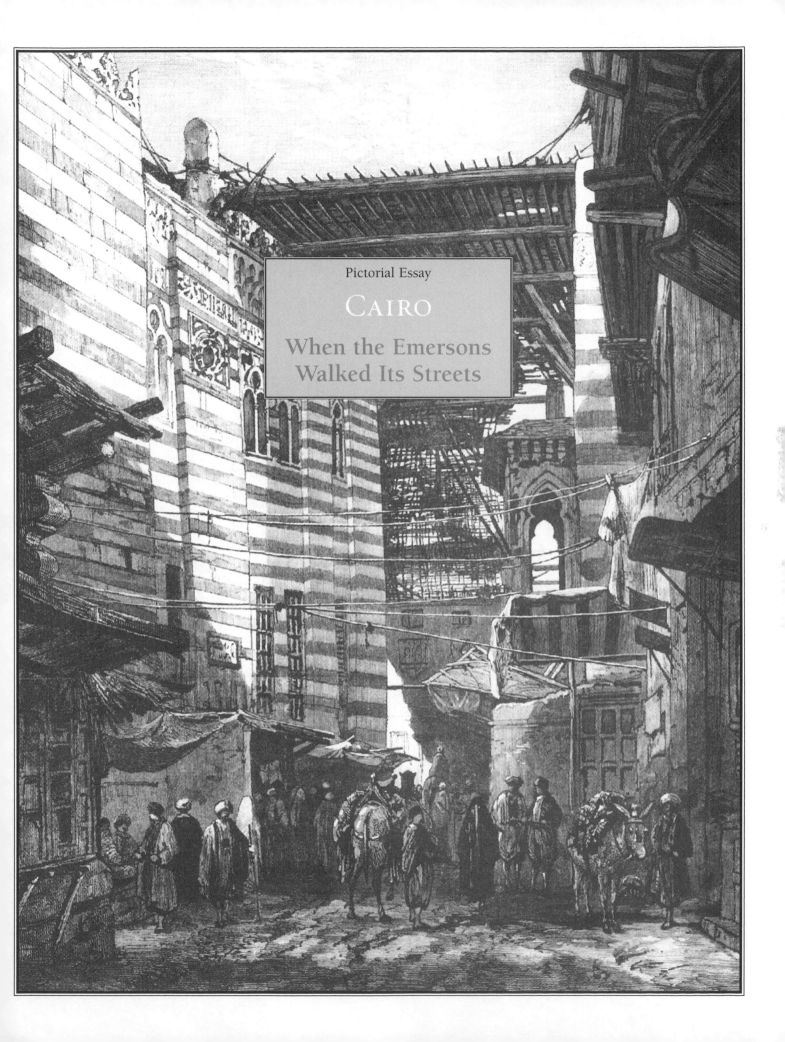

Pictorial Essay

Cairo

When the Emersons
Walked Its Streets

Late-19th Century engraved views of Egypt's capital.
Inset below, the city as seen from the Nile; Inset
opposite, the skyline looking northwest
from the Muslim cemetery
on the city's outskirts.

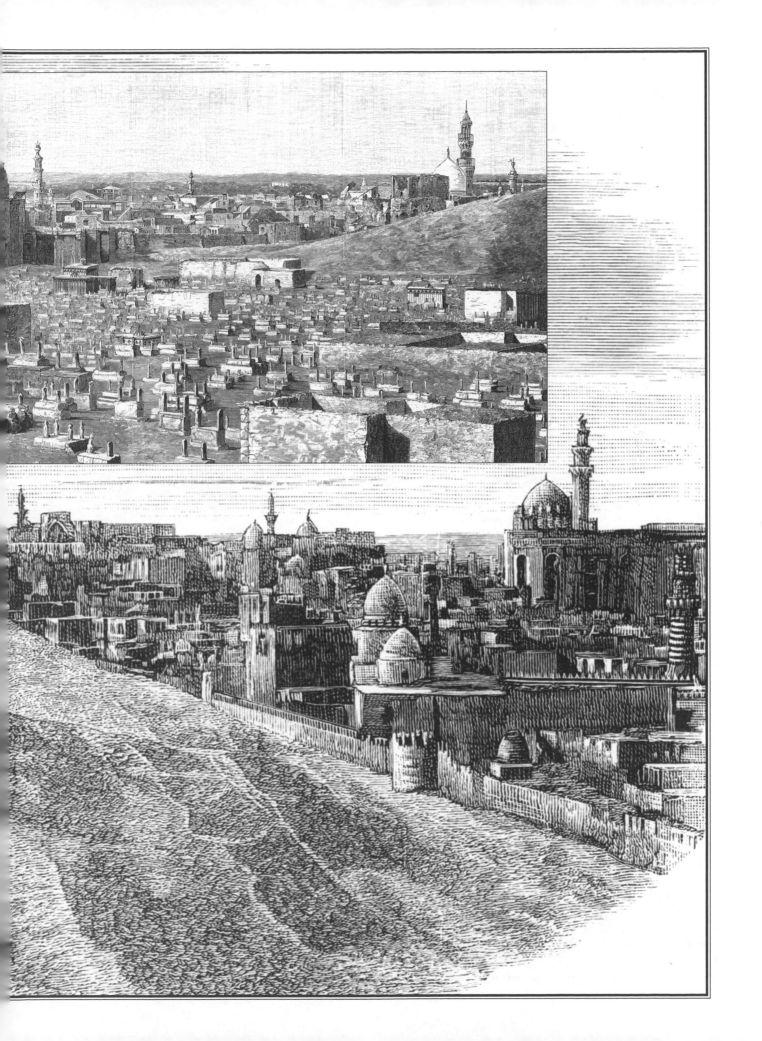

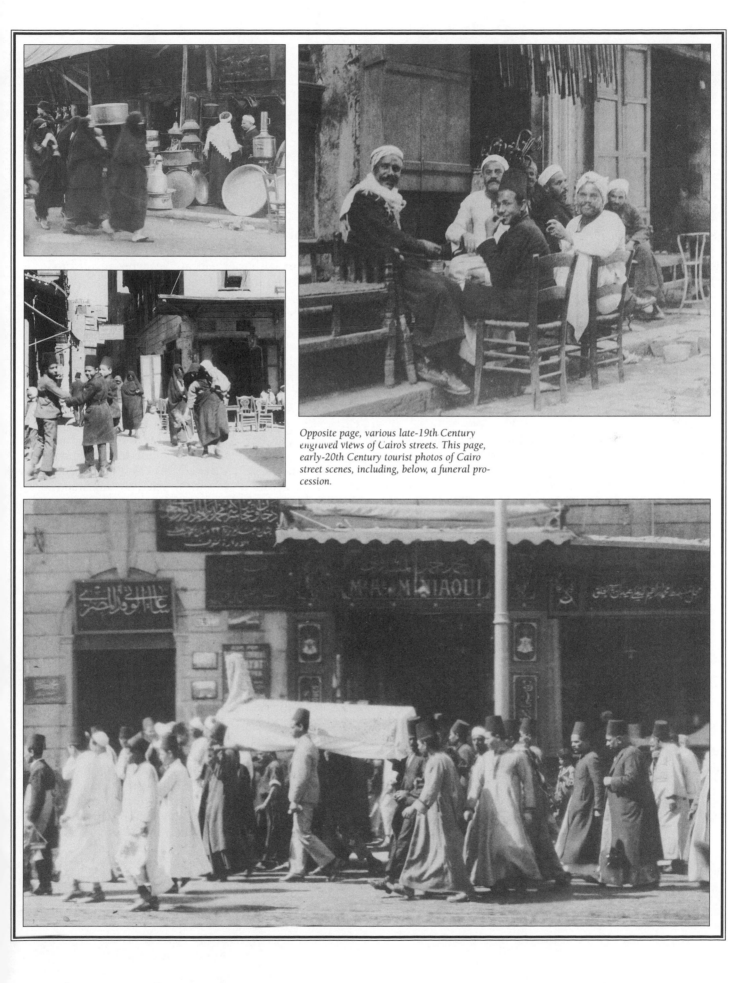

Opposite page, various late-19th Century engraved views of Cairo's streets. This page, early-20th Century tourist photos of Cairo street scenes, including, below, a funeral procession.

Chalfont in Yorkshire. It was inherited by Evelyn Barton Forbes after the death of her grandfather, the last Duke, and became the favored residence of Evelyn and her husband, Walter Emerson. A venerable old pile, retaining many of its medieval features; however, the family living quarters were modernized and comfortable. Its extensive grounds included a menagerie, a ha-ha and a maze.

Chalfont Castle

Chalfont House The London home of the younger Emersons, on St. James Square. One of the oldest houses in the neighborhood, it was built in the late 18th Century, but was extensively and ostentatiously remodeled in the 1860s, with a grand staircase inspired by one in the Palazzo Braschi in Rome and a ballroom modeled on the Palace of Versailles. The renovations included one of which Amelia approved — private bathrooms for each bedchamber. However, the device which was intended to supply hot water seldom worked, so the chambermaids still had to haul cans of water upstairs. Emerson referred to the house as *"the cursed catacomb,"* since it had over 50 rooms and not enough windows.

Chalfont House

Colossi of Memnon Gigantic statues of Amenhotep III in the western plain of Thebes on the road which stretches from the Nile to the Valley of the Queens and Medinet Habu. Originally the colossi flanked the entrance of the king's temple which no longer remains. During Greek and Roman times the North Colossus was reported to utter a musical note (not always reliably) at sunrise and was believed to be calling to Memnon's mother, the dawn, who in turn settled her tears (the dew) upon him. The base of it (up to the height of a human's normal reach) is covered with graffiti by those (including emperors with their entourage) who traveled to hear the phenomenon. The statue has been silent since Emperor Severus clumsily restored it in order to propitiate Memnon.

Coptos Now the modern town of Qift. In ancient times, the site of the Temple of Min. The main pharaonic highway to the Red Sea through Wadi Hammamet started in Coptos.

Cush (Kush) Strictly speaking, it was the ancient name for the part of Nubia south of the 2nd Cataract at Wadi Halfa. Lower Nubia, the Egyptian administrative district between Aswan and the 2nd Cataract, was called Wawat. Amelia does not make this distinction, using Nubia and Cush more or less interchangeably. Modern Sudan includes Upper Nubia.

The Land of Cush was the source of ivory, incense, ebony, gold, and slaves, and naturally attracted the attention of Egypt's pharaohs. By the end of the New Kingdom, large areas of Cush had been under Egyptian political and commercial control for centuries. As Egyptian influence declined, local rulers rose in power, culminating in the 8th Century BC, when the king of Napata, Piankhi, conquered Egypt, declared himself pharaoh, and established the 25th Dynasty. This occupation did not last, however, as only 50 years later the Assyrians invaded Egypt and the Cushites were driven back to their ancient capital, Napata, and then eventually to Meroe. A new African kingdom arose in Meroe, developing Meroitic script, and architecture with Greek, Roman, and Indian influences. In 23 BC the Romans invaded and weakened the empire. In 350 AD the Ethiopian Empire invaded, delivering the final blow to the Kingdom of Meroe. It was during this time that the royal house of Meroe and a number of their people retreated to the Lost Oasis, which was discovered by the Emersons

Late-19th Century tourist photo of the southernmost Colossus of Memnon & (insets) two late-19th Century engraved views of the pair of statues.

in 1897.

During Amelia's time the Sudan was once again in tremendous upheaval, heading toward war and eventual occupation by the English and Egyptians — an occupation which lasted until 1956, when England ceded control and the Sudan declared its independence.

D

Dahshur (Dahshoor, Dashur) The site is near Cairo, on the west bank of the Nile, south of Giza. There are two large Old Kingdom pyramids there, built by Snefru, the first king of the 4th Dynasty. The Red Pyramid is the second largest in Egypt, exceeded only by the Giza tomb of Snefru's son,

The Bent Pyramid at Dahshur.

Khufu. The Bent Pyramid got its name from the fact that the slope changes about halfway up, presumably because the builders discovered the original angle was unstable. The later 12th Dynasty pyramids at Dahshur were not so sturdily built; all have collapsed into piles of shapeless rubble. It was into the sunken burial chamber of one of these, the so-called Black Pyramid, that Amelia and Emerson were tossed by the Master Criminal's henchmen. In their day Dahshur was one of the most sought-after sites in Egypt. (It is still largely unexcavated.) De Morgan, the then-director of the Service des Antiquités, discovered the exquisite jewels of several Middle Kingdom princesses in their forgotten tombs near the pyramids. At least he got the credit; Amelia correctly suspected her incorrigibly inquisitive son found the jewels first.

Dakhla One of the Egyptian oases in the Western desert, approximately 100 miles west of Luxor. (In Amelia's time it was a three-day march from Kargha Oasis.)

Damascus In 1917 the capital of the Turkish province of Suriya, situated in a great oasis which was known for the beauty of its surroundings and the excellence of its markets. A very ancient city.

Darb el Arba'in The Forty Days' Road, a caravan trail from the western oases to Darfur. It was a hazardous journey through arid desert, marked by the bones of men and camels.

Darfur A province in western Sudan.

Deir el Bahari (Bahri) The term is generally used to designate the mortuary temple of the female pharaoh Hatshepsut (18th Dynasty) at Luxor. Its unusual design and beautiful proportions make it one of the most remarkable temples in Egypt. The site, which occupies a large bay in the cliffs of the west bank, also includes the tomb and mortuary temple of Montuhotep II of the 11th Dynasty, and a temple of Thutmose III.

Deir el Medineh (Medina) Luxor, west bank. The site of the village of skilled workmen who constructed and decorated the royal tombs in the Valley of the Kings. Occupied from the beginning of the 18th Dynasty until late Ramesside times, it is one of the few surviving village-sites in Egypt, though possibly not typical, since its inhabitants were craftsmen working for the state. They built their own tombs, elegantly painted and crowned with small pyramids, in the hillside overlooking the village: one of them, the tomb of an architect named Kha and his wife, Merit, had not been disturbed since the original burials and contained a wealth of objects of all kinds. Perhaps the most important materials from Deir el Medina are the masses of papyri and inscribed *ostraca*, which include everything from literary texts to lists of supplies and rude letters. The path the workmen followed over 3,500 years ago, along the cliff from the village to the Valley, continues in use today.

Demerdash One of the stations on the railroad between Cairo and Heliopolis.

Denderah Located on the west bank of the Nile 39 miles north of Luxor; in ancient times the town was the principal center for the cult of Hathor, wife of Horus, whose temple is at Edfu, some 110 miles to the south. Originally the site of Old and Middle

The great cliff bay at Deir el Bahari with the ruins of the Mortuary Temple of Hatshepsut, seen in a late-19th Century engraving & (inset) a tourist photograph taken after clearance of the monument had begun in the 1890s.

19th-Century photograph
of the Temple of Hathor
at Denderah.

Kingdom temples, the current structure was built during Greek and Roman rule — a date too late to interest Emerson.

Denshawai Of political rather than archaeological significance, an incident which occurred in this small village in the central Nile Delta marked a turning point in the Egyptian struggle for self-determination. The villagers at Denshawai bred pigeons for food. In the summer of 1906 a group of five British officers were invited by a local landowner to shoot pigeons. As a result of village protests and an ensuing scuffle, a number of villagers were killed. One British officer died during his escape. Fifty-two villagers were arrested and tried before a special court. Severe sentences were passed on the accused: four were sentenced to death, two to penal servitude for life, six to seven years in prison, and the remaining to 40 to 50 lashes. The hanging and flogging were carried out the next day, and the villagers were forced to watch. Following this, the tide of national sentiment against the British rose, even among Egyptians who had previously supported the Occupation.

Dir el Balah Lit. "the house of dates." A small village a few miles north of Khan Yunus.

Dongola A province of the Sudan. See Merawi.

Dra Abu el Naga Part of the cliffs extending from the temple of Hatshepsut to the road leading into the Valley of the Kings. As is true of most places on the Luxor west bank, the hillside is honeycombed with tombs, including those of the royalty of the

17th Dynasty. It was in the upper slopes of this range that the Emersons found the Tomb of Tetisheri.

Dronkeh A Coptic village near Mazghuna, where the Emersons first encountered the Master Criminal and an ill-fated group of American missionaries. Schools and missions operated by various Christian sects were tolerated in 19th Century Egypt, but the Muslim authorities did not look kindly upon proselytizers. They were less concerned about outsiders trying to convert the Copts, who were Christians (though not the right sort of Christians, according to the missionaries).

E

Edfu A market town known for its pottery establishment, 65 miles south of Luxor. The Ptolemaic Temple of Horus stands here, and while impressive and beautiful — its pylon gateway formerly flanked by huge black-granite falcons, one of which remains — it was, nonetheless, of a period later than would have warranted Emerson's interest.

Ezbekieh A district in Cairo, originally a lake, turned into elegant gardens in 1870. They contain a variety of rare shrubs and trees and several cafes and restaurants.

F

Farafra The smallest of the western oases, between Bahariya and Dakhla. Because of their distance from the river, all oases were convenient prisons for malcontents, even in pharaonic times. They are depressions watered by deep springs or wells; if

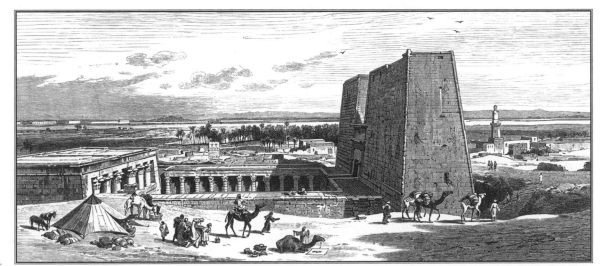

The well-preserved Temple of Horus at Edfu, as seen in a 19th-Century engraving.

19th-Century engraved view of the great pyramids on the Giza Plateau.

improperly drained, the fertile land may become swampy breeding grounds for disease-carrying insects, as Sethos unfortunately discovered.

Fayum (Fayyum) Strictly speaking, it is an oasis connected to the Nile by a branch of the river. On the west bank, just south of the Delta, it contained a large lake which was, over the centuries, gradually drained to provide cultivable land. The kings of the 12th Dynasty moved their capital to the nearby town of *Itj-tawi* and carried out extensive work in the Fayum. Their pyramids are, for the most part, located at sites nearby.

Ferdan, El A town on the Suez Canal. There were a lot of towns on the Suez Canal — most of them of more importance to the inhabitants than to the Emersons.

G

Gabbanat el Qirud "Cemetery of the Apes." One of the southwest wadis on the west bank at Luxor. It was in this wadi that local thieves found the tomb of the three wives of Thutmose III.

Gallipoli A Turkish city on the European side of the Dardanelles, scene of one of the most disastrous (for the British) battles of WWI. The idea was to cut Turkey off from its European allies by forcing the Straits and taking Constantinople. Miscalculating the terrain and the strength of the opposition, British and Empire troops (primarily Australians and New Zealanders) found themselves pinned down on a narrow strip of land between the sea and the hills. After terrible casualties the operation was finally abandoned and the survivors removed by sea.

Gaza Because of its position on the great commercial and military highway between Egypt and Northern Syria, and its lush vegetation, this ancient city has been the prize of conquerors since its founding in the Bronze Age. It was part of the Ottoman Empire in 1917 when British armies first besieged and then took it on their way to Jerusalem. Ramses's fears for its medieval monuments were, unfortunately, justified.

Gebel Barkal The Holy Mountain. Site of the great Temple of Amen built near Napata in Cush by Thutmose III and Amenhotep II in the 13th Century BC. A religious center for over 1,000 years.

The Emersons excavated the nearby pyramid fields of Nuri in 1897-98.

Gezira One of the islands in the Nile between Cairo and Giza. A fashionable area, it was reached from Cairo by the Kasr el Nil bridge. Khedive Ismail built a palace there for the Empress Eugénie of France, when she came to the opening of the Suez Canal; it is now a hotel. The Gezira, or Khedival, Sporting Club was on the island.

Giza The largest and best known of the cemeteries of ancient Memphis. The Great Pyramid, tomb of Khufu of the 4th Dynasty, was one of the wonders of the ancient world — the only one still standing. The sights of the site include two other pyramids, built by Khufu's successors, Khafre and Menkaure, and the Sphinx, which is believed to have been constructed by Khafre. These are only a few of the funerary monuments at the site; temples, smaller pyramids, and huge cemeteries of private tombs surround the major pyramids.

In Amelia's time the village of Giza was located not far from the archaeological site, and a new suburb was growing up around it. The Giza area was on the west bank across the river from Cairo, and could be reached by road and by train from the city. A number of bridges now connect Cairo to the west bank. In her day there were only two.

Guibri, El A mosque in Luxor dedicated to a holy man of that name.

Gurneh (Qurna) Used by Amelia and her contemporaries to designate a village on the west bank at Luxor, the home of the southern branch of Abdullah's family. The hill on which it stood, Sheikh Abd el Gurneh, was the burial site of the nobles of the New Kingdom, and the houses of the modern inhabitants are intermingled with the tombs. This situation proved irresistible to the Gurnawis, who had a reputation as expert tomb robbers. As Emerson once remarked, *"A man likes to be close to his work."* Attempts to remove the present occupants to New Gurneh, a handsomely designed settlement, have not been entirely successful.

H
Haggi Kandil One of the villages at El Amarna.

Hayil City in Arabia, the seat of the *emirs* of the Rashadi tribe.

Heliopolis Now a suburb of Cairo, it was the site of a great temple dedicated to the sun god, Re. All that remains today is an obelisk of 12th Dynasty date.

The Obelisk of Senusret I at Heliopolis.

Helwan A settlement approximately 17 miles south of Cairo, famous in Amelia's day for its baths, in the Moorish style. Thermal springs were believed to be efficacious for cases of rheumatism, gout, lumbago, sciatica, and neuritis. They probably were.

Hilmiya A suburb of Cairo, during WWI the site of a detention camp for Cairo's prostitutes and their pimps. Efforts to suppress the trade, from which a large number of Allied troops had contracted fatal diseases, were never successful.

The Karnak Temple of Amen complex is the largest religious site anywhere in the world, seen here in an early-20th-Century tourist photograph general view below & in 19th Century engravings of the Great Hypostyle Hall of the main temple (opposite left & above), & the still-standing obelisks of Hatshepsut (l.) and her father, Thutmose I (top right).

Holy Mountain, City of (**The Sacred Mountain, The Lost Oasis**) Massifs in the Western Desert south of Napata surrounded an isolated oasis originally inhabited by an ancient desert tribe. As a result of the decline in royal and religious power in Egypt and the subsequent upheavals during the 22nd Dynasty, a number of the priests of Amen took refuge here and established an Egyptian theocracy. A thousand years later, during the time of the incursions by the Ethiopian and Roman empires, the royal family of the kingdom of Cush escaped to the Holy Mountain, forming another element of the Egyptianized upper class. At that time, if not earlier, the original inhabitants were reduced to the status of slaves. It was around the time of the incursions by the Ethiopian and Roman empires (between 500 and 200 BC) that the royal family of the kingdom of Cush established at Meroe, escaped to the City of the Holy Mountain. First discovered by the western world in 1883 (by the famous explorer Willoughby Forth and his wife), it was rediscovered by the Emersons in 1897, during their search for the missing Forth.

House of the Doves The most popular brothel in Luxor. The name is either a euphemism or, as Ramses pointed out, ironic.

I

Ismailia (**Ismailiaya**) A town on Lake Timsah, at the southern end of the Suez Canal.

Ismailiaya Quarter An area of Cairo, built by the Khedive Ismail, a confirmed Francophile, in an attempt to rival the elegant districts of Paris. The city's fashionable hotels and business establishments were here.

K

Kantara Even before the construction of the Suez Canal, this town was a "bridge" (its Arabic meaning) on the the great highway between Egypt and Palestine. It was an Egyptian frontier station in pharaonic times. The Emersons crossed the Canal here, on a pontoon bridge.

Karnak, Temple of Temples would be more accurate; the structures make up what is probably the largest religious complex in the world. There are three major complexes, dedicated to Amen-Re, his consort, Mut, and their son, Khonsu; there are also shrines to various other deities. The structures visible today date primarily from the 18th Dynasty to Roman times, but there were earlier monuments, a few of which have been reconstructed from the pieces found inside pylons and walls of later kings, who used them for fill. During the 1899 season, a number of the monolithic columns in the Hypostyle Hall collapsed. As Ramses remarked, *"Lucky for me I was not there at the time."* This did not refer to his safety, but rather to his mother's tendency to suspect him of any and all catastrophes.

Kashlakat Village on the road between Cairo and Helwan.

Khan el Khalili The historic bazaar of Cairo, which began as a trading center and expanded over the centuries. A *khan* was a large building that incorporated living quarters and storage areas for merchants. The present-day area includes not only innumerable shops but historic structures such as mosques, fountains, and the facades of several of the medieval *khans*. It was one of Amelia's favorite haunts, where she found fabrics, rugs, illegal antiquities, and, on one occasion, a corpse.

Khan Yunus A town several miles south of Gaza. In the spring of 1917, it marked the northernmost point of the British advance against Turkish forces in Palestine. The Emersons used the house of an "old friend" here as the base for their private operations in Gaza and the vicinity during the War.

Kharga The southernmost of the Egyptian oases in the western desert, almost due west of Luxor. In the early 20th Century it was the only oasis accessible by rail. Travelers on the trains from Cairo to Luxor could make connections at Kharga Junction near Nag Hammadi. The remains are primarily Roman in date.

Khartoum Modern capital of the Sudan, located immediately above the confluence of the Blue and White Niles. It was built in 1823 by Mohammed Ali, destroyed during the Mahdist revolt, and rebuilt after the Sudan was retaken by Anglo-Egyptian armies.

Kom Ombo Site of an imposing temple designed symmetrically — the right half of the temple honored Horus, the left half, Sobek. Primarily of the Ptolemaic period, it is located 25 miles north of Aswan. In ancient times Kom Ombo was a strategi-

Entrance to the Khan el Khalili, Cairo.

The Temple of Horus & Sobek, Kom Ombo.

cally important trading town on "The Forty Days Road" from Nubia northward.

Kordofan A province of the Sudan. Prior to Amelia's arrival in Egypt, an Egyptian force under the command of Colonel Hicks was annihilated while attempting to seize the capital of El Obeid from the Mahdi. (For the details of this conflict see the article, "A Commanding Perspective: The British in Egypt 1884-1917" by Jocelyn Gohary.)

Kubbeh A station on the railroad from Cairo to Heliopolis, 1-1/4 miles east of Demerdash.

Kubri Town at the head of the Gulf of Suez, just north of the city of Suez.

Kurru One of the cemeteries of the Cushite kings, near Gebel Barkal in Nubia.

L

Lisht, El A site near *Itj-tawi*, the capital of Egypt during the 12th Dynasty, not far from the entrance to the Fayum. Kings of that period built pyramids at Lisht, Dahshur, and Hawara. None of them have held up well.

Lost Oasis, the See Holy Mountain, City of.

Lower Egypt The northern part of Egypt, from Cairo to the Mediterranean. It is called "lower" because the Nile flows from south to north.

Luxor The modern name of the city on the east bank at what was Thebes in antiquity. Nothing survives of the ancient city except the two great temples, Luxor and Karnak. When Amelia first visited Egypt, Luxor was a small village, centering around the Temple of Luxor. Karnak was some distance away. The city has grown to include both temples, and stretches for some distance north and south. There is now a bridge connecting east and west banks, but until recently the only way of crossing

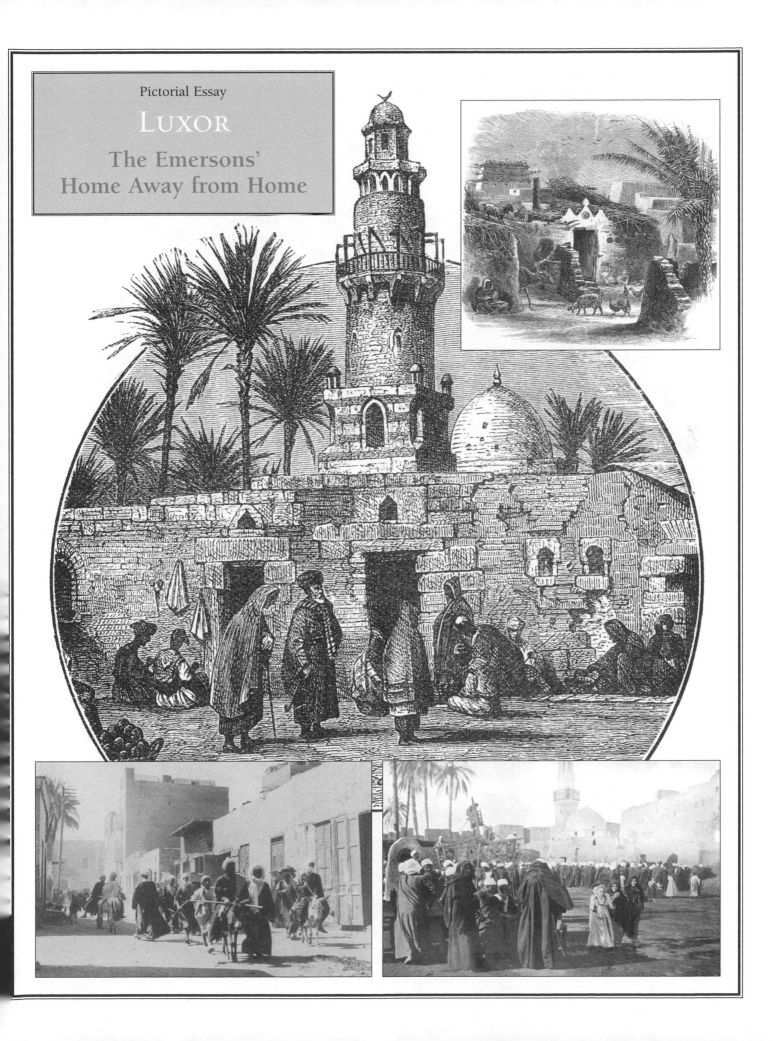

Pictorial Essay

LUXOR

The Emersons' Home Away from Home

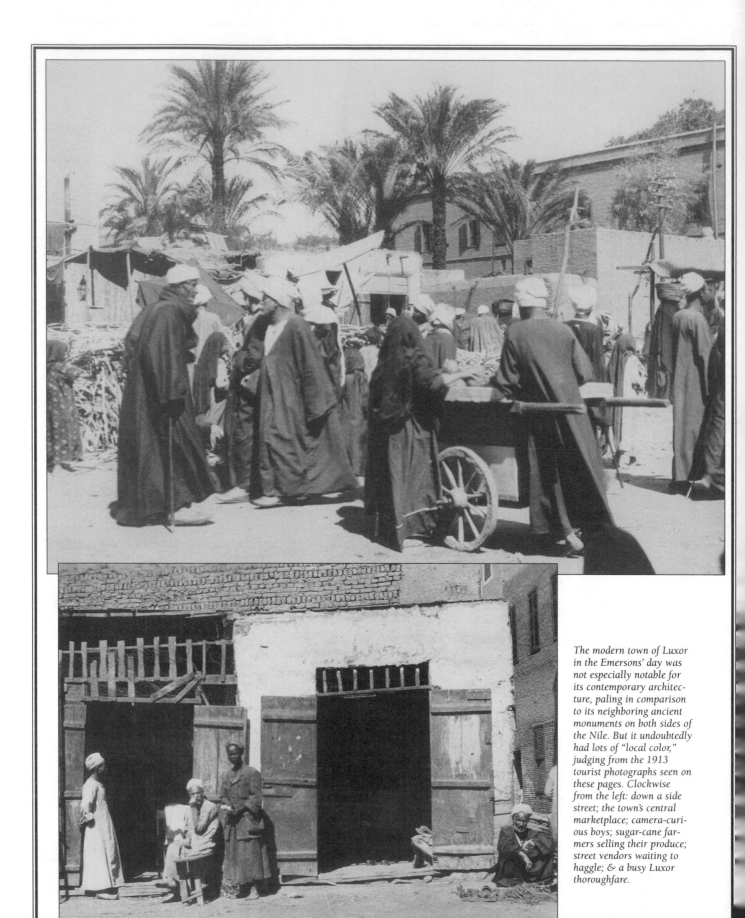

The modern town of Luxor in the Emersons' day was not especially notable for its contemporary architecture, paling in comparison to its neighboring ancient monuments on both sides of the Nile. But it undoubtedly had lots of "local color," judging from the 1913 tourist photographs seen on these pages. Clockwise from the left: down a side street; the town's central marketplace; camera-curious boys; sugar-cane farmers selling their produce; street vendors waiting to haggle; & a busy Luxor thoroughfare.

When the Emersons started going out to Egypt in the mid-1880s, Luxor Temple was undergoing excavation from the debris accumulation of the millennia (above), as well as from human habitation among the ruins. A decade later the temple built by Amenhotep III & Rameses II had become a principal tourist attraction (left & right). Located Nileside in the center of Luxor, the massive structure became a backdrop (as in the 1905 photograph below) for the dahabiyas & tourist steamers which docked nearby.

Above, the migdol-gate entrance to the Mortuary Temple of Ramses III complex at Medinet Habu on Luxor's west bank. In the 1880s engraving of the temple's interior, right, the scale of the human figure is far too small. The small 18th Dynasty Temple of Amen within the Medinet Habu compound is seen below in an 1896 tourist photograph.

the river was by private boat or public ferry, which is still the favored method of transport for many tourists.

Luxor Hotel Until the construction of the Winter Palace, it was the most popular and elegant hotel in Luxor. Famous for its gardens, it is still there.

Luxor Temple It stands today on the east bank at Luxor, in the middle of the modern city. Begun by Amenhotep III (18th Dynasty), it was enlarged by Ramses II (19th Dynasty). There are also remains of a Roman camp and a Christian church, as well as the medieval mosque of an important local saint, Abu el Haggag. When Amelia first arrived in Egypt in late 1884, the magnificent structure was disfigured by fallen debris and the mud-brick houses of the modern inhabitants. Gaston Maspero, head of the Service des Antiquités, began clearing the temple in 1885, eventually removing all the intrusive structures except the mosque, which is still in use.

M

Maadi A village south of Cairo on the road to Helwan. It gave its name to one of the predynastic cultures of Lower Egypt, the remains of which were first found there.

Mauldy Manor The ancient seat of the Earls of Liverpool, noted for its dungeons. Once on the river near Richmond, it has since been replaced by a modern shopping center.

Mazghuna The site had *"nothing whatever to recommend it"* to Amelia, but it was all they were able to get during the 1894-95 season, after Emerson had antagonized the then-director of Antiquities, Jacques de Morgan. It was and is only a few miles east of the much more desirable site of Dahshur, which Emerson wanted and de Morgan kept for himself. Cemeteries of various periods surround two pathetic excuses for pyramids; nothing remained of their superstructures, even in Amelia's time.

Medinet Habu The Mortuary Temple of Ramses III. One of the most impressive and best recorded of all the west bank temples at Luxor. It included storerooms and shrines to various gods, plus a set of private apartments used by the king when he was there on (religious) business. An earlier temple, begun by Hatshepsut and finished by Thut-

mose III (who was given to taking over his aunt's monuments), and the chapels of the Late Period God's Wives of Amen are also there.

Medum (Meidum, Meydum) Another of the cemeteries of Memphis, its most outstanding monument is the oddly shaped "pyramid" which was built by Huni or his son, Snefru, or both. The cemeteries of nobles surround it. Many of the private tombs are large and elegant; from one came a magnificent painted life-sized statue of the nobleman Rahotep and his wife, Nefret.

The Medum Pyramid.

Memphis Located at the junction of Upper and Lower Egypt, a few miles south of modern Cairo, it was the capital of united Egypt for a large part of its history, and always an important religious and political center. Tradition has it that it was founded by Menes, who united the Two Lands and was the first king of the 1st dynasty. The actual site (known in antiquity as Mennufer, "White Walls") was moved several times over many thousand years, as the Nile shifted its banks. There is very little left today, since the remains of the ancient city were used as a quarry by later conquerors. The modern village of Mit Rahina now occupies the site.

Mena House One of Cairo's most elegant hotels, located at Giza at the foot of the pyramids. Formerly a royal hunting lodge, it was turned into a hotel by the Lodges, an English couple, in 1880.

Merawi Capital of the province of Dongola, near Sanam Abu Dom; it was a rest stop for steamers from Wadi Halfa to Khartoum, and that's about all it was.

Meroe Three hundred miles south of Napata, as the Nile flows (in this case almost due north for 100 miles before the river bends south again), it replaced the latter city as the royal residence of the Cushite kings from ca. 600 BC until its decline in the 4th Century AD. Pyramids of the characteristic steep shape surrounded temples and residential areas. It was a cause of regret to Emerson that he never found the time to excavate there.

Mit Ukbeh Village on the west bank of the Nile where the Giza road crosses the road from Cairo.

Mokattam Hills East of Cairo, almost 700 feet high, from their summit they provided a magnificent view of the city and pyramids. Limestone quarries.

Muski, El The main thoroughfare of the old part of Cairo. Even during Amelia's time, it had lost many of its picturesque characteristics and was lined with European shops selling everything from cigars to clothing.

The Pyramid of Queen Amenishakheto at Meroe.

Mena House & the Pyramids in 1905.

The Temple of Isis at Philae, as seen in a 19th Century engraving of the Kiosk of Trajan (also known as "Pharaoh's Bed"). Below, another engraving of the same period of the main temple's hypostyle hall (bottom left); & an 1896 tourist photograph of that temple's pylon gateway.

The Mortuary Temple of
Ramses II on the Luxor
west bank is seen in two
19th Century views. The
gigantic fallen colossus of
the king — inspiration for
Shelley's famous poem
"Ozymandias" — is seen
on the right in the photograph & at the far left in
the above engraving.

N

Napata The ancient capital of the kingdom of Cush from about 900 to 600 BC, at which time the capital was transferred to Meroe, farther south. The ruins are near Gebel Barkal. The pyramid cemeteries nearby include Nuri and Kurru.

Nubia The Greeks were the first to use this name for the region between the 1st and 4th cataracts. It may derive from the ancient Egyptian word for "gold." See Cush.

Nuri Site of the pyramid cemeteries of the Cushite kings of Napata. The Emersons excavated there during the 1897-98 season.

O

Omdurman Originally founded to be the capital of the Mahdist regime, it is across the river from Khartoum. The Battle of Omdurman in 1898 ended the occupation of the Sudan by the Mahdists. The Anglo-Egyptian forces under Sir Herbert Kitchener lost 46 killed and 329 wounded, while killing and wounding 26,000 of the enemy and taking 4,000 prisoners. (So Baedeker claims, anyhow.)

P

Philae The site of temples to Isis, the majority of them dating to the Greek or Roman period. Following the completion of the first Aswan Dam in 1912, the island was covered with water for much of each year. When the second dam (the High Dam) was contemplated, it was realized that the temples would be permanently submerged. As a result of an international effort headed by UNESCO, from 1972 to 1980, they were moved in their entirety to the nearby island of Agilka, which had been configured to match the terrain of Philae. The present temples can be reached by boat from Aswan and feature a sound and light performance, of which none of the Emersons would have approved.

Place of Beauty The ancient name for the Valley of the Queens.

Place of Truth One of the ancient names for the Valley of the Kings. It was also called The Great Place.

Port Said The Egyptian port of call for many of the shipping lines between Egypt and the east, after the opening of the Suez Canal in 1869. It was connected to Cairo by rail.

Punt The country to which the ancient Egyptians went to procure exotic flora and fauna. Its exact location is still in doubt, though it was probably located in Somalia on the Red Sea coast.

R

Rafa (Rafah) A town on the coastal road, near the old Egypt-Palestine border. The battle fought here in January 1917 cleared the Turks out of the Sinai. Mounted troops were a decisive factor.

Ramesseum The Mortuary Temple of Ramses II, on the west bank at Luxor. It has always been a popular tourist site.

Red Blind District Moderns would use the term "Red Light." Included El Wasa and Wagh el Birka.

Roda (Rodah) An island in the Nile at Cairo, which contained nothing of interest to the Emersons — i.e. no pharaonic remains. A bridge (Abbas II) crossed it, connecting east and west banks.

Romani Egyptian town in the Sinai on the coastal route to Palestine. There was a particularly fierce battle here in July of 1916, which destroyed the optimistic belief of the British that the Turks could not get troops through the desert during the heat of summer.

S

Sakkara (Saqqarah) One of the necropolei of ancient Memphis, south of Giza on the west bank. It is a huge site, containing monuments from almost every period of Egyptian history. The crumbled remains of the "royal tombs" of the 1st Dynasty; the Step Pyramid — the first monumental stone building in Egypt; pyramids of the 6th Dynasty — badly ruined but containing the famous Pyramid Texts; the Serapeum — burial place of the sacred Apis Bulls; and many beautiful private tombs of the Old Kingdom make this one of the most visited sites in Egypt. Excavations are still going on, and discoveries will probably continue for years to come.

Sanam Abu Dom A small village in Nubia near Gebel Barkal which was, briefly, the headquarters of the Expeditionary Force that eventually reconquered the Sudan after the Mahdist revolt.

The Step Pyramid, principal monument at Sakkara.

Semiramis One of Cairo's best hotels, on the riverbank, as it still is today.

Serapeum Massive subterranean tombs of the sacred Apis Bulls at Sakkara. (For more information see, "A Splendid Overview of Egyptology: Napoleon to WWI" by Dennis Forbes.)

Serapeum Town on the west side of the Suez Canal, a few miles south of Toussoum.

Sharia Clot Bey (**Blvd. Clot Bey**) The principle street of the northwest quarter of Cairo, which starts at the central railroad station.

Sharia el Kamal (Sharia Kamel) A street in Cairo that passed Shepheard's and the west side of the Ezbekieh. A favorite shopping area for Amelia.

Sharia Suleiman Pasha A main thoroughfare in Europeanized Cairo, near the hotels and the English church. Someplace along the way it changes its name to Sharia Qasr (Kasr) el Ain.

Shellal A village on the east bank of the Nile opposite the Island of Philae, where both the desert and railway route from Aswan end. Ferries could be taken from Shellal to Philae in Amelia's day.

Shepheard's Hotel This famous Cairene establishment was prominently featured in the journals.

Founded in the 1840s, for many years it was the hotel in Cairo most favored by English and American visitors, and Amelia remained faithful to it even after newer hotels, such as the Semiramis and the Savoy, had become the mode. Over the years it was extensively remodeled, and it was one of the first hotels to have electric lights installed. The Moorish Hall and the life-sized statues of Nubian maidens that stood at the foot of the grand staircase were among its features, and the famous terrace was a popular meeting place. The present Shepheard's does not stand on the same site as the original, which was destroyed by fire in the 1950s. (See sidebar, pp. 58-59).

Siwa The northernmost, largest and farthest west of the oases. It was visited by Alexander the Great seeking the oracle of Amen. Nobody knows what Amen told him, but he went on to conquer a large part of the known world.

In the Serapeum.

Sudan See Cush. (For an overview of the modern history of this region see the article, "A Commanding Perspective: The British in Egypt 1884-1917" by Jocelyn Gohary.)

Vessel in the Suez Canal.

Suez The isthmus connecting Africa with Asia. The advantages of a canal cut through the isthmus at its narrowest point and connecting the Mediterranean with the Red Sea were evident even in ancient times, but the first historically verified attempt was made by the pharaoh Necho, in 600 BC. It was left to Darius, the Persian, to finish it. No attempt was made in modern times, until Ferdinand de Lesseps, a French engineer, presented his scheme to the viceroy of Egypt. The present canal was completed in 1869. Poetically referred to as "Britain's lifeline to the east," it shortened the voyage between England and "the jewel in the crown," India, by many weeks.

T

Tanis A town in the eastern Delta, Tanis became the capital of the kings of the 21st and 22nd dynasties. Sporadically excavated by Mariette between 1860 and 1880, it was being investigated by Petrie when Amelia first traveled to Egypt in 1884. Subsequent excavations have yielded important information about the New Kingdom and 3rd Intermediate Period including the undisturbed tombs of of 21st and 22nd Dynasty kings found there in 1939-40 by Pierre Montet, complete with gold and silver coffins, mummy masks, and canopics, as well as a great quantity of gold jewelry, all of which can be seen today in the Cairo Museum.

Tanis.

Valley of the Kings, 1905.

The Winter Palace Hotel in 1905.

Thebes The Greek name for the Luxor area, on both banks of the Nile. Strictly speaking, Luxor is the "modern" town on the east bank. Its ancient Egyptian name was Waset.

Toussoum Town on the west side of the Suez Canal. The first Turkish attack in 1915 occurred between Toussoum and Serapeum to the south.

Tumbakiyeh The old tobacco warehouse district in Cairo.

Tura One of the quarries near Cairo from which was extracted a particulary fine type of white limestone. It was used to case the sides of the pyramids and mastabas.

U

Upper Egypt The Nile valley, from Aswan to the Delta. See Lower Egypt.

V

Valley of the Kings (**Biban el Moluk** — lit. "Gates of the Kings") There are two of them in fact, but the West Valley contains only a few royal tombs and is not as accessible as the East Valley, which is the one meant when people talk about the Valley of the Kings. It was the royal burial place from the beginning of the 18th Dynasty to the end of the 20th. The rock-cut tombs, some of which have been known to visitors since Greek and Roman times, have been numbered more or less in the order of their discovery. Thus far, the last one numbered is that of Tutankhamen, no. 62. Egyptologists refer to the tombs by number, i.e., KV (for King's Valley) 55. It makes them sound cool. To be fair, the names of some of the occupants of the tombs are unknown or uncertain. Not all were kings; a few favored nobles and royal relatives were awarded the privilege of burial in the royal valley, and some of the numbered tombs are small and uninscribed.

Valley of the Monkeys The local name for the West Valley of the Kings. The monkeys are more properly baboons; they are found in the Tomb of Ay, successor of Tutankhamen and next-to-last king of the 18th Dynasty. Not to be confused with Cemetery of the Monkeys.

Valley of the Queens A large wadi or "valley" on the Luxor west bank, used for burials of queens and princes from the 19th Dynasty on. "The Place

of Beauty" in pharaonic times.

W

Wadi Halfa City at the 2nd Cataract, south of Aswan.

Wadi Natrum A large depression in the western desert, from which the salt natron, used in mummification, was procured.

Wadiyein "The two wadis." Narrow gorges, the southernmost of which led from Dra Abu el Naga into the Valleys of the Kings.

Wagh el Birka Some of the tourists who came to Egypt were in search of the exotic pleasures they were too cautious to sample at home (though most of them could have been found in London). The Wagh el Birka, like el Wasa, was part of the notorious Red Blind district of Cairo, where the brothels there were worked by European women (though not English). Because these brothels were run by Europeans rather than Egyptians, they were outside the jurisdiction of the Cairo police.

Wasa, El Another part of the Red Blind district, located embarrassingly (and conveniently) near several of the most fashionable hotels. It was featured on certain tours, though not those of the

respectable Mr. Cook. Most of the women were Sudanese, Egyptian, or Nubian. The British administration of Egypt didn't exactly legalize prostitution, but it was tolerated. In theory the women (and boys) underwent some medical control, but during WWI the incidence of venereal disease among the troops rose to such a point that the Cairo police attempted to shut down some of the establishments. It was in this area that Nefret Forth opened her first clinic for prostitutes and impoverished women.

West Valley One of the two Valleys of the Kings at Luxor. It contains some of the most ruggedly grand scenery in the area and a few royal tombs, notably those of kings Amenhotep III and Ay.

Winter Palace Hotel Opened in 1886, it immediately became the leading hotel of Luxor, where it is still in operation on the corniche, with splendid views of the river and the eastern mountains. Famous for its gardens.

Y

Yam The goal of the valiant caravan leaders of the 6th Dynasty, a source of exotic flora and fauna highly prized by Egyptian kings. Its exact location is unknown, but it was probably in Upper Nubia south of the Third Cataract.

Z

Zawaiet el Aryan In 1911, Amelia remarked that it was *"one of the most obscure archaeological sites in Egypt. For obscure, read 'boring.'"* It is still one of the most boring sites in Egypt. One of the "pyramids" consists only of a substructure, with a sarcophagus still in place. The other, attributed to King Kaba of the 3rd Dynasty (whoever he was), has a collapsed superstructure and a substructure with complex passages and a presumed burial chamber. In 1911 the Emersons discovered the remains of the royal burial, hidden under the floor of one of the passages. Until recently Zawaiet was a military zone, and at present writing it is still almost impossible to get permission to visit the site. Its cemeteries have never been properly excavated.

Zerzura A legendary city which held fabulous riches. The key to the gates hung on the beak of a carved bird beside the portal, but if the discoverer woke the sleeping king and queen he was in for big trouble!

Bedouins on the move.

WORDS YOU MAY NOT FIND IN WEBSTER
(Foreign Words & Phrases)

The editor had hoped, in this commentary, to produce definitive spellings of Arabic and ancient Egyptian words. She has concluded this is impossible. Neither script writes the vowels and both have certain sounds that do not correspond exactly to English letters. Transliteration into English is subject to variations over time and the conventions of different languages. Mrs. Emerson was as inconsistent about this as she was about a number of other things. The following list gives several variants. The definitions and some of the spellings are those of the period.

ARABIC & TURKISH
A

aba (**abayeh**) Loose, long robe, usually open and held with a belt or sash.

abadamu (**abadmun**t) Meaning unknown. It is the language of the Lost Oasis. If Ramses Emerson ever completed his dictionary, the manuscript has been lost.

abu Father.

Abu Shita'im Father of Curses; Emerson's Arabic sobriquet, which refers not only to the richness of his vocabulary but the power of his voice.

Adan The call to worship, recited five times each day by the muezzin. "God is most great."

adar ya-yan A peremptory command to a camel.

afrit, afreet, efreet (pl. *afareet*) An evil *djinni*.

agab The twisted band that holds the *khafiya* in place on the wearer's head.

Akhu el-Afareet Brother of Demons. Ramses's Arabic sobriquet. It was meant as a compliment, though his mother didn't see it that way.

Alemani German.

Alhamdullilah "Praise be to God."

Allah isabbekhum bilkheir "God grant you a good morning."

Allah warabakatu "May God be merciful."

Allah yibarek f'iki "May God preserve you."

Allah yisallimak "May God protect you."

antaree Short vest reaching just below the waist and cut quite low across the bosom. Usually worn over a shirt or other garment and always covered by a robe when the wearer appeared in public. It was when her captor and bitter enemy demanded that Amelia assume this garment, together with the long loose trousers (*shintiyan*) that Amelia realized his motives might not be quite what she had assumed.

antika Antiquities.

Ayet el Kursee The 256th or "Throne Verse" of the 2nd chapter of the Koran.

aywa Yes.

B

bab-sirr Secret door.

baksheesh Tip, gratuity.

Woman wearing a burko & tob.

be made with okra (although why anyone would want to is questionable).

bedouin Nomadic people of the desert.

Beiti beitak "My house is thy house."

Bey Turkish title: lord or governor. Turkish titles were used in Egypt which was, until 1914, a province of the Ottoman Empire. They were bestowed on British officials and military persons as well as on Egyptians. Such titles followed rather than preceded the name.

Bimbashi A Turkish title corresponding to the rank of major.

Bismallah "In God's name." (An invitation from the host to begin eating; the **Bismillahi**, "the blessing.")

bokra (**bukra**, **bookra**, **boukra**) Tomorrow.

bamiyeh An Egyptian dish of hibiscus pods lightly cooked and sprinkled with lime juice. It can also

burko Face veil; a long strip of white muslin reach-

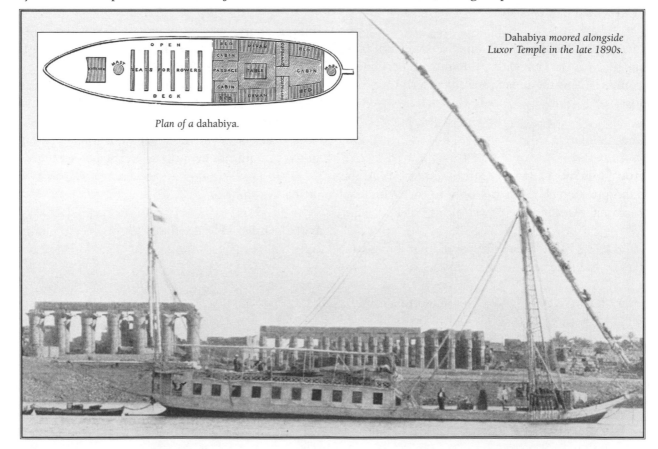

Plan of a dahabiya.

Dahabiya moored alongside Luxor Temple in the late 1890s.

*Feluccas under sail,
in late-19th-Century
tourist photos.*

ing from the bridge of the nose to the feet. Lower-class women wore one of coarser black cloth. The women of southern Egypt, particularly peasant women, often left off the face veil, but generally covered their heads with a separate piece of cloth or with a fold of their garment.

C

Copt Egyptian Christian.

Coptic The latest form of the ancient Egyptian language, written in Greek letters with some additional characters; also, the Christian church of Egypt, which used the Coptic language in its liturgy.

D

dahabiya (dahabeeyah) Essentially a houseboat; the favored means of Nile travel for wealthy tourists and officials in the 19th Century, varying in size and elegance depending on the means of the traveler. They were sailing ships, using the north wind to travel upstream (south) from Cairo. When the wind failed, the unfortunate crewmen had to row, or tow, the vessel. On the return voyage downstream, the current served as motive power. Motorized *dahabiyas* were used at a later time, but Amelia never approved of them.

Dervish Member of a Muslim religious order; the Dervish orders, (equivalent in some ways to Christian monks) believed in attaining religious ecstasy through various repetetive motions (such as the spinning of the "Whirling Dervishes").

dilk The tattered robe of a Dervish or *fakir*.

djinni (pl. djinn) Supernatural being. Of pre-Adamite origin, it is an intermediate species between men and angels and may be either good or evil. See *afrit*.

E

Effendi A Turkish title, used more indiscriminately than Bey or Pasha: lord, master.

el hamdu lillah See *Alhamdulillah*.

F

fahddling Gossiping.

fakir An Islamic holy man, an ascetic and beggar.

fantasia A celebration involving music, dancing, and occasionally performances by magicians and jugglers; in best cases, a good deal of food and general rejoicing.

feddan A measure of land equal, in Amelia's time, to slightly over an acre.

fellah (pl. fellahin) Peasant.

felucca (felukah) Small sailing boat (often used by the Emersons as a ferry for crossing the Nile).

Feranzawi Frenchman.

fez See tarboosh.

footah Napkin, towel.

fuul medemes A popular dish made of broad beans (usually fava beans), boiled and mashed, seasoned with butter, linseed oil, or lime juice.

G
gaffir Guard.

galabeeyah (**galabia**, **jellabiyah**) Full-length shirt or robe with long sleeves. The basic garment of the poorer classes. Amelia tended to use it as a generic term, instead of distinguishing between the various types of robe-like garments.

gebel Mountain, hill.

Steamer cabin boy wearing a galabeeyah & a fez.

ghurza Opium den. Smoking facilities are provided by the *ghurzazi*.

gibbeh (**jubba**) Floor-length coat-like robe worn by men and women, usually over a kaftan. The women's version is not as wide as the man's.

Gurnawi Resident of the village of Sheikh el Gurneh, on the West Bank at Thebes.

H
habara (**habarah**) A woman's garment worn when she is outside the house; black silk and voluminous, covering head, hands, and body.

habib Friend.

hakim Physician.

haremlik The women's part of the house.

harim Popularly used to refer to a man's wives, more properly the private part of the house where the women lived.

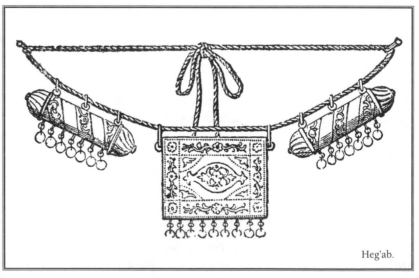

Heg'ab.

heg'ab An amulet most often containing an excerpt from the Koran enclosed in a case of gold or silver, some cylindrical, some square and flat, usually beautifully ornamented. Worn at the girdle on a chain or cord that passes over the left shoulder.

Hemet najurahmen Title for the high priestess of the Lost Oasis. Derived from the ancient Egyptian title, *hemet netcher Amen* ("God's Wife of Amon").

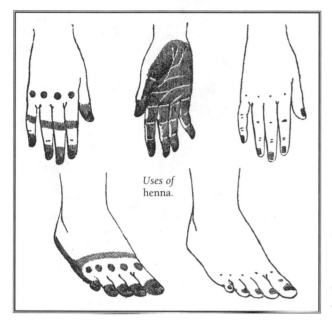

Uses of henna.

henna A reddish dye made from the leaves of *Lawsonia inermis*, sometimes called "Egyptian privet." Ground and made into a paste by adding water, it was used to color the palms and soles of the feet, the fingers and toes, and/or the nails.

hezaam Girdle, a colored shawl or long piece of figured muslin.

howadji Traveler, tourist.

Huquq al Ma'ra Equal rights for women.

I

Inglizi Englishman.

Inshallah "As God pleases."

J

jemedar A rank in the Anglo-Indian army, equivalent to lieutenant.

Jihad The root of the word is struggle, exertion. *Jihad* is the struggle of the individual against his lower self (*nafs*). The lesser *jihad* means war against infidels under the conditions defined by the Koran. The word can also be used metaphorically, like "crusade."

K

ka'ah Large, elegant reception room or salon, in the harem or elsewhere.

Entertaining the howadji.

A ka'ah.

kaf Coffee.

kaftan (**kuftan**, **caftan**) Long-sleeved, floor-length garment open down the front and held by a girdle.

Kaikoman Turkish word for governor.

keif halak Lit., "How is your health?"; generally, "How are you?"

kemengeh Stringed instrument played with a bow.

Musician playing a kemengeh.

A bedouin wearing a khafiya.

khafiya (**khafiyeh**, **khufiyeh**) Bedouin headdress; a scarf arranged over the head and held in place by a cord called an *u'kal* or *agab*.

Koran (**Quran**) The holy book of Islam, given by the angel Gabriel to the Prophet Mohammed.

kunafeh A dish made of wheat flour vermicelli fried in clarified butter and sweetened with honey.

kurbash A whip made of hippopotamus or crocodile hide.

L

la No.

la lahu illa-Allah A funeral procession chant.

lebbkah (**lebbek**; **Albizzia lebbek**) A splendid shade tree which can reach 80 feet (they line roads along the Nile).

libdeh Brown felt cap worn under turban.

liwan Roofed colonnades used for prayer, around the court of a mosque.

M

Maas salama (**Ma'as-salama**) "Peace be with thee."

Mahshallah "What God pleases."

makhba Secret room or cupboard.

malesh A catch-all word meaning, among other things, "it's okay," "too bad," "never mind," "that's life"...add your own! (Instructions for use: accent on the first syllable with a simultaneous shrug of the shoulders.)

Mameluke Originally male slaves trained by the Ottomans as soldiers and guards of the caliph. In

A Mameluke.

Mashrabiya.

mashrabiya Wooden window screens with intricate lattice work.

the 13th Century AD, they overthrew the sultan and formed their own dynasty, of which there were two: the first from 1250-1382 AD; the second from 1382-1517 AD, during which year Egypt was conquered by the sultan (Selim I of Constantinople) and became a Turkish province.

mandarah A reception room for male visitors.

mankaleh Game played with shells or pebbles on a board. The rules are far too complicated to explain, but if the reader is interested he can find a description in Lane's *Modern Egyptians* (modern for 1836, that is).

marhaba Welcome.

mastaba A simple stone bench, a flat lintel supported by two stones, found outside modern Egyptian homes and shops.

mudir Governor, boss.

muezzin The officiant who chants the prayers from the minaret of a mosque. Many have very fine voices, which are now amplified by loudspeakers. Ramses proved his claim that he could distinguish the voices of the different muezzins by imitating them at stupefying length.

Muslim (Moslem) Follower of the faith of Islam who worships a sole god (Allah) and His prophets, the last and greatest of whom was Mohammed. See article on Islam by Salima Ikram.

N

na'am Certainly.

nargeelah (narghileh) Water pipe.

Relaxing with a nargeelah.

nishuf wish-shak fi kheir "May you be fortunate at our next meeting."

Nur Misur Light of Egypt, Nefret's Egyptian sobriquet.

O

Omdeh (Omda) Head man of a village.

P

Pasha Turkish title indicating a rank higher than bey.

R

Ramadan The Muslim holy month, commemorating the time when the Prophet first received the

The hour of prayer during Ramadan.

revelation. No food or drink may be taken between sunrise and sunset. See the article on Islam by Salima Ikram.

reis The word can refer to the captain of a ship, or, as in the case of Abdullah, the foreman of a work crew.

rekkit Peasant in the language of the Lost Oasis; derived from ancient Egyptian *rekhyt,* "common people."

ruhi min hina, ya bint Shaitan "Get away from

A sha'er *entertaining his audience.*

here, daughter of Satan."

S

saffragi (suffragi) Hotel servant.

saiyid Gentleman, sir.

Salaam alkeikhum (Essalamu 'aleikhum) "Peace be upon you" (greeting).

salah The prescribed hours of prayer for Muslims: dawn, midday, mid-afternoon, sunset, night (about an hour and a half after sunset).

Sayyida Madame (Mrs.).

sebil An elaborate ornamental fountain (erected as a charitable act by one wishing for favor with God).

sha'er Storyteller.

shahid Small monument placed over a Muslim's grave.

Sharia Main street, boulevard.

Sheikh Head of a village or tribe; a title of authority; an honorary title given a holy man, a venerable old man, or one learned in the sacred writings.

Sherif Arab title, held by some princes and governors. It indicates a descent from the Prophet, through his daughter Fatima.

shintiyan Wide trousers worn by women; tied round the hips with a cord or sash, so long in the legs they have to be hitched up by strings tied around the calves.

shukran Thank you.

siim issaagha The argot or secret language used by the guild of gold- and silversmiths, largely based on Hebrew.

Sirdar Commander-in-chief.

sitt Honored lady.

Sitt Hakim Lady doctor (Amelia's sobriquet).

sudarayee Long, full drawers.

A suk of Cairo, early 20th Century.

suk (suq, sook) Market, bazaar.

T

tafl Strata of shale-like rock.

taiyib "It is good."

taiyib matakhafsh "Don't be afraid."

taftish A checkpoint or office.

takhtabosh A recess open on one side to a court,

on the ground floor.

tarboosh Fez; red felt upside-down flowerpot-shaped hat.

Egyptian official in a tarboosh.

tarhah Head veil.

tariqa The path of spiritual development followed by a particular Muslim sect.

tob Long, loose woman's gown with voluminous sleeves, worn out of doors.

Touareg A tribe of desert raiders known for their ferocity. Called "The Forgotten of God" by their despairing victims, or "The Veiled Ones," because of the blue veils that protected their faces from blowing sand.

tukhul Nubian hut.

tumbak A variety of coarse Persian tobacco.

Tumbakiyeh The old tobacco warehouse district in Cairo.

turab Dirt, dust; used to describe tomb fill.

U

ukaf! Halt!

U'aleikum es-salam warahmet "And with you be God's peace."

W

wadi Canyon.

Wadi leading to the Valley of the Kings.

wah Exclamation of surprise.

Wahyat en-nebi "By the life of the Prophet."

Wallahi-el-azem "By God the Great."

Y

Ya salam Heavens!

yalla! yalla! Forward! Quickly! ("Giddy-up" to a donkey).

yelek A long-sleeved garment, like a man's kaftan but tighter fitting and lower cut in front. Buttons down the front, open on each side from hips to floor. Worn over other garments.

Yimessikum bilkheir (Allah yimessikum bilkheir) "Good evening" (lit., "God grant you a good evening").

Z

zaboot A long shirt or gown open nearly to the

waist; worn by poorer classes.

zabtiyeh Police station.

EGYPTOLOGICAL TERMS

amulet A small ornament or charm meant to protect the wearer from bad luck or evil spirits. Ancient Egypt boasted quite a variety of amulets.

ankh The hieroglyphic sign meaning "life."

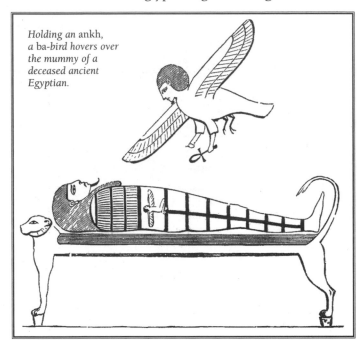

Holding an ankh, a ba-bird hovers over the mummy of a deceased ancient Egyptian.

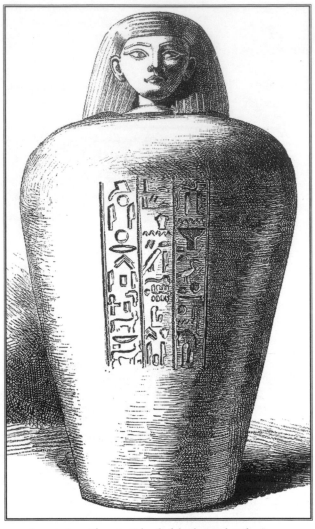

Canopic jar with portrait-head of the deceased as the stopper.

ba One aspect of the human personality which was depicted as a bird with human head and arms, and which appeared after death and visited the tomb to receive offerings.

canopic jars A set of four stone or ceramic vessels used to hold the viscera — the liver, lungs, stomach, and intestines — removed during mummification, thus preserving them for later use in the Hereafter. The heart, which was the seat of intelligence, was left in the body.

cartonnage Substance made of layers of linen or papyrus soaked in paste, molded into shape and

Cartonnage mummy mask of Thuyu, mother of Queen Tiye.

allowed to harden; used for mummy masks and coffins at certain periods.

cartouche An oval shape that enclosed certain royal names; it's supposed to be a loop of rope; the word is derived from the French word for cartridge.

demotic An extremely abbreviated script used to write a late form of the Egyptian language; used from about the 7th Century BC.

faience A glazed composition appropriately named *tjehnet*, "that which gleams," by the ancient Egyptians. Technically, faience is powdered quartz which has been coated or mixed with a glaze of sodium or potassium calcium-silicate, and then fired; more often it describes sand which has undergone the same process. This material was used to make the polished, brilliantly colored beads, statuettes, amulets, and jewelry.

false door Carved or painted doorway found in tombs, through which the spirit of the dead person could pass in order to receive offerings.

Mastabas.

hieratic Cursive script derived from the hieroglyphic signs; written with pen (brush) and ink on documents.

hieroglyphs (adj. *hieroglyphic*) Formal Egyptian script used for monumental inscriptions; means "sacred carvings."

hypostyle hall A large temple court filled with columns and lit by clerestory windows.

ka Another aspect of the human personality (see ba). The creator god Khnum shaped an exact double of each individual at birth; this was one's ka.

mastaba A rectangular tomb of stone or mud

19th-Century reconstruction of the Hypostyle Hall of the Amen Temple at Karnak.

brick. The word is Arabic, referring to the benches (*mastabas*) outside Egyptian houses, which were of the same shape.

natron Carbonate salts which, because of their dehydrating properties, were particularly useful in mummification.

obelisk The tall, pointed, four-sided shaft used to ornament temples and proclaim the power of the monarch by means of carved inscriptions. Ideally, obelisks were not pieced together but consisted of a single shaft of stone, the bigger the better; it was no mean trick to cut these massive objects out of a quarry and transport them.

Obelisk standing in front of the pylon gateway of Luxor Temple, prior to the monument's excavation in the 1880s.

ostrakon (pl. **ostraca**) Scraps of stone or pottery which have writing on them. Papyrus was expensive; schoolchildren used *ostraca* for practice, while scribes used it for jotting down notes or (occasionally) drawing vulgar pictures.

papyrus The ancient Egyptian version of writing paper, made from the pulp of the papyrus plant, in rectangular sheets or rolls, usually many feet long.

Anthropoid stone sarcophagus of the 19th Dynasty.

pharaoh The title comes from the Egyptian words *per-aa*, meaning "Great House"; it was not applied to the king until the early 18th Dynasty.

pylon Monumental temple gateway consisting of two massive towers with sloping sides. The surfaces were covered with reliefs and inscriptions praising the god and glorifying the pharaoh who built the monument. In their heyday they were brilliantly colored and gaudy.

Saite The 26th Dynasty (664-525 BC), which reunited the country after a period of upheaval. The name is derived from the city of Sais in the Delta, which was the northern capital of Egypt at the time.

sarcophagus The outermost stone (sometimes wooden) box containing up to three coffins fitted one inside the other, and, finally, the mummy.

scarab A popular amulet in the shape of the *scarabaeus* beetle. The flat underside was used for inscriptions or cartouches.

logical interest turns up — at which point one excavates. A somewhat hit-and-miss method, it is not used by responsible excavators.

19th Dynasty stela.

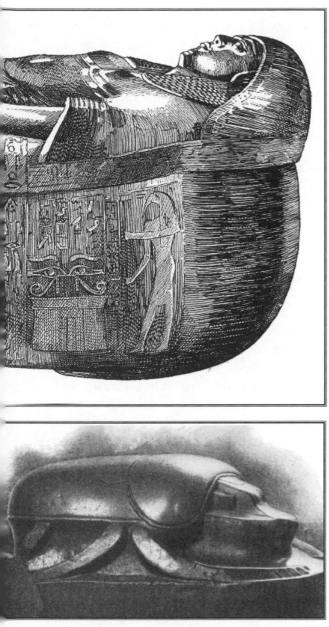

Colossal black-granite scarab in the British Museum.

serdab Small room in a tomb containing a statue of the owner; a narrow opening in the wall between the *serdab* and the room where offerings were placed enabled the spirit of the dead to receive offerings.

sistrum A rattle-like musical instrument which was played in the presence of certain divinities.

sondages French term referring to the practice of digging pits in an area until something of archaeo-

stela Rectangular inscribed stone slab, typically with a rounded top.

tell Artificial mound consisting of successive layers of occupation, one on top of the other.

titulary The formal names and titles of an Egyptian king. In its fully developed form, it consisted of five separate elements: the Horus name, the prenomen, the nomen, the Golden Horus, and the Two Ladies' names. The prenomen and nomen were written in cartouches. The prenomen was a king's throne name. The nomen or personal name is the one most people know: Thutmose, Amenhotep, etc.

uraeus Cobra image worn on the brow of the king, symbolizing the protection of the goddess Wadjet, one of the patron deities of Lower Egypt; at some periods queens wore a double uraeus.

A pharaoh wearing a uraeus *on his brow,
two of which also decorate the frame of this 19th-Century engraving.*

ushabti (**shabti**, **shawabti**) Small, inscribed funerary servant-statues of wood, faience, or other material, found in innumerable tombs. When the proper spell was pronounced the animated statue performed the tasks required of the dead person in the Hereafter.

MISCELLANEOUS

Circassian A tribe of people from the Caucasus; many settled in Turkey and Egypt.

dragoman A guide and, in some cases, general factotum for inexperienced travelers in Egypt.

Journal d'Entrée (French) The register of objects acquired by the Cairo Museum and kept up-to-date (usually) by the curator or another official.

Red Crescent The Islamic equivalent of the Red Cross.

Sahib "Master" in Hindustani. A title of respect for Europeans (especially the British in India), it came to be used by the British as a self-congratulatory designation of moral and social superiority. A *sahib* was "one of us," an upper-class person.

Sublime Porte (Ottoman Turkish) refers to the great gate before the government offices in Constantinople and hence, by extension, the government itself; there are parallels in "White House" and "Number 10 Downing Street."

terrassieurs (French, "terrace guys") Attractive Egyptian men who hung around the terraces of the big hotels attempting to pick up women tourists who were, in most cases, perfectly happy to be "picked."

*Engraving of a
Late Period* ushabti.

Opposite, tourist & his dragoman pose together in the Horus & Sobek temple at Kom Ombo in 1896.

INTRODUCING SOME ANCIENT EGYPTIANS
(Human & Divine)

As in the case of Arabic, transliterations from the Egyptian vary, which is why you will see Amen, Amun, and Amon, Zoser and Djoser, etc. The name Amenophis for Amenhotep is a bastardized form, half-Egyptian and half-Greek. It is still favored by English Egyptologists, as is Thutmosis (Thutmose), but Emerson refused to countenance it. A complete biographical dictionary would fill several volumes; included here are only the names of key importance to Readers of the journals. For further information on the ancient Egyptians, see: "Ancient Egypt 101: A Quick Refresher Course" by Betty Winkelman and "A Splendid Overview of Egyptology: Napoleon to WWI" by Dennis Forbes.

A

Ahmose A Theban prince, grandson of Queen

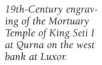

Akhenaton

Amen-Re

19th-Century engraving of the Mortuary Temple of King Seti I at Qurna on the west bank at Luxor.

Tetisheri, he completed the expulsion of the Hyksos begun by his father, Sekenenre Tao II, and reunited Egypt, starting the 18th Dynasty.

Akhenaton Late l8th Dynasty. The heretic pharaoh who abandoned the worship of the old gods in favor of Aton, the sun disc, and founded a new capital at El Amarna.

Amen (**Amun, Amon**) Originally an obscure and indistinct god — the Hidden One was one of his epithets — he amalgamated with Re and became Amen-Re, great ruler of Thebes, and just about everyplace else. Lord of the silent, ruler of Karnak. His sacred animals were the goose and the curly-horned ram. Depicted as a human figure, sometimes with a ram's head.

Amenemhat 12th Dynasty. There were four of them. The dark-gray mud-brick pyramid of Amenemhat III at Dahshur, familiarly known as the Black Pyramid, is the one with which Amelia and Emerson became only too well acquainted.

Amenhotep 18th Dynasty. Three of them, if you don't include Akhenaton, who was for a time Amenhotep IV, before he changed his name along with his religion. Amenhotep III was his father, also known in modern times as "the Magnificent."

Amnit Crocodile-headed monster who stood behind the scales in the Hall of Justice and devoured the souls of those who failed the Judgment of Osiris. We don't know of anyone who did, although the ancient Egyptians would probably have considered Akhenaton a prime candidate for the oblivion that befell the guilty.

Ankhesenamen Queen of Tutankhamen, third daughter of Akhenaton and Nefertiti. She may have had two female children, both of whom were stillborn. She disappeared from the scene shortly after the death of her husband, when the throne was taken over by Ay, one of his courtiers. Her ultimate fate is unknown.

Anubis God of cemeteries, patron of embalming. He escorted the souls of the dead to the Judgment. His sacred animal was the jackal (or possibly a wild dog; it's hard to tell from his representations).

Apophis Serpent deity of darkness and enemy of Re. Attacked the boat of Re as it passed through the realms of darkness before its journey across the sky and had to be defeated by Set, who was a good guy that day (in one version of the tale, anyway; in another version the gods pooled their magic for the battle, and in still another the Great Cat of Re defended the Bringer of Light).

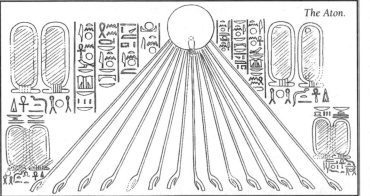

The Aton.

Aton Akhenaton's "sole god." For a brief period he was identified with Re and shown as human with a falcon's head, but before long all anthropomorphic representations were abandoned in favor of a sun disk with rays ending in human hands that held

out the sign of life to his son, Akhenaton, and to the latter's family.

Ay (Aye) Tutankhamen's short-reigned, non-royal successor, who took the throne after the young king died without issue. His unfinished tomb is in the West Valley of the Kings.

B
Bastet Cat goddess of Bubastis. Shown as a woman with a cat's head. An amiable deity who shared many of the attributes of Hathor.

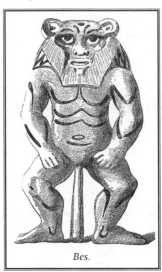

Bes.

Bes Depicted as a bow-legged dwarf and always full face (most unusual in Egyptian art). A jolly god, who looked after women in childbirth and — although Amelia never actually said so — the pleasures of the bedchamber.

C
Cheops Greek form of Khufu.

Chephren Greek form of Khafre.

D
Djoser (Zoser) 3rd Dynasty. Builder of the Step Pyramid at Sakkara, the world's first great construction in stone.

G
God's Wives of Amen Also called the Adorers of the God, these women, some of whom were Saite princesses, occupied the position of high priestess of Amen at Thebes during the Late Period dynasties. Their tomb chapels are located within the temple enclosure of Medinet Habu.

H
Harkhuf One of the adventurous princes of El-

ephantine during the 6th Dynasty, who led caravans into Africa in search of the exotic treasures the Egyptians enjoyed — including a dancing pygmy. His tomb is at Aswan.

Hathor in her form as the Divine Cow.

Hathor Daugther of the sun god, Re. A benevolent goddess, patroness of love and beauty, music and pleasure, and one of the guardians of the dead. The cow was her sacred animal and she is sometimes shown as a human female with the ears of a cow, at other times as wholly a cow.

Hatshepsut 18th Dynasty. Daughter of Thutmose I, wife of Thutmose II, she co-ruled as king with her nephew Thutmose III. Scholars are still arguing about the precise relationship between Hatshepsut and Thutmose III. While she lived he was certainly the lesser of the two kings, and at some time after her death he destroyed or usurped many of her monuments; but the virulent hatred he was supposed to have felt for his aunt may be only a romantic theory. The magnificent temple at Deir el Bahari on the west bank at Luxor is her mortuary monument.

Horemheb Last ruler of the 18th Dynasty, non-royal successor of Ay. He was not related to the previous Thutmosid royal house, whose last scion was Tutankhamen.

Horus One of the greatest and most confusing of Egyptian gods. As the son of Osiris and Isis, he fought his murderous uncle, Set, for the kingship. He was also a sun god — Horakhte, Horus of the Horizon — shown as a falcon or falcon-headed human. The Egyptian king was the "Horus," until he died and became an "Osiris."

Hyksos Line of Western Asiatic rulers of northern Egypt during the 15th and 16th dynasties (c. 1648-1539 BC). They were driven out by Ahmose, king of Thebes. The word means "rulers of foreign countries."

I

Isis Wife of Osiris, mother of Horus. She was the ideal wife, tracking down the body of her murdered husband and restoring it to life; and the ideal mother, often shown nursing the child on her lap. Al-

Isis.

ways one of the great goddesses of Egypt, her cult became very popular in the later period and spread throughout the Roman empire.

The intact burial chamber of the Tomb of Kha.

K

Kha An architect whose remarkable intact 18th Dynasty tomb was found at Deir el Medina.

Khafre 4th Dynasty. Builder of the 2nd Pyramid and probably the Sphinx, which is believed to be a portrait of him. Not much else is known about the rulers of this period, but with monuments like those, what else do you need to know?

Khufu 4th Dynasty. Predecessor, probably father, of Khafre; builder of the Great Pyramid.

Khnum Creator god (one of them) who modeled the *ka* of the newborn baby on his potter's wheel. Sacred animal, the ram.

M

Maat Her name is usually translated as "truth," but this was a complicated concept in ancient Egypt, as it is today. She was the daughter of Re, and it was

Maat.

against her symbol, a feather, that the heart of the deceased was weighed at the Judgment. Maat is usually depicted as an attractive lady with that feather on her head.

Menkaure (Mycerinos) 4th Dynasty. Builder of the third and smallest pyramid at Giza.

Menes Traditionally, the first king of a united Egypt, who began the 1st Dynasty.

Min The one with the enormous..... Amelia would say no more, nor did she ever allow Emerson to do so. Obviously a god of fertility. The correct word for his remarkable condition is ithyphallic.

Montu (Mentu) A war god. Sacred animals, the falcon and the ram.

Montuhotep (Mentuhotep) There were several of them. The greatest was Montuhotep II, who began the 11th Dynasty and reunited the country after the 1st Intermediate Period. The remains of his remarkable mortuary temple lie next to that of Hatshepsut at Deir el Bahari, Luxor.

N

Nefertari Chief wife of Ramses II, whose beautifully decorated and recently restored tomb is located in the Valley of the Queens.

Nefertiti Queen of Akhenaton, known to the world from her exquisite painted-limestone portrait head found at El Amarna.

Neith A warrior goddess, shown in human form, her symbol a bow and crossed arrows.

Nekhbet Predynastic vulture (and mother) goddess of a portion of Upper Egypt, became the protector of the king in Dynastic Egypt. Eventually came to symbolize the White Crown of Upper Egypt.

Nephthys Sister of Osiris and Isis, wife of her brother, Set. Regardless of her marriage, she took the side of her brother, Osiris, during the conflict between evil Set and good Osiris.

Nut Sky goddess. Her body spanned the heavens; she swallowed the sun each night and gave birth to it each morning.

O

Osiris According to legend he was a primeval king of Egypt who brought peace and plenty. Murdered by his jealous brother, Set, he was revived by his sister-wife, Isis, who bore him a (very) posthumous son, Horus. The gods appointed him king of the Afterworld and he presided over the judgment which had to be passed before a dead man or woman could enter into eternal life.

Osiris, king of the Afterworld.

P

Ptah Patron of craftsmen, one of several creator gods. He is easy to identify because his body is shrouded like a mummy; he wears a curious sort of skull-cap and carries a combination of sceptres. His home base was Memphis.

R

Ra (Re). The sun god par excellence who became amalgamated with Amen and, as Amen-Re, was top god of Egypt during and after the 18th Dynasty. He was depicted as a man with a hawk head crowned by a sun disk.

King Ramses II.

Ramses (Rameses, Ramesses) There were eleven of them, but only two are of interest to Readers of the journals: Ramses II, builder of Abu Simbel and innumerable other temples, whom Amelia considered conceited even for an Egyptian pharaoh; and Ramses III, whose mortuary temple at Medinet Habu Emerson lusted after.

Ramose One of the high officials of Amenhotep III and Akhenaton, whose beautifully decorated tomb at Gurneh is still popular with tourists.

S

Saite Princesses See God's Wives of Amen; also Shepenwepet.

Engraving of the mummy of King Sekenenre Tao II.

Sekenenre Tao II A courageous but unfortunate ruler of Thebes at the end of the 17th Dynasty, who began the struggle against the Hyksos — a people of Asiatic origin who had occupied Lower Egypt for over 100 years. His mummy shows the marks of horrible wounds, and it is assumed he died in battle. Son of Queen Tetisheri, who was regarded as the grand matriarch of the 18th Dynasty.

Statues of Sekhmet at the Mut temple-complex.

Sekhmet Lioness-headed warrior goddess. Many statues of her have been found around the Temple of Mut at Karnak.

Senenmut This is now the accepted reading, rather than Senmut as before. One of Hatshepsut's (q.v.) favored officials, who was responsible for many of her monuments. Was he also her lover? We will probably never know.

Senusert (Senwosret, Sesostris, Usertsen) A popular name for 12th Dynasty pharaohs. Senusert I was the lad who almost lost his throne when his father Amenemhat I was assassinated. Amelia "translated" the story of Sinuhe, which describes this event.

Seshat Goddess of writing.

Set Bitter enemy and murderer of his brother, Osiris. After the child Horus (son of Isis and the temporarily reanimated Osiris) came to manhood, he fought his uncle for the kingship. It was eventually awarded to Horus, but Set was neither condemned nor punished; Re apparently forgave him and

The mummy of King Seti I, as displayed in the Cairo Museum early in the 20th Century.

Colossal granite statue of Senenmut, photograph-ed by a tourist shortly after its 1896 discovery in the Temple of Mut precinct at Karnak. The kneel-ing figure holds a rebus of the name of his patron, the female pharaoh Hatshepsut.

awarded him his own place as a god of storm and chaos. Set is thus, in one sense, a force of evil opposed to the noble Osiris; yet he was the patron of the royal house during the 19th Dynasty. A typically confusing bit of Egyptian theology.

Seti (old form, **Sethos**) Man of Set. The name of two 19th-Dynasty pharaohs, the foremost being Seti I, whose temple at Luxor was the scene of one of Ramses and David's more unlucky encounters. His mummy was found in the Deir el Bahari cache; and, as mummies go, it is extremely handsome.

Shepenwepet One of the God's Wives of Amen,

Sobek.

whose reburial with that of three other Saite princesses was found by Bertie Vandergelt at Deir el Medina.

Smenkhkare A mysterious, short-lived king, predecessor of Tutankhamen, who was probably his brother or half brother. His may be the skeletal remains found in the strange KV55 tomb, with which the Emersons were involved in 1907. Some people still think the bones are those of Akhenaton. They are wrong.

Sneferu First king of the 4th Dynasty. He built two of the greatest pyramids in Egypt, at Dahshur. His third one at Medum may have been started by his predecessor.

Sobek The crocodile god. His centers of worship were in the Fayum and at Kom Ombo in Upper Egypt.

T

Tausert (**Taweret**, **Thoueris**) Protector of women in childbirth. For some reason she is always shown as a monstrous-looking, pregnant hippopotamus. Also the name of the queen of Seti II, who ruled briefly after him as pharaoh.

The hippo goddess, Tausert, as depicted on a furniture piece from the Tomb of Yuya & Thuyu.

Statue of the god Khonsu with the features of King Tutankhamen.

Tetisheri Queen of Senakhtenre Tao I, mother of Sekenenre Tao II, grandmother of Ahmose I (q.v.). Her hidden tomb at Dra Abu el Naga on the west bank at Luxor was found by Radcliffe Emerson in 1900.

Thoth God of wisdom and learning, the divine scribe. He sometimes is shown as a man with the head of an ibis, one of his sacred animals. Otherwise depicted as a baboon.

Thutmose Four 18th Dynasty pharaohs; Thutmose III — the warrior king, who extended the boundaries of the Egyptian Empire to the Euphrates — is the most famous.

Thuyu Non-royal mother of Queen Tiye. See Yuya and Akhenaton.

Tiye (Tiyi, Ti) Queen during the later 18th Dynasty and chief wife of Amenhotep III; mother of the heretic pharaoh, Akhenaton. Theodore Davis believed he had found her tomb in 1907. He was wrong.

Tutankhamen A successor of Akhenaton, possibly his son. His name was originally Tutankhaton. He came to the throne at approximately nine years of age and married his (probably) half-sister, Ankhesenpaaton/Ankhesenamen. Shortly thereafter he changed his name, as did his wife, to honor Amen instead of the heretic's god, Aton, and abandoned Akhenaton's religious beliefs. He died at the age of 18, cause unknown (the theory that he may have been murdered is provocative but completely unsubstantiated) and was buried in the Valley of the Kings. The discovery of his tomb in 1922 was the archaeological sensation of the 20th Century. Amelia thought they had found it some years earlier, but Emerson always harbored doubts.

Y

Yuya Non-royal father of Queen Tiye and husband of Thuyu. His and his wife's joint tomb was found virtually intact in the Valley of the Kings in 1905 by James Quibell, who was working for Theodore Davis.

The well-preserved mummy of royal father-in-law Yuya.

Opposite, raised-relief depiction of Queen Tiye in the tomb of an 18th Dynasty Theban nobleman.

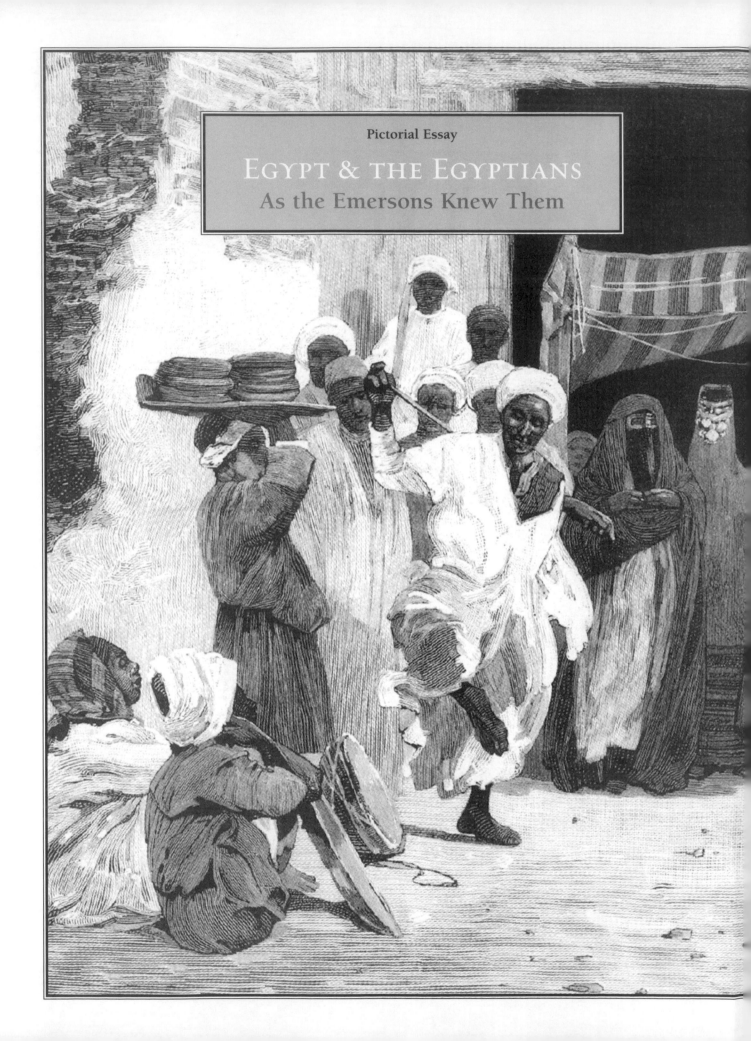

Pictorial Essay

EGYPT & THE EGYPTIANS
As the Emersons Knew Them

Above, a belly dancer performs for her audience, in a 19th-Century engraving; left, a group of fellahin youngsters are captured by a tourist early in the 20th Century; &, opposite, a European artist depicts snake charmers & onlookers in the courtyard of a Cairo residence; preceeding 2 pages, the start of a wedding procession.

Top, both pages, various Cairene occupations captured in 1905 photographs, left to right: a coffee vendor, cutlers, a wood turner, a sword maker, & cobblers. Below, 19th-Century engravings of, left, a bakery, &, right, a woman grinding grain while her husband relaxes with a nargeelah, or water pipe. Below opposite, water sellers at an urban well.

Opposite, the interior of a Turkish bath depicted in a 19th-Century engraving; Above, a funeral procession, the mourners & coffin preceded by a group of young boys; Below, con-
sulting a fortune teller; Bottom right, a barber
shop with fahddlers.

The Great Sphinx of Giza.

ANCIENT EGYPTIAN TEXTS
Referred to in the Journals

The assiduous Reader interested in the full literary and historical documents referred to in Amelia Peabody Emerson's journals is offered the following list. It should be noted that Mrs. Emerson's translations were often free and selective. The modern sources for these documents are:

Lichtheim, M., *Ancient Egyptian Literature*: Vol. I, *The Old and Middle Kingdom* (Berkeley, c. 1973); Vol. II, *The New Kingdom* (c. 1976); Vol. III, *The Late Period* (c. 1980).
Referenced below as * plus volume number (I, II, III) and page number.

Simpson, W.K., *The Literature of Ancient Egypt* (Yale, 1973).
Referenced below as #S plus page number.

The early version of the Boundary Stela has been translated most recently in:
Murnane,W.J., *Texts from the Amarna Period* (Atlanta, 1995).
Referenced below as +M plus page number.

Unfortunately, there is not a readily available translation of the *Dream Papyrus*. An excerpt and discussion will be found in: Brier, B., *Ancient Egyptian Magic* (New York, 1980), 216 ff.
Referenced below as ^B.

(The fragment of poetry quoted by Sethos — *"Let down your hair..."* is not ancient Egyptian. It appears to have been an original composition.)

THE QUOTES
Crocodile on the Sandbank *"The love of my sister...."* From a collection of New Kingdom love poems. *II 193; #S 130.

Curse of the Pharaohs "The Tale of the Two Brothers." *II 203; #S 92.

Lion in the Valley *"Set upon his mountain...."* From the Kadesh inscription of Ramses II. *III 63.

Deeds of the Disturber "The Hymn to Osiris." *II 81.

The Last Camel Died at Noon "The Wisdom of Ani." *II 135.

The Snake, the Crocodile and the Dog El Amarna Boundary Stela (first version). +M 73; "The Doomed Prince." *II 200; #S 85.

The Hippopotamus Pool Correspondence between Apophis and Sekenenre. #S 77.

Seeing a Large Cat "The Dream Papyrus." ^B.

The Ape Who Guards the Balance *The Book of the Dead*, "Chapter 125: The Declaration of Innocence." *II 124.

The Falcon at the Portal "The Story of Sinuhe." *I 222; #S 57.

He Shall Thunder in the Sky "The Contendings of Horus and Set." *II 214; #S 108.

Luxor Temple early in the 20th Century.

A first camel ride.

THE WIT & WISDOM OF AMELIA PEABODY
(& Some Others)

ON MARRIAGE

Some concessions to temperament are necessary if the marital state is to flourish.

Marriage should be a balanced stalemate between equal adversaries.

The combination of physical strength and moral sensibility combined with tenderness of heart is exactly what is wanted in a husband.

Husbands do not care to be contradicted. Indeed, I do not know anyone who does.

ON MARTYRDOM

One may be determined to embrace martyrdom gracefully, but a day of reprieve is not to be sneezed at.

Martyrdom is often the result of excessive gullibility.

A fondness for martyrdom, especially of the verbal variety, is common to the young.

Unnecessary discomfort is a form of martyrdom with which I have no sympathy.

I am sure even the early Christians raised no objection if Caesar postponed feeding them to the lions until the next circus.

ON MEN

No woman really wants a man to carry her off. She only wants him to want to do it.

Men are frail creatures, it is true; one does not expect them to demonstrate the steadfastness of women.

Men always have some high-sounding excuse for indulging themselves.

A man does not have to be a hero to gain confidence in himself. He only needs a woman to think he is one.

It was just like a man! They always invent feeble excuses to keep women from enjoying themselves.

ON CRIME & CRIMINALS

The worse a man is, the more profound his slumbers; for if he had a conscience he would not be a villain.

The trouble with unknown enemies is that they are so difficult to identify.

Candor is not a conspicuous characteristic of criminals.

Most people obey the orders of an individual who is pointing a gun at them.

Hired thugs are never reliable.

I have known several villains who were perfect gentlemen.

No mystery is insoluble--it is simply a matter of how much time and energy one is willing to expend.

ON LIFE, LOVE & CATS

He had an ulterior motive. Everyone does.

Particularly clever ideas do not always stand up under close scrutiny.

Once in the hansom cab she was at his mercy.

A woman's instinct, I always feel, supercedes logic.

I do not scruple to employ mendacity and a fictitious appearance of female incompetence when the occasion demands it.

When one is striding bravely into the future one cannot watch one's footing.

All is fair in love, war, and journalism.

Once a man has taken refreshment in your home and a chair in your sitting room, you are less likely to pitch him into a pond.

Superstition has its practical uses.

A lady cannot be blamed if a master criminal takes a fancy to her.

Abstinence, as I have often observed, has a deleterious effect on the disposition.

There is nothing so futile as regret for what cannot be mended.

Another shirt ruined!

No innocent person can lead a life so free of harmless vice.

It is better to have a demon as a friend than an enemy.

Humor is an excellent method of keeping a tight rein on unproductive displays of emotion.

Godly persons are more vulnerable than most to the machinations of the ungodly.

I hope I number patience among my virtues, but shilly-shallying, when nothing is to be gained by delay, is not a virtue.

A man asking for help ought at least give directions.

There is a layer of primitive savagery in all of us.

Love has a corrosive effect on the brain and the organs of moral responsibility.

If someone lies down and invites you to trample on him, you are a remarkable individual if you decline the invitation.

Cats cannot be held accountable for their actions, because they have no morals to speak of.

There are advantages to being notorious.

Even a woman of iron nerve may be taken aback by a dead mouse six inches from her nose.

It is difficult to be angry with a gentlemen who pays you compliments...especially impertinent compliments.

There are occasions on which a frank expression of opinion may be counterproductive as well as rude.

I always say there is nothing more comfortable or commodious than a tomb.

It is impossible for a writer to do herself justice if she is only talking to herself.

Though I deplore in the strongest possible terms the slightest deviation from straightforward behavior, there are occasions upon which moral good must yield to expediency.

There is never any excuse for violence. It is the last resort of people and nations who are too stupid to think of a sensible way of settling their differences.

EMERSON ON RELIGION
High minded individuals are much more dangerous than criminals. They can always find hypocritical excuses for committing acts of violence.

Cursed religion!

AND AS DAOUD OFTEN SAID,
The soft voice of the Father of Curses is like the growl of an angry lion.

Cairo street scene, 1905.

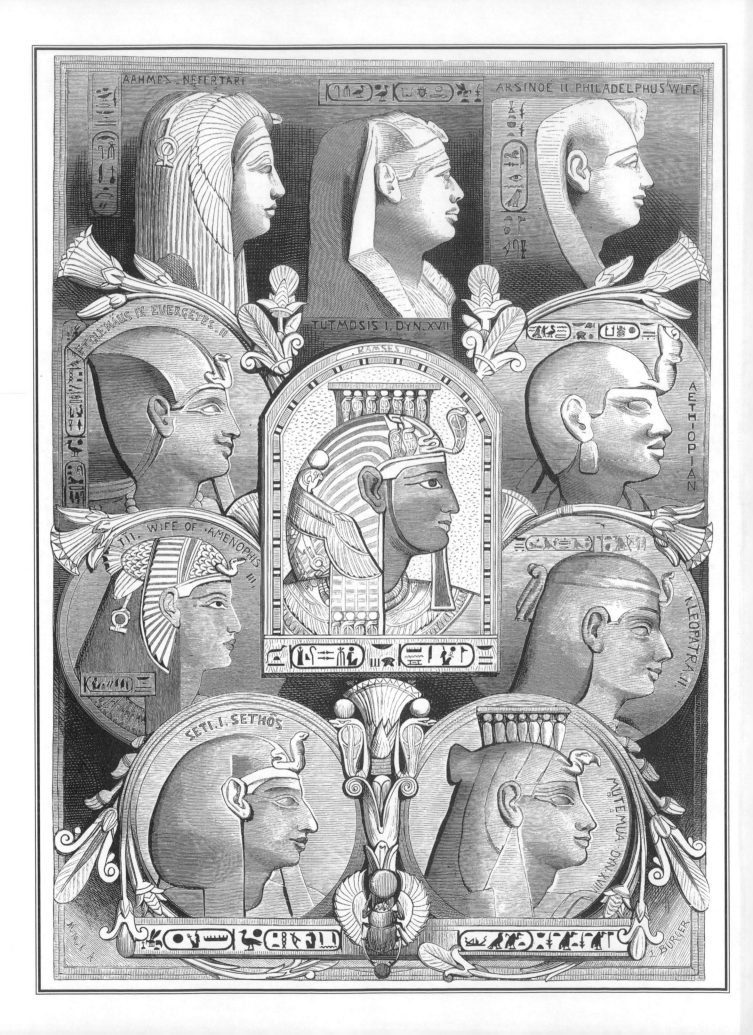

ANCIENT EGYPT 101
A Quick Refresher Course

The civilization of the ancient Egyptians lasted longer than any other in the world. Today we look at their works of art and the monuments to their gods and their dead and see them as unchanging, a land and people frozen in a way of life. Change did occur, not as rapidly as it does today and possibly not as dramatically, especially to our untrained eyes; but like any other civilization, ancient Egypt evolved.

The foundations of the Egyptian civilization were laid during Predynastic times, perhaps as early as 4500 BC, long before pharaohs ruled the Nile valley. As no written records exist because writing had not yet been developed, this is a rather murky period of Egyptian history. People who had relied on hunting and fishing and the gathering of edible wild plant materials began to settle down in one place, where a more stable life allowed them to cultivate crops and raise animals. Simple oval huts made of light materials were abandoned in favor of more permanent, rectangular mud-brick structures. Pottery reached a high level of skill, especially in the south, and a primitive form of art was developed. People began to dwell closer together, forming towns. Later, these towns were walled, indicating conflict among them.

Instead of simple, individual burials in the sand, as had long been the custom, the dead were placed in cemeteries, with a baked clay pot or two, a few weapons and some jewelry buried with them to accompany them to an afterlife. Since no religious texts from this period exist, one cannot be certain how the Egyptians envisaged an afterlife at this time. Later concepts of the afterlife included joining the sun god as he sailed across the sky, *"becoming one with the imperishable stars,"* and dwelling in a Paradise of endless food, somewhere in the West. A few people were given more elaborate burials, indicating the existence of a growing social elite. By about 3300 BC, centers of political power had formed in both Lower Egypt (the Delta) and Upper Egypt (the Nile valley south of the Delta to Aswan).

By 3050 BC (though dates vary somewhat), the local traditions of the villages and towns along the Nile had merged into a single culture and many of the features of pharaonic Egypt had developed. Large areas were ruled by local chieftain-kings, houses were arranged along streets rather than being randomly placed, and writing was in its infancy. The scene had been set for unification.

According to tradition, a powerful chieftain-king from Upper Egypt, named Menes, conquered and subjugated a northern king and united Egypt. The tale probably simplifies reality, but whatever the truth, beginning sometime around 3050 BC, a line of hereditary kings (known today as the 1st Dynasty) ruled the Nile Valley from Aswan to the Mediterranean. The basic attributes of kingship that were to survive throughout pharaonic history were developed at this time. Mastabas, large flat-topped rectangular tombs, were built to contain the bodies of kings and their grave goods, raising them far above their subjects in death as well as life.

By the end of the following dynasty, a tightly controlled, centralized state was ruled by a king from the capital of Memphis (Mennufer), located near modern Cairo. He associated himself with the gods Horus and Set, wore distinctive clothing, and surrounded himself with symbols and rituals that would set him apart from the people. These included the Double Crown denoting Upper and Lower Egypt, and the *Sed* festival, a ritual of renewal and regeneration performed by the king. An elaborate bureaucracy began to be formed, aided by the use of the rapidly developing system of writing. Many of these officials were members of the royal family. The Nile Valley was divided into a series of provinces whose chiefs reported in person to the king or to his closest and most important representative, the vizier.

With its foundations firmly laid, Egypt moved into one of the grandest periods of its existence, known today as the Old Kingdom, the age of the pyramids. By this time, the kings had developed into semi-divine beings, ever-present and all-powerful, and the gigantic pyramids in which they were buried reflect this notion. Statuary depicts solid, self-assured men embraced by the gods. As even a god-king could not possibly rule all facets of life, representatives in the form of priests and administrators performed the actual tasks in his place. Members of the royal family were appointed to all important positions, including that of provincial chief.

The energy and power of the Egyptian state during this time was exemplified by the pyramids, massive construction projects that required a large, well-organized work force supplied with materials, tools, housing, and sustenance. The capital was surrounded by cemeteries where nobles were buried in handsome tombs near that of the king. The Step Pyramid of the 3rd Dynasty king Djoser was the first massive construction in stone. It was followed by "true" pyramids at Dahshur and Giza; the Great Pyramid at the latter site was considered one of the Seven Wonders of the ancient world. Its builder, Khufu (Greek: Cheops), was succeeded by Khafre (Chephren) and Menkaure (Mycerinus), whose pyramid tombs are of slightly smaller size.

Military expeditions, using troops conscripted as needed from the provinces, were sent south to Nubia, not to occupy and settle the land but to ensure access to Nubia's rich gold mines, and to provide an uninterrupted flow of luxury items from farther up the Nile.

The progressively smaller pyramids built after the 4th Dynasty reflect a gradual social decline and a weakening of royal authority. A major factor was probably the growing independence and power of the provincial chiefs, who were no longer required to report regularly to Memphis and who now occupied posts that had become hereditary. Rainfall decreased after about 2900 BC, which in time reduced agricultural resources and therefore the wealth of the country. As the kings' economic power declined, royal control dwindled.

With the government decentralized and powerless, the provincial chiefs waged war among themselves. During this time, known as the 1st Intermediate Period, the land was in turmoil, the people suffered, and tombs and monuments were damaged or destroyed. Ephemeral kings, seeking legitimacy, clung to the old symbols, customs, and rituals, inadvertently preserving them for another, more stable time. By about 2100 BC, a powerful family of Thebes controlled the southern part of Egypt, while another family held the north. Battles raged between them until, as had happened almost 1,000 years earlier, south conquered north and the land was united once again.

Though staggered by the events of the past, the Egyptians were a resilient people. Under a new dynasty from Thebes, the Amenemhats and Senusrets, they rose to a second period of grandeur, known today as the Middle Kingdom.

The new kings were no longer considered semi-divine, and this is clearly shown in their statues, where they have ordinary human faces, often deeply lined and with down-turned mouths, reflecting the burden of leadership. They reigned long and well, appointing their sons as co-regents to ensure continuity of the dynasty. The land was prosperous and immigrants came from both the south and the east, resulting in a more cosmopolitan outlook. The capital was moved to Itj-tawy near the Fayum, an oasis-like area south and west of the Delta and a more central location from which to control the provincial chiefs.

All was not perfection however. The mud-brick pyramids built

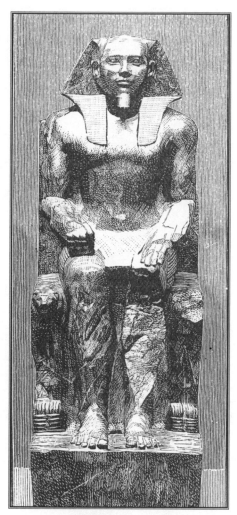

King Khafre of the 4th Dynasty.

*12th Dynasty sphinx
with the features of Amenemhat III.*

at this time — located at Dahshur, El Lisht, Mazghuna, El Lahun, and Hawara, not far from the new capital — had to contain elaborate mechanisms to foil thieves intent on stealing the rich grave goods buried with the king and his family.

The need to control trade, immigration, and intrusion from beyond the borders resulted in the creation of a national standing army. A chain of great fortresses was built along the Nile at the 2nd Cataract, a long stretch of rapids 200 miles south of Aswan that were impossible to navigate much of the year; and a defensive barrier known as the "Walls of the Ruler" was raised in the eastern Delta.

During the succeeding dynasty, this stability grew fragile and the country once again began to break up, this time due to external forces as well as internal dissension. The northern part of the Nile Valley was occupied by Asiatic people known as Hyksos, probably not as a result of war but through gradual incursion. They allied themselves with the Nubians to the south of Egypt, sandwiching the Egyptians between them. This situation, known as the 2nd Intermediate Period, lasted for over 100 years and was a source of constant irritation to the proud Egyptians, who finally marched off to war.

The Theban king, Ahmose, finally succeeded in driving the Hyksos out of Egypt and in bringing Nubia to its knees. Thus began a third era of grandeur, known as the New Kingdom, or the Empire period. For the first time, Egypt went far beyond its borders and became an international power, both militarily and economically.

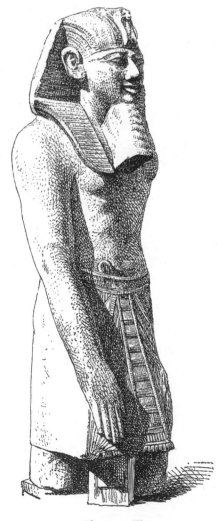

Thutmose III.

The 18th Dynasty is often called the Golden Age of Egypt. Ruled by kings whose power was absolute and a bureaucracy that functioned from the lowest to the highest level, it was, until near its end, a time of stability, prosperity, and achievement. Its artwork is elegant; statues of the rulers show self-satisfied men and women with Mona Lisa-like smiles. The capital was moved back to Memphis, and Thebes was the dynasty's religious center, primarily for the god Amen, who was favored by the the New Kingdom rulers. Temples to Amen and the other gods were built or expanded and mortuary temples were built for the kings. Huge temple bureaucracies were supported by immense quantities of food, goods, and landed estates.

The 18th Dynasty kings, having realized the vulnerability of pyramids, were buried in rock-cut tombs far below the surface of the earth in an isolated valley west of Thebes. Their sepulchers contained vast wealth destined to accompany them to a netherworld beautifully depicted on the tomb walls.

Under a series of strong, dynamic rulers, especially Thutmose I and Thutmose III, the Egyptian war machine, using the horse-drawn chariot — introduced by the Hyksos — and the powerful composite bow, marched into battle time and time again, to fight Nubians and Asiatics alike. Each time the the Egyptians returned victorious. Nubia was colonized, while the city-states of the Middle East were held as a loose alliance, each under the leadership of an Egypt-friendly ruler.

Luxury items, obtained in exchange for gold mined in Nubia and the eastern mountains, flowed into the capital and into the royal tombs. Advancement was often by meritorious service rather than noble status. Royal women achieved a new recognition, culminating in Hatshepsut's rule as female pharaoh early in the dynasty.

The reign of Amenhotep III near the end of the 18th Dynasty is often considered the apex of Egyptian civilization; and he has been called the Sun King, an epithet that reflects not only the glorious, gilded lifestyle of royalty and nobility at that time, but also a new royal iconography showing the rejuvenation of the aging king through his association with the sun god Re. Clothing changed drastically from the traditional simple kilt of the men and the plain sheath dress of the women to long kilts, tunics, and dresses of multiple pleated layers. Wig styles became more elaborate and jewelry larger and more showy.

Amenhotep III's son, who changed his name from Amenhotep to Akhenaton, took sun worship several steps further. He adopted the solar disk Aton as his sole god, forbade the worship of all other gods and built a new capital in a location previously uncontaminated by any other god, a place he called Akhetaton. New temples were constructed as gigantic courts open to the sun rather than the enclosed dark spaces common to the other gods. The artwork of the time, though still subject to previous conventions, depicted nature in a more realistic manner, although statues and reliefs of the king, his family and even courtiers were grotesquely deformed.

Within a few years, Akhenaton vanished from history. The last kings of the dynasty restored the old temples of the gods the ordinary

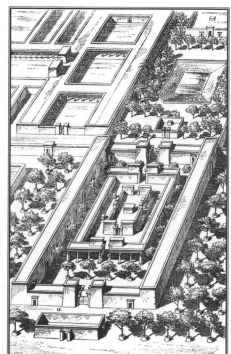

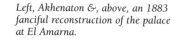

Left, Akhenaton &, above, an 1883 fanciful reconstruction of the palace at El Amarna.

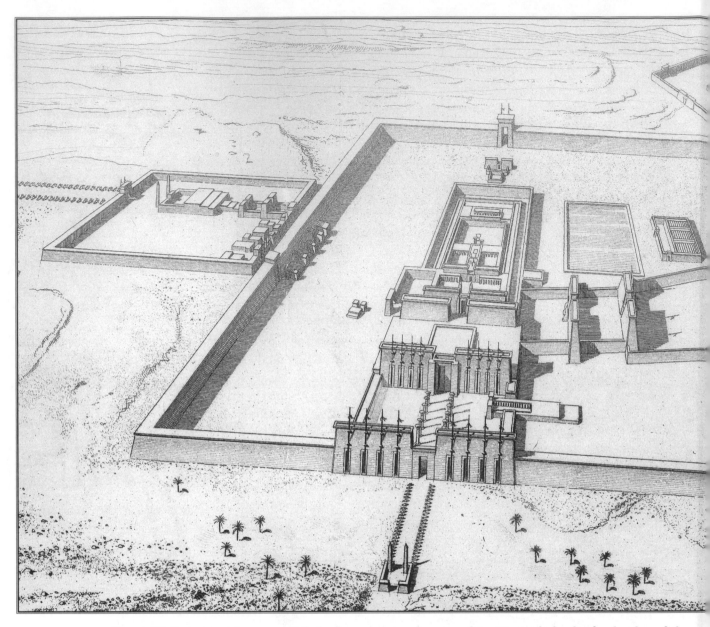

Above, a 19th-Century reconstruction of the great temple-complex at Thebes as it would have appeared towards the end of the Pharaonic Period. The sprawling Temple of Amen-Re, with its many pylon gateways, is surrounded by a massive wall (called a temenos) & is connected to the adjacent Temple of Mut (at far right) by an avenue of sphinxes, which also extends (out of the picture) to the Temple of the Southern Harim (modern Luxor Temple), a few kilometers to the south

people had never ceased to worship. Horemheb, the final ruler of the dynasty, reorganized the army and bureaucracy, and reformed administrative activities throughout the land.

The powerful kings of the next dynasty, the 19th, poured unimaginable wealth into the temples of Egypt's many gods, especially those of Amen. Fanciful wig and clothing styles remained in vogue. While artists were creating lovely, delicate reliefs and paintings, statues of the king, especially those used to adorn the many temples of Ramses II, were heavy and massive, the facial features often coarse.

Although life in Egypt appeared stable and secure, a dark cloud loomed just over the horizon. The Hittites had become a major power in the Middle East, and the strength and influence of the Assyrians was growing. Realizing the danger, Ramses II moved his capital from Memphis to the Delta, building a new city he named Pi-Ramesses. Early in his reign, he marched off to battle the Hittites, who

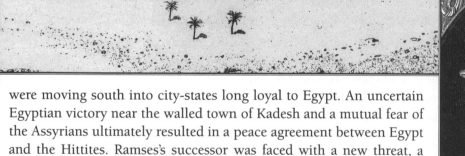

were moving south into city-states long loyal to Egypt. An uncertain Egyptian victory near the walled town of Kadesh and a mutual fear of the Assyrians ultimately resulted in a peace agreement between Egypt and the Hittites. Ramses's successor was faced with a new threat, a confederation of people from the Aegean and coastal Western Asia we now call the Sea Peoples. They, too, were defeated.

The vast donations to the temples gradually sapped the strength of the government, leading to political instability and civil disobedience. Workmen's strikes, harem conspiracies, terrible inflation, and tomb robberies are recorded during the 20th Dynasty. By its end, Herihor — who was not only the high priest of Amen but also commander of the troops — claimed the right to use the titles of the king. The land was once again torn asunder.

The 21st Dynasty marked the beginning of the 3rd Intermediate Period. The capital was moved to Tanis and its temples were built

Ramses II.

Engraving of the unwrapped mummy of 21st Dynasty Priest-King Pinudjem I, found in the Royal Mummies Cache in 1881. It is missing today.

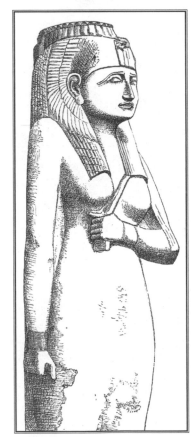

*Ameneritis,
25th Dynasty God's Wife of Amen.*

of stone taken from nearby Pi-Ramesses. While the kings ruled the northern part of Egypt from there, the high priests of Amen-Re at Thebes ruled in the south. By the 22nd Dynasty, the land was further fragmented with additional rivals assuming power in other cities. The small tombs at Tanis reflect a poverty of resources and power.

Finally a Nubian king, Piankhi (Piyi), marched north and conquered the several rival dynasties in Egypt, once again reunifying the land. To better control the power of the priests of Amen, these 25th Dynasty kings from Nubia appointed their daughters as God's Wives of Amen and left the administration of the country in their hands.

Having conquered much of Palestine, the increasingly powerful Assyrians were looking toward Egypt, which, though floundering, still appeared rich in the eyes of the rest of the civilized world. The Nubian pharaohs attempted to avoid the unavoidable, but the Assyrians took Memphis in 674 BC. They were beaten back, more by a tremendous rainstorm than by the Egyptian army, which by this time employed many mercenaries of foreign origin. A few years later, the Assyrians again entered Egypt. This time they sacked Thebes, chased the Nubian king back to his homeland far up the Nile, and left behind a vassal king, Psammethicus. He threw off Assyrian rule as soon as the army departed, and claimed the throne for himself.

Egypt recovered once again, moving into what is known as the Late Period, though without the same energy and freshness as in previous ages. The 26th Dynasty was a time of renaissance looking back to a greater, more glorious past. The temples were restored and the artwork of the period, especially the elegant-yet-solid statuary, reflects a conscious effort to identify with times long past. The Egyptians became dependent upon Greek and Phoenician mercenaries to fight their battles.

The Egyptian government fell 125 years later to the Persians, made a brief recovery, and fell again. In 332 BC Alexander the Great conquered the Persians and took as his own the age-old symbols, customs and rituals of Pharaoh. Until the middle of the 20th Century, Egypt would never again be ruled by a native leader.

While Egypt was being torn asunder by rival native rulers and by foreigners, the heirs of the 25th Dynasty were building a new kingdom on the foundations of a colonial society established south of the 1st Cataract by the rulers of the 18th Dynasty. This kingdom of Kush clung to the gods and symbols of the Egyptians. Its capital was located near the 4th Cataract, and across the river at Gebel Barkal was a large Egyptian-style temple to the god Amen. Small, steep-sided pyramids housed the burials of kings in nearby Nuri and El Kurru.

About midway into its 1,000-year history, the kingdom of Kush moved its capital southward to Meroe, which lies between the 5th and 6th cataracts. The rulers and priests continued to cling to

Egyptian models, but the resemblance was becoming ever more difficult to recognize as native customs and Greek and Roman ideas and imports overwhelmed the older symbols and rituals.

Finally, as had happened with Egypt itself, Christianity and Islam successively overwhelmed the ancient culture of Meroe and its gods. For over 1,500 years after this, Egypt was a lost civilization, admired but uncomprehended by visitors from Europe. By the time the Emersons arrived in Egypt, exploration of the ancient civilization of the Egyptians by European scholars — particularly the decipherment of the hieroglyphs by Champollion early in the 19th Century — had exposed to an astonished world the wonders of Egyptian history as we now know it. However, the succeeding century was to add greatly to Western knowledge, and it is certain Professor Radcliffe Emerson and his spouse/partner Amelia Peabody Emerson played no small part in the advancement of our understanding today.

Betty Winkelman

Mid-19th-Century drawing of the royal pyramid-cemetery near Meroe, which was published in Lepsius's Denkmäler aus Aegypten und Aethiopien.

Karnak's Hypostyle Hall under the stars.

FOR FURTHER READING
(Resources for the Articles)

Egyptology: Napoleon to WWI

Breasted, C., *Pioneer to the Past: The Story of James Henry Breasted, Archaeologist* (New York, 1943).

Donadoni, S.C. & A.-M. Donadoni Roveri, *Egypt from Myth to Egyptology* (Milan, 1990).

Drower, M.S., *Flinders Petrie, A Life in Archaeology* (Madison, WI, 1995).

Forbes, D.C., *Tombs. Treasures. Mummies. Seven Great Discoveries of Egyptian Archaeology* (Sebastopol & Santa Fe, 1998).

Hankey, J., *A Passion for Egypt: A Biography of Arthur Weigall* (London & New York, 2001).

James, T.G.H., *The Archaeology of Egypt* (New York, 1972).

—, *Excavating in Egypt: The Egypt Exploration Society, 1882-1982* (London, 1982).

—, *Howard Carter: The Path to Tutankhamun* (London & New York, 1992).

Maspero, G., *New Light on Ancient Egypt* (London, 1908).

—, *Ancient Sites and Modern Scenes* (London, 1910).

Petrie, W.M.F., *Seventy Years in Archaeology* (London, 1931).

Reeves, N., *Ancient Egypt, The Great Discoveries: A Year-by-Year Chronicle* (London & New York, 2000).

— & J.H. Taylor, *Howard Carter Before Tutankhamun* (New York, 1993).

Romer, J., *Valley of the Kings* (New York, 1981).

Smith, J.L., *Tombs, Temples & Ancient Art* (Norman, OK, 1956).

Wilson, J.A., *Signs and Wonders Upon Pharaoh* (Chicago, 1964).

Wortham, J.D., *The Genesis of British Egyptology, 1549-1906* (Norman, OK, 1971).

The British in Egypt

Annesley, G., *The Rise of Modern Egypt* (Durham, 1994).

Barthorp, M., *War on the Nile* (Poole, 1984).

Boyce, J., *Bayt al-Lurd* (Cairo, 2001).

Carmen, B. & McPherson, J., ed., *The Man Who Loved Egypt* (London, 1983).

Cecil, Lord Edward, *The Leisure of an Egyptian Official* (London, 1921).

Cromer, Earl of, *Modern Egypt* (London, 1908).

Mansfield, P., *The British in Egypt* (London, 1971).

Marsot, Afaf Lutfi al-Sayyid, *A Short History of Modern Egypt* (Cambridge, 1985).

Moorehead, A., *The Blue Nile* (London, 1962); *The White Nile* (London, 1962).

Rodenbeck, M., *Cairo* (Cairo, 1998).

Sattin, A., *Lifting the Veil* (London, 1988).

Vatikiotis, P. J., *The Modern History of Egypt* (London, 1969).

Warner, N., *An Egyptian Panorama* (Cairo, 1994).

Welch, W.M., Jr., *No Country for a Gentleman* (Westport, 1988).

Islam

Armstrong, K., *Islam* (New York, 2000).

Denny, F.M., *Islam* (San Francisco, 1987).

Esposito, J.L., *Islam: the Straight Path* (Oxford, 1991).

Waines, D., *An Introduction to Islam* (Cambridge, 1995).

Lesser Breeds

Cecil, Lord Edward, *The Leisure of an Egyptian Official* (London, 1921).

Drower, M.S., *Flinders Petrie. A Life in Archaeology* (London, 1985).

Eliot, T.S., ed., *A Choice of Kipling's Verse, made by T.S. Eliot. With an Essay on Rudyard Kipling* (New York, c. 1943).

Haggard, H.R., *King Solomon's Mines* (Pleasantville, New York, 1994).

Higgins, D.S., *Rider Haggard, A Biography* (New York, 1981).

Mansfield, P., *The British in Egypt* (New York, 1971).

McPherson, B., *A Life in Egypt*; B. Carman and J. Mcpherson, eds. (London, 1983).

Petrie, F., *Seventy Years in Archaeology* (New York, 1932).

Russell Pasha, Sir T., *Egyptian Service, 1902-1946* (London, 1949).

Wilson, J., *Lawrence of Arabia. The Authorized Biography* (New York, 1990).

Personal communication from Elizabeth Peters, editor of the Amelia Peabody Emerson journals, 2002.

Upstairs, Downstairs

Beeton, I., *Mrs. Beeton's Book of Household Management* (New York, 2000).

Dawes, F., *Not in Front of the Servants: A True Portrait of English Upstairs/Downstairs Life* (New York, 1973).

Deary, T., *The Vile Victorians* (London, 1994).

Huggett, F. E., *Life Below Stairs: Domestic Servants in England from Victorian Times* (New York, 1977).

The Women's Movement

Amin, Q., *The Liberation of Women and The New Woman.* Translated by S. S. Peterson (Cairo, 2000).

Baron, B., *The Women's Awakening in Egypt: Culture, Society and the Press* (New Haven, 1994).

Bonner, T. N., *To the Ends of the Earth: Women's Search for Education in Medicine* (Cambridge, MA, 1992).

Fokkena, L., "Linkages between Feminism, Nationalism, and Third World Development: The Case of Egypt."

http://www.stygmata.net/~slit/ jael.html (1995).

Manchester, W., *The Last Lion: Winston Spencer Churchill. Visions of Glory 1874-1932* (Boston, 1983).

Manton, J., *Elizabeth Garrett Anderson* (New York, 1965).

Rubenstein, D., *Before the Suffragettes: Women's Emancipation in the 1890s* (Brighton, 1986).

Shiman, L. L., *Women and Leadership in Nineteenth-Century England* (New York, 1992).

Strachey, L., *Queen Victoria* (New York, 1921).

Tucker, Judith E., *Women in Nineteenth-Century Egypt* (Cambridge, UK, 1985).

Wallach, J., *Desert Queen: The Extraordinary Life of Gertrude Bell: Adventurer, Advisor to Kings, Ally of Lawrence of Arabia* (New York, 1996).

Evolution of Fashion

Bryk, N.V., ed., *American Dress Pattern Catalogs, 1873-1909, Four Complete Reprints* (New York, 1988).

Buxbaum, G., ed., *Icons of Fashion: The Twentieth Century* (New York, 1999).

Cunnington, C.W., *English Women's Clothing in the Nineteenth Century* (New York, 1990).

Cunnington, C.W. and P. Cunnington, *Handbook of English Costume in the Nineteenth Century* (Boston, 1970).

Etherington-Smith, M. and J. Pilcher, *The "It" Girls: Lucy, Lady Duff Gordon, the Couturiere 'Lucile', and Elinor Glyn, Romantic Novelist* (New York, 1986).

Ewing, E., *History of Twentieth Century Fashion* (New York, 1992).

Farrell, J., *Umbrellas and Parasols* (London, 1985).

Olian, J., ed., *Victorian and Edwardian Fashions from "La Mode Illustrée"* (New York, 1998).

Schroeder, J. J., Jr., ed., *The Wonderful World of Ladies' Fashion: 1850-1920* (Chicago, 1971).

Shep, R.L., *The Great War: Styles and Patterns of the l910's* (Mendocino, 1998).

Waugh, N., *Corsets and Crinolines* (New York, 1970).

Seen But Not Heard

Chandos, J., *Boys Together: English Public Schools 1800-1864* (New Haven, 1984).

Deary, T., *The Vile Victorians* (London, 1994).

Gathorne-Hardy, J., *The Old School Tie: The Phenomenon of the English Public School* (New York, 1977).

Miall, A., *The Victorian Nursery Book* (New York, 1981).

Reader, W. J., *Victorian England* (New York, 1973).

Modern Inconveniences

Colman, P., *Toilets, Bathtubs, Sinks, and Sewers: A History of the Bathroom* (New York, 1994).

Josephson, J.P., *Umbrellas* (Minneapolis, 1998).

Morris, J., *The Spectacle of Empire* (Garden City, NY, 1982).

Ochoa, G., and M. Corey, *The Timeline Book of Science* (New York, 1995).

Owls Head Transportation Museum. Information on safety bicycles. http://www.ohtm.org/1887safety.html.

Porazik, J., *Old Time Classic Cars 1885-1940* (New York, 1985).

Rubin, S.G., *Toilets, Toasters & Telephones: The How and Why of Everyday Objects* (San Diego, 1998).

Schneider, S., "The History of Flashlights," http://www.geocities.com/~stuarts1031/flashlight.html.

Vercoutter, J., *The Search for Ancient Egypt* (New York, 1992).

Wilson, A., *Visual Timeline of Transportation* (New York, 1995).

Musical Heritage

Chapple, J.M., ed., *Heart Songs: Melodies of Days Gone By* (Boston, 1909).

Eastman, A.M., et al., *The Norton Anthology of Poetry* (New York, 1970).

Lee, C. C., *...the grand piano came by camel: Arthur Mace, the neglected Egyptologist* (Edinburgh, 1992).

Russell, D., *Popular Music in England, 1840-1914* (Manchester, 1987).

Taylor, D., ed., *A Treasury of Gilbert and Sullivan* (New York, 1941).

The Best of Wonder

Elwin, M., *Victorian Wallflowers* (Kennikat Press, Port Washington, New York, 1966).

Ernle, R.E.P., Lord, *The Light Reading of Our Ancestors* (Hutchinson, London, 1927).

Schlik, W.J., *The Ethos of Romance at the Turn of the Century* (University of Texas Press, Austin, 1994).

The works cited by author and title in the article are not included, since there are innumerable editions of the majority of them.

Ancient Egyptian History

Brewer, D.J. and E. Teeter, *Egypt and the Egyptians* (Cambridge, 1999).

Fagan, B., *Egypt of the Pharaohs* (Washington, D.C., 2001).

Kemp, B., *Egypt: Anatomy of a Civilization* (London, 1989).

Shaw, I. (ed.), *The Oxford History of Ancient Egypt* (Oxford, 2000).

Strudwick, N. and H., *Thebes in Egypt* (Ithaca, 1999).

Welsby, D.A., *The Kingdom of Kush* (Princeton, 1998).

Fellahin near the Giza pyramids, time of the Inundation.

SOMETHING ABOUT THE CONTRIBUTORS

A life-long Egyptophile and the editorial director of *KMT, A Modern Journal of Ancient Egypt*, a quarterly which he founded in 1990, **Dennis Forbes** is also the author of the 1998 tome *Tombs. Treasures. Mummies. Seven Great Discoveries of Egyptian Archaeology* (which incidentally covers the same time frame as Mrs. Emerson's journals). In preparation is his three-volume study, *Imperial Lives: Illustrated Biographies of Significant New Kingdom Egyptians*, as well as *Scepters & Trowels*, a collection of his caricatures of ancient Egyptians and famous Egyptologists.

A cofounder of Malice Domestic® Ltd. and a regular contributor to "Mystery Scene," **Elizabeth Foxwell** has published several mystery short stories and edited or coedited nine anthologies, including *More Murder They Wrote* (Berkley) and *Malice Domestic* (Avon). She believes the finest line in the Amelia canon is *"Emerson scuttled sideways, like a crab."*

Dr. Jocelyn Gohary is a British Egyptologist with degrees from Liverpool University in the U.K. She has lived in Cairo for almost 30 years, during which she worked for the Akhenaten Temple Project, and taught at a number of universities and colleges, including Helwan University and the American University in Cairo. She has traveled extensively throughout Egypt, often as a lecturer/guide for the American Research Center in Egypt and the Egypt Exploration Society. Dr. Gohary is the author of several books and articles on various aspects of the pharaonic civilization, her latest being the *Guide to the Nubian Monuments on Lake Nasser* (AUC Press, 1998).

Dr. Salima Ikram is an associate professor of Egyptology at the American University in Cairo. She has excavated in Egypt, Sudan, and Turkey, and has authored and coauthored numerous articles and several books, including *The Mummy in Ancient Egypt* with Dr. Aidan Dodson, with whom she is also writing *The Tomb in Ancient Egypt*. Her forthcoming publications are: *Death and Burial in Ancient Egypt* and *Divine Creatures: Animal Mummies in Ancient Egypt*. She is currently director of The Animal Mummy Project for the Cairo Museum and co-director of the North Kharga Oasis Survey Project.

Although employed as a webmaster at a law firm, **Margareta Knauff** has always had a passion for history. She is also co-webmaster of mpmbooks.com, the official website for Mertz/Peters/Michaels, and remains deeply indebted to her aunt for introducing her to Amelia Peabody.

Dr. Barbara Mertz considers herself to be a historian and Egyptologist. She is the author of two popular books on ancient Egypt (*Temples, Tombs and Hieroglyphs* and *Red Land, Black Land*) and articles in various encyclopedias.

Like Rider Haggard, **Barbara Michaels** has often been accused of being "prolific," though she has only written 29 works of popular fiction — "romances," as they would have been called in Amelia's day.

Elizabeth Peters is the editor of the journals of Amelia P. Emerson. She has also perpetrated a number of works of popular fiction.

A costume designer and faculty adjunct at New Jersey City University, **Florence Rutherford** lives with her husband, daughter, and three cats.

Lisa Speckhardt is managing editor of *Landscape Architecture*, and is co-creator and assistant webmaster of the official Elizabeth Peters website, www.mpmbooks.com.

Kristen Whitbread is Ms. Peters's personal assistant, a vocation which has been variously described by readers of the author's works as "glamorous" and "exciting." While she does not care to disabuse them of this notion, it is, quite possibly, a different sort of "exciting" than such readers have imagined. In addition to a spectrum of disparate duties (about which one individual remarked, *"I'd like to see that resume!"*), she also edits Ms. Peters's trimester newsletter.

Under the pen name of Lauren Haney, **Betty Winkelman** writes the Lieutenant Bak novels, which combine her enjoyment of the mystery genre with her passion for ancient Egypt. Her works include: *The Flesh of the God, The Right Hand of Amon, A Face Turned Backward, A Vile Justice, A Curse of Silence, A Place of Darkness*, and *A Cruel Deceit*. Under her own name she has published a number of non-fiction articles and book reviews for *KMT, A Modern Journal of Ancient Egypt*.

Avenue of Sphinxes at Karnak early in the 20th Century.

ILLUSTRATION SOURCES

(Code: t=top, b=bottom,c=center, tr=top right, tl=top left, cr=center right, cl=center left, br=bottom right, bc=bottom center, bl=bottom left).

Annales de Service des Antiquités de l'Égypte: 33 b, 40 tl, 46 b, 200 cr, 222, 291 r, 304 t, 305; Anonymous Archival Images: 14, 16, 18, 18 inset, 20 all, 21 all, 22 both; 25 tl cl cr, 26 tl bl, 27 all, 29 cl, 30 both, 39 b, 40 br, 44 both, 45 t c, 48-49, 50, 67 both, 68t, 72, 73 t, 80 t, 86 t, 141, 143 tr cr, 181, 182, 211 b, 220t, 222, 225 both, 226 c, 228, 229 bl, 231 both, 232, 235 t, 236 l, 267 t; F. Bedford Photograph: 252; C.F. Moberly Bell, *From Pharaoh to Fellah* (Philadelphia, 1888): 323 t, 328 t, 24 b, 29 cr both, 35, 109 t, 168 tl, 244-245, 246 tr, 254, 257 tl, 259, 264 t, 265 br, 271 b, 278 t, 301 tl, 310 bl br, 311 b, 324; Birmingham City Library: 41 b, 42 t, 235 br; F. Bonfils Photograph: 23; F.H. Brooksbank, *Legends of Ancient Egypt* (New York, n.d.): 185 all; J. Chesney, *The Land of the Pyramids* (London, Paris, New York, n.d.): 54 b, 102 l, 103 br, 108 r, 109 b, 121 bl, 128 b, 261 c, 271 t; *Daily Mirror* (London): 139; *Daily Sketch* (London), 143 l; N.G. Davies, *El Amarna* I (London, 1903): 296 l; T.M. Davis, *Excavations Bibân el Molûk* (6 vols., London, 1904-1912): 37 bl br, 38 both, 42 b, 43 all, 288 b, 302 r. 304 b; A.-B. De Guernville, *La Nouvelle Égypte* (Paris, 1905): 8, 25 bl, 39 tl tr, 40 tr, 55, 57 b, 68 b, 73 b, 75, 76, 77 both, 79 both, 86 b, 87, 108 l, 118 b, 121 tl tr, 168 tr, 199 br, 200 bl, 221 l, 229 t, 267 b, 273, 274-275, 287 l, 310 tl tr, 311 tl tc tr; *Description de l'Égypte*: 51; Dover Pictorial Archives: 140, 147, 148, 149, 150, 152, 155, 166 both, 169, 172, 175, 177; M. DuCamp Photograph: 269 b; G. Ebers, *Egypt: Descriptive, Historical, and Picturesque* (London, Paris, New York, n.d.): 2-3, 4, 12, 320, 322, 323 b, 325 b, 327 b, 24 t, 36 t, 37 cl both, 52, 53, 95 b, 97 t, 100, 102 r, 103 tr c, 104-105, 106, 107, 110 tl, 111 both, 112-113, 114, 115 all, 116 all, 117 all, 118 tl tr, 119, 120, 121 br, 123, 125 t, 164, 190, 191 all, 192-193, 194, 195, 238 inset, 240, 241, 242, 244 inset, 246 tl, 250, 251, 253, 255, 256, 257 tr, 260, 265 t, 266, 269 t, 276, 280 bl, 282 l, 283 both, 284 r, 285, 292 both, 294, 295 both, 297 both, 300 both, 301 bl, 312, 313 t bl, 316; Emerson Library: 196, 197, 198 both, 199 tr, 200 tl, 201 both, 202, 204, 205 all, 206 r, 208 all, 209, 210, 211 r, 212, 213 all, 214 both, 215, 216, 217, 218, 219 both, 220 b, 221 r, 223 both, 224, 226 t b, 227, 229 br, 230, 233, 234 both, 235 bl, 236 r, 237 t bl, 248 both, 308 b; F. Frith Photograph: 7; *The Graphic* (London): 29 both, 30, 33 t, 61 tl bl, 82-83, 88-89, 102-103, 301 r; T. Gray, *"And in the Tomb were Found—"* (Cambridge, 1923): 183 both; *Harper's New Monthly Magazine* (1882): 26 tr, 29tl br; A. Hoppin, *On the Nile* (Boston, 1874): 94 b, 95 t, 96 tr bl cr br, 125 b, 127; Hulton Picture Library: 64, 66, 80 b; *Illustrated London News*: 32, 54 c, 56 tr, 58 both, 60, 61 tr br, 62-63, 70-71t, 71 b, 74, 91 t, 94 t, 110 b, 142, 179, 180 all, 186, 187, 189, 243, 306-307, 308 t, 309, 313 br, 314, 335; *Journal of Egyptian Archaeology*: 199 cl, 225 l; T.W. Knox, *The Boy Travellers, Egypt and the Holy Land* (New York, 1883): 121 cl, 128 t, 290 l; E.W. Lane, *The Manners and Customs of the Modern Egyptians* (London, New York, 1877): 280 r, 281 t br, 282 r; K.R. Lepsius, *Denkmäler aus Aegypten und Aethiopien*: 329; V. Loret, *Bulletin de l'Institut d'Égypte* (Cairo, 1898): 34 t; D.A. MacKenzie, *Egyptian Myth and Legend* (London, 1907): 184 both; S. Manning, *The Land of the Pharaohs* (London, 1887): 29 tr bl, 36 both, 55, 56 tl cl bl, 100 b both, 96 tl, 124, 126 b, 237 br, 238, 245 inset, 246 bl br, 249 tr inset, 261 tr inset, 268 t bl, 272 b, 278 inset, 284 l, 288 l, 302 l, 330; Metropolitan Museum of Art: 46 t; Motoring Picture Library: 167 all; Oriental Institute Museum Archives: 45 b, 203 t; G. Perrot and C. Chipiez, *A History of Art in Ancient Egypt* (2 vols., London, 1883); 324, 325t, 326-327, 328 b, 288 tr, 289 both, 290-291, 296 r, 299; Period Postcards: 264 cl, 272 t, 286, 315, 332; W.S. Perry, *Egypt, The Land of the Temple Builders* (Boston, New York, Chicago, 1898): 25 bl, 37 tr cr, 90 t, 278 b, 279 tl, 287 r, 319; Player's Navy Cut Cigarette Cards (1915): 84 both, 85 both, 126 t ; Private Collections: 91 b, 110 tr, 131, 132, 135, 136, 137, 157, 159, 160, 162, 163; Private Photo Albums: 10, 17, 57 c, 59 all, 97 b, 129, 247 all, 249, 251 inset, 257 b, 261 bl br, 262 both, 263 all, 264 cr b, 265 bl, 268 br, 279 tr, 280 l, 293, 303, 333; Redwood Library and Athenaeum: 206; E. Schiaparelli, *Relazione II* (Torino, 1927): 40 bl, 41 t, 298; J. Ward, *The Sacred Beetle* (London, 1902): 291 cl; E.L. Wilson, *In Scripture Lands* (New York, 1890): 28, 239, 249 tl inset.

A storyteller's captive audience.